The Legend

The Armor of God

Book 1

The Legend

JEFF BOLES

ISBN: 978-1-6653-0783-3 - Paperback
ISBN: 978-1-6653-0784-0 - Hardcover
eISBN: 978-1-6653-0785-7 - eBook

These ISBNs are the property of BookLogix for the express purpose of sales and distribution of this title. The content of this book is the property of the copyright holder only. BookLogix does not hold any ownership of the content of this book and is not liable in any way for the materials contained within. The views and opinions expressed in this book are the property of the Author/Copyright holder, and do not necessarily reflect those of BookLogix.

⊗This paper meets the requirements of ANSI/NISO Z39.48-1992 (Permanence of Paper)

101723

Acknowledgments

The writing of *The Armor of God* was a thirty-year process during which there were many starts, stops, and lengthy periods of dormancy. The one constant throughout this endeavor was the never-ending support and encouragement from my number one fan: my mother, Faye Boles. She has always had much more faith in my talents than I ever have, and without her, I don't know that this story would have ever been completed and published. Perhaps it was the pride of a mother that fostered her steadfast nudging for me to complete the story, or perhaps it was the light-hearted promise (which I just might have to make good on) I made to take her on a vacation to Ireland once the book was published that produced such persistent prodding. Her enthusiasm and excitement when I discussed the story with her ever encouraged my dedication to finishing the book. Thank you, Mom. Your approval means more to me than any level of success that this book may have.

I also have to thank my brother, Timothy, and his wife, Ginger. *The Armor of God* would not be what it is without their gift to me for Christmas of 1989: *Roget's Thesaurus*. Of all the gifts I have received in my life, I truly have never valued one as much as this book. Well, with the possible exception of the train set I received when I was eight years old. I still have both. Thank you, Tim and Ginger.

There is another person who has been a great encouragement and a solid wall off of whom I bounced many ideas over the years. My nephew, Trey. I could always depend on him to provide good feedback and ideas when I would come to a bit of an impasse. I always enjoyed it when we would talk about this story, trying to figure out where to go with it and how to write it. Thanks, Trey.

I cannot leave out the rest of my family, for their support and encouragement has been invaluable. My father, my brother Aubrey Jr., and my nieces and nephews Ariel, Christian, Jorden and Christopher Lee.

Finally, this book would not exist had the Lord not put it on my heart to write it and had not given me the tools to do so. I did my best to write this story in a manner that would be pleasing to God and be glorifying to him. I can only pray that he is pleased with it and somehow, it will be edifying to the people who read it and be an encouragement for them to put on the full armor of God. To God be the glory. Amen.

Prologue

The little hamlet bustled with activity as dozens of men, women, and children went about their daily routines. Bright white clouds floated across the blue sky, casting the land in shadow one moment and then allowing the sun to bathe it the next. It was a reasonably warm day, and the winter rains had not yet commenced, giving the town a few more days of sure footing before being turned into a land of mud and stench. A young woman of sixteen years exited a building upon which's front doors were slats of wood arranged in the forms of crosses. A steeple and bell gave further testimony to the nature and purpose of the structure. A covered basket was draped across one of her arms, and she smiled and greeted the townsfolk as she walked down the street. She came to an elderly, crippled man who was sitting in a rickety chair in front of a building that looked as crippled as the man himself. The man's expression had been one of weariness and loneliness as he stared into the distance, but as the young lady approached, his face brightened, and he managed a toothless smile. Her compassionate greeting further lifted his countenance, and he looked as if he would jump up and dance a jig as she retrieved some bread and a small flask from her basket and handed them to him. She laid a comforting hand on his shoulder, spoke a few more words, then continued down the street.

The young man watched the girl as he had done countless times over the month that he had spent in the town. Her smile mesmerized him, and her laughter was music to his ears. Her long, wavy black hair bounced as she walked—no, floated—

down the street, and her hazel-colored eyes always appeared to be smiling. He had yet to speak with her, but from gentle inquiries of the people in the village, he had learned that she lived, worked, and studied in the care of the church. It seemed that nearly every day she was out visiting the people of the town, especially the elderly, taking food to them and helping care for them when they were ill. There had been many occasions when, while speaking with someone who appeared to be sad or dejected, she would retrieve a book from her basket and begin reading to them. Most times, the people appeared to receive encouragement and were smiling when she finally had to leave their company. Today, he decided, would be the day he mustered the courage to speak with her. After all, he was no ordinary commoner, and at twenty-five years old, there was no reason to be bashful.

It was later in the afternoon as the young woman was returning to the church when the young man spotted her again and decided he could no longer delay speaking with her. He casually strode across the street and fell in step with her.

"It would appear that your basket is empty," he said, peering at the basket she was freely swinging back and forth as she walked. "It was truly a perfect day for a picnic."

"Why do you presume that I went on a picnic today?" she asked suspiciously.

"Your basket was full this morning, and now it is empty. Therefore, I assumed you had taken advantage of such a beautiful day for a walk and a picnic. Perhaps down in the glade by the river?"

"I see," she replied. "Indeed, it was a nice day for a walk and even for a picnic. I can understand how you might make that deduction. My question to you, though, is how did you know my basket was full this morning?"

"Well," the young man started, "I ... you see, I was just ... I mean, this morning," he stammered, not sure what to say and how to explain himself.

"You could simply say that you were standing across the street and saw me exit the church, carrying this basket covered with a colorful cloth this morning," she said almost accusingly.

"You saw me?" he asked, surprised.

"I saw you," she admitted with a nod of her head. "I saw you watching me yesterday and the day before yesterday. It has taken you long enough, I must say, to make your presence and interest known."

"Interest?" he repeated, as if not knowing to what she was referring. "What do you mean *interest*?"

"Come now," she replied. "It is no secret that you have been making inquiries about me. It is a small village, and I am well acquainted with all its inhabitants. You have been here nearly a month now and watching me for three of those weeks, though never venturing closer than the other side of the street. Truth be told, had you not finally approached me, I was going to march across the street the next time I saw you and ask your business. A woman does not appreciate being spied upon."

"Forgive me. It was not my intention to spy upon you," he said with genuine sincerity. "I just could not decide the best manner in which to make your acquaintance."

"Well then, I shall make it easy for you. I am Theresa McMaster."

"Theresa," the young man replied as if relishing the name. "I take it that you live in the church."

"What would lead you to that deduction?" she asked.

"I have seen you enter and exit the building many times, in the mornings and evenings. I have not seen you spend so much time anywhere else."

"Ah, yes, a good spy would certainly take notice of my comings and goings," Theresa replied. "Or perhaps your intentions are not so honorable."

"I am not a spy, and my intentions are nothing less than fully honorable," the young man insisted, his feelings bruised, "although in retrospect I can understand how you have come to that opinion. When one stands out in a crowd such as you do, well, it is difficult to not notice you."

"Hmm," Theresa grunted in response. "Yes, the church is my home."

"Do you not have any family in the area?"

"My mother and father passed many years ago, and I have no other relatives that I know of. The priests took me in as an orphan and have cared for me to this very day."

"And in turn, you help minister to the people," he surmised.

"Yes, I do help in the church's mission to the people. I consider it a privilege, though, and by no means a chore. However, not all my days are filled wondering the streets with a basket full of goodies and handing out gifts to people," she answered. "I spend a good bit of time studying, and I have had the fortune of traveling with the priests from time to time. I am quite taken with history and learning of kingdoms and peoples of the past. I do take great satisfaction in helping people near and far, yet I also enjoy learning. Peoples, lands, languages, I study them all."

"Very impressive," he replied, nodding his head. In the few minutes of conversing with Theresa, his interest had grown greatly, and he knew he would invest however much time it took for the interest to become mutual. He had just scratched the surface of who this young lady was, and he could not wait to learn more about her.

"And what of you?" she inquired. "What has brought you to this little borough called Buckington? Most strangers simply pass through town, yet you have been here a month at least."

"My father sent me here to study," he answered.

"Study?" she repeated. "In Buckington? It is not exactly a mecca of knowledge and learning. The church's library is quite impressive, and the priests are very knowledgeable to be sure, but I have not seen you take advantage of those resources. What, therefore, could your father possibly expect you to learn here?"

"You have me there," he replied. "The truth of the matter is that I have had somewhat of a disrespectful attitude toward my family, and my father thought it best that I spend some time away to reconsider my thoughts and disposition. I would say, in complete honesty, that I am here to learn humility."

"Then I hope your studies go well, for this is quite the humble town," Theresa said.

"I would say that I am off to a good start," he replied. "However, I can be a slow learner. I may have to stay here for an extended period to ensure I learn all that I can."

"Have you found our village to your liking thus far?" she asked.

"It is very impressive from the standpoint of activity and opportunities," the young man replied, "but there appears to be a coolness toward outsiders. While the people have been cordial, I can certainly detect an underlying suspicion in them, though I have done nothing to warrant such scrutiny."

"You, as a stranger, come into town one day and spend the next thirty or so days walking about the village, conducting no business, and interrogating the townsfolk about one of the young ladies in town. You then wonder why there is a coolness to the people, an air of suspicion hanging over your head?" Theresa replied matter-of-factly.

"Well, I would not describe my inquiries as an interrogation," the young man responded in his own defense. "Just an innocent question here and there."

"Suspicion of a stranger by the people is well to be expected," she replied. "Several years ago, another young man came to our town for what he described as studies. He was welcomed and spent a number of days taking advantage of the church's rather extensive educational resources. However, his curiosity overcame his conscience, and he ventured into areas that were specifically off-limits to anybody but the priests. He became quite indignant at being reprimanded and was banished from not only the church but the community as well. So I trust you can see why the people here can be cautious when it comes to strangers."

"Yes, that would be reasonable," he replied, nodding his head. "I assure you I have no intentions of misbehavior or malintent. I am simply here as a visitor. Perhaps I, too, can find a way to help the people and become a part of the citizenry during my stay and alleviate some of the wariness they have for me."

"Perhaps," Theresa replied thoughtfully. "Not to be rude," she said as they approached the doors to the church, "but I still have several chores to complete before I am able to end my day. It has been a pleasure speaking with you."

"I understand," he said. "I do not wish to get you in trouble with the priests. Perhaps we will have future opportunities to visit with each other. Good evening."

"I am sure we will," Theresa said as he turned to leave. "However, if we are to continue our conversations, I think it only proper that I know your name."

"How discourteous of me," he replied, feeling chastised. "My name is Richard. Richard Talbot."

"Talbot?" Theresa asked, wrinkling her brow. "Certainly not of the Talbot line that currently reins over Wellington."

"Aye, the one and same," Richard said, pausing his departure and turning back to face her.

"Then you are quite removed from home," Theresa replied. "Wellington is at least a two-week journey from here."

"What can I say?" Richard replied with a shrug of his shoulders. "My father's dissatisfaction with my disposition was of no small matter." He looked at her inquisitively. "How do you know of my family name?"

"As I said earlier, I love studying history. It is full of fascinating times and fascinating peoples. You would be surprised to learn what I know."

"Then I look forward to hearing more," Richard said, and with a courteous bow, he turned and walked away.

Theresa watched him until he disappeared down a side street. "More but not all," she said thoughtfully, then opened the door and disappeared into the church.

Chapter 1

The bright afternoon sun floated high in the midspring sky, bathing the rolling landscape with welcomed warmth while chasing away a harsh and stubborn wintry season. The highlands were accustomed to winters long and cold, but this year, winter had been fiercer and colder than any season in recent history. Lakes that had been frozen several feet thick were now dotted with masses of ice patches, which should have completely disappeared several weeks earlier. Rivers and streams fought against their boundaries as runoff from the thawing, high-altitude ice and snow poured into them. Small animals and rodents, noticeably fewer in number than in previous years, romped through fields sparsely decorated with blooming flowers and plants. Trees still striving to spread their verdant veils played host to a population of birds returning after a prolonged absence. The soft blue sky was spotted with tiny, billowy clouds pushed along by a whisper of a breeze. Spring, though a bit late, had finally arrived in this peaceful land.

A man and woman walked hand in hand through a field of tall grass, setting scores of butterflies and insects to flight with every step they took. They, like the wildlife, were out to greet the long-awaited warming. Two energetic children, a young boy and a girl just a few years older, ran along the edge of the forest playing tag.

"I would that we could store up the warmth and save it for winters long and cold," the woman said with a sigh.

"That would be a wonderful trick," Douglas Knox replied to his wife. "However, we can enjoy the day only as long as it lasts and hope the morrow smiles brighter. I feel as if the sun shines on my very bones." He stretched his arms wide and lifted his face to the sky. After a moment, he turned his head and checked on his children, a ritual he repeated every few minutes. "It is good to see Robert and Stephanie playing again. Young ones need fresh air and sunshine."

"So do old people," the woman replied teasingly with a smile.

"We are not old yet, Melanie. We are between young and old, in the happiest time of our lives. The aches of old age have not yet riddled our joints, our eyes are still sharp and clear, and our ears still tell us when our children are having fun." He paused for a moment as the children's romping brought a smile to his face. "And our stomachs tell us when we need to fill them again. I believe it is time for lunch."

"The children will be happy to hear that," Melanie agreed.

The couple called to their young ones, and the foursome rendezvoused at a small clearing several yards deep into the forest. The children arrived first, being that they were nearer to the site than their parents were, yet waited patiently until the man and woman joined them. After a few minutes, all four were seated in a circle around a basket overflowing with delicious-looking food.

"Father, may I give thanks?" Robert asked. The boy had sandy-colored hair and blue eyes and was about ten years old. Although he was not physically developed beyond his years, there was an air about him that caused most people to overestimate his age by a few years.

"Do let him, Douglas," the boy's mother urged.

"Very well, Robert. You may give thanks."

Excited by the honor, the boy quickly clasped his hands together, closed his eyes, and concentrated for a moment prior to speaking.

"Our Father in heaven, we are most gracious for this wonderful day you have given us. We thank you for protecting us through this terrible cold season and for this food we are about to eat. May we bring glory to you in all things. Amen."

"Amen," the others repeated.

"That was very good," Melanie complimented her son. "Where did you learn to pray like that?"

"Father Dante, at church. He taught me. I am going to miss him," Robert said sadly. "Are we ever going back?"

"Maybe one day," Douglas answered. "One day when the violence ceases and it is safe."

"Are we going to stay here?" Stephanie asked.

"Now that spring is here, I believe we should move on to my brother's village. As you will recall, that was our original intention. The McDaniels were nice enough to provide us shelter for the winter, but it would not be right to continue inconveniencing them. We will leave within the week."

"How much longer will it take us to get to Uncle Hewlitt's village?" Robert asked.

"I am not sure," Douglas replied. "My original estimate was six weeks of travel. Early winter caught us by surprise after only three weeks. We should be there in about three more weeks if all goes well."

"What is it like there?" Stephanie asked.

"Not too different from our village. The weather is warmer, and there are more people. But the important thing is that there is peace in the land — and has been for many years. I am sure that ..." Douglas paused and lifted his head, scanning the surrounding area with alert eyes.

"What is it?" Melanie asked, seeing concern in her husband's face.

"Hush," he replied, holding his hand up. He cocked his head to the side, straining to again hear what he thought he had heard before. A strange expression crept across his face, an expression born from the union of worry and fear. His hand slowly reached over to a small sword by his side.

"What is it, Father?" Stephanie whispered.

"Stand up," Douglas commanded as he rose to his feet, "but do so slowly. Very slowly." He took a stance of defense and cautiously turned to his right, then to his left. "Pick up a thick stick or a rock or something to defend yourselves. God help us."

"Douglas, what is it?" Melanie asked again, her voice laced with fear.

"Wolves," he answered, spitting the word out. "I do not know how many there are, but I can hear them. They must be starving as a result of the long winter. We may be able to hold them off." As he finished speaking, four monstrous wolves appeared like ghosts amid the trees. Three of them had coats that were a mixture of light and dark gray. The fourth, noticeably larger than the others, was as black as the deepest depths of the deepest cave. Slowly they approached their prey with teeth bared and saliva dripping from long, bone-crunching fangs. A deep, terrifying growl paralyzed the humans. His voice threatening to flee him, Douglas addressed his children.

"Robert, Stephanie, listen to me. There are only four of them. When they attack, your mother and I will draw their attention and hold them off. You two are to run back to Mr. and Mrs. McDaniels' home. Run as fast as you can. Do not look back. We will join you as soon as we are able to, Lord willing."

"Father, we can help. We will not leave you," Robert argued.

"You will do as I say," his father replied firmly. "No questions." The wolves were now only forty feet away, slowing their approach even more. Attack was imminent.

"Maybe they will not attack," Melanie weakly suggested. "If we stand very still, they may go away."

"I would that it was so. They will charge, however. I have seen wolves like this hunt. It is only a matter of seconds now. We must do something." Putting his own survival secondary to that of his offspring, Douglas strained for a plan that would help his children get away safely. There were not very many options. Here they were, the four of them, in the woods, no other people around, and facing four hungry, vicious, monstrous beasts that were about to attack. When they did, all would be over. He had to make the first move and catch the animals off guard.

"Listen to me. Listen closely. We have but a few moments left. This is what we must do. Melanie, you and I will rush the wolves—"

"Have you gone mad?" the woman asked incredulously.

"Be still and listen! We must make the first move and startle them. They will concentrate on us. The children will then be able to flee, hopefully unnoticed. With luck, they will be able to make it back to the McDaniels'. We must give them every chance!"

"I understand," Melanie answered softly, her voice quivering. She was terrified and felt all but completely paralyzed. Her hands shook noticeably, and her knees threatened to buckle. There was a feeling within her that surpassed fear, a sensation she had never previously felt. She was going to die. It was inevitable. She was powerless to do anything about it, and no matter how direly she wished to be somewhere else, anywhere else, no matter how strenuously she tried to awaken, this was not a dream. She reflected on her life, on her husband and her children. As she thought about her children, anger began to well up beside the fear. Their precious lives were only moments away from being ripped from them before they had the opportunity to taste all the wonders life could offer. Though a tingling numbness had engulfed her entire body, she knew that the love she held for her offspring would rise above her fear of the beasts. Love would vault her forward and into death's savage, indiscriminate jaws. There was no other way.

"Children, do you understand?" Douglas asked as he glared at the salivating demons that were creeping ever so slowly forward. He made himself hate the animals. He hated their yellowish teeth, their evil eyes, their gray and black coats. He hated everything about them and hated even more that these creatures would threaten his family. The adrenaline began racing through his entire body, priming his muscles and feeding his courage. His heart pounded heavily in his chest, and though the day's temperature was not above sixty degrees, a bead of perspiration trickled down his brow, over his cheek, and into his thick black beard. The doomed man tightened his grip on his only weapon. These animals would retreat or die. "My, son, my daughter, you will run when we charge forward."

"We understand," Stephanie answered. The children knew that the chances of seeing their parents alive again were very slim. As badly as they desired to stay, Father's word was law. They had to do as told.

"We will see you again, someday, somewhere. Ready, my love?" Douglas asked his wife.

"Upon your command," Melanie replied, her body tensing in preparation of the charge.

"One ... two ... three ... *now!*" With a terrific shout, Douglas sprang forward. Melanie followed on his heels, waving a rather unintimidating stick in front of her as if it were the deadliest sword ever crafted by man. Her legs felt weak, yet they did not fail her. Her arm felt heavy, yet she kept it raised. Cold terror gripped every muscle in her body, straining to make her turn and run the other way. She knew, however, that to run would be in vain. She had to make sure that her children's running was not.

Robert and Stephanie did not hesitate. They turned and raced away from their parents, away from the horrible nightmare — and away from their only possible refuge. Overwhelmed by fear, the children failed to check their direction and ran not to the McDaniels' but in the opposite direction. Although Stephanie was older and had longer legs than Robert, the boy took the lead as they darted across the open field and headed for the forest on the other side. As a result of obeying his father's word and not looking back, Robert had no way of knowing that his sister was slowly falling farther and farther behind as he entered the trees.

This part of the forest was thicker than that which they had been in previously. Branches slapped him in the face, and thorn bushes grabbed his clothes as he vaulted haphazardly through the dense brush. Twice he successfully hurdled over fallen trees, but his third attempt failed. His foot caught on a branch that reached up like a bony, skeletal arm from the grave, and Robert plummeted to the soft forest floor. Uninjured, he sprung to his feet and paused to look back.

The world had suddenly grown deathly quiet. He fully expected to hear Stephanie crashing through the brush behind him, yet there was not a sound anywhere. He considered backtracking to locate his sister, but a distant, blood-curdling howl forced him to abandon any such notion. The fear and panic in him intensified, and once again he bolted forward. He could only hope that she had found a tree and climbed to safety. After several more eternal minutes of running, his chest pounding and his lungs aching, Robert knew that he could not flee any farther and began looking for a tree to climb. As he frantically searched for a tree that could provide a safe haven, the boy heard a twig snap behind him. Robert froze. If it had been his sister behind him, she would have called out. He knew what he would see as he slowly turned around. The huge black wolf slowed its approach even more and stopped thirty feet from Robert. Those eyes of death pierced the boy and petrified him. He could not force himself to look away. He could see the bared, devilish fangs, and for a moment, it appeared that a vicious, malevolent grin spread across the beast's face. He could see the red-stained muzzle and chest. That was when the powerful reality of his futile situation hit him. Robert looked around, praying to see some avenue of escape. There was none. Knowing that a kill was finally at hand, the beast slowly approached its defenseless prey in preparation for the attack.

"I hate you," Robert blurted as the tears began to flow down his face. His voice was shaky and weak, ready to leave him any second. "I hate you for what you did to my family. Mother! Father!" he screamed, though he knew it was in vain. The only answer was a faint, distant echo of his pitiful plea. The wolf, sensing the weakness in its prey, picked up speed and began to run. With but a split second to spare, Robert bent over and with both hands grasped a two-inch-thick, three-foot-long limb. He closed his eyes and swung it as hard as he could at the beast. The wolf yelped in pain and surprise as the meager weapon struck it just behind its left ear. Robert opened his eyes in time to see the predator back away for a second, then resume its attack. Once again, the boy swung his only defense at the beast, but this time the wolf was wary and broke off the attack just in time. Now it circled the boy. Robert turned with the beast so that he was always facing it. His back brushed up against a large tree. His body quivered uncontrollably, and he wondered how much longer he could hold up. The world swayed ever so slightly in front of him, and he felt as if he was dreaming. He took a step forward, feigning an attack. The wolf did not hesitate. It took three running steps forward and vaulted into the air with its gaping jaws determined on ripping through the boy's throat. Weakly yet bravely, Robert swung the stick at the wolf, and in the last split second of consciousness, the boy thought he heard the beast yelp in pain. The massive body slammed into him, throwing him back against the tree and into darkness.

Chapter 2

E rie shadows danced across the wall cast by the soft glow of a lone candle's flickering flame. A faint trace of the receding daylight filled the small room's only window, offering little if any additional illumination. Two people occupied the diminutive chamber. A small boy, appearing to be asleep, lay on a cot in one corner of the room, opposite the room's only door. A damp cloth stretched across his forehead. A woman in her late twenties sat on a chair beside the cot. She reached over and gently lifted the rag off the boy's head. After dipping it into a bowl of water and ringing it out, she replaced it. A deep, concerned look covered her face.

"How is the boy?" a deep, masculine voice softly called from the doorway.

"He has not awoken," the young woman replied. "He has not moved." She checked underneath the crimson-stained bandage on the boy's chest as the man strode to her side. "We should at least be thankful that the bleeding has stopped. At his age, he does not have much blood to spare. What of the girl?"

The man reached over and gently grasped the woman's left shoulder. "I am afraid she will not awaken from her rest. Her injuries proved too severe. The boy is alone." He looked out the window and into the approaching night. "Cursed wolves. Tomorrow, we will hunt them down."

A faint groan from the small, still figure drew the man's attention. He looked down and saw the boy's closed eyes squeeze tightly in pain, then slowly open. They hovered a moment on the woman's face, blinking to focus, then moved to the man. Suddenly, they flew open wide as panic raced through him. The rag on his forehead dropped to the ground as he tried to sit up and back into the corner. The woman grabbed his shoulders and gently held him in place as she soothingly talked to him.

"You are safe now, little boy. Nothing is going to harm you. Lay back down. You are safe here."

Quickly the boy looked around the room. After a moment, he relaxed a bit.

"Where am I? Who are you?" he tentatively asked.

"You are safe now," the man answered. "I am Justin MacLean. This is my wife, Kristin. You are in our home."

"Why am I here?"

"You had an accident," MacLean replied. "You were injured, so we brought you here."

"An accident?" the boy repeated, obviously very confused.

"Yes, while you were in the woods. Do you not remember?"

The boy's eyes darted back and forth between the man and woman, the confusion slowly turning into panic. His breathing started to quicken.

"I want to go home. I want to go home!" Tears welled up in the boy's eyes.

"Yes, yes, I am certain you do," Justin replied. "We shall talk about that soon enough. Tell me, though, do you remember what happened in the woods?"

"The woods ..." the boy repeated, his eyes dancing across the ceiling. "When was I in the woods?"

"Earlier today," Justin answered, furrowing his eyebrows a bit. "You do not remember being in the woods?"

"What was I doing in the woods?" the boy asked innocently.

"That is what we were hoping you could tell us," Kristin answered.

"I ... I ... I do not remember being in the woods," the boy confessed.

"What do you remember about today?" Justin asked.

"Today? I remember ... I remember ..." the boy stuttered, fighting for a memory of the day that would not come.

"Where do you live?" Justin asked, pushing for information.

"I live ..." The boy paused for a moment as his brow wrinkled. "I live ... I do not know. I cannot remember where I live." Panic began to well up inside him again. "I cannot remember!"

"There now," the woman comforted him, patting his arm. "You have a nasty bump on your head. It seems to have affected your memory a bit. You will be okay when it goes away. Be calm. Do you remember your name?"

The boy thought for a moment, confusion rampant in his eyes. He slowly shook his head. "I do not know." A lone tear trickled down his face.

"Where are your parents?" Justin inquired.

"My parents. My parents ..." the boy replied, his lower lip beginning to tremble. He stared into the darkest corner of the room. "I do not know. I cannot remember!" He lifted his right hand and touched the bandage on his chest as tears rolled down his face.

"Let us speak outside," Justin said to his wife. She reached out to the boy's face and wiped the tears. He did not respond. She stood up and followed her husband out of the room.

"Poor lad," she said. "What are we going to do?"

"What can we do?" Justin replied. "I know of no villages within a week's walk of where we found him. His family name is a mystery, let alone his own. How can we determine where he is from or if he has any relatives? We can only hope he regains his memory." A sharp rap at the front door interrupted their conversation. Kristin returned to the boy's side as Justin strode to the front of their house.

"Who is there?" he called out.

"It is the king. Open your door," an authoritative voice answered. Justin quickly complied. He unlatched the heavy wooden door and pulled it open. Two burly, fierce-looking guards, fully armed, swept into the room and, after a brief scanning of the area, motioned to someone outside the house. King Edwin Gallard, also dressed as if ready for combat yet retaining his royal demeanor, boldly stepped into the home.

"Your Majesty," Justin said, bowing his head in respect.

"Justin, my friend," the king addressed him as he placed a hand on the man's shoulder. "I have only now heard of the tragedy you stumbled across today. Tell me what happened."

"Please, sit," Justin said, motioning toward a table in the middle of the room. The king moved over to the table and sat down. Justin followed.

"My family and my brother's family were returning from the seasonal gathering at Wicklethorpe. We had decided to take a shortcut through Bristle Forest to cut off a few hours of travel time. I was walking ahead of the group, keeping an eye out for any possible danger, when I heard a commotion a short distance away. I motioned for everyone to be silent and cautiously moved around some large rocks. That was when I saw them. The boy and the wolf. As I watched, the wolf lunged for the boy, but he beat it back with a stick. His small victory was short-lived. The lad never stood a chance. It was a full-grown, very hungry wolf intent on making a meal of the boy. I was about thirty yards away and could never have reached him in time. Before I knew it, my bow was in one hand and an arrow in the other. The wolf leaped, I shot ..." He paused for a second. "The boy and I both were lucky."

"Luck had nothing to do with it. You have proven yourself time and again as being the best bowman in the land. Had it been anyone else in your place, the situation would have ended more tragically. How is the boy? And the girl? I was told there was a young girl also found in the area."

"I am sorry to say that the young lady passed on just a short time ago. Her wounds were too great. We did everything we could."

"And the boy?" the king urged.

"The boy awoke a few minutes ago. He appears well except for one thing."

"What is this one thing?"

"His memory, Your Majesty. He does not remember what happened or where he is from or even his own name. He received a terrible blow to the head, and I am afraid it has interfered with his memory."

"The man and woman you found. Can we assume they were his parents?" Gallard asked.

"I believe that to be a safe assumption," Justin replied.

"Was there anything on them or around them that would suggest where they were from or who they were?" the king inquired.

"No, my lord. We found a number of personal possessions but nothing that revealed their names or where their home may have been."

"Was there not an old man and woman living in that area? Perhaps they were relatives," Gallard suggested.

"Aye, the McDaniels. They were an old couple with no relatives of whom I am aware. They kept very much to themselves. My brother went to their home while the rest of us returned here. Unfortunately, the wolves had beat him there. He said it looked as though several people had been living in the house. I believe that this family had been living there for the winter. While they were out enjoying the spring weather, they were attacked by a pack of wolves."

"So we have a little boy with no name, no family, and no memory," the king summarized.

"That is the situation," Justin agreed. "What shall we do?"

"We can hope that he regains his memory. Perhaps if he sees his parents' bodies or his sister's body, he will recall his past. He may remember tomorrow. Then again, it may take a year or two. Since we cannot know, we must take care of him. You will take care of him, Justin MacLean. He is to be like a second son to you and your wife. You will be his family since he no longer has one. Raise him as you do your own son. If he asks questions about what happened to his family, whether now or in the future, tell him what you know. This may help his memory. If you need anything due to this extra responsibility placed on you, it will be provided. I will be around in a day or two and speak with the lad. What do you say, Justin?"

"As you wish, my king. He will be my own son. I am honored to be chosen by you."

"Very good," King Edwin said as he rose from the dining table. "Then we will speak again in a day. Good evening."

"Good night, Your Majesty." Justin closed the door behind the king and his guards. He walked to the back room and stood beside his wife as she comforted the young boy.

"Has he spoken again?" he asked his wife.

"Not a word," she replied. "What did the king say?"

Justin did not answer his wife. Instead, he spoke to the boy.

"Do you feel well enough to walk around a bit?"

The boy did not answer verbally. He looked up into the brawny man's eyes and nodded his head.

"He should not be on his feet," Kristin argued as the boy moved to rise from the cot. "His injuries may start bleeding again."

"Come with me," Justin instructed, ignoring his wife's objection. The boy stood beside Justin, and the man laid a guiding hand on the lad's shoulder and walked out of the room. They slowly strode down a short hall and turned into another room quite similar to the previous one. An old, worn blanket covered a figure lying on a cot in the far corner. The man and boy stopped by the cot's side while Kristin waited outside.

"I will try to help you remember your past," Justin told the boy. "Unfortunately, my knowledge of you and your family is quite limited. Therefore, I must do something that I would not do otherwise.

"This very day, you were in the woods not so distant from here with who I believe were your mother, father, and sister. It was a beautiful day, and you were having lunch near an open field. Before you could finish eating, a pack of starving, vicious wolves came upon the four of you. The wolves attacked. You and your sister ran. Your parents fought the wolves, killing two of them before they themselves were overcome. The other two pursued you children. One caught up with your sister, and the other continued after you. The last wolf caught up with you, and though you tried to fight, you had no chance against it. I stumbled upon you just as the wolf leapt for your throat. I shot the beast and killed it before it slammed into you and knocked you into a tree. That is how you got the bump on your head and scratches on your chest. Do you remember any of this?"

Speechless, the boy could only shake his head. He ran a hand over the bandage on his chest.

"Do you recognize this?" Justin asked the boy, pulling from his pocket a medallion with a thin leather strap. He handed it to the boy for a closer inspection. "We found it around your father's neck." The medallion was made of bronze, about an inch and a half in diameter. What appeared to be writing of some type was etched into both sides of the medallion.

The young man took the medallion and looked at it, though it appeared to be more of a reflex than an act of thought. He showed no expression as he turned the medallion over in his hand. He shook his head, but instead of giving it back to the man standing by him, he closed his fist around it, as though he were afraid to let it go.

"I regret that your family did not survive. We have brought them back here for a proper burial. Your sister, who lies before us, died only a few minutes ago. Perhaps if you see her, your memory will be regained." Justin reached over and gently pulled the blanket away from the girl's face. He was careful to leave the blanket at her chin and not reveal any more of her body. She had a young, pretty face that had been left untouched by the awful attack. She had died with a peaceful look, giving evidence that she had passed away in her sleep. The boy stared at the still form for several seconds.

"She is my sister?" he asked in a shaky voice.

"I believe so," Justin replied.

Shaking his head, the young lad backed away. "I do not remember a sister. I do not remember a family. Why can I not remember? Why?" He burst into tears and ran back into the room he had been in before.

"Go comfort him. I will join you in a minute," Justin instructed his wife. She obeyed wordlessly and followed the boy. Scarcely a minute went by before Justin entered the room. The boy was sitting on the cot with his knees drawn up to his chest. He was sobbing, and blood was visible coming out from beneath the bandage on his chest. His fist was closed tightly around the medallion.

"You must lie on your back," Kristin told the crying child. "Your wounds are opening again. Come now. Rest back." Reluctantly, the boy obeyed. Meanwhile, Justin stood beside the table. He held in his right hand what appeared to be a fire stoker. On one end of it was a round emblem, about two inches in diameter. Justin held the end of the slender, foot-long rod over the candle's flame. After about two minutes, he stepped over and gently nudged his wife away. He knelt by the bed and took hold of the boy's right arm. He exposed the delicate, almost fragile forearm.

"You may weep tonight, young one. Weep for your lost family and weep for your lost memory. Weep until no more tears fall from your eyes." Justin gazed into the innocent, red, puffy eyes looking back up at him. Despite the boy's fragile condition, Justin could see strength in those young eyes. He paused for a moment before continuing. "From this moment on, you are part of this family." He positioned the hot poker over the boy's arm. "You are my son. You are Andrew MacLean," he declared and pressed down.

Chapter 3

W ispy smoke from a sea of small campfires entwined with the early-morning mist to enshroud the wavy, verdure landscape in a gently flowing, wraith-like veil of white. The morning sun lay hidden behind the glowing horizon, only moments away from beginning its ritualistic trek across the immense sky. The air hung peaceful yet full of tension. An ominous silence gripped the land, a silence that belied the imminent carnage and death that would soon litter the face of this otherwise beautiful field. Two armies faced each other across a small valley, three hundred yards separating them. Despite the close proximity of the opponents, there were no threatening moves, no cries of war, only well-disciplined patience among the troops. They went about their preparations for war almost nonchalantly, almost as if the enemy did not exist. The scene was nearly identical on both sides.

Around each fire huddled three to four warriors, each fully arraigned in battle gear. They did not speak, nor did they survey their surroundings. Each had his attention focused on the task at hand, which was the final honing of the weapons of war. Swords were sharpened, and shields were inspected for strength to withstand the powerful blows from enemy weapons, which would come all too soon. There were easily three hundred such fires on both hilltops.

On the crest of both sides of the valley stood two large yet rather plain-looking tents, the obvious centers of power for both armies. Numerous identification banners and regal pennants denoting family, clan, and religion hung limp in the still air on ten-foot-tall poles surrounding the tents. As were the colors and insignias on the flags, so were the colors on the shields and garments of the armies. Several horses outside the tents wore cloaks with the corresponding colors. Along the southern end of the valley, a tall, strapping figure of a man rode a magnificent, large black stallion along the line of fires, surveying the preparations of the troops. As he reached the temporary shelter, he dismounted, and after being recognized by two armed guards, he strode boldly into the tent.

"The sword is the second key," a voice was saying as Andrew MacLean brushed the tent flap aside. The voice abruptly fell silent upon Andrew's entrance. There were four other men already in the tent. One was seated behind a small table, upon which a parchment was spread. There was a large object on the table, approximately two feet long by a foot wide, partially covered by a purple silk cloth. Andrew caught a glimpse of gold before the seated man quickly covered the object. He was a brawny man with an unmistakably royal demeanor. His clothing was a bit cleaner and better kept than those of the men opposite him, and his long, dark mustache was neatly groomed. He sat tall and proud, and it was obvious that he was highly respected by his comrades. A beautiful sword lay on the table beside the parchment, with its intricately designed hilt well in reach of the seated man. It was this man who had been speaking, and as the newcomer entered the tent, the seated man stood and quickly addressed him.

"How come the preparations, Andrew?"

"The men are ready, my lord," the newcomer replied, feeling uneasy as he realized he had walked in on a private conversation. "They are most anxious to defend their kingdom and their king."

"And you? How are your preparations coming?"

"I have been ready to defend my king since the day I was accepted as his servant, my lord. I would take on their whole army if need be."

"I pray that the need does not arise. You will do well today, Andrew. Your spirit is strong, and your sword is sharp. We will teach these barbarians a lesson this day, and when it is over, you will be well rewarded for your loyalty and bravery. Go to your brothers and ready them for battle. The hour has drawn nigh."

"As you wish, my king." Andrew turned abruptly and exited the tent. The four men remained silent for a moment longer until they heard the hoofbeats of their comrade's steed fade away. Then the king spoke.

"Donovan, you are sure the one whom we seek is among them?"

"Yes, my lord. My informant confirmed it to me earlier this morning."

"And he has it with him?" the king continued.

"He does indeed have it with him," Donovan confirmed.

"How foolish of the man to bring it to battle," King Edwin Gallard said, shaking his head. "He has practically handed it to us on a silver platter with his blessing."

"I will seek him out during the battle and bring him to you," Donovan informed the king.

"Bring him to me alive in case he chooses to hide it from us. We cannot divulge information from a dead man," King Gallard instructed.

"As you wish, my lord," Donovan answered.

"These men we face may be far more motivated than we first estimated, especially if they know of the sword," one of the other two men stated. "This battle may not go so easily."

"Andrew is a mighty fighter and trusted leader among the men," the king replied. "With his lead, we will have the sword before the sun reaches its peak."

"Does he know of the sword?" the third man asked. He stood well over six feet in height, and his broad shoulders gave him a solid, invincible appearance. His long, hard face was nearly completely hidden by a dark beard. His shield, which lay at his feet, bore the imprints of a dozen battles. Bright, penetrating blue eyes set firmly beneath heavy black eyebrows blazed with a confidence that would make any foe think twice of confronting him.

"I would think not, Walter, unless there has been a loose tongue among the three of you."

"My tongue has remained bridled," Walter answered faithfully.

"Nor have I spoken of it," Donovan answered.

"The secret is safe," the third man stated. "Only the four of us know of our plan."

"I hope you are right, John. If not, who would I have to blame but you three, and with each of you professing innocence? It would be sad to throw out all of the apples just because I did not know which one housed the worm." The king studied his advisers. "But enough of such talk. Our plan is perfect. After today we shall be yet one step closer to having the entire land under our rule, from east to west and north to south. You three shall have your own states to reign over. Let us ready ourselves. The battle shall begin soon."

Andrew MacLean rode his steed along the small ridge, calling his fellow warriors to readiness. As he gazed across the valley, he saw the enemy doing likewise. Fighting was a formal affair, and contrary to popular belief, there were certain rules to which the armies generally adhered. The battle was to take place during the day, for there was no honor in fighting after darkness. Only the lowest of a leader under the most extreme of circumstances would call his troops to attack in hand-to-hand combat after the sun had set. Representatives from each encampment would meet to determine if a truce could be arranged. If not, the two kings would meet and set a time for the engagement, with the result usually being dawn. Neither side would attack until both were ready. To do otherwise would indicate cowardice and weakness. After that, there were no rules. The fighting continued until either one of the kings was killed or one side surrendered, the former nearly always giving rise to the latter.

Since becoming a part of King Gallard's force at the age of sixteen, Andrew had participated in countless battles and earned many words of praise from his king. Through his heroic efforts, Andrew had been promoted several times in the king's army and now held a position that placed him under only the king himself and his three advisers. The glory and honor were secondary to Andrew. Fame was not his goal. He cared not for power. He was a warrior and would fight the same whether he was a leader or a follower. During his eighteen years in King Gallard's kingdom, and especially in the last twelve serving in Gallard's military, he had been faultlessly loyal.

As Andrew reached the end of the line, he turned his mighty stallion and headed in the opposite direction to rouse the rest of the army. Even though he had been a foreigner, the kingdom had accepted him well. He had made friends of many of the men along whose side he had fought, and even those who did not care for his friendship gave him their respect. Nods of acknowledgment greeted Andrew as he trotted by the small fires one by one. As he approached a particular fire, occupied by a lone man, he reined his horse to a stop.

"Are you prepared, Donald?" he asked the seated warrior.

"More than ready," the man replied as he stood. "I am anxious to get this day over with and get back to my wife. We have been gone too long. She will forget what I look like if my return is delayed much longer."

"Then I will take your place, and she will never know the difference," Andrew returned.

"Oh, she will know the difference," Donald answered, "but it will not be by your looks. She will know the difference when I hold her in my arms this evening and whisper in her ear sweet and tender poems of love."

"So that is why she chose you and not me," Andrew deduced. "You are a poet. I knew her choice could not have been based on looks, for she would have made a terrible decision." The two men laughed at the mutual insults as only the closest of friends could.

"Battle well and watch your hide," Donald advised as Andrew prepared to move on.

"Battle well," Andrew replied over his shoulder. "I look forward to celebrating our victory with you and your family upon our return."

"Cynthia will be glad to have two good-looking men for dinner," Donald called out and moved to gather his weapons.

"Two? Who else will be joining me?" Andrew yelled over his shoulder in jest as he continued to the end of the line. It had been Donald's family that had taken charge of Andrew as a young orphan. The two boys had grown up together, trained together, competed against each other, quarreled as brothers, and had even fought for the same girl's affection. While the fight had been a draw, Cynthia had taken a fancy to Donald for reasons unknown to anyone but her. Nevertheless, the two men were brothers again. For some reason, Andrew was bothered that he would not be fighting by his brother's side this day.

By the time he returned to the tent, the four men had emerged and were preparing themselves for battle. They mounted their heavily armored horses and discussed last-minute details. While the king rode into battle with his army, he rarely took an overly active part. Generally, he remained in the rear of the troops where he would be subject to less risk. The king was the leader and brains of the army and too great of an asset to lose, yet, as such, he was required to lead his men into war. Therefore, he was protected at all costs.

"All are ready, sire," Andrew reported. He paused for a moment, then continued. "My lord, shall we entreat for a peaceful resolution to our differences one final time? Perhaps the night has given our adversaries time to reconsider their path."

Gallard looked at Andrew, a look that could not belie the king's contempt at being questioned.

"Andrew MacLean, you have never before questioned going into battle. Why do you now give pause?"

"Forgive me, my lord. There is neither pause within me nor lack of confidence as to your leadership. We shall be victorious this day. To that there is no doubt. It was a mere suggestion, a suggestion born from the desire to preserve as many lives today as possible."

"They have been given every opportunity to turn from their wicked intentions of overtaking our land and spare their own lives," Gallard replied firmly. "They have refused every offer of a peaceful resolution. Andrew, I must be certain of your unbridled resolution to the defense of our homeland."

"My king, I would give my life here and now if it would turn this army from us and save the souls of my men on this battlefield and the soul of every one of our people. I shall fight to the death if necessary."

"Very well," the king replied, satisfied. "To victory, my countrymen!" he cried as he hefted his sword into the air.

"To victory!" those around him responded in a single, confident shout. They maneuvered their horses into position between the lines of warriors. Across the valley the enemy likewise was in position for action. The standard bearer for King Gallard's army hoisted the flag high into the air as a signal to the enemy. They did the same, indicating their readiness. The horses fidgeted about as if they were eager to plunge down the hillside and into the impending chaos. The men stood silent, offering silent prayers to their Maker and blocking out all thoughts not of war. The sun broke over the eastern horizon and began its fight against the smoke and morning mist.

"First infantry, report!" the king instructed, and Walter, who was positioned to the king's right, barked out the order.

The responses were quick and precise.

"Company A ready!"

"Company B ready!"

"Company C ready!"

"Company D ready!"

"Second infantry, report!" the king said. Again, Walter called out the order, and the ready responses came back as before.

"Archers, report!" the king ordered, and as before, the ready response sounded.

"Are the reserves in place?" King Gallard asked Walter.

"That they are, my lord," Walter replied. "Four companies are standing by just behind the crest of the hill, out of sight of the enemy. I should hardly think that they will be needed. Our scouts indicate that the enemy's numbers are half ours, and their weapons are little more than the toys of children."

"If you are ever to rule your own state, you must learn this lesson and learn it well: never underestimate your opponent. His weapons and numbers are plainly visible, but his heart is far from sight. Battles are won by the heart. The sword is merely a tool."

"Yes, my king," Walter replied with a trace of contempt.

"Give the signal for first and second infantry to ready position. I want this over quickly."

Walter obeyed and called out the order. Flag bearers holding pennants for the two infantry divisions hoisted their poles high, and the first and second infantries moved forward, weapons poised. The enemy across the valley stirred.

"Attack!" the king cried out, and a loud, shrill trumpet blast answered. The invisible barrier, which had held the armies in place, was violently shattered. The two countries rushed down the hillsides in blind fury, both intent on destroying the opposition and leaving no survivors. Cries of war and the thundering of hundreds of feet and hooves pounding the ground destroyed the early-morning peace as the tranquil landscape was metamorphosed into a vicious vision of slaughter.

The two armies met in the trough, and the cries of battle were drowned out by the clashing of swords and shields. Each man chose an opponent and struggled with him until one of them was knocked out of the battle. Each thrust of the sword was accompanied by a loud cry, which was intended to strike fear in the heart of the enemy, but within these battle-scarred veterans, there was no fear, only the desire to defend their respective kingdoms. If that meant forfeiting their lives, then so be it. The ground was soon badly scarred, and bodies began building up as the battle raged. Cries of pain born by the deadly carnage accompanied blow after blow. Men too seriously wounded to continue fighting struggled to pull themselves away from the violence to a place where their wounds could be tended. Even some of these received unsympathetic deathblows while attempting to escape the slaughter. Others chose to lie still among the dead, hoping to be overlooked until the battle came to an end. However, for the men still on their feet, there was no time for rest. As soon as one opponent was disposed of, another stepped forward.

Andrew guided his war-tried stallion into the middle of the chaos like the fearless soldier he was and put his deadly sword to use. Three opponents fell in a matter of seconds by its sharp edge. Andrew pushed his horse further and further, going in circles, stepping backward then forward again, avoiding blows while delivering them at the same time. Thick hides draped over the horse prevented the animal from suffering any seriously wounding thrusts. An enemy sword glanced off his shield and nicked Andrew in the side. Without a pause, he leaned over and returned the favor, although with a more fatal result. Somehow, above the shouting and deafening thunder of the conflict, Andrew heard his name called out.

Turning to his right, Andrew spotted his brother trying to defend himself against three of the enemy soldiers. So far, Donald had been successful in holding the attackers at bay, but they were beginning to move closer as he tired. Andrew kicked his horse in the side and guided it to where his best friend and brother stood. Before he could reach him, however, a sword snaked in from behind Donald and pierced him in the back. At almost the same instant, a club struck Donald in the side of his head. Before Andrew's horrified eyes, Donald fell to his knees, as if ready to say a prayer, and then slowly collapsed facedown. The display of cowardice on the enemy's part infuriated Andrew. To strike from behind was the epitome of weakness. Unable to contain his fury, Andrew cried out and began sweeping his sword from side to side. One of Donald's attackers was brutally cut down before he knew what hit him. Another tried to get away, but Andrew's horse reared up and kicked him in the temple. The third man had momentarily disappeared, but Andrew spotted him. He was the one who had stabbed Donald from behind. He was purposely working his way out of the confusion. After a moment, Andrew could see that the man was heading for the woods just off the battlefield. Quickly he scanned the battlefield to determine how the battle was progressing. Knowing that his countrymen were about to end the battle in victory, Andrew pursued the fleeing foe.

When he was about twenty feet from the forest, Andrew dismounted and cautiously approached the edge of the trees. The underbrush was not so thick that he could easily be ambushed, but the still early-morning sun provided less than a preferred level of light. The warrior cautiously entered the woodland. He used his sword to poke in front of him and to push aside the numerous branches that reached out to grab him. He kept his shield ready to defend against any sudden blows that might challenge him. The way of the escapee became increasingly apparent as more and more twigs and branches were broken. It appeared as if the man was having difficulty walking and had stumbled several times. Andrew had ventured about fifty yards into the growth when he noticed a clearing ahead of him. As the growth thinned, he could see his prey leaning for support against a huge boulder as tall as he was, then slowly slid down until he was sitting on the ground. Andrew stopped five yards shy of him.

The man looked to be about fifty years old. He was not a thin man but rather stocky, a good warrior's build. His long beard was mostly gray with a few strands of dark brown showing through. His dark eyes had a hollow, exhausted look that was the result of more than just the day's battle. The lined face seemed to hold the tales of a thousand journeys, and the skin was baked a dark, leather-like tan. An ugly scar stretched across his face from the bridge of his nose to the bottom of his left jaw. His left arm dangled limp at his side. There was a deep red stain across the man's midsection, and Andrew knew that this man would not live much longer.

"Stand, you coward, so that you may at least die a death a little more dignified than that which you handed my brother," Andrew spat at the perishing man.

"Stand I would if my feeble body were able to do so," the man replied in a resigned tone. "However, I am afraid, my friend, that I cannot. The years and the battle have worn me frail. I will meet death where I rest."

"So be it," Andrew replied callously. "With consideration to the way you took my brother's life, I will find no dishonor in slaying a man who is not on his feet." The warrior raised his weapon and poised it over his enemy, ready to deliver the merciless blow that would avenge his brother's cruel death. He then made the mistake every warrior is trained over and over not to make. He looked into the eyes of his enemy and hesitated. Did he see gratefulness in those dark pits, or perhaps relief? There was no fear, not even the hint of apprehension. The man merely stared back at his imminent slayer without flinching a muscle or batting an eye. In that briefest moment of time, Andrew caught a glimpse of something shiny hidden in the leaves about ten feet to the man's right.

The warrior lowered his weapon and slowly walked around his enemy. The seated man watched as Andrew circled around him toward the object. When he deduced what Andrew's intentions were, he struggled to rise to his feet, but his efforts were futile. He slumped back to the ground, exhausted.

"What is this?" Andrew queried as he stooped and reached for the shiny metal. "It is a sword, and unlike any I have ever seen," he answered himself as he lifted the weapon high into the air. Sunlight glinted off the mirrorlike blade and reflected back into Andrew's eyes. He lowered the sword and inspected it more closely. It was magnificent, unlike any weapon he had ever seen, much less held, in his own hands. The craftmanship was impeccable. Near the hilt were a dozen gems embedded in the blade itself, a great feat of workmanship. The handle itself was clearly designed for two-handed use and was made of gold with inlaid ivory. Carved in the gold were symbols unfamiliar to Andrew, yet he knew that they represented something of importance by their design. The value was beyond his comprehension.

"You tried to hide this so I would not find it."

"It is not a weapon for you," the man replied solemnly.

"And why is that? Is it not a part of the spoils of war? Do I not have a right to it after I kill you?"

"You have no right to it, neither now nor ever. It is not part of the spoils of war. What you hold in your hands is the sole reason for the war."

Andrew ran a hand along the flat of the blade. "How could a mere weapon precipitate a war?" he asked. "It is a beautiful sword, granted, but it is not worth the deaths of all these men." He turned his accusing eyes on the dying man. "This war was initiated by your country's plot to invade my kingdom. We captured several spies who confessed to that fact."

"My country is one of peace. We had no plans to invade your land or any other. We deployed no spies to your kingdom. They must have been set up by your king to justify this war. He had to have a reason to fight us, for he knew the sword was within our kingdom, and he was determined to possess it. A story of espionage and foul plots was created. Who would disbelieve it?"

"I disbelieve it," Andrew responded loyally. "King Gallard would not start a war just to obtain a simple weapon. It is a ludicrous notion. He even presented multiple pleas for a peaceful resolution to avoid war, but your king denied them all."

The man shook his head. "There were no offers of peace," he said. "I have been near my king's side for the past two days, hardly leaving it since dawn yesterday morn. You saw our numbers, our weapons. Why would we invade a kingdom such as yours?"

Andrew considered the man's claims but could not bring himself to believe that Gallard was anything but honorable. "Many lives have been lost today because of your king's aggression," Andrew replied. "Your claim that this battle was fought over this meager weapon is insulting at best."

"What you hold in your hands is not an ordinary sword, and it is worth more than all the lives on the battlefield today. In the possession of the right man, it can lead to great things, but in the hands of the wrong man, it can result in great evil and despair."

"How can a mere piece of metal, valuable as it may be, mean so much? Is it magical?" Andrew asked sarcastically as he turned the weapon over in his hands.

The old man looked closely at Andrew before replying. His gut instincts told him that Andrew was an honorable man, although there was nothing in Andrew's appearance that would justify such an evaluation. The dying man knew that he had to take a chance.

"Some think it is. Others scoff at the notion. There is a great history behind it, a history that gives uncertainties as to its qualities."

"Well, since I shall own this fine sword from this day forward, I believe I should know its history. Tell me about this weapon that you would not have me possess."

"I will tell you out of respect for the sword and what it represents so that you may comprehend what you have. I cannot keep it from you. Perhaps you will continue my quest." The man closed his eyes and took as deep a breath as his dying body would allow.

"There was a king, many years ago, now all but forgotten by time. Yet, in his time, he was one of the most righteous kings who had ever ruled in realms near and far. Reginald DuFay was his name. His kingdom flourished during his reign and became the virtual Eden. There was no fighting, no dissension among his people. The land produced bountiful harvests year after year, and there was more than enough for all. King Reginald was incredibly wise and, naturally, immensely popular. People of the countries around his kingdom took notice of his goodness and petitioned for him to come and help their own struggling communities. Reginald's kingdom grew larger, and soon he was the ruler of a thousand mountains, from where the sun rises in the morning to where it sets in the evening." Once again, the man hesitated in his story. He closed his eyes for a moment as if gathering his thoughts, then continued.

"A sword, shield, and breastplate were made in his honor. The blacksmith from one of the villages forged them from some of the tokens of payment he received for his services to others. When people learned of what he was doing, they voluntarily contributed some of their most precious possessions for his use. News of these magnificent items spread across the land, and soon they became a symbol of the king. He wore them at formal celebrations, when foreign dignitaries visited, any time he could. When he was ready to pass from this world, King Reginald gave the armor to his son, and his son became overlord of the land. And thus it continued from generation to generation." The man looked at Andrew, knowing that his time was short. The sword sparkled in the morning sunlight and seemed to give the speaker a little more strength. He spoke with more authority.

"However, several generations after King Reginald's death, his descendants became placid. Their power became their weakness, for their thoughts turned away from the land and the people to themselves. The moral fiber of each generation dissolved more than that of its predecessor until DuFay's descendants were not even a shadow of his righteous character. The kingdom relaxed, and its defenses were let down. Invaders from a distant land swooped down and devoured this weakened kingdom. They were barbarians. They burned and plundered and slaughtered their way to the middle of the kingdom. Legend tells that in order to prevent the sword, shield, and breastplate from falling into the hands of evil men, the king of that day summoned his three bravest, strongest, and wisest warriors. He gave each man one of the pieces of armory and charged them to flee the battle and protect their possession with their very lives. The men were supposed to rendezvous at an appointed time and place in order to return the sword, breastplate, and shield to the king's family."

"What happened?" Andrew asked, somewhat intrigued.

"Who knows? Destiny? Fate? For whatever reason, the three men did not come back together, and to this day, the royal pieces of armor remain apart."

"That is an interesting story," Andrew said impatiently. "I shall tell it to my children someday as I put them to sleep."

"You do not understand."

"I understand that you are only trying to prolong your own life in hopes that one of your comrades rescues you from my sword."

"My death is a foregone matter, and in truth, I welcome it," the man replied. He looked at Andrew and summoned his strength to continue the tale. "You do not understand the importance of what you hold."

"By all means, enlighten me," Andrew replied sarcastically, admiring the sword as he executed several fighting maneuvers. "What grand magic does it possess?"

"Many legends have been born over the years concerning these things. What is true and what is not, I am uncertain. Most people today know little of the truth, and what they do believe, they recite as fairy tales to their children at night. It has been said that the blacksmith who forged the sword, shield, and breastplate was also a sorcerer and placed within them spirits. For the sword, he placed within it a spirit of power. For the shield, he placed within it a spirit of knowledge. For the breastplate, he placed within it a spirit of perfection. It is said that the person who possesses all three items shall rule a thousand kingdoms. It is also said that King DuFay's own spirit dwells within them, a spirit of utmost courage and bravery. When the three are held together, the ancient spirits will awaken, DuFay's soul will be summoned, and he shall bring to the world righteousness, peace, and prosperity that have not been known for hundreds of years. Other legends say that they are the keys to timeless treasures, treasures mortal man cannot comprehend."

"What do you believe?" Andrew asked, enraptured by the tales.

"I believe my spirit is struggling to leave this broken body." The man sighed, and his eyelids began to slowly close.

"What of the shield and breastplate? Do you know where they are?" Andrew inquired.

"If I did, I would not be here now with my life flowing out of me. Many years I have wasted searching for them, hoping to return them to the rightful line. Legend says that only a descendant of

King DuFay, good in heart and soul, can summon the spirit and bring to the land prosperity, peace, and goodness. If anyone else attempts this, he will be consumed by the spirit's fire. He will be driven to insanity and irrationality, and he will conquer the world through violence and bloodshed. The world will be driven into darkness, depravity, and hopelessness for a thousand years." The dying man looked at Andrew with fading eyes. "Who knows what is true and what is not."

"So how did you come by the sword?" Andrew inquired.

The man struggled to respond as his strength continued to fade. He tried to stifle a coughing spasm but was not successful.

"Not in so different a manner than you," he finally answered, his voice soft yet raspy. "It was given to me by a dying man, a priest actually, when I was near your age. He had just returned from a journey during which he had obtained the sword, but there had been a fight. His injuries were taking his life, as mine are now taking my life. His breath was leaving him quickly. He managed to tell me where he had hidden the sword. He charged me with returning it to the heir of DuFay, and with his last breath, he managed two final words: knocks bucking."

"Knocks bucking?" Andrew repeated, a quizzical look on his face. "What does that mean?"

"I do not know," the man answered. "From that moment on, my life was spent trying to locate that royal line and to return the sword to whom it rightfully belongs. I believed I was close once, but greed and corruption, two of men's most despicable traits, thwarted my efforts. If it falls into the wrong hands, this land could be doomed forever. Imagine what an evil person who possessed all three would do if he knew of the legend and the legend was true. Ultimate control. Ultimate corruption."

"Hmm," Andrew murmured. "Ultimate power. So that is the motivation for King Gallard's quest. You were trying to prevent him from finding it. Yet what good would it do him without the breastplate and shield? Even if he possessed all three, they would still do him no good unless he was the descendant whom you seek."

"Who is to say that he does not already possess one, or perhaps even both, of the others?" the man answered. "I have heard tales of Gallard and his past. He is not the right man. Your naïve loyalty has blinded you to the true man he is, for honesty and fairness are strangers to him. However, it is not inconceivable that he could fool the people. Everyone would believe that he is the overlord. He could make whatever claims he desired and dispel all the legends. As I said, few people remember the truth to begin with."

As the man's life slowly drifted away, his eyes drooped shut, and he gave a sigh of relief. "My life is over. I am afraid I failed in my task." He struggled to open his eyes and looked up at Andrew. "What is your name, young man?"

"I am Andrew MacLean," Andrew replied.

The man gazed deeply into Andrew's eyes and spoke. "Andrew MacLean, with my last breath, I charge you to find the descendants of King Reginald DuFay and return the sword to the rightful bearer. Protect it with your very life."

"Protect it I will," Andrew said with a slight grin on his lips as he beheld the object in his hands. "Do not worry about that."

The old man closed his eyes, and the last remnants of his life ebbed away. He breathed his last, and his head slowly drooped forward.

Andrew shifted his unsympathetic gaze back to the deceased man. "I regret that I was not able to avenge my brother's death on you, old man. That you did not live beyond the battle gives me little consolation. I will leave you where you spoke your last and let the beasts of the field dispense with your remains. Since you were not honorable as you murdered Donald, you will not receive an honorable farewell." As he finished his speech, Andrew heard horses approaching from behind him. He whirled with his own sword drawn, expecting to see the enemy, but was only partially relieved to see his own countrymen. King Gallard and his three officers dismounted their horses.

"So this is where you disappeared to, Andrew," the king said.

"It was this man I followed," Andrew said, indicating the corpse. "My intentions were to slay him."

"A field full of enemy soldiers for the killing was not enough for you? You had to pick out one fleeing old man to pursue into the forest to slay?" Walter said accusingly.

"He stabbed Donald in the back, like a coward. I saw him running for the trees, and knowing that the battle was going well, I followed him. I wanted to pay him back for killing my brother in such an unworthy manner."

"I see," the king murmured, looking at the sword in Andrew's left hand. "You were successful in your efforts from all appearances. I have never seen that sword before. Did it belong to the dead man?"

"No," Andrew answered, for indeed it had not been the man's personal property. "I found it under some leaves several feet from him."

"Maybe he was trying to hide it from you," Donovan speculated.

"Why would he bother to hide a sword from me?" Andrew innocently asked. "Surely he would have no use for it after he died."

Donovan did not reply.

"May I see it?" the king asked.

"Surely, my lord," Andrew replied and handed the sword to his king. He disliked parting with his prize, but he had no other choice. The king hefted the weapon and inspected it closely.

"Yes, yes," he mumbled to himself. "I believe this is it." His advisers gathered closer to him and also peered closely at the sword. Andrew could tell that they were getting overly excited, and he did not like it. "This would be a fine gift to your king to show your loyalty," Gallard said to Andrew.

Now Andrew was in a corner. If he did not give in, he would be accused of being a traitor and killed. If he did give in, then the king would be in possession of the sword. If the dead man's words were true …

"It would be at that, my lord. But has not my brave fighting shown my loyalty over the years? Did I not do you honor on the field today?"

"Are you refusing to relinquish this fair weapon to your lord and king?" Walter asked in astonishment.

"I believe that I would like to retain this sword as compensation for my brother's death," Andrew answered.

"Many men died on the battlefield today. It is a part of life. Who are you to require compensation for one man's death?" Walter asked.

"What are we to do now?" John asked the king. "We must have it."

"And we shall," Gallard replied confidently. "Andrew will present this to me, as is proper for a servant to present his master an offering." The king handed the sword back to Andrew. "He knows that such a sacrifice on his part will be well rewarded in the future. *Very* well rewarded."

Andrew reached out and grasped the outstretched weapon. For a moment, he reconsidered his decision about keeping the sword. However, the thought quickly passed, and he knew that he could not surrender it.

"Good King Gallard, I regret that I will not be able to accommodate your desires today. I will fight a thousand battles for you, and I will gladly sacrifice to you any of my earthly possessions. Any, that is, except for my latest acquisition. I must retain this sword."

"I see." Gallard eyed Andrew deeply. "Then I regret what must now happen, but it is by your choice. Gentlemen, the sword please."

The three men slowly advanced toward Andrew and drew their weapons. Andrew laid his prize on the ground, picked up his shield, and raised his own sword. For some reason, he could not bring himself to brandish the beautiful weapon in battle. Walter moved over to Andrew's right, and John took to his left. Donovan remained in front. For a moment, there was no movement and complete silence as the men contemplated what course of action they were going to take. Then suddenly, in the blink of an eye, the melee began.

Donovan and John attacked simultaneously, raising their swords above their heads and taking several quick steps forward.

Andrew raised his shield and moved forward to meet John. The latter's downward blow glanced off the shield, and Andrew rapidly turned. He parried the thrust from Donovan and kicked him in the midsection, sending him tumbling off to the side. Andrew dropped to the ground and rolled several yards to his right, just avoiding another stroke from John. Quickly, Andrew jumped to his feet and turned to face his attackers. John's sword had momentarily embedded in the ground, but he tugged it free and sent a pivoting, waist-high slash at Andrew. The warrior stepped back and gave the off-balance attacker a tremendous kick to the side of his head. John crumpled to the ground, unconscious. Just as Andrew was about to finish him off, Donovan made another charge and forced Andrew to change his motion, throwing his balance off. He was barely able to deflect the incoming sword with his shield and stumbled to the ground. Sensing the kill, Donovan straddled Andrew and raised his sword high. He did not have a chance to bring it down. Andrew rolled backward and thrust his legs up, catching Donovan in the groin. With a scream of agony, the attacker dropped his sword and doubled over. Andrew brought his weapon up and sliced Donovan's midsection. As the dead man fell, Andrew rolled to the side and pounced onto his feet to face whatever else was next.

To this point, Walter had not taken part in the battle but had merely watched. Now he took a battle stance, his legs spread apart and slightly bent at the knees. He held his weapon out in front of him, pointing it at Andrew.

"You have held yourself well, traitor, but those two were always the weaker. Let us see how you do against a real man."

"Should one appear, I would be more than happy to show you," Andrew replied, not the least bit intimidated. "Until then, I will just have to keep fighting you pathetic women."

With a cry of rage, Walter raised his sword and attacked. He covered the fifteen feet between them in the blink of an eye and brought with him a blow intended to kill instantly. The defender raised his shield and braced for the impact but nevertheless was knocked back several feet. It was followed immediately by another and then another until all Andrew could do was hope that the big man tired quickly, for he could not take any sort of offensive position. His sword dropped from his right hand, as it took all his concentration just to hold his shield. Suddenly Andrew felt a boulder at his back and could retreat no farther. His arms ached from holding the shield, and he nearly panicked from the unyielding situation.

"The man is here, boy, and has taught you a lesson. Too bad you will not be around to learn from it." Walter smirked evilly as he raised his weapon for a mighty stroke. Andrew was not a man to submit to defeat so easily. He lunged forward and punched his adversary in the midsection, knocking his breath out of him. Without a moment of hesitation, Andrew swung his shield up and connected with Walter's face. Walter stumbled back, completely taken by surprise. Andrew took two quick steps and swept his sword from the ground. At the same time, he caught a glimpse of a figure ten feet to his right. It was John. He had regained consciousness, and the prized sword was in his possession. Andrew reached into his right boot, and a six-inch dagger magically appeared in his grasp. With a flick of the wrist, he sent it flying at the man. The deadly weapon embedded itself deep into John's back. He took three steps forward before crumbling to the ground. That was all the fighting Gallard needed to see.

"Enough!" he cried. Walter froze in place, coiled to spring on Andrew again. He looked at his king with a quizzical and almost contemptuous glare but said nothing.

"Take the cursed sword, you traitor. I have seen enough killing for today. Be warned, however. This is not the last of the fight. I will have that sword along with your head. For years, I have battled for it and will not give up now. A little more time will not matter. I will track you down. You shall never have a moment of peace as long as you hold that sword. When the day comes that we meet again, you will dearly wish that you had relinquished it to me here and now."

"You shall never have this sword. It does not belong to you, and you do not deserve it. I shall do with it as I please." Andrew walked over and picked up the sword from beside John. He pulled his dagger from the man's back and wiped it off.

"Another day," Walter hissed as he mounted his horse. "Another day."

King Gallard turned his horse and raced out of the woods without another word. Walter followed, leading his fallen companion's horses, leaving Andrew alone with the two dead men. The warrior, tired and sore, pulled himself up onto his own steed and left the gloomy scene. He headed opposite of Gallard and his army, not knowing where to go or what to do.

Chapter 4

The early-afternoon sun beamed brightly in the cloudless, azure sky, and the gentle whisper of a breeze carried its warmth across the land. A small, well-traveled road wound its way through an ocean of colorful, aromatic flowers before vanishing into a thin forest of small, fat trees. Just as the field was alive with the buzzing of insects and bees, so was the forest alive with the fanciful flights of its feathered inhabitants. Puffy, parachuting spores and seeds littered the air as they were caught up in the wind and carried away. A small rabbit hopped into the middle of the road and paused, then barely managed to scramble out of the way of the huge beast bearing down the path.

The rider reined his horse to a halt as the tiny rodent disappeared into the thicket. Slowly he dismounted and reached for a bulging water skin dangling from the saddle. He gave the horse a tender slap on the hind section, and the beast moved over to the side of the road and began munching on the rich, sweet honeysuckle that bordered the way. The man took a long swig of water, and a small stream trickled down his short, sandy-colored beard. He took a few steps over to his horse, retrieved a small bowl, poured some water into it, and lifted it to the animal's mouth. The horse took a break from its feasting to slurp the water, then returned to the vegetation.

"I know you are tired, Annon," he said to his companion as he surveyed their surroundings. "So am I. It has been a long journey, and for all we know, it may be longer still. Perhaps we will find a place where we can rest for a while."

The man took the reins loosely in his hand and continued down the road at a leisurely pace. The horse obediently followed, occasionally stretching its neck out to grab a mouthful of succulent greenery. Within minutes, the man and beast had reached the boundary of the forest and without pause entered the woodland.

The ground was a soft mosaic carpet of pink and white and lavender. The midsummer flowers were in bloom everywhere. For a moment, the man almost regretted tromping on the beautiful pattern woven by the flowers, but his masculinity arose to conquer the effeminate emotion, and he stepped with a little more authority. His steed tugged on the reins to the man's right, and knowing that his horse smelled water, he followed.

About thirty yards beyond the road, a twenty-foot-wide stream snaked through the woodland. So clear was the water that the man could see the bottom of the stream in areas that were several feet deep. Annon moved into the middle of the cool, slow-flowing water and drank deeply. His master stayed several yards upstream and, after taking off his clothes, proceeded to wash off the grime that had built up over the previous week. The refreshing coolness felt as if to wash away some of the weariness and melancholy along with the dirt. The man's body was almost completely relaxed when his horse suddenly lifted his head. The relaxation was chased away by apprehension.

"What is it, Annon? Trouble?" he asked his steed as he climbed out of the stream and quickly donned his clothes. The horse's ears twitched, and he nodded his head up and down quickly several times. The man, fully clothed, stood still and listened intently. At first, he could hear only the trickling of the water, but after a couple of seconds, he detected faint, feminine squeals of panic which were clearly originating from upstream. Swiftly, the traveler swooped up on his steed and charged upstream. After about one hundred and fifty yards, he slowed down and carefully approached the scene.

Three lovely young ladies, their clothes soaked through, stood in the water along the stream's rocky bank, confronted by four very dirty, very savage-looking men. Two of the ladies had dark hair, and the third was blond. They were all well developed, the stranger noted, probably in their early to mid-twenties. Three of the men held onto strands of fabric, which they had obviously ripped from the girls' attire, and looked quite intent on removing the rest of the girls' coverings. The attackers were all large in stature, each one standing over six feet tall, with broad shoulders. They all had long, blondish hair that extended below their shoulders and beards of varying lengths. The lighter complexion of their skin was not completely lost under the filth that covered their bodies. Being downwind of the men, the stranger could smell the strong odor of unwashed bodies.

Helpless and terrified, the maidens hunched together and tried to cover themselves as best they could. The men moved closer. While two of the maidens took a step backward, one of them, the one with flowing black hair, stood her ground, a look of staunch defiance on her face. The closest man reached out and grabbed her by the hand. Her companions grappled for her, but their efforts were in vain. She was roughly jerked into the middle of the stream. With her free hand, she lashed out at her captor and just grazed his rough face. He backhanded her across her cheek and immediately grabbed her loose hand. The spectator had seen enough. He nudged his horse, and they proceeded at a rather nonchalant pace toward the action.

"We have uninvited company," one of the men said to his companions. Everybody turned his or her attention to the horse and rider. The four men breathed heavily in malicious hostility. The three women held their breath in dire hope.

"You have wandered in the wrong direction, stranger. If you value your life, you will not interfere in our business and continue your journey. Perhaps you will find other women further upstream for yourself. Move on and live or stay and die. Those are your only two options," the largest of the men told the rider.

The newcomer did not respond immediately but remained stoic in his saddle. He was obviously not intimidated and took several seconds to assess the threat in front of him. He then casually scanned the banks of the stream. There was a slight bow of the head as he contemplated what course of action to take. He nodded a couple of times, coming to a decision. He addressed the man who had spoken.

"I am afraid that I see things a bit differently," he replied calmly. "You see, I cannot simply ride on and let you have your sadistic way with these young ladies. What kind of man would I be to abandon them in their time of need?"

"The kind that lives," the man replied.

"Is there any chance that you and your comrades might have a change of heart and go on your way, leaving these young ladies to themselves?" the newcomer asked.

"None," the man replied with a grin that displayed pure wickedness.

"I was afraid of that," the newcomer replied, resigning himself to the course of action that was being forced upon him. "I would rather not have to kill you to save these maidens, but the choice is yours."

"You cannot be serious. There are four of us."

The rider looked at each of the men in turn. The girls gripped one another a little more tightly. The one who had been slapped had been allowed to rejoin her companions upon the appearance of the rider. He finally responded.

"Yes, there are four of you, but only two of you have much, if any, experience in hand-to-hand combat. The other two will quickly fall out of the fight, leaving yourself and one other. While you may have experience in bar room brawls and alley fights, you do not have much if any formal training in hand-to-hand combat. I beseech you one last time, go on your way. I do not care to take any lives today."

"You are mad," the speaker of the foursome said. His body language indicated that he was ready to fight. The rider gripped the horse's reigns tightly with his left hand placed his right hand on the hilt of his sword, which was strapped to the right side of his saddle.

"I would hate to be so desperate for a woman's company that I would be willing to die before I had a chance to enjoy her. But looking at you, I see the epitome of desperation and loathsomeness and am not surprised."

The two vagabonds closest to the newcomer shouted in anger, produced their weapons, and charged clumsily. The rider tugged on the reins, and his horse reared up, kicking the closest man in the temple, knocking him back several feet and into unconsciousness. In a flash he dismounted. The second man brandished a long sword and after dodging the horse's hoofs, sent a clumsy strike toward the stranger. The newcomer quickly stepped back, and the blade met only the bottom of the stream. Off balance, the man tumbled headfirst into the water. The stranger used the hilt of his sword and whacked the man in the back of his head, knocking him out. He quickly looked at the other two men, taking a strong defensive posture.

A third man took up the attack, but he moved more slowly and carefully. A huge sword was in his grasp, and it was obvious from the way he waved it that he knew how to use it. The newcomer stood ready, waiting for the man to make his move. The fourth man circled around the stranger and unhooked a tough, painful-looking leather whip from his side. The newcomer, now situated between the two men he had previously assessed as being the stronger fighters of the four, looked his undesirable situation over and tried to form some sort of plan. Before he could begin to think, the whip cracked, and he felt a sharp sting on his right arm. It was followed almost immediately by another crack, and this time his back was the target. He tensed for a third attack, but his body was not the target this time. The whip wrapped tightly around his sword, and it was ripped from his grasp. Now he was weaponless.

"You should have taken option number two, stranger," the man with the whip said with a snicker.

"And you should have gone on your way, peacefully," the stranger replied. "Now I must kill you. Ladies, this may not be pretty, so I would suggest that you go on your way." The women did not budge but merely stared at the battling men, too frightened and too mesmerized to move.

The whip snapped again, and a streak of pain shot up his back. Immediately, the swordsman attacked, but his target stepped to one side, and the blow missed. While the attacker was pulling back for another stroke, the stranger moved in and with a strong forward kick sent the man reeling backward. The stranger quickly turned to face the other man and was met with a weak scourge to his cheek. The fallen man had quickly regained his footing and was preparing for another attack. Seeing this, the man with the whip lashed out again and entangled his prey's left foot, just below the knee. With a mighty jerk, he sent his opponent to the ground. The would-be hero tried to unravel the strap of leather, but it was wrapped around his leg too tightly. Out of the corner of his eye, he caught sight of the other man quickly moving in for a final, fatal blow. Without a second to lose, the stranger grasped a dagger from his right boot and flicked it at the attacker. It embedded itself in the man's chest and stopped him cold. As he fell, his sword splashed a foot from the entangled man. The fettered man immediately picked it up and cut the strap around his leg. Leaping to his feet, he faced the last attacker. Knowing that he had no chance, the vagabond dropped the whip and raced out of the water. He quickly disappeared into the woods. There was neither movement nor sound from the women or their savior as they watched the man run. The victor tossed the sword beside its dead owner and retrieved his own, several feet away. He turned to face the women. They seemed to have forgotten their ability to speak for the moment. Silent and still, they stood, their eyes wide open, unblinking.

"It is a bit cool under the shade of these trees, and the water is none too warm. I would suggest you step into the sun and dry yourselves lest you catch ill," the stranger said, breaking the silence.

The women did not move at first but only stared wide-eyed at the stranger. They were still recovering from the attack and did not know quite what to do. It was the blond-haired girl who seemed to gather her senses together the quickest and took a couple of steps forward.

"I … I do not know what to say," she stammered. "Those awful men. We never stood a chance. It seemed so hopeless. We could never thank you enough for what you have done. Who are you? Where are you from?" she inquired.

"The road has been more of a home to me than any land. Many years ago, I called a place far away from here home, but now I have no permanent dwelling. My name is Andrew. Andrew MacLean."

"We owe you our dignity, if not our very lives, Andrew MacLean. How can we ever show you our gratitude?" another girl asked.

Andrew looked at the girls closely. The one who had just spoken had curly, dark brown hair that was nearly shoulder-length. She had the fullest figure of the three yet carried it well and did not look the least bit chunky. She had dark blue eyes and an exceptionally soft-looking face with the faintest hint of an overbite. Her complexion was naturally darker than that of the other two girls. To describe her, Andrew would use the word *sweet*, and as far as he was concerned, she was by far the most attractive of the three, although it was a tough contest to judge.

The blond-haired girl was simply beautiful, and there was no other word that would better describe her. Her golden, wavy hair stretched nearly to her waist and looked to be as soft as the clouds in the sky. Her eyes were light blue and mesmerizing, almost having a mystical quality to them, and they scrutinized Andrew as he gave her a quick visual inspection of his own. Her lips were a bit on the thin side, and her cheeks were not as narrow as those of the first girl. As Andrew looked at her, she could not help but smile gently. She was the tallest, standing well over five and a half feet tall. Her skin was a golden brown, giving evidence that she spent quite a bit of time outdoors.

The third girl was the one who had stood in defiance of her attackers. Her black hair flowed well below her shoulders. Her almond-shaped, dark brown eyes stared back at him, and her cheeks were set high and slender. Her tiny, slightly upturned nose added just a touch of youthfulness to her facial features. Her body was quite lean, yet he knew that she would be soft to the touch. She was the shortest of the girls, standing just a few inches over five feet tall. *Cute* would be the word that Andrew would use to describe this female. She was also the shyest, for she stood a step behind the others, and as he looked at her, she diverted her eyes to the ground and shifted her stance so as not to fully face him. This struck Andrew as a bit odd, being that she was the one who had bravely defied their attackers. There was something in her eyes, in the way that she had first looked at Andrew, that gave him the impression that there was more to her than met the eye. He took only a second before he answered.

"You need do nothing. However, I could use a warm meal and a bed to lie in for the night. Is there a place in your village where I may find such comforts?"

"We will ensure that you have the grandest meal and the softest bed you have ever known. I shall tend to your injuries also," the blond answered, spying a red welt on Andrew's cheek. "It is the least that we can do."

"That sounds fair enough to me," Andrew responded. The girls finished drying themselves and walked over to a quilt that was spread out on the ground about ten feet from the stream. Their half-eaten lunches were strewn over the blanket and ground, proving that they had been interrupted while feasting. The young ladies talked quietly among themselves, and an occasional giggle floated from their huddle as they cleaned up the mess and packed everything into a small basket. As they went about their business, Andrew busied himself with dragging the unconscious men from the stream. He took some lengths of rope from one of his saddlebags and bound their hands and legs as securely as he could. He also retrieved the dead man from the water and laid him by his former comrades. Andrew paused a moment and looked across the stream in the direction in which the last man had fled. There was no movement as he peered into the distance, no sign that the scoundrel had done anything but continue running as fast as he could without stopping. As Andrew turned his attention back to the men on the ground, the girls finished up their packing and in unison turned to face him.

"We are ready to leave. Have you finished what you were doing?" The blond-haired girl inquired.

"What of these men?" Andrew asked in reply. "Perhaps I should stay here until you can send someone to take them into custody."

"It appears that they are bound quite well. We can send someone back when we get to the castle," she answered.

"Their companion may return and loose them. It would be best to take at least one with us for questioning," Andrew argued.

"I care not to have one of those filthy men in my company, even if he is bound," the curly-haired girl said with a look of disgust on her face. "For all we know, there could be other strangers with less than the best intentions near who would not hesitate to complete what these wretches tried to start. Your continued protection would be much appreciated."

"Then we shall leave them here," Andrew conceded, not wishing to argue. "Lead the way home." The girls picked up their baskets and walked toward the road just beyond the tree line.

"I take it your afternoon picnic was rudely interrupted," Andrew said to the blond.

"If you had not ventured along, I hesitate to think what would have happened," she replied.

"I will spare you the details, but my guess is that you never would have seen home again," Andrew said. "Do you make a habit of wandering around alone, vulnerable to men like these?"

"We have been here many times, and not once were we challenged. These woods have always been safe for everybody. Those men were strangers, most certainly not from around here. Just like you, except you seem to be a gentleman. What brings you this way?"

"I am searching for someone."

"For whom are you searching? A friend? Perhaps we can be of assistance," the black-haired girl asked, having fallen slightly behind Andrew and the other two girls.

"No, he is not a friend," Andrew replied, slightly turning his head toward her. "The truth of the matter is that I have never met the man. I appreciate your offer of assistance. However, there are certain circumstances behind my search which dictate that it would be better for me to keep his name to myself," Andrew answered cautiously. "Speaking of names, what are yours?"

"I am Heather," the blond girl answered. "This is Elizabeth," she said, indicating the curly-haired girl beside her, "and this is Marie."

"Is your village far from here?" Andrew asked.

"A little over two miles. It is a pleasant walk, not the least bit tiring. We usually come this way once a week, sometimes twice."

"How large is it?"

"Around the central commons area, there live about thirty families, but there are perhaps two hundred more living under the king's rule throughout his territory."

"What is the name of this king of yours?" Andrew asked.

"You are asking a lot of questions," Marie said from behind the two who were conversing, her tone tainted with a tinge of accusation.

"Does that bother you? Does it make you suspicious of me?"

"Undoubtedly," she replied directly.

"As well it should. However, you may put your suspicions aside. As you can see, I am alone. If I were a spy, would I have wasted my time and put my life in jeopardy to save your lives? I think not. I am just making conversation, trying to find out a little about your home before I get there. There is always the chance that it may be a place where I would not care to go."

"Why is that?" Elizabeth asked. "It is a very peaceful place, and the people are quite friendly. Why would you not want to visit a place like that?"

"Perhaps he has enemies who are looking for him," Heather suggested.

"Is that it?" Marie inquired. "Is someone after you?"

"Not that I know of," Andrew answered immediately. "I tend not to make too many enemies, at least not the type that live long. I try to be a peaceful man. However, there are those who care not for peace, and to them, everyone is an enemy. I simply desire to know the type of place to which I am traveling."

"Our king's name is Richard Talbot," Heather informed him. "He is a great man and a wise ruler. The people under his care are quite peaceful."

"What makes him so great and wise?" Andrew asked.

"Before he came here, we were but a small village, maybe twenty-five or thirty families at most. Things were peaceful, and everyone was happy. The land had been faithful and produced good crops upon which we lived well. But one season, the crops began struggling for some unknown reason. To make things worse, bandits would raid us quite frequently, taking most of our food and some of our herds. The bandits always outnumbered us, and the men of the village were farmers and not trained fighters. We were at the mercy of the attackers. Then one day King Richard ventured along and saw the carnage left after a recent attack. He vowed to protect us and to show us how to farm and build sturdy homes if we accepted him as king."

"How very generous of him," Andrew said sarcastically. "What made you people think you could trust this man?"

"What choice did we have? Could we have been worse off? It was worth the chance," Elizabeth responded. "It was well that we accepted him. Now we have an abundance of food every year with no fear of bandits. We have good homes, and all the people are happy. The king is kind to all and extremely wise."

"Your king sounds like the perfect man. I do not suppose he

required anything from your people, such as half of all produce and a huge castle to dwell in."

"Not at all. He does request that we present to him a small portion of our crops and herds but nothing about which anybody has ever complained. As for a castle, he did not need to build one. There was one already standing, although it had been deserted for as long as any of our people could remember. He and his followers made some repairs and improvements and moved in right away."

"How convenient," Andrew noted. "How long has it been since he first came here?"

"Nearly twenty years have passed," Elizabeth answered. "I was perhaps five years old when he ventured upon us."

"And since that time, there has been nothing but peace and happiness," Andrew stated. "The attacks on your herds and crops ceased immediately."

"We did have one incident several years ago," Elizabeth replied. "A stranger came to the kingdom. He had several men with him. He went directly to the castle to speak with King Richard. None of the villagers ever knew what his business was, but he seemed a peaceful man, and we assumed it was some type of social visit. However, there arose a tremendous clamor in the castle, and all the king's men were called to arms. A huge fight erupted, and all of the strangers were killed, except their leader. He somehow managed to escape and was never seen again."

"Nobody ever found out who he was or what he wanted?" Andrew asked.

"Rumors were started, but I hesitate to believe any of them."

"Rumors, such as?" he prodded.

"There are those who say he was a brother of the king and demanded a share of the kingdom. Others say he was a descendant of the family that lived here many years ago and had returned to reclaim the land. Another rumor says that he was an assassin sent by another king. While each would be easy to believe, I accept none of them. There is no proof, only speculation."

"Very interesting," Andrew muttered. He then changed the subject. "Is this all that you young ladies do, have picnics in the wild and beat away men who attack you? Do you not have husbands and children and homes requiring your attention?" he asked, half turning to address all three girls.

"None of us are married," Heather replied, eager to wedge her way back into the conversation.

"That must be by choice. I would wager that there are many men who would be more than willing to take any one of you for a wife."

"There are plenty of men who would have us, to be sure, but none that we would have. A good man is a hard thing to find," Elizabeth answered.

"Where I come from, women are not so choosy. A good man is one who can provide food to eat, a safe shelter overhead, and stands a better than average chance of coming home every night."

"Here, there is more than enough to eat, shelter for everyone, and peace in the land. The men do not have to go away and fight. We have what is necessary. We can afford to be picky," Heather stated.

"That sounds a bit arrogant," Andrew replied. "Do all women in your village harbor this attitude?"

"Not at all," Elizabeth answered. "Many would be content with any man. It all works out."

"Your land sounds too good to be true," Andrew said, not entirely accepting the pretty picture the girls painted of their homeland. His extensive traveling through countless kingdoms had never revealed a place even remotely like what had been described to him. "I am eager to see this place for myself."

"It is not far now. These are the farmlands of one of our families," Elizabeth informed him, indicating a field to their left. "Corn is this family's crop. They have two acres to farm. Each family has about two acres, although the crops vary. The king provides tools and whatever else is needed. It is a very productive and efficient system. As I said, there is plenty to eat for everyone and a satisfying variety."

"Even a good system is not beyond improvement," Andrew stated.

"Oh?" Marie said, after having shied away from the prior conversations. "I sense you believe yourself to have some better ideas. Do share them with us."

"A person who travels as far as I have will undoubtedly see many examples of agricultural systems," Andrew replied vaguely, "and I am far from an expert on farming. Out of curiosity, how many different crops are grown?"

"I cannot say exactly," Marie answered. "Perhaps a dozen or more are grown across the region. Not all families use the land for crops though. Some raise swine, some raise cattle, some sheep, and so on. It depends on what the land is best suited for." As she finished speaking, the sound of trotting horses grasped the group's attention. They all looked up to see three horsemen approaching from the direction in which they were heading. Marie laid her hand on Andrew's arm as he tensed.

"You need not worry. They are some of the king's men," she assured him. Andrew relaxed a bit but remained poised to defend himself.

The horsemen reined their steeds to a halt ten feet in front of the group. They did not dismount. The man in the middle spoke with a gravelly voice.

"I see you have picked up a traveling companion, Marie."

"This man is more than a traveling companion, Martin. He is our savior. Four vagrants attacked us as we were having our picnic by the stream. This man saved our lives."

"Did he now? Well, we are certainly most grateful, stranger. The king will demand to see you, to thank you in person. What is your name?"

"I am Andrew MacLean. There is no need for the king's thanks. The ladies have already expressed their gratitude, and that is sufficient for me."

"King Richard insists on meeting all visitors, nevertheless. From what homeland do you travel, or perhaps travel toward?" Martin inquired.

"I have neither a particular destination nor a place I would call home," Andrew replied. "I am simply passing through. I do not foresee my stay to be a long one. Just a night or two, and I should be on my way."

"I see," Martin replied, not pleased at Andrew's vagueness. "What of this attack? Where did it take place?"

"The clearing where we picnic by the stream," Marie answered. "Just beyond Dwarf Falls. Andrew killed one of the men, and two others were knocked unconscious and bound. The fourth was able to escape."

"I know the place," Martin acknowledged with a short nod of his head. He turned to his two companions. "Garrett, return to the king. Inform him of what has occurred, that the young ladies have not been injured and that they will be there shortly. Tell him I suspect their attackers to be spies. Edward, you will accompany me to find these men." He turned his attention back to the girls.

"You should return to the castle immediately. After MacLean's horse is cared for, go at once to the king so that he shall not unduly worry over you. I will retrieve these three men and perform a short search of the area before returning."

Before the girls could answer, Martin and Edward bolted forward and were shortly out of sight. Garrett thundered off toward the castle.

"He does not appear to be a very cordial man," Andrew noted as they resumed their march.

"Martin is not an unfriendly person once you get to know him. It is not easy being captain of the guard," Marie replied.

"Of course not, what with all of the fighting going on in the land."

"That there is peace in the land does not mean his job is without troubles. He has his share of concerns. Martin is the king's eyes and must keep careful watch over the land to ensure that an enemy does not encroach upon us without warning. He also must keep the kingdom free of vagabonds and beggars and other undesirables who might jeopardize the safety of the villagers."

"Well, I must say he certainly has done an admirable job of that today. Would you not agree?" Andrew asked sarcastically.

"Those men likely wandered into the territory just this morning," Marie said in defense of her friend. "Martin would have discovered them promptly enough."

"Perhaps, but it would not have been in time to save you and your friends."

Marie gave up the battle. She knew that Andrew was right, but she also knew that she was right, and further debating the matter would not produce different results. Andrew did not pursue continued conversation on the subject.

The foursome passed several more homes and fields as they neared the village that the girls called home. The path on which they traveled became wider and smoother, indicating frequent traffic and maintenance. Eventually, the dirt path became a road of small, hard-packed pebbles that more than likely had been retrieved from the large stream that ran parallel to the road, about fifty feet away. Along the sides of the road were small huts, roughly ten feet by ten feet, spaced about three hundred feet apart.

"What is the purpose of such small huts?" Andrew inquired as they passed one of the structures. "Certainly they are too small to be dwellings."

"The king had those built a number of years ago," Elizabeth replied. "They are simply shelter for people who travel along the road and find themselves caught in terrible storms. There is room for three or four people to fit comfortably for a short period of time."

"How thoughtful," Andrew replied. "Your weather must turn foul quite often to warrant shelters such as this." He was impressed with the idea and wondered what other novelties he would encounter in this picture-perfect kingdom so brightly painted by the maidens in his company.

Chapter 5

T here were no discernible boundaries or gates that gave evidence to the beginning or end of the village. As they passed a field of apple trees, Andrew found himself on the edge of the common area, staring at the everyday life of the people dwelling in this land. There were at least a dozen small, sturdy-looking wooden huts situated around a central water well. Men, women, and children continually milled about, walking in and out of the huts, pausing and speaking with fellow commoners. It was a jovial scene, with laughter and shrieks of glee coming from young children as they chased one another around the well and adults pointing at the kids and smiling. Andrew's skepticism concerning Elizabeth's description of the village slowly ebbed away.

"Welcome to Durinburg, our home," Heather proclaimed proudly.

"Is today a day of celebration?" he asked, watching the people wander about.

"No," Elizabeth answered. "Why do you ask?"

"Everybody appears to be in such a festive and happy mood."

"It is like this every day," Heather butted in. "You will find that most people in our village are quite friendly."

"This is the most active time of day," Elizabeth informed him. "Everybody takes a midday break to come here and trade food and goods. These small huts are where people bring the fruits of their labors and trade for other food, clothing, or whatever else is needed."

"Surely there is not enough room for all the families at once. How is it decided which families get to bring their goods here?"

"King Richard established the system. Each day, only designated families occupy the huts. That way, everybody has a turn at least once a week. Most of the far-out families rarely come though. They generally trade among themselves."

As the foursome came upon the well, the girls stopped. Elizabeth grabbed a ladle that was one of several hanging on posts around the water. She dipped the utensil into the water and took a long drink. When done, she handed the ladle to Andrew. He hesitated for a moment before accepting the water. He gazed at the girl, then followed her example and tasted some of the purest water that had ever passed over his lips. He, in turn, handed the ladle to Heather. He was about to comment on the water when Garrett thundered up on his mount and stopped by the well.

"I have informed King Richard of what has happened," he said, looking at the group and trying to appear as authoritative as possible. "He is most anxious to greet the man who saved your honor, if not your lives. You must all proceed to the castle at once."

"Will you be coming with us?" Elizabeth inquired.

"I have other matters to which I must attend. The king has instructed me to rejoin Martin and bring the strangers back for questioning." He quickly turned his horse and galloped out of the village. Several small children just managed to scramble out of the way.

"He is not one for idle talk, is he?" Andrew commented as he watched the man disappear.

"Not while he is on duty. Truth be told, he is not much of a conversationalist when he is off duty. That is just his nature. He is a decent man," Elizabeth answered. "We must hurry. King Richard is a good man, but his patience tends to run short. It would not be wise to keep him waiting any longer."

"Why do we all have to go?" Heather asked. "Surely we are not all needed to tell what happened."

"I do not know," Marie replied. "Perhaps you should question King Richard when we see him."

"I do not think so," Heather answered and fell silent. Elizabeth led the group through the extent of the common area and followed a road that was a bit wider than the one they had traveled on into town. To their right was a forest of evergreen trees, and to their left were more homes and crops, but there was no castle to be seen. Andrew was about to inquire as to its location when his attention was diverted by something coming into view off to his right, just beyond the tree line.

The castle was an ominous sight, dominating the surrounding landscape and taking the breath away from all first-time visitors. Andrew was no exception. His eyes followed the wall that surrounded the structure. It extended at least two hundred yards both north and south of a huge wooden door before turning and heading to the rear of the complex. The wall stood at least thirty feet high, and there were numerous small openings dotting the wall's face. On each of the four corners of the square stood a watchtower that rose another forty feet above the top of the wall. Of the castle itself, four floors were visible from Andrew's point of view. The stone that had been used to construct the castle was lighter in color than that which had been used to build the surrounding barrier. There were no more towers other than those on the wall, yet the castle itself was well over forty feet taller than the wall. As he drew closer, Andrew realized that the castle was not all one building but rather several buildings of almost equal size connected by walkways. He could also see the thirty-foot-wide moat encircling the outer walls. He presumed the moat was supplied by the huge lake he could see a short distance behind the castle.

"For a land that lives in peace, your king sure has himself well protected," Andrew commented.

"Most all of this was in existence when he moved into the castle," Elizabeth answered. "Whoever lived there previously built the moat and wall."

"This must have been a violent land at one time," Andrew said. "It would be interesting to know who originally built this place."

"I do not believe that anybody knows," Elizabeth replied.

"Surely there was something inside to identify the previous dwellers before King Richard moved in," Andrew countered.

"I remember seeing some things when I played there as a small child, but the exact details escape me," Elizabeth responded. "We were never permitted to roam too far in there. The king has never made mention of the earlier inhabitants even if he knows who they were. I doubt that anyone knows for sure."

"I would wager that there is at least one person within those walls who knows. You just have to know the right questions to ask the right person."

"And you know those questions?" Marie asked suspiciously.

"Perhaps," Andrew replied.

"What does it matter to you who lived here in the past? You are just a wandering traveler, per your own admission. Or perhaps you do have a destination and we now approach it?"

"I told you, I have a destination, but what or where it is, I do not know. It could very well lie before me now as easily as a hundred miles from here."

"And there you will find this person for whom you search under such mysterious circumstances," Marie said.

"I do not know where I shall find him," Andrew responded.

"Perhaps King Richard will be able to assist you. You should discuss this with him," Heather interjected from behind Andrew and Elizabeth.

"I do not think it would be best for me to do so. I believe we should keep my personal quest to ourselves if I make myself clear. There could be others looking for the same man with less than kind intentions. Your king may know of him, and he may not. I have learned that even kings are not always what they seem to be on the outside."

"Then I would advise you to speak carefully," Marie said.

"Remember what I told you of the one stranger who called upon the king."

"I am not the one doing the calling but the one being called," Andrew responded as he looked intently at the monstrous wall that was now only a hundred yards away. He scrutinized the top of the barrier and the towers to either side yet was not able to identify any watchmen. He was beginning to wonder how they were to announce their presence when the huge door in the center of the wall began a slow descent. Its bottom remained stationary as its top swung out and stretched across the strip of water. The road had been extended via a stone bridge beyond the mote's bank to a third of the way across the water. Less than two minutes elapsed before the bridge finally touched the road's surface as the group reached it. Andrew paused for a moment as he looked around and surveyed his situation. He had not been physically intimidated in any way, yet his guard was up, and he proceeded cautiously. His stallion, which had obediently followed his lead so far, now balked as Andrew stepped upon the wooden bridge.

"What is it, Annon?" Andrew asked, stepping back off the bridge. The horse snorted a couple of times and shook its head from side to side.

"I do not care for strange places either, but we must proceed. We will be all right. We are just visiting, so nothing should happen," Andrew said soothingly as he stroked the horse's neck. The warrior stepped back onto the bridge, and his horse followed without further hesitation.

"So you have conversations with your horse," Heather said, looking questioningly at Andrew.

"It is not a matter of language. It is knowing where we are and how he reacts to certain circumstances. In turn, he does not understand what I say, but he can sense how I feel, whether it be anger, happiness, calmness, or excitement."

"Or fear," Elizabeth added.

"I would think so," Andrew responded. The foursome passed

through the opening in the wall, and Andrew slowed to a near standstill as he took in the surroundings.

There were two buildings in front of him separated by an alley about fifteen feet wide that stretched as far as he could see. About thirty yards in front of him was a well quite similar to the one he had drunk from in the village. Forty yards beyond the well stood the main structures. The buildings themselves were sixty yards wide and built in a staircase fashion. The first step was three stories tall, the second was two stories tall, and the third was two stories also. His original guess as to the dimensions of the structure had been greatly conservative. Each level had at least two stone walkways stretching across the alley. The building to his left contained what was apparently the main entrance to the castle. A series of steps had been carved into a foundation of stone and led to a fifteen-foot-tall set of wooden double doors. Four huge statues, lions from their appearance at this distance, guarded the entrance to the castle. Two statues sat at the bottom of the stairs, and two sat at the top. Two immense stone columns, both containing intricate chiseled designs, bordered the doorway.

To his right, Andrew noticed another structure thirty yards wide and separated from the main building by about sixty feet. It was but one story tall, with small windows spread out every fifteen feet.

"Impressive," Andrew stated casually, trying to hold back the awe that the grandiose surroundings struck upon him.

"More than just impressive," Marie said proudly as she moved up from behind Andrew and stood beside Elizabeth. "There is no other castle in the known world as magnificent as this one."

"It must have taken a very long time and monumental effort to build," Andrew mused. He surveyed the crowd and various types of people milling about the courtyard. Several women were standing around the well, chattering while they drew water. Four well-dressed men exited the alley between the buildings and walked in Andrew's direction, although they expressed no acknowledgment of the little group. A dozen burly-looking men strode casually toward the small building to the far right. In all, there were perhaps a hundred people in view, including many children performing various chores.

"The outer wall and watchtowers were already here when King Richard moved in," Marie informed him. "Most of the buildings were here also, but many had been damaged in some long-forgotten war and were little more than ruins. Some sections were still standing quite soundly, and construction was directed around these parts. I would guess that a quarter of the castle had to be brought to the ground and rebuilt. The stables were not originally here, and they were designed by King Richard." As if on cue, a young boy ran from the single-story structure to which Marie had just pointed and headed for them.

"With your permission, Steven will see to your horse," Marie said as the lad came to a stop beside them. "It will be well fed, watered, and washed off."

"Annon is a *he*, not an *it*," Andrew corrected her. Marie's expression gave evidence that she did not take well to being corrected. He turned to the boy. "You will take good care of my horse," he said matter-of-factly. It was not a question or a request but more like an order.

"Yes, sir. He is a beautiful stallion and deserves nothing but the best." Andrew was not sure if the boy was serious or just trying to get a little something extra for his trouble.

"His name is Annon. He will not give you any trouble unless you give him trouble. What you see is all that I own. It would make me very unhappy to return to my horse and find anything missing. I believe I can trust you, Steven." Andrew squatted down until he was eye to eye with the boy. He reached up and touched the prized sword he had come to possess years before, now wrapped up in a cloth and attached to the saddle. "This is extremely special to me. I won it a long time ago, and it is a unique weapon, none other like it in the world. You will ensure that it does not mysteriously disappear while I am gone. You will be rewarded should it be here when I leave, and if it is not ..."

"My life should anything happen to it," Steven replied sincerely. "It will be safer than a baby in its mother's arms."

"Good." Andrew stood and said a few soothing words into his stallion's ear. He then handed the reins to the waiting boy. "Go and take good care of my friend," he instructed. Steven took the reins and led the horse away, all the while speaking softly to the animal.

"You need not worry," Marie said to Andrew. "Thieves are not tolerated here. You will find everything when you return to your horse, just as you left it."

"Good," Andrew replied. "Let us not keep the good king waiting any longer."

"Follow me," Marie ordered and took the lead. Surprised at her initiative, Andrew fell in line behind her, and the two other girls brought up the rear. She led them into a wide alley and past several doors before stopping in front of one seemingly no different from the others. A guard stood in the doorway blocking their entrance but quickly stepped aside after seeing who it was entering the building.

"Where is the king?" Marie asked. "He has requested our presence."

"He is in the tactical room on the second floor," the guard responded in a deep voice.

The group had entered a large hallway ten feet wide by ten feet tall, and their footsteps echoed back and forth as Marie led them on. The corridor was rather gloomy despite flaming lanterns that lined the walls every ten feet and an occasional window that allowed a few rays of sunlight in.

After several minutes of walking, the foursome approached a set of double wooden doors guarded by two lightly armored, tough-looking young men. The guards had been relaxed and conversing between themselves in hushed tones, but as the group came into view, they ceased their talking and came to attention.

"We are here by direction of the king," Marie informed the watchmen. "Let us pass."

"Wait," the guard on their right commanded. He opened one

of the doors and entered the chamber. Andrew tried to capture a glance of the interior of the room, but the door closed immediately. A minute passed, and the door opened once again. The guard exited the room and moved out of the doorway.

"Now you may go in," he directed to the visitors. Marie shot him a contemptuous glare as she whisked by him and proceeded into the room. Andrew followed, with Elizabeth and Heather trailing him.

The room was not as large as Andrew had expected, judging by the doors leading into it. Walls extended fifteen feet to either side of the door and curved around to form the sides of the room and ran for about thirty feet before curving in and coming together in the far end. Three columns, each nearly two feet in diameter and decorated with exquisite carvings depicting battles, individual warriors, and celebrations, were evenly spaced along both sides of the room. A single torch glowed in what appeared to be copper brackets on each column. Andrew shifted his gaze to the ceiling, fifteen feet above him. An intricately detailed painting of a grand battle appeared to encompass every visible square inch overhead. At the far end of the room, a chandelier boasting two dozen candles hung over a sturdy oak table, around which three well-dressed men sat. As the group entered the room, one of the men stood and approached them.

"Marie, my little girl! Are you okay? Did they harm you?" he asked excitedly, embracing her tightly.

"I am not your little girl, Father. I am a woman," Marie replied, slightly embarrassed. "I am unharmed. They scared us a bit, but that was all." The king released his daughter and turned to the other girls.

"Elizabeth, Heather. I trust that you were not harmed in any way either."

"No, sire," Elizabeth replied. "We have but a few scratches here and there."

"I am relieved. I assume this is the gentleman whom we have to thank for your well-being," King Richard said, turning to Andrew.

"Father, this is Andrew MacLean. Andrew, this is my father, King Richard Talbot." Andrew grasped the king's outstretched hand and received a vicelike handshake. With his other hand, the king gripped Andrew's shoulder.

"Thank you, Andrew. Thank you for my daughter's safety and that of her friends as well. Many years have passed since troublesome vagabonds ventured into our lands. You have done the kingdom a great service today. The people of Durinburg, the people in this very home, are eternally in your debt."

"You are most welcome, my lord," Andrew responded cordially. He stole a sideways glance at Marie. "I did not realize that I was in the presence of royalty at the time."

"She is my only child," King Talbot said, looking at Marie with the eyes of a proud and loving father. "It is fortunate for me, as well as the kingdom, that you happened by." The king released Andrew's hand and returned to his seat at the table. "Come now, young maidens. Recount to me your harrowing episode. Let no detail be spared."

"Heather, Elizabeth, and I were peacefully picnicking by the stream just as we always do," Marie began. "Four men approached us and innocently inquired as to directions to the castle. Though a bit suspicious of their sudden appearance, I saw no reason to respond other than with the truth. While I was providing them with directions, they surrounded us, and before we knew it, they were closing in. We had nowhere to run. They grabbed at us and tried to rip off our coverings." As she said this, her right hand reached up to her chest as if to hold her blouse up. She was shaking ever so slightly. "That was when Andrew ventured upon us. The men told him to leave or die." She looked at Andrew. "He responded in kind, and the men attacked him. He killed one of them, subdued and bound two of them, and the fourth ran away." There was a moment of silence before the king spoke.

"What a frightful experience," King Talbot said, shaking his head. "Andrew, you must be a great fighter to take on four men."

"I am just a humble traveler, no more skilled or brave than most other men. I perceived no other course of action when the men refused to leave. I would rather they had turned away. I take no pleasure in separating a man from his life; however, they made their choice, and the ending of a life was unable to be avoided. I could not let them violate these young ladies."

"Of course you could not," King Talbot said. "How did you happen to be nearby? Were you also looking for our borough?"

"I was merely traveling along the road, looking for no particular place. I heard the girls' screams and investigated."

"I see. Well, since you have no destination, I insist that you stay as our guest for a few days at least and allow me and the kingdom to fully express our gratitude. Our people are very generous and hospitable. Relax from your journey and visit our land. You can see the advances we have made in farming and building, methods unknown elsewhere. Perhaps you will even decide to make this place your home. We can always use strong, brave young men like yourself," the king offered.

"I could use a few days of rest," Andrew replied. "I would be honored to be your guest."

"I am sure Andrew would be quite interested in seeing our systems of farming and agriculture. He seems to have some ideas of his own concerning improvements in farming and other things," Marie said to her father. At this, the two men seated at the table seemed to straighten up and take a bit more interest in the conversation.

"I am sure he does. Everybody knows how to do things better, more efficiently," King Talbot replied. "Maybe while he is in our company, he will volunteer some of his criticisms and superior designs."

"I am sure that I know nothing that has not been considered previously by Your Majesty. I am anything but a farmer. Should anything novel should come to mind, I will consider it a privilege to share such an idea with your kingdom."

"Very good. Marie, will you see to Andrew's comfort and

entertainment? We will hold a great banquet this evening in his honor."

Andrew looked into the king's eyes and was not sure exactly what he saw in them. Gratitude, yes, but there was something else. Suspicion? Or was it something more malevolent hidden in his charm? Andrew abandoned his wariness for the moment as Marie gently grasped his arm and led him out of the room. Heather and Elizabeth followed.

"I would have never known," Andrew said to Marie as they walked.

"What would you have never known?" Marie asked.

"That you are the king's daughter. After all, it seems quite irresponsible on someone's part for the king's one and only heir to be so far from home without any type of protection. Also, your mannerisms are not those of royalty. At least they were not until we passed through the castle's gates."

"There are patrols that periodically scout the land for intruders and nomads. In fact, that was why Martin and his men were riding today. I would venture that they were out to check on us. There has not been the least bit of trouble from vagabonds in many years, so Father allows me certain privileges with my friends."

"What makes you so sure they were simple vagabonds?"

"What do you mean? What else could they have been?"

"What exactly did they ask you when they first appeared?" Andrew inquired.

Marie reflected for a moment before answering. "They said, 'How much farther is it to the castle?'" she replied.

"And you have never seen these men before?"

"Never."

"But if they had been in this area for any length of time, they would undoubtedly have known just where the castle was. I am also sure that Martin, if he is as responsible as you say, would have known about them."

"Okay, maybe they were not vagabonds. They could have been visitors looking for the village."

"If that had been the case, would they have attacked you?" Andrew asked. He did not wait for an answer. "I doubt it. We have four men who are complete strangers by your own admission. Obviously, their intentions were completely hostile. They were not sure where the castle was, or perhaps they were, and by inquiring, they hoped to relax you, to put you off-guard. I tend to believe the latter." Andrew paused in his speech.

"What exactly are you inferring?" Marie asked, confused.

"I would venture to say that those four men are spies. They attacked you because, first, you are beautiful young ladies, and second, because you saw them. They could not let you report seeing four strangers. They would have either killed you after their malicious intentions had been fulfilled or would have kidnapped you."

"That is a fairly fanciful conclusion," Marie said, although she could not completely dismiss it from her mind.

"Perhaps. However, I would wager that when the prisoners are questioned, if done effectively, that is the truth to be discovered."

"What do you mean by *effectively*," Marie asked.

"Spies are trained to resist interrogations," Andrew replied simply. "Sometimes they must be—let us just say *motivated* by different means to provide answers."

Marie changed the subject, not liking where this topic of conversation was headed. "Just how is the daughter of the king supposed to act? You said that I do not act like royalty."

"Not that I have met many princesses, but I would say that a king's daughter would act a little more authoritative and be more outspoken, as Elizabeth is. If I were to guess which one of you three was royalty, she would be my choice."

"Being that I am the king's only child, should I draw attention to that fact when confronted by a stranger?" Marie responded.

"Then you are not the introvert you first appeared to be?"

"I am when I need to be," she replied.

"It strikes me that you enjoy playing games," Andrew stated and looked at her slyly.

"It depends on the game."

"Is deception a game you enjoy playing? You did well today."

"Today was not a game," Marie replied seriously. "When I am away from the castle, I am no longer the king's daughter. Had those men known that I was the daughter of a king, they most certainly would have kidnapped me and held me for ransom. Worse, they could have threatened the entire kingdom. After today, my father will surely forbid me from gallivanting about with my two friends. Either that or insist that one or two of his guards accompany us."

"If your father is as wise as Elizabeth seems to think, then I am sure he will take action in that direction," Andrew agreed.

"He is a wise man. How else could he become such a respected and beloved king? He would never accept complete credit for the well-being of the kingdom though. He attributes much of his success to his wise and loyal advisers."

"Loyalty can change unexpectedly at any moment," Andrew informed her.

"Not my father's men," Marie countered, looking up at Andrew as they walked along. "They have been with him for many, many years. Since before we came here."

"I have known men to turn against their leader after many, many years, men who owed their lives to that very leader. Sometimes it takes that long to discover who a person really is." Andrew paused, then spoke again. "When your father took to this land, did he accept any of the local people as advisers or counselors? Were any of their leaders taken in by him?"

"Not that I recall. I was quite young then and did not have much concern for the affairs of the kingdom. It would strike me as odd if he did not keep at least one of the local leaders as an adviser."

"Who were those men with your father?"

"The one with the reddish hair is Angus, my father's military adviser. The other one is Malcolm. He oversees the land and food production."

"Did we interrupt an important meeting?"

"No, they are always getting together and talking about one thing or another. Usually they regale each other with stories of the old days, when a man could prove himself in battle and be a hero. Their conversations are generally quite boring," Marie answered.

"You are privy to their meetings?" Andrew inquired.

"Well, sometimes," Marie answered hesitantly.

"It seems that your friends disappeared some ways back," Andrew noted, changing the subject.

"I did not notice," Marie replied as she turned her head. "They must have gone to get ready for tonight's banquet. Wait until you see it. There will be a great crowd of people and endless tables of food. There will also be dancing and singing and entertainers galore. It will be a grand event."

"Do you have such celebrations often?"

"Twice a year, a banquet is held to celebrate harvest and the new year. If an event in the meantime warrants another, the king so declares it." Marie stopped in front of the door that marked the end of the passageway. "This will be your room while you are here."

She opened the door. Andrew stepped into a huge, lavishly decorated room. The main living area was nearly twenty-five feet square. A fireplace was set in the wall to his left, and a thick, four-foot square sheepskin rug covered the floor in front of it. Around the rug were two elegant, cushioned mahogany chairs. Marie led Andrew into another room, this one being the bedroom. Just by looking at it, Andrew knew that the bed was softer than anything upon which he had ever lain. Four corner posts supported a canopy over the bed, drooping lazily in the middle. Drapes were attached to the top of the frame and could be untied to completely conceal the sleeping person. At the foot of the bed, a large, cedar chest rested on the floor. A dresser, also made of cedar, stood beside a window along one wall. Andrew was quite impressed with what he had seen already and was astonished as Marie led him into yet another room. This one was smaller and had a two-foot-deep pit that was about five feet in diameter. The room itself was about fifteen feet square, and another fireplace was cut into the wall. A large metal tub hung over a pile of kindling, with a lever attached to one end.

"What purpose does this serve?" Andrew asked.

"It is for taking a bath. Have you never seen anything like this before?" Andrew shook his head. "You fill it up with water and wash yourself off. When done, you pull out the cork stopper in the bottom, and the water drains outside. This way, you do not have to go to the river to wash."

"I have seen wooden tubs and metal tubs but never anything like this," Andrew confessed.

"If there is anything that you need and do not find already here, simply pull the cord beside your bed. Someone will come and take care of whatever it is. I will return and escort you to the banquet in a few hours. Do you have any questions?"

"Just one for now. How do you get water into the pit to begin with?"

"There is a rope outside the window in the bathroom. It has a large bucket tied to one end, and the bucket reaches to the water. I will send someone to fill the bath. They will also bring some extra clothes for you and fetch your belongings from your horse. Anything else?"

"That will do for now," Andrew answered.

Marie reached up as if to touch the deep red welp on Andrew's right cheek but stopped just short of contact. "Then I will see you in a few hours," she said in barely more than a whisper. He watched the young lady seemingly float across the floor as she left the room.

Andrew took another tour of the magnificent living quarters. They were unlike anything he had ever seen, to say the least. As a boy, he had slept in a room with three other people and ate in the only other room in his house. There were no tapestries hung on the walls, nor were there any portraits as this place had. His home had but two lanterns to be lit after dark, yet this place had three in every room. He ran his hands over the arm of one of the chairs.

Such craftsmanship he had never seen. The wood had been carved faultlessly with intricate detail. The cushions were smooth and soft to the touch, and he dared not sit on them in his dingy condition. Andrew had tried to conceal his awe when Marie had been in the room with him, but now he freely gawked over the decorations and grandeur of the rooms. He moved into the bathroom and was inspecting the rope hanging from the window when he heard two knocks on the main door. He walked across the living room and opened the door. Two young boys of about thirteen years stood outside. One was carrying some garments.

"We were instructed to bring these clothes to you and fill your bath, sir," the empty-handed lad informed Andrew.

"I am most grateful. Lay the clothing on the bed," Andrew directed and moved aside to let them pass. The boy with the clothes headed for the bedroom, while the other one steered for the bathroom. Once there, he busied himself with lighting a fire in the fireplace. Andrew watched, but by now he had pretty much figured out what was going to happen. The second boy brushed by Andrew and took up position by the rope. A pulley, through which the rope was threaded, was attached just above the window on the outside wall. The boy loosened the rope from its mooring and let it slowly snake through his hands. After a couple of seconds, the rope's descent stopped.

"What are your names?" Andrew asked.

"I am Jonathan," the boy by the fire answered, "and he is Mark."

"Well, Jonathan, is this not women's work that you do?"

"No, sir, it is not. Women are too weak to pull the bucket of water up and carry it to the fire. It takes strong men to do it."

"I see," Andrew replied. "Then by all means proceed."

Both boys grabbed the rope and began pulling the bucket back up. It only took a few seconds for the large bucket, now filled, to appear outside the window. Jonathan reached outside and swung it in. It took both boys to carry the water over to the fireplace, where they emptied it into the metal tub. Andrew could see that it was going to be some time before he would get to wash. He left the young men to their chore and closely examined the tapestries in the other rooms.

There were three of them in all. Two were in the main room, and the third was in the bedroom. The first two were quite different, one being rather new looking and the other obviously quite old, with tattered edges and faded colors. The latter was a very intricate design of connecting circles, thirty in all, enclosed by an even larger circle. Though it was faded, Andrew could still discern the scarlet and lavender coloring in the body of the tapestry, while the edges had been embroidered in gold.

The second piece of artwork was not just a design. It was a portrait of a grand celebration painted on a large cloth. The castle in the background was without a doubt the very one in which he now stood. A huge crowd had gathered around a central table on which food was piled high. Off to one side, a group of dancers performed. In the distance, there appeared to be a contest of swords and skills being held. The detail was stunning. Andrew could almost make out the individual faces in the crowd. He was ready to move into the bedroom when the boys addressed him.

"Your bath is ready, sir," Jonathan informed him. "Is there anything else that you may require?"

"Not at the moment," Andrew replied. "Thank you."

Jonathan and Mark gave each other a questioning look as they left the room. They were not accustomed to being thanked for doing their chores. As the door closed, Andrew walked into the bathroom. He squatted down and felt the water. It was quite warm and would be a pleasant change from the ice-cold river baths he had known most of his life. He slid out of his dirty clothes and stepped into the small pool. A large groove was cut into one side of the pit's edge, and Andrew positioned himself so that his head rested in the groove. It was almost a perfect fit, and he knew that he had correctly guessed its purpose. Within minutes, the tired nomad was completely relaxed and drifted into a light slumber.

Chapter 6

T he voice seemed to come out of a dream.

"As guest of honor, it would be quite rude of you to deny the banquet your presence, would it not?"

Andrew slowly opened his eyes. Marie was standing in the threshold, and although she was staring out the window, Andrew did not doubt in the least that she had let her eyes wander before she had spoken. Her deliberate distant gaze did not fool him. Thankfully, the soap-soaked water hid all that was beneath its still surface. His stiff neck protested with a twinge of pain as he tried to lift it from its place of rest.

"You are not the rude type, are you?" she asked as she shifted her gaze to him.

"I am when I need to be," he replied, returning her stare. He stretched his arms behind his head and took a deep breath. "Do not worry," he said. "Tonight is not one of those times."

"Good," Marie responded. "The tale of your heroics has no doubt attracted the curiosity of many villagers. You would not want to disappoint them."

"Is it customary for the king's daughter to wander into the room of a strange man while he is bathing?"

"I knocked quite loudly several times, I assure you," Marie replied, keeping her eyes on his. "When you failed to answer, I feared that perhaps you had fallen asleep and drowned. I saw no recourse but to enter and confirm your well-being."

"I expect that is as good an excuse as any," Andrew answered with a teasing grin, clearly disbelieving her explanation. He expected her to retreat from the room so he could get dressed, but she showed no signs of moving. He waited perhaps half a minute before speaking again.

"While I make no boast of prudence or excessive modesty, there are people who might consider it improper for the king's daughter to unabashedly observe a total stranger bathing and getting dressed. I would not desire that your reputation be soiled on my account, as I have the utmost confidence that your reputation is one of pure modesty and discretion beyond question. Now, shall I climb out of the water and dress while we continue our banter, or would you rather wait somewhere else?"

"Oh," she quickly said, as if being brought out of a daydream. "Indeed, I think it would be proper for me to wait outside." She turned and not too quickly left the room. Andrew rose and walked over to the bedroom. He did not bother checking to see if Marie had actually left his quarters. Within five minutes, he was dressed and joined the young lady in the hall.

"You look very nice in those clothes," she complimented him.

"They fit well enough. To whom do they belong?"

"They are yours to keep. We have an extensive wardrobe of clothes that are donated by various people in the castle. Garments get old, and people tire of wearing the same clothing over and over. Periodically, we give excess clothes away to the people in the village."

"How very generous," Andrew remarked as they started off down the hall. "You simply give them away."

"Sometimes the people give a little something in return, such as a bushel of food or some other small token of thanks, but we never require anything in payment."

They continued down the corridor in silence. Andrew noted an abrupt change in architecture as Marie led him around a corner and down another hall. The color of the stone blocks lightened, and supporting arches crossed the passageway every twenty feet.

Tall, fat candles glowed in cavities, dotting the walls of the corridor in an alternating pattern, providing illumination and a bit of warmth to the otherwise cool hallway.

"How many people will be at the banquet?" Andrew inquired.

"See for yourself," Marie answered as they reached the end of the corridor and stood on a balcony overlooking the massive banquet hall.

It was a huge, three-story-tall arena approximately two hundred feet long by a hundred and fifty feet wide. Four rows of tables ran the length of the room, with one long table intersecting the two innermost rows at one end. Chairs were situated at the tables so that everyone seated would be facing the center of the room. An aroma floated up to Andrew that was a mixture of baked hams, roasted chickens, and fresh bread. His stomach reminded him that it had been quite some time since his last meal. In one of the nearest corners of the room, several musicians skillfully played various instruments, and their uplifting, melodic notes floated throughout the auditorium. There were easily three hundred people present, either seated at the tables, standing in small groups, or just milling about. Andrew could see young people, old people, and even small babies clutched in the arms of their mothers.

"That many," Andrew muttered to himself.

"Does it make you nervous?" Marie grinned.

"Should it?"

"If you are not accustomed to being displayed in front of hundreds of people, I would think so."

"Then perhaps just a little," Andrew replied as Marie directed him down a set of steps to his right. This whole charade was nonsense as far as Andrew was concerned. If there had been any way around it, he would have foregone the banquet. But as it was, he had no choice. After descending the stairway, they moved along another short corridor, which led them to the head of the banquet hall where the single table reached across the room. They received scarcely a glance from the crowd as a server accompanied them to their seats. As they lowered themselves onto the highly ornate, cushioned, high-back mahogany chairs, the other attendees began filling their seats around the room. The heretofore noisy auditorium slowly quieted, and the musicians' instruments faded into silence. Within three minutes, the auditorium was deathly quiet. Not a soul moved about, and not a spoken word was to be heard. Andrew wanted to ask Marie what was going on, but his better judgment restrained him. He sat in silence, as still as one of the dozens of life-sized marble sculptures lining the room's walls.

Somewhere off to his left, a door slowly swung open, the groaning of its hinges echoing across the vast room. Still, nobody moved; nobody looked to see what was going on. Andrew turned his head slightly to his right so he could capture a glimpse of Marie. She sat as still as everybody else. He could not help admiring her picturesque profile or inhaling her delicate, sweet perfume. As he looked at her, he was startled to see that she was looking at him out of the corner of her eye. Angered at himself for being caught staring, Andrew quickly shifted his gaze and kept his eyes forward. No sooner had he done this than he felt someone pass behind him. The person stopped behind the chair to Marie's immediate right. Andrew knew that it was King Richard without having to look. It was obvious from the admiration and respect that saturated the room. The potentate addressed the crowd.

"My countrymen, today I came close to losing a daughter, and you a future queen. Four strangers with who knows what foul intentions viciously attacked my daughter and her two friends. It would have been a tragedy for us all. One man is the reason why Marie, Heather, and Elizabeth are with us tonight, safe and sound. One man, a stranger to our country. One man, honorable and compassionate. One man, strong and courageous. Here, in this room this evening, we have gathered our hearts together to express our eternal gratitude to this most worthy soul and to praise this one man who considered his life a little less that he might drive away the four foul scoundrels who maliciously attacked our daughters." The king turned to Andrew.

"Stand, Andrew MacLean, and be recognized. Today you have done for a country not yours that which many would not do for their own country. We are indebted to you." King Richard looked back to the audience. "My countrymen, I present to you Andrew MacLean, the savior of your daughters' lives and honor. Regard him as a hero, for he is nothing less. To the hero!"

The crowd burst into a deafening cheer, and Andrew felt his cheeks grow warm as hundreds of smiling eyes bathed him in praise and adoration. He was as much a stranger to them as a man could be, but their enthusiasm and roaring would not give any such indication. Strangely, he felt at home, as if he already knew these people, as if he belonged here. His initial nervousness faded away, and he let a grin of acknowledgment creep across his face. He bowed his head several times to the crowd. The king let the revelry continue for nearly an entire minute before holding his hands up in a gesture for the crowd to silence themselves. They immediately responded.

"Eat, drink, and enjoy this festive occasion, yet do not forget why you are here." He turned and addressed the musicians. "Minstrels, let us hear music fit for a celebration," he ordered. The bandleader turned to his small orchestra, and after some brief instructions, they erupted with a capricious melody that floated throughout the entire arena.

A female server stood by the king, waiting for his order, but King Richard brushed her off and directed her toward Andrew. She tapped the hero on the shoulder, and a surprised Andrew turned to her.

"What is your pleasure tonight?" she asked.

"I beg your pardon?" Andrew replied.

"What would you like to eat?" Marie inquired. "There is chicken, turkey, venison, and beef. It is your choice. My father has honored you by letting you choose first. No one will eat until you are served. Tell her what you desire."

"Uh," Andrew started, still not sure of himself. "I believe I would like the turkey."

"Excellent choice," Marie chirped. She whispered to the server. "Make that two, but do not tell my father I ordered before him." The girl winked at Marie and returned to the king, who quickly made his own choice.

"Forgive me if I appear inordinately intrusive, Andrew, but what might be the business that directs your path through our country?" the king asked casually. "The timing of your travels could not have been better."

"At present, I have no particular business," Andrew replied. "It was Providence only that guided me in this direction today."

"Providence is an interesting term," Talbot said. "Your use of it would lead me to believe that you are a religious man."

"The king is correct," Andrew responded.

"Is your homeland Christian?" Talbot continued.

Andrew thought a moment, then responded. "My homeland is but a shadowed memory, Your Majesty. I have been on the road for so long that I truly have no land that I would refer to as home."

"You have no family, no friends, no king?" Talbot asked. "No place to which you would return after a long journey?"

"My father, mother and sister await me in Heaven. I have no family of my own, my friends are long forgotten, and there is no king to whom I have an allegiance," Andrew confirmed.

"What does a man have to live for if he has no family or king, no country to defend?" King Talbot persisted. "How could such a life be more than a burden?"

"Every man lives for his god," Andrew replied. "Some men live for their families because that is their god. Some men live for their country because that is their god. Some men live for their king because he is their god."

"But you have none of these," Talbot countered. "What is it, therefore, that you live for?"

"This is true," Andrew answered. "My God is none of these. He has laid a path in front of me, and that is what I live for."

"And what is this path?" prodded Talbot.

"I would that I could offer Your Majesty a precise answer,"

replied Andrew. "However, my path changes direction quite often, and I could not begin to say where it may lead or what meaning it may have."

"Well," King Talbot said as he decided to turn the conversation, "it has led you here, and for that we are most grateful. I shall offer a toast: may your path be full of success and happiness." He lifted his goblet in a toast, and the others at the table followed the gesture. After drinking, the king turned to Angus, who was seated at his right side, and began a conversation with his military adviser. Andrew's mind dwelled on the words he had just exchanged with the king even as he struck up a conversation with Marie.

"Your people appear to be quite amicable and happy," he noted to the king's daughter.

"They are, and why should they be otherwise? They lack nothing. Peace is known throughout the land, food is plentiful, and none lacks shelter over their heads at night. I think you will find it most comfortable and inviting here. The people do not even know you, yet they are ready to accept you."

"How do you mean?" Andrew asked inquisitively.

"Just wait and see," Marie replied. Even as she spoke, a trio approached them. Andrew recognized Elizabeth and assumed that the older couple accompanying her were her parents.

"I am Leonard MacGregor," the gentleman began, "and this is my wife, Melody. Our daughter was one of the girls you rescued today. We could never fully express our gratitude for what you have done. We are indebted to you, good sir."

"You owe me nothing," Andrew answered. "It is always my pleasure to play savior to young ladies in distress."

"She is too old to be running around, playing like a little girl," Leonard continued as if lightly scolding his daughter. "We have told her on many occasions that it is time to find a man and settle down, yet she delays for some unknown reason. We would truly regret having to arrange something for her ourselves. If you had not come along, she may never have had another chance. Again, our deepest thanks. If you need anything, if we can be of any help, what is ours is yours." The man and two women backed away a few steps, bowed, then turned and headed for their seats.

"That was subtle," Marie said with a snort.

"What do you mean?" Andrew asked.

"He was trying to pawn his daughter off on you. It was quite obvious. Could you not see?"

"Why would he do that?" Andrew inquired. "For all he knows, I may be gone tomorrow, never to return."

"Elizabeth is an only child. Her mother went barren after she was born, and her two older brothers were killed years ago when the barbaric raids started. From what I have been told, her father was quite successful at one time and was gaining much respect in the village. In fact, he was well on his way to becoming one of the village's elders. However, that all changed with the onslaught of the raids, his sons dying, and the arrival of my father. He lost nearly everything. Now he is pretty much just like everyone else. He misses that respect. MacGregor is gambling that my father will offer you a position in the kingdom and that you will stay. It would not be the first time that it has happened. If you were to stay and marry his daughter, and you thrived here, he might regain some of that respect via his association with you and better his position."

"He uses his only child, his daughter, as a tool for his own ambitions. His love for her is astounding," Andrew said sarcastically.

"Of course he loves her," Marie replied. "That is a happy family. But once one is exposed to the world of power and gets involved, the hunger never leaves. Naturally, he wishes that this unfortunate event today had never occurred, but since it did, he will take advantage of it. It has always been that way and always will be."

"It is too bad. I do not care for the egotistical self-seekers who make up the ruling class. They work only for themselves and not the people who actually support them," Andrew fumed, his voice taking a sharp edge. His grip tightened on the mug of ale in his hand. "Rulers are all the same. They profess a concern for those who look up to them yet plot behind closed doors as to how they can further their own desires at the expense of those very people. That is the way it always has been, but that is not the way it always will be."

"Well," Marie said, slightly taken aback. "I believe we have a crusader as well as a hero with us tonight. And just what do you plan on doing about this situation you have described? Dispensing with all selfish, corrupt kings and statesman and taking their places? It would be a big job."

"I do not plan on doing anything," Andrew replied after a slight hesitation. "I have no desire for power or high positions. It will be up to the people to make changes if they desire change. Not me."

"Not all kings are corrupt and selfish. Look at my father. He seeks only the provision for and the protection of the people of his kingdom. This is what brings him joy, not acquiring more wealth and power."

Andrew forcibly calmed his nerves. Conversations like this one tended to make his blood boil. The time was not right for hostility or friction. He looked into Marie's eyes, relaxed his muscles, and softened his tone.

"You are right. Your father is an exception to my otherwise well-founded opinion. It pleases me to find a man such as him." As Andrew finished speaking, King Richard leaned forward and broke into the conversation.

"What might you two young people be discussing so intently?" he asked.

"It was nothing important, Father," Marie replied, turning to the king.

"Indulge me," King Talbot insisted rather strongly.

"We were discussing the position and duties of women," Marie responded quickly.

"And what is the view you have been offering, guest of honor?" Talbot inquired.

Andrew answered without pause. "Women are best suited for taking care of the household, which includes educating and training the children."

"And your response to this, daughter?"

"I am of the mind that the man should help care for the children, for are they not equally his? And the wife should have time of her own to do as she pleases."

"That has been the argument between man and woman since the beginning of time." The king laughed. "It still has not been resolved, nor shall it ever be." His voice took a less jovial tone. "Think of something better to converse about, something not so serious," he recommended.

"Yes, Father," Marie replied as King Talbot resumed his conversation with Angus. She took note of the three villagers approaching the king's table. The trio consisted of Heather and her parents.

"Here comes proposition number two, not to be outdone by proposition number one," she said. Andrew looked to see to what Marie was referring.

The villagers stopped in front of the king first, greeted him, and then approached Andrew. Andrew did not really care to be the benefactor of another proposition, nor did he desire their profuse gratitude. However, he kept his expression neutral and let them speak.

"I am Carl Bergman. This is my wife, Annette. You have met our daughter, Heather. Met? What am I saying? In truth, you saved her life. Words could never express the gratefulness our hearts hold for your brave actions in rescuing our daughter," the man said, half bowing to Andrew.

"To know that I have done good for another is thanks enough," Andrew politely replied.

"Perhaps you will stay a few days and allow us to serve you in whatever way you may need. I am a blacksmith and could provide new shoes for your horse, a new sword, or any other item of metal that you may desire. My wife and daughter are wondrous cooks, and Heather is a talented seamstress. She could mend your garments or make you new clothes if you wish. She has too much time on her hands as it is."

"Thank you. I will certainly keep your generosity in mind and perhaps will find an evening to visit your home."

"Please do not hesitate," Carl replied as he, his wife, and his daughter backed away, bowed once, then turned and walked to their table.

"He is good." Marie smirked as she watched the trio leave. "Very good."

As Andrew was about to reply, the server returned with his plate of food. The turkey looked and smelled delicious. It was accompanied by a potato that had been heated and a steaming ear of golden corn.

"It has been a long time since I have seen such an elegant plate of food," Andrew informed Marie. "I would almost regret disturbing it if I were not so hungry."

"Then enjoy it and do not hesitate to ask for more," Marie told him as her own plate was set before her.

Andrew dug his fork into a slice of the white meat and lifted it to his mouth. The tender and succulent meat was like none other he had ever tasted. His stomach growled in eager anticipation of the forthcoming treat, yet Andrew chewed slowly, determined to savor every morsel.

"So what do you think?" Marie asked as she lifted a smaller portion of the turkey to her own mouth.

"It is most delicious. My mouth has never been treated this well."

"I am glad you like it. However, I was addressing the recent propositions presented to you."

"I must say it has been interesting so far."

"So far?" Marie questioned. "What more do you expect?"

"I believe there were three young ladies rescued," Andrew replied.

"Of course. What is your point?" Marie asked, although she had an idea of what he was going to say.

"Three girls, only two propositions. Is there to be a third?"

"I should think not," she replied with a hint of indignation. "I am the king's only daughter after all, heir to his throne. There will be much more to consider in the man I shall one day marry than whether or not he is an accomplished swordsman who can subdue four weak, starving, filthy, clumsy men."

"Good," Andrew said. He looked into her eyes, trying to hide the amusement in his own. "That means I will have to turn down only two offers instead of three. Besides, there is more to consider in a potential wife than whether or not she shall inherit a throne."

Marie looked back to her plate, stunned. He had just insulted her, and the sting of such a discourteous remark was unfamiliar to her. If such an insult had come from anybody else, she would have taken great offense and retorted. However, for some reason, she actually felt a twinge of amusement ... and a challenge. Quickly she continued the conversation so as not to appear hurt.

"Then you do not plan to tarry here long."

"I could not make such a decision in so short a time. I shall rest a few days prior to making a decision." He looked back to his plate. "In the meantime, I plan to sample the different dishes available here."

Marie was not convinced that he was speaking about the dishes of food but said nothing. She did not like the way the conversation had turned and decided to sit through the rest of the meal in silence. However, the king was quick to end the silence in which Andrew had hoped to finish his meal.

"How does your food compare to that which grows in your country, Andrew?"

"It would be difficult to compare. A long time has passed since I ate a meal in my own home, and the flavor, I am afraid, is no longer so familiar. Rest assured, though, your meal is more delightful than any I have partaken of in the last several years."

"Are there any dishes here that may be unfamiliar to you or your country?"

"No, I am quite familiar with the bounty presented here," Andrew replied after a brief hesitation.

"Perhaps your native land has something that is lacking here, maybe a particular fruit or vegetable?"

"No, Your Majesty, I believe the cuisine is about the same," Andrew warily answered. The king's interest in food rang of more than pure curiosity. The questioning had taken on the aroma of interrogation, and that did not sit well with Andrew. It was obvious that the king was attempting to stumble upon some information that would help him decipher Andrew's homeland. Considering his hostile departure from home so many years ago, Andrew was not ready to share such information. With his lack of intimate knowledge about this people and land, he could not know if they had any type of ties or interest in his former homeland or king.

"We pride ourselves on our variety and abundant production of foods," King Talbot informed Andrew. "Surpluses such as we have are known virtually nowhere else. There is not a belly in the whole kingdom that goes to sleep empty at night. With abundance comes choice. It would not be an exaggeration to say that a person could go nearly an entire week and not have the same dinner twice, if he so desired."

"Your accomplishments are quite remarkable," Andrew responded, although he was hardly impressed. "How have you been able to achieve all of this? Is the land so fertile?"

"Granted, the land we have here is good, but it is no richer than ground elsewhere. No, I believe the prosperity lies in the agricultural system we have." King Richard turned to the man on his immediate right. "Malcolm, enlighten Andrew as to our systems." He turned back to Andrew. "Malcolm is our minister of agriculture."

"When we first came here," Malcolm began, "the people were just barely surviving. Each family was able to provide just enough to live on without any surplus whatsoever. It was King Richard's idea of specialization that turned things around. Instead of growing a little bit of everything, each family was assigned a certain crop. By doing this, energy could be focused on one thing, one task, and improvements would surely arise in growth techniques. By becoming experts in one area, the people have given themselves a much-enriched existence."

"A good system, no?" King Richard asked Andrew.

Before answering, Andrew took a short draw on his goblet of wine. It was a good drink, but he had tasted better. He thought of what to say before he voiced his opinion, for he did not wish to insult the king or say the wrong thing.

"If the people are happy, if the people are content, then it is a good system. From what I have seen, the people are indeed happy."

"And content," Talbot added. "Malcolm has done an outstanding job of his administration in this position. I doubt that there is a man who could perform better."

"Of course, if you have any ideas that you would care to propose," Malcolm said, looking to Andrew, his voice laced with sarcasm, "I would be more than happy to entertain them."

"I have none I would care to propose," Andrew responded, not desiring to oppose the man in front of so many people and get on his, and possibly the king's, bad side. "Even so, such discussions are best left for after dinner when words are less likely to be misconstrued by peripheral conversations and ideas are more easily exchanged. Do you not agree?"

"I think this is as good a time as any," Malcolm challenged. "Your Majesty?"

"Andrew is our guest. If he would rather concentrate on the fruits of farming instead of farming itself at this time, then we shall let him enjoy his meal. I would venture that he has not enjoyed such a feast in many months, if ever. Let him partake of our richness in silence and save conversation for another time. Let us not interrupt this time of socializing with conversation."

The king's sarcasm was not the least bit veiled. He had not even bothered looking at Andrew while speaking, and his smirk was enough to ignite a spark within Andrew. He decided to answer Malcolm.

"I would gather that you have had a rather dry year," he said to the minister of agriculture.

"No. As a matter of fact, we have had a bit more rain than in past years. So far, it has been a good growing season. The harvest will be plentiful. What moves you to believe otherwise?"

"I noticed a plot just outside of town on which corn was being grown. The corn appeared to me to be a bit on the short side, what with harvest time being so close at hand." Andrew took another drink as Malcolm replied.

"Truth be told, the corn crops are doing extremely well this season. Never have they grown taller or faster. You are partaking of this year's first fruits. I think you are mistaken."

"No," Andrew answered. "I am sure my observations were correct. The color is good, and the flavor is good, but I have known better."

"Where have you known better?" Malcolm asked.

"It was a long time ago and far away. But corn is a favorite vegetable of mine, and I have a good taste for it. Tell me, what is your timetable for crop rotation?"

"Timetable?" Malcolm repeated, obviously confused. "What do you mean?"

"How often do you switch crops on a tract of land? Every two years? Three years? Five years?"

"There is no switching of crops. One family, one home, one crop. Otherwise, there would not be the developments we have experienced through specialization."

"I see," Andrew acknowledged. "How often and for how long do you let the land rest?"

"Every four years, the land is left bare for one year."

"It just sits there, unused for any purpose?"

"Of course. We plow the ground twice during the fallow year, but it is otherwise unused. What is your point?"

"You asked for my opinion, and now I shall present it. You presently have an open-field system. You need to fence off each field and employ a new four-year system. The first year, you plant wheat, and in the second, turnips or potatoes. The next year, you should plant barley and under sow it with clover and rye grass. After harvesting the barley, allow your cattle and sheep to graze the clover and rye grass. Being better fed, your cattle will be healthier and will provide better milk and meat. Also, their manure will be richer and will better fertilize the land. Following the fourth year, you simply begin again. You will notice your crops to be larger and healthier if you care to experiment a little." Andrew paused to gather in the reactions of those around him.

It seemed as if the erstwhile blustering arena had calmed to a whisper. Malcolm's face reflected bitter enmity. King Richard appeared surprised and impressed. Marie kept her eyes to her plate and failed in her attempt to appear unimpressed. Her chewing slowed noticeably, and she straightened ever so slightly in her chair.

"That is ridiculous," Malcolm finally managed to blurt out, yet he knew that it all made sense. He also knew that what the king said next could drastically damage his prestigious reputation, one for which he had worked long and hard.

"Your ideas sound reasonable yet are quite different than anything we have ever seen or heard. It would be a major alteration of a proven system to adopt any of your ideas," King Talbot said to Andrew. "Where did you learn of such ways?"

"I have picked up ideas here and there. If you think about it for a moment, it almost seems common sense. Do you not think so, Marie?"

His unanticipated calling upon her caused Marie to choke on the wine she had just sipped as it went down her windpipe instead of her throat. It took a moment for her to recover.

"I know very little about farming," she finally sputtered. "I do not generally think about such things."

Andrew took pleasure in seeing the king's aggressively self-confident daughter put off-balance. He stifled an amused grin with a piece of turkey.

"What are your other ideas in this area? Have you any?" the king prodded.

"I noticed some lowlands down near the stream that have been left untouched. That land is some of the richest you will find. It would be good for growing corn. After a couple of years of use, the land could be flooded by deliberately diverting the stream. This will help replenish the minerals in the ground. That, coupled with fertilizing the land with a compost of animal and human waste, leaves, weeds, and leftover foods, will produce an extremely rich plot of ground."

"You sound like a well-educated man, Andrew MacLean," King Talbot surmised.

"My travels have taught me more than books have. Experience is said to be the best teacher."

"That it is. I would like to discuss more of these things with you in the morning," the king said, ending the conversation. "However, now it is time to enjoy the celebration." He motioned to the musicians, and once again, music filled the chamber.

"I would never have known," Marie said to Andrew mockingly.

"What would you have never known?"

"That you are from an aristocratic family."

"Now what makes you say that?" Andrew replied, laughing.

"The things you just said. No mere soldier or nomad could begin to conceive of the ideas you have. You are educated, no matter if you claim otherwise. That means you are aristocracy or royalty, more likely the former. What I cannot figure out is why you are here."

"Perhaps I am nothing more than a simple farmer," Andrew replied with a grin, "and my knowledge has come from a lifetime of tilling the soil. Truth be told, there was nothing profound in what I said. The methods I described are quite common in other lands."

"That may be true," Marie answered, "but though I have known you for less than a day, you are anything but simple and most definitely not a farmer. There is more to you, Andrew MacLean."

"I assure you the blood flowing through my veins has not a

drop of royalty in it, nor am I from a family of high standing. As for why I am here, your village just happened to be in my path. My presence here is nothing more than happenstance. You shall deprive yourself of reason and wit seeking pattern in chance."

"Maybe," Marie said, returning to her meal. "Maybe."

Chapter 7

T he heavy, soft coverings smothered his body as Andrew rolled over onto his stomach. Never had he slept in a bed that was as warm or as comfortable as this one. The chill in the air prompted him to pull the thick spread over his head so that no part of his body was exposed to the air. How long it had been since he experienced this degree of warmth and security he could not remember. He tried to drift back to sleep, to prolong the blissful slumber from which he had just awoken. It was not to be allowed. Somebody pounded at his door and called out his name. It was a feminine voice, although he could not quite identify who it was. Maybe if he ignored her, she would go away and let him return to his dreams. Andrew did not answer but merely rolled onto his side so his back was to the door. The tactic did not work, and the pounding continued. Knowing how persistent women tended to be, Andrew was about to answer when the woman, obviously fed up with getting no response, simply opened the door and entered his room.

"Andrew MacLean. Do you intend on sleeping all day or shall you enjoy this most delightful morning as are the rest of us?"

Suddenly Andrew knew to whom the voice belonged and was not a bit surprised that she had invited herself into his room. It was not the first time she had done so.

"Just a little longer, Mother," he replied. "I promise I shall get all my chores done."

"I am not your mother," Marie spat at him. "I have been instructed by my father to escort you around and show you our castle and land. The morning is already half past us, and I grew weary of waiting for you. I will pull you out of that bed myself if I must. Now, on your feet and make use of those clothes at the foot of your bed."

"I venture you would enjoy doing that," Andrew murmured to himself as he rolled over.

"I beg your pardon?" Marie asked.

"I said that if you leave, I will get up," he lied.

"If that is what you said, then I really am your mother." Marie glared at him for a moment. "I will be waiting outside your room." She turned and walked over to the door. She tried to sneak a quick glance at him as she closed the door, but he saw her and smiled. She quickly looked away and pulled the door shut none too gently.

Andrew deliberated whether to stay in bed a little longer and antagonize Marie a bit more. He decided it would be best not to vex his hostess any further and reluctantly rolled out from under the mountain of warm covers and onto the cold stone floor. A shiver shot from his toes to his head as soon as his feet touched the ground. A small basin of water and a towel were sitting on a table beside the bed. He splashed some of the cool water onto his face and rubbed the sleep out of his eyes. After drying off, he walked to the foot of the bed and opened the trunk. Inside were numerous articles of clothing, none of which were his. After sifting through the contents, he pulled out several pieces and slipped into them.

"So you were granted the unpleasant task of babysitting me today, I gather," Andrew said as he joined Marie in the hall.

"It was not exactly a job for which my father entertained volunteers," Marie answered, "although I am sure he could have found a few young ladies more than willing to sacrifice their day after last night. He rather firmly requested that I spend the day with you and give you the grand tour."

"He must be quite proud of his kingdom," Andrew said.

"My father was impressed with you last night. He figures that once you see what all our lovely borough has to offer, you might decide to stay. He knows that although our systems and ways are much superior to those of other people's, there is always room for improvement. Since you are more familiar with me than anyone else, he thought it best that I be the one to lead you around. I had nothing better to do today."

"You mean you have no important picnics or romps with your friends scheduled for today? I would not dare interfere with such preeminent plans," Andrew parried.

"My father has forbidden such adventures for an 'indefinite period of time,' as he put it," Marie replied. "This leaves me free for whatever petty tasks he requests I do for him." Touché.

"Where shall we start?" Andrew asked.

"Since we are here, I will show you the rest of the castle first. That should take the rest of the morning. Then will we have some lunch and resume our tour outside."

"The castle is that big?" Andrew marveled.

"It is that big," Marie confirmed. "The upper level, in which we are now located, is exclusively for living quarters. The second level contains more living quarters, meeting rooms, and libraries. The lower level is comprised of recreation rooms and banquet rooms."

"Libraries? You have more than one?" Andrew inquired.

"We have three," Marie replied proudly. "Each has its own character. We have an extensive collection of books and parchments. One library contains quite a few pieces of art, most of which are extremely old."

"In my room, there was a tapestry on the wall that appeared to be quite old. Where did it come from?"

"It was here when we first arrived many years ago. Most of the sculptures, paintings, and tapestries displayed throughout the castle were found in the ruins upon which we built."

"Has anybody tried to interpret from them who may have

---

inhabited this place before you came? It would be fascinating to inspect them."

"I am afraid that would be quite difficult to do. Some of the objects have been scattered throughout the castle as decorations. They offer little information as to the past. My father has locked away many of the pieces though. He has never explained why. He refuses to let even me see them, which is odd."

"That is quite interesting," Andrew mused. He decided to change the subject for the moment. "On which level might the kitchen be located?"

"That depends on which kitchen you wish to visit," Marie replied with a twinkle in her eye.

"The closest one, of course," Andrew answered, trying to sound unimpressed.

"Then that would be this way," Marie responded and turned down a corridor to her right. "I do not see how you could be hungry though. After all, you practically ate a whole turkey, half an acre of corn, and a loaf of bread by yourself last night."

"Usually, my morning appetite is quite modest. Why this morning is different I cannot say. I was neither stiff nor sore when I woke up, unlike most other days. Perhaps a night of solid sleep is the difference."

"It is certainly possible," Marie said. "Here is the kitchen. Grab what you desire, and we shall keep moving."

Andrew spotted some bread and sausage and loaded himself with a generous portion of each. He ate and mostly listened as Marie led him through corridor after corridor, into room after room. She knew the castle intimately and did not miss an opportunity to display her knowledge of art as they encountered numerous statues and paintings. Andrew was impressed with this ability of hers, which spoke of more than a casual interest in art. She had obviously spent much time studying this particular discipline. He began to listen closely to her as the tour continued.

Two hours and what seemed like two miles later, Marie and Andrew had reached the lowest level of the castle. They were in a section that appeared to have last seen human passage some years before. The lanterns the explorers carried revealed damp, mildew-stained walls and a thin coating of dust on the stone floor. Marie stopped, and Andrew waited for her next move.

"This is the end," she said. "These rooms around us are used mainly for storage. As you can see, there is little traffic that ventures this far into the castle's bowels." Andrew took a few more steps down the corridor beyond Marie. The glow of his torch revealed an iron gate that guarded against further exploration.

"What is beyond this gate?" he inquired.

"More passageways and rooms," Marie answered.

"Why are they blocked off?"

"They are parts of the ruins upon which our castle was built. When we first came here, I started exploring them little by little. When my father discovered my secret journeys, he had the blacksmith forge a gate to keep me out. He said it was too dangerous for me to be down here."

"You came down here by yourself? Were you not scared of the darkness, the solitude?"

"Oh, most certainly. It was frightening yet exhilarating. I would spend hours at a time down here. It was fascinating to see things so old, left untouched for who knows how many years."

"What kinds of things?" Andrew asked, his curiosity peaked.

"Many, many different things. Armor, weapons, works of art, parchments, books, et cetera. It has been so long I cannot be any more specific than that."

"Did you take any of these things out before your father sealed off the corridor?"

Marie hesitated for a second, then answered. "No. They were not my things to take, so I left everything alone."

"Do you know if your father took out any of these artifacts before barring the passageway?"

"No, not that I am aware of, although I am sure he performed a thorough search for anything of value. I have not seen any of the articles around the castle."

"History itself is valuable, not just the objects it leaves behind. I would not be surprised by the stories and lessons that could be learned from what lies beyond those bars. Sometimes it just takes a trained eye to see them. Is there another way into this part of the castle?" Andrew inquired.

"I do not know," Marie said rather quickly. "Perhaps there is, perhaps there is not. We can search for another entrance some other time. Right now, I am chilled and would prefer to continue the tour in the warmth of the sun."

Andrew hesitated for a moment but did not argue. He followed Marie as she led the way back to the more populated sections of the castle. His mind was preoccupied with the dark, secret parts of the castle, and the bright sunlight caught him by surprise. He squinted his eyes as he surveyed the activity in the courtyard.

The scene was much the same as it had been the prior day upon his passage through the castle's gates. People milled about, some taking care of business, some merely socializing. Although the day was not hot, the sun felt extremely warm after the coolness of the stone walls.

"I would like to check on my horse," Andrew informed Marie.

"I can assure you that he is being well cared for," Marie replied.

"I do not doubt that he is. However, I would not want him to get anxious or upset. If I stay away from him for too long a period of time in unfamiliar surroundings, he tends to get most unreasonable."

"Well now, we would not want to upset him, would we?" Marie responded. Andrew did not take the bait her taunting tone offered and followed her in silence. They were about halfway to the stables when he stopped. He cocked his head slightly, and a look of deep concentration blanketed his face.

"What is it?" Marie asked.

"I hear a low rumbling, almost like thunder." He listened for a moment longer. "But it is not thunder. It sounds like ..." Again, he paused. "Horses," he finally finished. "Dozens of horses riding hard. It is getting louder." There were several shouts of warning from the stable area, and people began to dive out of the way. Suddenly, a flood of horses and riders burst from around the corner of the castle. The horses were in full battle dress, as were the riders. It was a magnificent and frightening parade.

"Is the castle under attack?" Andrew quickly asked.

"No, not at all. This is a practice routine the men undergo a few times per week. They ride out to a field about two miles away. There they go through mock battles and sharpen their fighting skills."

"I would like to watch this training exercise sometime," Andrew said. "Would it be possible?"

"Most certainly. I feel like a good ride."

"You ride?" Andrew asked, surprised.

"Of course. Why would I not?"

"It is just that I do not often see a woman ride a horse. Especially one in your position."

"I am quite an accomplished rider, as a matter of fact. Even though I am a woman, my father taught me many things that he would have taught a son."

"What kinds of things?" Andrew asked.

"Just things," Marie answered, intentionally being vague. She addressed a stable boy who had stepped out to meet them.

"Our horses, please. Andrew's is the magnificent black stallion that arrived yesterday afternoon."

"Right away, my lady," the youth answered and trotted away.

"I try to get out and ride at least three times a week. It is a wonderful experience, what with the wind whipping through your hair and the ground flying beneath you. I am the best female rider in these parts."

"How nice," Andrew answered. "But then again, it is all relative to the level of competition. Just how many female riders are there in these parts?"

"Granted, there are not many," Marie replied, undaunted, "but I am also better than a respectable number of the male riders."

"Then I am impressed," Andrew said. "I am in the mood for a

good ride myself." The challenge had been made. It only took a few minutes for the young boy to return with both horses in tow. Marie's was a fine-looking three-year-old mare, dark brown with a splash of white on its nose. She wasted no time swinging up on its back. Andrew was not as quick to mount Annon. He took a minute and inspected his horse.

"Are they treating you well, my friend?" The stallion snorted once. "Good. It appears that your saddle is snug enough. Do you think everything is in order for a nice workout?" The horse nodded his head up and down. Andrew gracefully swung up onto Annon's back. His hand reached down and felt the familiar outline of the special sword wrapped up where he had left it. "If you are ready," he said to Marie.

The princess gently nudged her horse in its rib cage, and the beast obediently moved forward. They kept a leisurely pace through the courtyard and over the drawbridge. When they reached the main roadway, Marie turned her mare to the right, opposite the way from which they had approached the castle the day before. A rolling meadow stretched out before them, lined by a forest of evergreen trees on its left. Marie veered off the main roadway and stopped beside a patch of lavender flowers. The horses did not hesitate at the opportunity for a change in menu. They immediately began munching on the rich green meadow grass.

"Such a beautiful day," Marie exclaimed as she took a deep breath. "A most favorable day to give a horse a workout. It is neither too hot nor too cold. Would you agree?"

"I would," Andrew replied. "It is much more enjoyable than an arid desert baked by the sun or a snow-covered mountain that has not seen the sun for weeks."

She looked at his large, muscular horse and his own stout form. An idea crept into her mischievous mind.

"Do you see that lone tree on the crest of the hill, about four hundred yards distant?"

Andrew looked into the distance. "It would be difficult to—"

Marie thrust her heels into the ribs of her mare, and the horse bolted forward. Andrew hesitated for a moment, taken off-guard, but quickly recovered and gave his stallion a kick in the sides. Annon had been enjoying a feast and reared up in a blatant show of disapproval at being interrupted. By the time the horse was finished with his tantrum, Marie had a good fifty-yard head start. Andrew leaned forward as Annon bolted. The beast knew that the race was on and needed no human guidance. His legs were a blur as he flew over the meadow grass, instinctively avoiding the scattered rocks lying on the ground, any one of which could cause a fatal fall. Marie's horse vaulted in the air as it reached a small stream of water that was not readily visible. As he approached it, Andrew questioned Annon's ability to leap over the obstacle. The stream was about ten feet wide, and Marie's horse had cleared it with little room to spare. Annon was a larger horse and had a heavier rider on its back. Andrew considered slowing, but Annon showed no signs of reducing his pace. The stallion approached the water at a full gallop. Andrew held on tightly as Annon vaulted into the air. For a split second, it seemed that all motion stopped; then the horse landed and continued on without missing a step. The distance between the two horses slowly dissipated. Marie stole a quick glance back and urged her mare on as she saw Andrew only twenty yards back. Their finish line loomed closer and closer. With fifty yards left, Andrew pulled up to Marie's side. He knew that he could easily win the race, but to do so would only put Marie in an impossible mood for the remainder of the day. If he let her win, that, too, would result in a foul mood on her part. He decided that a tie would be the best thing and kept his horse's nose even with its counterpart's. The racers were side by side as they passed the lone tree. Believing the contest to be over, Andrew began to rein his stallion in. Marie, however, showed no signs of slowing and continued at a full gait.

"So that is how you play the game," Andrew mused to himself as he prompted Annon to resume the race. Once again, the horse broke into an all-out gallop. Marie traveled another two hundred yards and then slowed to a stop before Andrew could catch up to her.

"Why did you stop?" she asked him as he reined Annon in beside her.

"For some reason, and I cannot tell you exactly why, I was under the impression that the finish line was that tree on the crest back there," he replied.

"It was, but that would have resulted in a tie."

"And that is so bad?"

"I do not believe in ties," Marie answered as she patted her horse on its neck. "There has to be a winner and a loser, and the race goes on until it is so decided."

"Decided by whom?" Andrew inquired. "You raced until you were winning, and then you quit. You cannot call that a contest."

"Since you were not clear on the rules, I will declare the race a draw," Marie answered, "but just this once. We shall have a rematch some time."

"How kind of you," Andrew responded.

"The training field is still about a mile and a half away. It is a rather boring scene, to be honest. There is nothing to see but a bunch of men using wooden swords, pounding on each other. Are you sure you wish to see them? I know of other more interesting, more secluded places we could visit."

"We can visit those places some other time. Do you come out and watch the men often?"

"When I was younger, I would. I have more intellectually stimulating and profitable activities to fill my time now."

"You were quite an adventurous girl in your early years," Andrew surmised.

"I still am. It can get boring sitting around the castle, doing nothing. I like to go places and do things. I do not want to be the sweet little princess who stays in the castle all her life, waiting for a charming prince or hero to come along. I feel so closed in there."

"I was like that once, but after years of wandering around without a home, I would not mind staying in a place for a while."

"But you are prevented from doing that until you find the person for whom you are searching, right?"

Andrew nodded his head. "It is especially important that I find this person. I cannot tell you why. It was a task bestowed upon me by a dying man, a task that I did not want and cannot ignore. I fear his last breath fled him too soon. If only he had told me more, my journey would not be so challenging."

"If you would tell me more, perhaps I could be of help," Marie suggested.

Andrew looked at her closely. It would be a relief to be able to share his seemingly insurmountable quest with someone, to have a partner in his search. But she could never leave her father when it came time to continue his journey. His secret was extremely powerful and could be badly exploited by the wrong person. Who could he trust? The slightest slip of the tongue on her part could result in disaster.

"Maybe one day I can tell you more, but for now, it is best that I keep the reason for my journey to myself. I hope you understand."

"I understand. I have secrets of my own, which I have never told even my closest friends. Even so, I have a feeling that someday I will know your secret, Andrew."

"Perhaps," Andrew replied.

As the two riders topped a small knoll, the busy training field spread out before them. The men were paired off and sparring with each other. Just as Marie had described to him, the fighters were using wooden swords to train. Even from a distance, the moves appeared to be orchestrated and mechanical. Some of the men were engaged in what appeared to be wrestling maneuvers without weapons. A section of the field was dedicated to archery practice. Several men on horses weaved among the fighters. Occasionally they would dismount, provide some instruction to the men, then proceed with their rounds.

"This is how they train?" Andrew asked Marie.

"Rather boring, would you not say?"

"What I would say is that it is a good thing there is peace in the land."

"Why do you say that?" Marie inquired with a curious look.

"If this is how the men train, they would not stand a chance against an attack by experienced warriors. Your kingdom would fall."

"From what do you form such an opinion? These men come out here three times a week for a full day, and they have been doing this for several years. Surely you cannot form such a negative assessment from but a few seconds of observation."

"Unlike many of these men, I have fought in numerous engagements since I was hardly more than a boy. I know how battles are fought and what it takes to overcome an opponent, especially on a one-on-one basis. Experience forms my opinion. See how they fight? It is as if they know the routine and are simply going through the motions. There is no emotion, no intensity, only boredom. And to fight with wooden swords is a child's game. I have not used such a toy since I was ten years old. I venture your king's men could be bested by well-trained men with no battle experience whatsoever."

"You must remember that there has been peace in our land for many years," Marie reminded him. "There are few veterans among them."

"Yes, and that is their weakness. Battle-scarred warriors would know how to push their younger comrades and instill fire in their veins. The lack of veterans is all the more reason to train hard with continuous challenges. This type of training is inadequate."

"Do not let Angus hear you say that. He might take offense. This regime is his fabrication."

"By all means, let us not offend the king's military adviser," Andrew sarcastically replied. "Pride is far more important than the lives of these men and the safety of your kingdom."

Andrew and Marie's attention was captured by a rider approaching them from the battlefield. Andrew recognized the man on the horse as King Richard's military adviser himself.

Perspiration masked his face, and he wiped his brow as he stopped before them.

"Out for a ride today, are you?" Angus inquired.

"It was too nice of a day to stay in," Marie replied. "Andrew was curious as to the training exercises, so we came out to observe."

"At least three times a week, we train," Angus informed Andrew. "Never less. There are also spontaneous sessions held at my discretion, day or night. We spar most of the day, working on technique and strategy. It is a good workout, no?"

"It does appear to be a good workout. I must say you are perspiring quite a bit," Andrew answered.

"The intended effect is not to produce sweat but quickness and strength," Angus retorted in a firm tone. "It is a battle-training exercise. Quite effective, I assure you."

"It would be difficult to say how effective until proven in something other than a staged conflict," Andrew replied. "Would you not agree?"

"I would not disagree." Angus thought for a moment. "I take it you are not impressed with our efforts."

"In all truthfulness?" Andrew asked.

"I would be offended if you offered anything less," Angus replied.

"Then I would have to say no, I am not overly impressed."

"I assume you have some suggestions for me, as you did for Malcolm last evening."

"I have my own ideas, as any man does."

"I do not doubt so. Perhaps you will entertain me with them some time," Angus said. It was obvious that he did not care to have his methods questioned, nor was he too anxious to hear what Andrew's ideas were. He was startled to hear a voice from behind him. The king's approach had been silent.

"I would be interested in hearing them now," King Talbot said. He had ridden up the small hill and now stood beside Angus.

"Your Majesty, it is time to begin the next exercise. We should return to the training field."

"After we have heard Andrew speak," the king replied. "Proceed," he directed, looking at Andrew. After a moment of thought, Andrew complied.

"You said that you were trying to build quickness and strength," he began. "How can you build strength while training with wooden swords? Is not steel heavier than wood?"

"Wooden swords are used to prevent injuries on the practice field. The movements of the warrior are the focal point on which we are concentrating," Angus replied.

"A good warrior knows how to avoid injury," Andrew countered, "for otherwise he would be a dead warrior. A warrior who fights with dull wood develops dull reflexes. He knows that he cannot be seriously harmed. Steel teaches wariness; wood, carelessness. After sparring with a lighter weapon here on the practice field, how long could a warrior last having to heft a heavier weapon in a real battle?"

"The warriors practice with swords back on the castle grounds," Angus responded. "They go through strength-building exercises, sometimes by themselves, sometimes with a partner."

"The moves they are performing out there," Andrew said, indicating the field, "they look too practiced, too boring. Are your opponents going to have attacks so orchestrated? I think not. I am afraid that a true battle would be exceedingly difficult for your men to win and could be potentially devastating to the very land you have sworn to protect." Andrew's words stung Angus, and the king's adviser was heavily insulted. His anger was so severe that he could not respond right away.

Marie was not used to hearing such hard, direct words being spoken to any of the king's advisers, and she was initially taken aback. The anger on Angus's face was frightening, and yet somehow, she found it humorous at the same time. Recovering more quickly than Angus or the king, she was the first to break the silence. She looked at Andrew and spoke softly, yet not so softly that the others could not hear.

"Do not lay such a coat of sugar on your words the next time you offer your opinion," she said. "My father prefers that a man say what he means."

"Now that you have totally destroyed the carefully constructed training scheme created by my trusted and proven military adviser," Talbot said to Andrew, "what would you suggest in the way of improvements?"

Andrew stole a glance at Marie. "I will try to be direct," he said.

"I would first of all insist that real swords be used in place of those wooden children's toys. A warrior vulnerable to injury during practice will develop better muscular control, reflexes, and stamina, all vital components in any battle. Granted, there will be many cuts and nicks at first, but that will only serve to improve the men. They will learn how to use the sword and how to avoid it. They will also learn how to use their shields as weapons of attack and not just weapons of defense."

"And you have been in many battles, no?" King Richard inquired. It seemed an innocent question, but Andrew knew that the king was trying to delve into his past.

"I am no stranger to the battlefield," Andrew replied.

"Then perhaps you would like to demonstrate the superiority of your training," Angus suggested in a challenging tone. "I have trained just as my men. Shall we spar a while?"

Andrew recognized the challenge for what it was. This was no innocent joust. There was no friendliness in Angus's eyes, only malevolence. He intended to put Andrew in his place, being the visitor that Andrew was. This was understandable. If Andrew succeeded in showing Angus up, Angus would lose some of his prestige and power to the newcomer. Andrew was sure that he could soundly beat Angus. However, to do so would create an unnecessary enemy. Now that the challenge had been presented, to turn it down would be cowardly, and Andrew did not care to be labeled a coward. Talbot sat on his horse, and although he did not say a word, his face fully spoke of his enjoyment of the confrontation.

"It would hardly seem fair," Andrew taunted. "You appear

quite spent on this morning's session. Maybe you would prefer to postpone the joust until you are fresh."

"I have but warmed up. I doubt that I would need all my strength anyway. Dismount," Angus commanded.

Andrew swung off Annon and pulled his sword out of its scabbard. The blade was honed to a mirrorlike surface, and the edge was razor sharp. The warrior inspected his blade, turning it over several times and running his hand along the smooth surface. He thrust the point into the ground, and the weapon stood perfectly upright. Andrew shed his outer cloak, threw it up to a startled Marie, and grabbed his sword. After a few warm-up maneuvers, he addressed Angus.

"Three hits?"

"As you wish," Angus replied without emotion. He had also dismounted and pulled out his weapon. It was an impressive-looking sword, similar in size to Andrew's yet appearing smaller due to its oversized handle. Andrew noted Angus's large hands, the reason for the custom-made handle. It was obvious that the sword received much care.

"If my king would be kind enough to be judge," Angus said, bowing to King Richard.

"Proceed," Talbot commanded. He knew that to urge the opponents to exercise due care would be useless. Angus was an angry man by nature, and fighting only made him worse. That was what made him an excellent warrior and instructor. Talbot almost pitied Andrew yet was too curious about him to interfere in the duel. Whatever happened, happened.

The two fighters approached each other and stopped with less than ten feet separating them. Angus's face portrayed unshakable confidence and arrogance, with a touch of evil thrown in to intimidate his adversary. Andrew was a veteran to battle, and no man intimidated him so easily. His statuesque face revealed no emotion and almost complete indifference to the situation. He did not need scare or intimidation tactics to get the upper hand on his foe. His abilities would speak for themselves and prove sufficient for any fight."

The battlefield had grown deathly quiet as the warriors paused to view the match between their respected trainer and the newcomer. Andrew and Angus were unaware of the stillness around them as they concentrated on each other. Neither fighter wasted his breath by attempting to talk his opponent off-guard. They were both too well trained for that. Words were not the weapons here. Experience, pride, and desire were the tools that would decide the winner of this melee. An entire minute of silence passed when, with the suddenness and anger of an explosion of thunder, Angus bellowed and threw himself toward Andrew.

The tactic was obvious to Andrew before Angus had taken two steps. By his maddening charge, Angus was attempting to force his opponent to take a step back and therefore destroy his balance. Instead of retreating, Andrew himself moved forward into Angus, swinging his sword high to intercept the steel arcing toward him. Angus altered the path of his sword, trying to glance it ever so slightly off Andrew's weapon and guide it down toward Andrew's hands. Andrew twisted his body and hands enough so that the incoming sword narrowly missed his grip and slashed harmlessly into the ground. Immediately, the two men whipped around and faced each other again, the first pass ending in a draw.

"Their intensity is astounding, is it not?" King Richard whispered to his daughter.

"This is no sparring match," Marie observed. "Angus is out for blood."

"I would not be surprised to see crimson before the match is over," Talbot said. "However, despite his nature of fierce fighting, Angus knows restraint. He also knows that Andrew is a guest and that to injure him would be an insult to me. There will be no serious cuts."

"I would that I had your confidence in Angus. Restraint is not what I see pouring from his eyes."

"Are you so concerned for your new friend?" the king

inquired. "Surely he is a suitable match for Angus if he fought off four vagabonds all by himself, especially if they were near starved to death and had no formal training. I would wager that those men could not have fought off Stephen and three of his friends."

"I care not whether Andrew wins, loses, or draws," Marie retorted, turning her attention back to the fighters.

His first pass being unsuccessful, Angus pondered a new strategy. His foe was quick and strong, probably as much so as himself. He would have to think his way through this one, as brute strength would not be enough.

Andrew saw the hesitation in Angus and knew he was rethinking his strategy. Not being one to miss an opportunity, Andrew took an unexpected offensive position and charged Angus. However, instead of charging on past, as Angus had done previously, Andrew stopped short and swung his sword on a horizontal plane aimed for Angus's midsection. Angus took a step back, not at all phased at Andrew's aggressiveness, and brought his sword down to parry the blow. Andrew's hands stung as if he had struck a wall of rock. The vibrations shot up his arms and into his head, jeopardizing his grip on the sword. He recovered just in time to narrowly avoid Angus's thrust at his gut. Andrew parried the blow, twisted in a full circle, and brought his sword up, slapping Angus's thigh with the flat side of the steel blade. Angus roared in anger.

"One for Andrew," Talbot announced. The fighters backed off and took a few deep breaths. Andrew decided to let Angus be the aggressor and wear himself down. It was a role that Angus seemed eager to play. In the blink of an eye, he was again charging Andrew, backed this time not only by anger but also a damaged ego.

The conflict was fast and furious. For every move one fighter made, the other parried and countered with his own move. The two men appeared to be equally matched, and neither could get the upper hand. Slowly Andrew began giving ground and backing up. Angus saw this as a sign of weakness and exhaustion on his foe's part and pressed that much harder. Andrew had actually intended to incite Angus to push harder, and the ploy was working—until Andrew stepped on a rock and momentarily lost his timing and balance. He fell to the ground and immediately raised his sword to ward off an attack. However, Angus was quicker, and before Andrew had attained any type of defensive position, Angus's steel was pressing at his throat, threatening to break the skin. A slight gasp rushed by Marie's lips.

"Point!" Talbot shouted, stopping the action before it went any further. Angus hesitated a moment, then withdrew his sword and backed off without offering Andrew a hand up. Andrew stood and casually brushed himself off, appearing completely indifferent to the fact that he had been momentarily bested. He took several deep breaths to regulate his breathing, then prepared for another round.

A smug expression rode Angus's face as he stared at Andrew. Although his breathing was visibly deeper than Andrew's, he was still full of energy and ready to continue. He looked to his king for approval, and Talbot gave him an almost imperceptible nod. Angus charged again.

Andrew had noted a particular consistency in Angus's style of fighting during the first two engagements. Angus was right-handed and therefore almost always initiated his attacks from the right side. Counting on this to happen again, Andrew charged in, angling to his left. He caught Angus's sword before it could gain any momentum, kneed Angus in the midsection, and rested his sword on the nape of Angus's neck as the big man doubled over.

"Point," Andrew said before King Richard could speak. The king sat with his mouth open, the word taken off his tongue.

"I see how you fight," Angus growled as he straightened up. "It seems you must result to other than skillful methods to win."

"I have used no methods that are not common to the battlefield," Andrew replied. "I have seen far dirtier fighting with more deadly results. The sword is but one weapon at your disposal in a fight."

"I will keep that in mind," Angus retorted with a menacing smirk on his face.

"Continue!" Talbot commanded, eager to see how Angus would respond to Andrew's words.

Angus feigned an attack, attempting to determine a pattern in Andrew's response. Andrew, seeing the false start, remained still. The two men moved in a circle, buying a little time to catch their breath and plan their next moves. This time, Andrew started the action.

With an unexpected cry, Andrew rushed Angus. The suddenness of the move caught Angus by surprise, though not unprepared. He quickly moved and countered Andrew's stroke. The ensuing battle lasted for five minutes, an eternity to the warriors. Suddenly they found themselves in a deadlock, nose to nose. Muscle strained against muscle as both men refused to give an inch. Sweat dripped off their brows, and each breathed the other's stale breath. Finally, Andrew conceded, dropping to the ground and doing a backward somersault. He was instantly on his feet and defending against another powerful blow from his opponent. He lifted his sword high and brought it down at a slight angle, just enough to avoid doing any real harm. Angus side-stepped the strike and brought his sword down over Andrew's, pinning it to the ground. He threw a forearm at Andrew's chin and knocked him back several feet. Knowing that to hesitate meant to lose the advantage, Angus swiftly vaulted forward and plunged his head into Andrew's midsection. Andrew was knocked to the ground and again found the point of Angus's sword at his Adam's apple.

"Point," Angus spat. He pulled his sword away, leaving a tiny indentation in his opponent's throat. He took several steps backward and stood triumphantly, waiting for the final round.

"Two points apiece," Talbot called out. "Next point wins." Marie shifted in her saddle as an uneasy feeling crept through her body. The sparring match had taken an ugly turn, now becoming an all-out battle of pride. She was certain that blood would be spilled, and it was not likely to be Angus's.

Andrew took two steps forward. He held his sword with the

hilt chest high and the tip pointing up at a forty-five-degree angle. Angus strode forward and took an identical position. The blades touched near their tips. Andrew was at an immediate advantage because his sword was to the right of Angus's, therefore blocking the natural motion of his enemy. Andrew was beginning to ponder why Angus would position himself at an obvious disadvantage when Angus exploded into action.

With a mighty flick of his wrist, Angus knocked Andrew's sword aside and slashed toward Andrew's chest. Andrew pulled his sword back just in time to block his opponent's weapon. Angus's sword slid across the blade of Andrew's and stopped at the hilt, a fraction of an inch from Andrew's hands. Andrew planted his weight on his right foot and pushed forward with all his strength. Angus stumbled back two steps and immediately rushed back in. He pointed his sword at the ground to his right and slightly in front of him, blocking the horizontal slash from Andrew. Andrew then pivoted on his right foot, turned a full circle, and brought another mighty blow to Angus's left side. Angus successfully parried this blow also and backed off a step in an effort to form a plan for an offensive maneuver.

Andrew denied Angus any opportunity to form a strategy as he continued his onslaught. Blow after ringing blow rained upon Angus until he was doing all he could to maintain his own balance and protect himself. Talbot was about to call a halt to the action when a totally unexpected turn of events took place. Just as he appeared to be in complete control, Andrew suddenly seemed to lose his balance and lunged to his right. Angus, seeing the golden opportunity, took a quick yet weak stab at Andrew. Andrew tried to dodge the blow, but the steel tip of the sword grazed his chest.

"Enough!" Talbot cried. "The contest is over. Angus has won the final round."

The chest of Angus heaved heavily as he gulped for air. He let his sword fall to the ground as he moved over to his horse for support. Andrew, breathing not quite as deeply as Angus, examined the wound on his chest. Marie had vaulted off her horse and rushed to his side.

"That certainly is a nasty wound," she observed with genuine concern as she gingerly parted Andrew's ruined shirt.

"I have received worse," Andrew nonchalantly replied. "A needle and a little thread will fix it."

Talbot addressed Angus. "I had complete confidence in you and was not disappointed. I am proud of you. Return to your men and send the surgeon to attend to Andrew."

"Yes, my lord," Angus replied. He turned his head to Andrew and gave a slight nod of admiration that only a warrior would recognize. Andrew returned the favor. Angus picked up his sword, mounted his steed, and galloped down the hill. He was met with a victorious roar from his men.

"You fought extremely well," Talbot said to Andrew.

"Not quite well enough, it would appear," Andrew replied.

"I disagree," Talbot continued. "You were beating my best man quite handedly when you suddenly lost your balance, certainly of your own accord. That was highly uncharacteristic of you."

"Any man can lose his balance," Andrew responded.

"Yes," the king agreed, "but not you, not today."

"Is it your opinion that I purposefully lost my balance and the fight? Why would I want to have my chest split open? I have no death wish."

"I am saying that your skills are superior to those of Angus. It was obvious. As to why you chose to lose, I cannot say." He looked at Andrew for a moment before continuing. "I must return to the daily activities. I will speak more with you later." Talbot turned and galloped down the hill.

"He keeps saying that," Andrew noted to Marie.

"My father fully intends to speak with you at greater length, but his timetable is his own." She eyed Andrew curiously. "Why did you let Angus win?"

"You too?" Andrew asked.

"Do not attempt to fool me, Andrew MacLean. I am not blind. I have seen you fight twice now. He was yours to do with as you wished. I ask again: why?"

"I thought it would be better not to get on his bad side. If it should happen that I stay here more than a few days, I would prefer to have more friends than enemies. In his case," Andrew said, nodding toward the battlefield, "perhaps not friend but certainly not enemy. I have already offended Malcolm, one of your father's advisers. I would prefer not to show up another."

"Malcolm is a foolish old man. If he cannot take criticism or accept fresh ideas, he deserves to be offended on occasion. Does this mean that you plan to stay here?" Marie asked. "I know of several people who would be extremely gleeful to hear that."

"So do I," Andrew said as he looked directly into her eyes. "However, I said *if* I am to stay." Before another word could be spoken, the surgeon approached them.

"Nice fight, young man," he said as he opened a bag he was carrying. "Too bad you lost."

"Andrew, this is Ian, the royal surgeon."

"There is nothing royal about me," Ian said as he inspected Andrew's wound. "Angus keeps his blade very sharp and smooth. I see you have been injured before," he continued as he spotted several scars on Andrew's chest. "And not from a sword. These look more like claw marks. Wolf I would guess."

"So I am told," Andrew replied, then immediately regretted the response he had chosen.

"You mean you do not know for sure?" Marie asked. She did not miss much.

"It happened a long time ago, when I was young," Andrew said. "It was nothing."

"They may be old, but these scars tell of quite a serious injury, especially to a young boy. A life-threatening injury to say the least. Do not tell me it was nothing," Ian said.

"I was knocked unconscious and remember nothing of the

incident," Andrew said. "I am told by others it was a wolf that attacked me. That is all I know."

"Not much, but it is something," Marie mused aloud.

"What did you say?" Andrew asked.

"This is going to hurt a bit," Ian said as he prepared to put some powder on the wound.

"Nothing," Marie replied with a smile.

Andrew did not pursue the issue any further. He drew in a deep breath from the pain as the surgeon began treating the wound.

Chapter 8

T he next several days passed with welcomed serenity as Marie and Andrew continued their tour of the countryside. Marie was more than pleased to show Andrew some of her favorite hideaways and picnic spots away from the castle and regale him with stories of her adventurous childhood. Two places captured Andrew's curiosity, as they were extremely old dwellings that had obviously been abandoned many, many years ago. The homes were larger than the one in which he had grown up. Marie had no special knowledge of these places, and despite his desire to investigate for even a few minutes, Andrew did not stop the tour. He would return sometime on his own.

There was about an hour of daylight remaining as the twosome approached the stables, and Andrew's chest was throbbing in pain with every stride of his horse. Although the wound was slowly healing, it was still somewhat sore, and the more activity in which he engaged, the more it ached. As they dismounted, Steven stepped to their side and took the horses' reins.

"Thank you for the tour," Andrew said to Marie as they walked to the castle.

"It was my pleasure. I do not get out and ride enough these days. There are a few matters I must attend to now," Marie said to Andrew as he turned to her. "Will you be returning to your room?"

"I should think so," Andrew answered. "And to the kitchen as well. Exercise tends to make me hungry."

"We generally eat around sundown," Marie informed him. "I will come by your room in about an hour." Without waiting for a reply, she turned and hurried away. Andrew watched her until she was out of sight.

"Pretty, is she not?" Steven asked as he led the horses to their stalls.

"Very much so," Andrew answered, following him. "She is not your average young lady. Quite mysterious I would say. One moment, there is a playful little girl in her eyes, the next a full-grown, driven, ambitious, intelligent woman."

"You could not be more correct," an unseen man called from the stall that Andrew and the boy were passing. A man of about Andrew's age and build stepped from behind the horse in the stall. He had reddish-brown hair cut somewhat short and a dark, thick mustache and beard. His clothes were dusty and ragged looking, telling of a busy day.

"She is a very mysterious and desirable young woman. It is a captivating combination of characteristics she possesses. I would be careful if I were you." He offered his hand to Andrew. "I am Lawrence Morecraft."

"Andrew MacLean," Andrew replied, grasping the strong hand offered to him.

"I saw your little melee with Angus the other day. You were quite impressive against the old man."

"He moves extremely well for an 'old' man," Andrew replied.

"As a matter of fact," Lawrence continued, "I do not believe that there is a man here who has stood up so well to him in one-on-one combat."

"That is of little wonder," Andrew said.

"Why so?" Lawrence inquired.

"It was obvious to me that Angus was trained in methods quite different than those he teaches you, methods far superior to what he shows you out there. If a man's only training comes from what Angus teaches him, his skills will not be as sharp and developed as they should be for a true warrior. He would stand little chance in a melee against Angus or someone of his fighting caliber."

"Yet you performed quite well," Lawrence reminded him.

"I was not trained as he trains you," Andrew replied directly.

"I see," Lawrence said with an air of curiosity. "I was about to have a mug of ale or two at the tavern. Would you care to join me?"

"Never let it be said that Andrew MacLean turned down a mug of ale," Andrew answered. He sensed a genuine offer of friendship from Lawrence, the first of its kind since he had arrived at the castle. "Lead the way."

"We can walk to the village," Lawrence said as Andrew moved toward his horse. "It is not far. There have been occasions, however, when my horse was the only one who remembered the way home. I try to limit those nights to few and far between."

"Do you live here in the castle?" Andrew inquired.

"I live here but not exactly in the castle. Most of the unmarried soldiers, including myself, have rooms in a building behind the stables."

"Are you required to stay there?"

"Not at all," Lawrence was quick to reply. "We can live anywhere we desire, outside of the castle. Most of the unmarried men elect to stay in the bachelor's quarters where there is little upkeep required. The king provided the building to us so we could be near our horses. When a man who lives there gets married, he builds a home and moves out."

"Are you planning to move out anytime soon?" Andrew asked.

"I have not met the woman who would have me." Lawrence laughed. "Until then, I shall stay where I am."

"Have you lived in this area all of your life?" Andrew inquired.

"All of my life, from my first breath till now," Lawrence answered proudly.

"How long has your family been here?"

"I believe my father told me once that the Morecraft family has lived on and farmed this land for four or five generations. At one time, our family was one of the largest landowners in the area. Before Talbot's arrival, my father was one of the more prominent men in the area. That was primary attributable to his education and knowledge. He was a farmer by trade but a historian by passion. He knew everything about this land and its people, dating back five hundred years or so."

"That is impressive. How did he gain such knowledge?" Andrew asked.

"He loved to read. Every night before going to bed, he would read out of this book or that book or whatever he could get his hands on. The walls of our home were lined with shelves stacked with books. His knowledge and wisdom impressed the other families in the area, and he was chosen as one of the local elders. It was not much more than an honorary title, but people respected him."

"That sounds like quite an impressive collection of books. How did he come to possess so many?" Andrew asked.

"He told me that in his youth he traveled quite extensively, and whenever the opportunity presented itself for him to obtain interesting reading material, he could not resist the temptation. He also obtained a number of books from the castle, well before Talbot arrived."

"What happened to him?" Andrew asked, intrigued by the tale.

"A terrible accident," Lawrence replied. "It was not long after Talbot arrived, as a matter of fact, perhaps six months or so later. My mother, my two younger brothers, and I were visiting my aunt and uncle who lived about a day and a half ride from here. Upon our return, we discovered that our house had caught fire one night while my father slept. It was believed that he had fallen asleep at a table while reading, and somehow his reading candles were knocked over. By the time the fire was discovered and people arrived to douse it, it was too late." Lawrence paused, and Andrew allowed him a moment of reflection.

"That truly was a terrible accident. I am sorry for your loss. He certainly would have proven valuable to Talbot and his administration and the future of this land."

"I do not see how," Lawrence replied. "Talbot treated my father with no more regard than any other man who lived here at that time, whether they had been prominent men or not."

"Do you mean that Talbot did not take any of the existing leaders of the land into his administration?"

"Not that I recall. We had four local elders before Talbot arrived. It is no important matter, in retrospect. Three of the four elders met with accidents well within a year of Talbot's arrival, so in the end, they would not have done him much good. He had his own people whom he put in charge of the various aspects of the land and people."

"What sorts of accidents?" Andrew pushed.

"First, my father's life was taken by that fire. Another elder, Connor O'Banion, drowned in the lake. A third, Patrick Jergen, was trampled by one of his horses. It was a time of greatly conflicting emotions. We had been saved by Talbot and were finally protected from the devastating raids that had plagued us for nearly six months. However, we lost three of our most respected men within that first year of Talbot's reign. Joy and grief—a combination that can be terrible yet wonderful."

Intrigued by the history lesson but not wanting to appear overly inquisitive, Andrew decided to change the subject.

"How many men are there who live in the same quarters as you?"

"Nearly thirty, ranging in age from sixteen to almost forty."

"Are there not enough women for these men or do they simply choose to stay unmarried?" Andrew inquired.

"Women. Now there is a subject for a mug of ale if I have ever heard one," Lawrence said as he directed Andrew toward a building on the outskirts of the village. "It will be refreshing to hear from a stranger on females. The conversations with my friends have grown boring, though I doubt your perspective will be much different. Perhaps the women where you are from tend to be less finicky than those here."

A dank, musty smell reminding Andrew of old, wet clothes greeted him as he passed through the doorway behind Lawrence. The tavern was not crowded to capacity yet was full of laughter and loud conversations. Lawrence sat down at an empty table against the far wall. Almost before Andrew had a chance to sit, a barmaid rushed over to them.

"Rachael." Lawrence smiled as he snaked an arm around her not-too-slender waist. "This is Andrew MacLean. Andrew, this is Rachael. You must watch out for her, my friend. This one is full of mischief."

"Pleased to meet you," she said with a twinkle in her eye.

"The pleasure is mine," Andrew answered. "Are you truly as mischievous as he thinks?"

"More so, I am sure," she replied.

"We need two ales and a loaf of bread with some cheese, my lady," Lawrence ordered.

"Be right back," she answered and rushed off.

"She most certainly is an enjoyable girl, and quite playful," Lawrence said as he watched Rachael disappear. "A bit plump perhaps, but she can certainly keep a man warm at night. The way she eyed you, you may find that out for yourself."

"I think not," Andrew stated firmly.

"Why not? A little too much meat on the bones for your taste?" Lawrence teased.

"Her figure does not have anything to do with it," Andrew replied.

"Do you not like the company of women?" Lawrence asked with an inquisitive expression.

"I like their company as much as the next man, but I prefer the type of company that is enjoyed outside of the bedroom."

"What is this?" Lawrence asked incredulously. "Are you saying that you do not take a woman to bed from time to time?"

"That is precisely what I am saying," Andrew replied.

"Inconceivable! A man of your young age and good looks refusing the one thing that makes life interesting? I have never heard of such a thing. Do not tell me it is your respect of females that inhibits you."

"Respect has a part to play but is not my primary consideration. I believe such intimacy is for the marriage bed only."

"You cannot be serious! You have no idea what you are missing!" Lawrence bellowed. "There is nothing like holding a woman against you in the cold of the night."

"Perhaps not," Andrew replied, "but when I do, it will mean that much more when shared with one woman only."

"Rachael will be disappointed to hear that," Lawrence said as the barmaid wove her way back to their table.

"How is the cheese?" Lawrence inquired of Rachael.

"Like it always is, good sir," she replied with a devilish grin. "Fresh." As she hurried to another table, she threw back over her shoulder, "If you care for more, just let me know."

"Are all women around here like her?" Andrew asked as he pulled off a chunk of bread.

"Some but not all. Most of the girls are, shall we say, more discreet? More along your lines I should say. You have already met two of the best prospects in this neck of the woods."

"Which are?" Andrew urged.

"Heather and Elizabeth. They are excellent around the house, sweet, and beautiful."

"If so, then why are they not married?"

"It is not by lack of offers. I can tell you that," Lawrence said as he downed half his mug of ale.

"What of Marie?" Andrew asked.

"She is the reason Elizabeth and Heather are not married, in my opinion. She is a unique girl to say the least. Has she caught your eye perhaps?"

"I would not say that," Andrew answered vaguely.

"I would warn you away. That girl has no intentions of getting married, or even near so, in the immediate future. She has plans and dreams." Lawrence leaned over the table, closer to Andrew, and lowered his voice. "Her father has agreed to send her away to study music, but what he does not know is that she intends on studying much more."

"More, as in …" Andrew prompted him.

"She wishes to study languages, sciences, philosophy, and theology. Things that women are not meant to study. She is quite ambitious. She has influenced her two closest friends to remain unmarried, at least until she goes away."

"Would her father send away his only child and heir to his throne?" Andrew asked. "That would appear to contradict the wise nature that so many people have attributed to him."

"She will not be going far. It is but a two-day journey from here. As heir to his throne, he wants her to know something more about the world than what she has seen here. She is quite sheltered here, as you can imagine, and has few opportunities to travel. But you can rest assured that her identity will be a closely guarded secret, and she will have bodyguards near her every minute of the day. I must tell you she fully intends to go, and nothing will stand in her way."

"And you know all of this how?" Andrew inquired.

"There are any number of signs. First, you must know Marie's personality. She has a thirst for knowledge, and what she does know, she likes to flaunt. You can generally see that when you have a conversation with her. She is very intelligent; I will give her that. She is rather independent, also, and does not appreciate being told what to do. Pay attention sometime to the conversation subjects you address with her. You can tell that she leans toward intellectual topics and not simple, casual conversation. The town where she plans on studying, while known for its expertise in music, is also known far and wide for these other things. Plus," he said, a mischievous twinkle lighting his eyes, "one of her friends happened to mention something along these lines not too long ago while we were, well, spending some time together."

"And which friend might that be?" Andrew asked with a bit of a grin.

"I will not mention any names, as I am a gentleman and would not want to soil the reputation of a beautiful young lady with brown hair and blue eyes."

"I see," Andrew answered, not really wanting to pursue that topic. "When will all of this happen with Marie?" he asked, getting back to the primary subject of their conversation.

"Nearly a year from hence," Lawrence replied.

"A lot can happen in a year," Andrew said thoughtfully.

"That is what I thought too," Lawrence told him. "She has so many great qualities, more than any girl around. The man who captures her heart will be a blessed man; of that you can be certain. However, she has no intention of letting that happen. You would be wise to look elsewhere if you desire female companionship for an extended period of time. I would suggest Elizabeth," he added with a knowing smile.

"I shall keep that in mind," Andrew mused. A shout of greeting from across the room ended their conversation.

"Lawrence!"

Andrew looked up to see a rather short but stocky man approaching their table. Lawrence turned in his seat to see who had called.

"Louis, come join us," Lawrence beckoned. The short man pulled up an empty seat and sat down.

"Louis, this is Andrew MacLean. He is the one who gave Angus a difficult time the other day. Andrew, this half-pint is Louis Connor."

"So you are the one," Louis said as he scrutinized Andrew.

"Word travels fast," Andrew noted, drawing on his ale.

"I was on the practice field and saw the melee but was too far away to see who you were. You wield a skilled sword. Everybody was impressed."

"It is merely a matter of training," Andrew replied, bored of the praise he was receiving.

"You mentioned that earlier," Lawrence said. "Would you

mind telling us the kind of training you have received and how it differs from ours? We are always looking for ways to improve."

"I would not want to infringe on Angus's territory and offend him," Andrew answered after a swig of ale.

"Forget Angus. He is an angry man anyway—and boring. It is always the same with him. We need something fresh, a new idea or two."

"I will tell you how I was trained," Andrew conceded, "but you are not to mention to Angus, nor anyone else, what I say here and now."

"Agreed," Lawrence said.

"Agreed," Louis echoed.

"Very well," Andrew said and began to recant the techniques that had been used during his training. The issue was not that these were big secrets meant only for certain ears. Andrew was pleased to be of help to these men. However, he did not want to put on an air of superiority and arrogance and get a bad reputation. He also did not wish to appear as if he was attempting to worm his way into the chain of command. His desire of remaining in the background had already been thwarted.

Over the next few hours and countless mugs of brew, the conversation ran from training to women, back to training, then to battles and contests of skills. The pain in Andrew's chest had been dulled by the bittersweet liquid that was continually offered to him. Rachael tended to squeeze a little closer to Andrew every time she visited the table and ended up in his lap on one occasion.

"Are you saying," Louis started in a voice slurred by too much ale, "that you can hit a three-inch target with a dagger from twenty-five feet?"

"I have done it," Andrew stated in agreement. He had not downed as much ale as the others but was nevertheless feeling its effects.

"I challenge you!" Louis declared loudly, slamming the table with his fist and nearly knocking over their half-full mugs. "Clear the throwing area!" he bellowed. Slowly the crowd parted along the wall to Andrew's right.

"Here and now?" Andrew asked, surprised.

"And why not?" Louis replied. "Are you not up to the challenge?"

"No reason, save for this gash in my chest and over a half dozen mugs of ale in my head."

"Well, I have had at least eight mugs of ale, and that should make us about even. As for that scratch on your chest, I have seen house cats impart worse wounds than that."

"Then throw I shall," Andrew answered and rose to his feet. The room swayed a bit, and it took him a moment to get oriented. He followed Louis over to the throwing area. About twenty-five feet away, on the far wall, a target had been painted. The bull's-eye was a black circle almost three inches in diameter.

"There is your target," Louis announced as he grabbed another mug of ale from Rachael, who had followed the men. "Whenever you are ready."

"There was a challenge," Andrew said as he pulled his dagger from his boot. "Are there no stakes?"

"Oh, there most certainly are," Louis replied. "The stakes are the same as always. Loser buys the ale."

"Perhaps you would prefer to go first," Andrew suggested. "I fear after another mug you may not be able to throw, let alone stand."

"Then move aside, scoundrel, and watch the tavern champion in action!" He set his mug on the nearest table and pulled a six-inch dagger from his belt.

"Champion?" Andrew asked Lawrence, who was paying more attention to Rachael than the contest.

"Three years running," Lawrence confirmed without taking his eyes off Rachel. "He is the best anybody has ever seen."

Andrew turned his attention back to Louis, who was eyeing the distant target. At the end of his outstretched right arm, the dagger wavered toward the bull's-eye. He held the blade firmly for a few seconds, then with a quick motion let it fly. The blade embedded in the wall with a thud. It was nearly ten inches from the bull's-eye.

"One point!" someone cried from beside the target. Louis's dagger was pulled free and returned to him.

"I cannot remember the last time I got but a point," Louis grumbled as he took another gulp from his mug.

"From the way you are drinking, I doubt that you will remember this time!" Lawrence chided him. Several onlookers laughed, but Louis did not respond. He repositioned himself and took careful aim. Again, he let the dagger fly.

"Bull's-eye!" the caller yelled. The crowd roared. Louis beamed.

"Much better," he declared as he reached for his dagger, which had been swiftly returned to him. "That gives me six points. Another bull's-eye shall give me the contest."

"I see confidence is not his weak point," Andrew said to Lawrence. Lawrence was too busy with Rachael to reply.

For his last throw, Louis took more time than his previous two. He kept changing his grip on the dagger's blade and shifting his weight. Finally, he was ready. The crowd was dead silent. Louis brought the dagger back until it almost touched his shoulder, then threw it with authority. The silence continued as the onlookers waited to hear the result.

"Three points!" The crowd erupted in approval, but Louis looked downcast.

"This ale has affected me more than I thought. Nine lousy points." He turned to Andrew with a smile. "Your turn, my friend." He stepped, or rather staggered, aside, and Andrew took his place. Louis moved over to Rachael and whispered in her ear. She giggled, disengaged herself from Lawrence, and walked up to Andrew. She rubbed up against his side and gave him a big kiss on the cheek.

"Good luck," she said in a sultry voice and slowly pulled herself away with a final pat on his posterior. Andrew shook off the momentary distraction and concentrated on the target. With the wound on the left side of his chest, and him being right-handed, his throwing motion was not seriously impeded. He quickly took aim and wasted no time in letting the dagger fly. It sunk deep into the wall as the whole tavern looked on.

"Three points!" the same person as before called. He struggled for a moment with the dagger before succeeding in pulling it from the wall. In a moment, Andrew had it back.

"Not bad," Louis commented. It was an understatement, as the dagger had been less than an inch from the center of the target. Andrew took no time at all in resetting and throwing again. This time, the caller hesitated before judging the throw as he peered more closely at the position of the dagger.

"Three!" he finally yelled.

"Look again!" Lawrence bellowed. "I can see it is dead center from here!"

"You are too drunk to see your own hand in front of your face!" Louis responded. "I doubt you could hit the wall with a spear!"

"It is close, but that is not enough. Three points," the judge replied to the challenge.

Andrew hesitated for a moment before his final attempt. He took a deep breath, released it, and flicked his dagger. Again, there was a moment of silence as the result was discerned.

"Three more! A tie!" The crowd erupted in disapproval and immediately demanded another throw to break the deadlock. Louis plopped down in the closest chair.

"No more throws tonight," he said. "I fear I would stab my own foot after that last mug." He looked up at Andrew. "Good show. Another time, we shall continue, yes?"

"Assuredly," Andrew replied. He then spoke to Lawrence, who was not even aware that the contest was over.

"I shall be heading back now. What of you?"

"Another mug of ale for me."

"Remember, you left your horse in the stall this evening," Andrew reminded him.

"I believe I can talk Rachael into escorting me home,"

Lawrence replied as the barmaid returned with another full tray. Andrew was sure that Lawrence would not even have to ask her. She was getting more friendly and frisky with every trip to the table.

"Then I will see you another time." He turned to Louis. "You, too, my friend." Louis grunted a reply. Andrew shook his head, took a last gulp from his mug, and wove his way out of the boisterous tavern.

Chapter 9

T he mesmeric monotony of the burning candle threatened to lure King Talbot to sleep as he stared into the yellow flame. His hands were clasped together across his stomach, and his feet rested comfortably on a large oak table as he mused over the events of the past several days. The virtual buffet of the kingdom's best food he had just consumed for dinner in no way aided his efforts to escape slumber. The serene silence that had snuggled around him for the past ten minutes was chased away by the purposeful footsteps echoing up and down the corridor outside his tactical room. The king heard voices from beyond the door, quickly followed by three rapid knocks. Without waiting for a reply, the door opened, and the king's top two men, Malcolm and Angus, strode in. They closed the door behind them and approached their leader.

"You wish to speak with us?" Angus inquired.

"Yes, I do," Talbot replied, becoming fully alert and straightening up. He motioned for the two visitors to sit, and they immediately complied. "We have two matters of some importance that require our thoughts. One is of no small importance and is the reason for my request of your counsel this evening. The second has not such an urgent appeal, yet I shall offer it for discussion, as we are already gathered." A rap on the door interrupted the king.

"Come," Talbot called out, and in obedience, the door opened. Martin walked in and approached the king.

"Have you completed your search?" Talbot inquired as Martin bowed in respect.

"Yes, my lord," Martin replied. "For each of the last four days, we have canvassed more than a half day's ride around the kingdom quite thoroughly."

"And your findings?"

Martin hesitated for a moment, as if dreading the response he was about to give the king.

"We found nothing, sire. Not a trace of the scoundrels who attacked the young ladies was to be found. Not even the supposed corpse lay where we were directed. No campsite was evident within the area. Nowhere in our search did we find evidence or even indications of vagabonds or visitors."

"My daughter was quite precise in the location of the event, was she not?" the king asked.

"Yes, she was definite in her description. We scoured that area most thoroughly on the first day of our search. Nothing out of the ordinary was found."

"There were no tracks whatsoever that would testify to the presence of persons other than the girls?"

"We found tracks of one horse and one man. They would belong to MacLean," Martin answered.

"This is a most peculiar report," Talbot mused, more to himself than to his companions. He leaned back in his soft, ornate chair and thought for a moment while once again staring into the flame in front of him. He looked back at Martin.

"As of tomorrow, you are to arrange for regular patrols of the kingdom, encompassing a half day's ride out to the north, south, east, and west. They are to be deployed at least twice per week. Concentrate on the less-traveled roads and trails. To you I leave the other details. That will be all."

"Yes, my lord," Martin replied. He gave a slight bow of respect and marched out of the room. As the door closed, Angus spoke.

"Was it not Martin himself who had delivered this account, I would doubt its accuracy. Yet I know Martin and his abilities are honed as sharp as any man's, more than most. His report is most interesting."

"That is a grave understatement, for I would that it was merely interesting," the king said with deep concern.

"I can see how such events would pose as puzzling but scarcely more than that," Malcolm said. "What about the matter do you find so foreboding?"

"Does it not strike you as odd, the whole ordeal?" the king replied. "How many years has it been since such trouble reared its head in our land? Never have we had ill issue with nomads, yet now four of them appear, attack our women, and disappear with not a single trace left behind. One greeted death, one fled, and the remaining two were bound and gagged, yet what smallest tidbit of physical proof do we have of their mere existence?"

"There is no mystery therein. MacLean's knots were not sufficient to hold the men. They loosened themselves and made good their escape," Malcolm suggested.

"Possible but doubtful," Angus said as a different scenario developed in his mind. "Were they nomads or vagabonds, their concern would not be to erase all traces of their passage, as was done, but rather to flee from the trouble into which they fell. Upon freeing themselves, they would run as fast and as far as their legs would carry them to elude potential pursuers."

"I agree," Talbot said. "If this indeed is the case, we must ask ourselves what type of men would display these actions."

"I would venture them to be men trained in elusiveness and covert operations," Angus replied.

"Such men would make ideal spies," Talbot said, continuing Angus's line of thinking. "Only in this case, their lust of the flesh superseded their professional training, and they made themselves known. One paid the price with his life. His comrades fled in shamefast failure."

"The one who eluded capture returned and untied his comrades," Malcolm deduced.

"Exactly," Angus agreed. "They retrieved the one Andrew slew, covered their tracks, and vanished."

"To my ears, such a story sings truer than that of nomadic, uncivilized scoundrels, though these men can also be named as such," Talbot said. "Therefore, the question now becomes one of identity. Who were they? What country or kingdom sent them forth?"

"We could send spies of our own to search the country and perhaps determine who sent them," Malcolm suggested.

"I would venture every country has spies deployed at any given time," Angus said. "With not a shred of identifying evidence, how could we know to whom their loyalties belong and where to begin?"

"It is a fair idea, one that necessitates further consideration," Talbot said, agreeing at least in part with Malcolm. "We must determine where hostilities lie and prepare ourselves, lest we fall prey to assault."

"I will implement a more rigorous training scheme immediately," Angus volunteered. "The men shall grow stronger and be able to defend their king and country. We will build stronger defenses."

"You have unwittingly led us to the second issue to be discussed this evening," Talbot said to Angus. The king stood and walked around the table. "You gentlemen are my most trusted aids. The strength and prosperity of the kingdom are as much in your hands as they are mine. You have exceeded all of my demands and expectations, and your accomplishments are remarkable." He posed as if to examine the decor on one of the supporting columns. "I know there are limits to every man's knowledge, and we must learn from others when opportunities to do so arise. Only by doing so may we continue to grow and prosper even more. Only by doing so may we be prepared to defend against any and all onslaughts."

"What is on the king's conscience?" Malcolm asked.

"What are your thoughts concerning this newcomer, Andrew MacLean?"

"He is arrogant and subtly pompous," Malcolm replied, visibly defensive. "He has an irritating air of self-importance."

"Such an opinion you form in the wake of one meeting, one brief conversation?" Talbot asked.

"My judge of character has more often than not been quite accurate, given one meeting or many," Malcolm answered.

"And you, Angus?" the king prompted.

"My thoughts travel the same path as Malcolm's, though of less passion," Angus replied. "I also do not think these qualities are bad in this particular man if they can be justified by his abilities. He is skillful and intelligent, yet I stop short of naïvely giving him my trust or friendship."

"Trust and friendship indeed go hand in hand and must be earned," Talbot said. "As you say, he is intelligent, and even Malcolm cannot disagree that Andrew has some worthy ideas."

"I have given great thought to his words, and they make nothing less than perfect sense," Malcolm conceded.

"You have seen proof of his strength and skill, for he nearly bested you in a joust," Talbot said to Angus.

"What are the ends to this discussion, my lord?" Angus inquired, obviously not wishing to dwell on his near defeat.

"It is my opinion that the kingdom would benefit greatly from fresh perspectives. Therefore, I am giving much consideration to requesting Andrew extend his stay here and take an active, yet certainly limited, role in our administration."

"You have known the man less than a week, yet already you are willing to invite him into the affairs of the kingdom?" Angus asked, taken aback.

"Not all at once, to be sure," Talbot answered. "I envision a gradual merging. He will be under close scrutiny until he proves his loyalty. That is where you, my trusted eyes and ears, my voices of good counsel, will be of service."

"You wish us to spy on him?" Malcolm asked, as if the task was beneath him.

"Not at all. He will work with you, learning our system of food production under your instruction, and offer what ideas he can for improvement and growth. Whether or not you implement any of his concepts is entirely up to you. I trust your judgment." The king turned his attention to Angus. "I had also envisioned Andrew working with you and your men. He has certain skills that could prove quite valuable for our men to learn. Would you agree?"

"That may be true," Angus replied. "He has strength and stamina for sure. As for what other skills he may possess, I cannot testify."

"The Skills Contest is scheduled to take place in less than two months. Perhaps we would be witness to what skills he has should he tarry his journey that long," Talbot said.

"I would advise great caution, my lord," Angus said. "What do we know of this man? Where is he from and to what destination does he now travel? Is he loyal, or is his sword for hire? By acting on impulse, we could very well invite a serpent into our nest."

"I am not a man of blunt wit, and the matter has been given thorough thought," Talbot replied with a tone of rebuke. "I have spoken with Andrew on a number of occasions and have paid close attention to the way he conducts himself. Truly, there is something about this man that strikes a chord of caution in me. I do not trust that his appearance here is completely of chance. If we are able to convince him to extend his stay, I venture the longer he is here, the more we shall come to know of him and his allegiance. I do not want him staying here without reasonable supervision. You two will carefully watch his attitudes and mannerisms. If his behavior appears odd or in any way less than loyal to us, we shall deal with it. Until then, we would be wise to learn what we can from him. If indeed we are being spied upon for reasons of war, we need to be prepared. I believe Andrew could be of great service in that preparation."

"Are you so certain war is imminent, my lord?" Malcolm asked.

"There is no way of knowing at this juncture. Assumptions are all we have. Let us nonetheless be wary of such a possibility and not be caught unguarded."

"You are firm of mind in this issue of MacLean then?" Angus asked.

"I am. The kingdom is our concern, and my senses tell me he could be of benefit to us while he is here. In the morn, I shall summon him and present a proposition. It will be his to accept or reject. If he declines, then he will move on his way. If he accepts, then appropriate arrangements shall be made." Talbot yawned and stretched his back. "The evening draws late. When MacLean makes his decision, we shall discuss the issue further."

"As you wish, my lord," Angus said as he and Malcolm stood. "Good night." The king's two aids turned and strode out of the room.

Talbot paced in silence for a few minutes as he contemplated the issues a bit more. Then he departed for his private chambers.

Chapter 10

Despite the late evening and the numerous mugs of brew he had consumed, Andrew awoke fairly early the next morning with no lingering effects from the ale. He walked into the bathing area and to his surprise found the pit full of water. A test of the water revealed that it was room temperature, and Andrew concluded that it must have been filled for use the previous evening. Being accustomed to rinsing in cold streams, Andrew was not about to complain. He slipped into the water and, after a few minutes of scrubbing and shaving, stepped back out, clean and refreshed. He pulled the stopper and watched the dirty water disappear, a trick that still amazed him. A fresh pair of clothes lay on top of the chest at the foot of the bed, and Andrew wasted no time in getting dressed. As he was pulling his boots on, a knock came at the door.

"She is quite the early riser," Andrew said to himself as he crossed the room. He reached for the door and spoke aloud as he opened it. "What do you have in store for today?"

A young boy, perhaps ten years old, stood in the doorway with a look of confusion.

"I beg your pardon, sir?" he asked.

"My apologies," Andrew answered as he peered down the hall. "I was expecting someone else." He turned his attention to the lad. "And what might your mission be this morning?"

"His Majesty instructed me to escort you to him after you had partaken of breakfast. He wishes to speak with you this morning."

"Your timing is perfect, for as you can see, I am washed, dressed, and hungry as a bear. Lead the way."

Without another word, the boy turned and walked down the hall. After a quick breakfast of sausage and bread, the pair headed for another section of the castle. Andrew took careful note of where they were every step of the way, drawing a mental map of the castle. The boy finally stopped in front of a door, outside of which a single guard stood watch.

"King Richard is expecting us," the boy informed the guard. Without hesitating, the guard opened the door and allowed them to pass. As soon as they were through the doorway, the door closed.

"Good morning," King Talbot's voice boomed in greeting from the far end of the room. He was sitting at a table upon which a book lay open. Sunlight from several small windows illuminated the area around the table, and several torches offered light to other parts of the small room. The room was quite barren of furniture and decorations, save the table and two chairs. "That will be all, William," the king called out. The boy bowed respectfully and left the room.

"How is your wound this morning?" the king asked as Andrew strode toward the table.

"A bit on the sore side but healing quite well," Andrew answered.

"And your head?"

"My head?" Andrew asked, confused.

"From your evening at the tavern. The morning following an evening at the tavern tends to be not so pleasant for quite a few people, if you know what I mean. Please, sit down."

"I see." Andrew nodded as he pulled up a chair. "My head is no worse for the wear, and my eyes are quite clear. It would appear that your eyes are quite clear also and miss little if anything."

"I assure you, I have no spy watching your every move," the king answered, slightly offended. Andrew was not entirely convinced but did not wish to pursue the matter. "Last night, Marie seemed a bit concerned that you were not around at dinnertime, being that she had extended an invitation. She insisted that we determine your whereabouts, so I dispatched one of my aids to appease her."

"Dinner completely slipped my mind," Andrew answered as he reflected on the previous evening. "I was invited to a mug of ale, and the ensuing conversation pushed all thoughts of dinner to the side."

"She was quite disappointed, I assure you," King Talbot informed him. "An invitation from her rarely goes to waste."

"An invitation is not how I would describe her words of last evening. It was more of an order, which I did not appreciate."

"Ah, yes, she can be like that." The king sighed in understanding. "She can be quite spiteful too. She refused to escort you to me this morning, claiming that she had 'things' to do. She is just like her mother." The king paused for a moment, and Andrew did not ask the question that immediately came to mind. As if reading his mind, Talbot continued.

"Marie's mother, Theresa, died of ill health nearly fifteen years ago. She was a hard worker, that woman, constantly moving about and having her hands in one thing or another. To sit still was to be bound hand and foot to her. She was not your typical queen, as she could never stand to leave even the smallest of tasks to the servants."

"How did you meet her, if you do not mind me inquiring?" Andrew asked.

"Not at all," Talbot replied. "It was before my father passed away and I inherited his crown and the responsibilities of governance. I had an insatiable curiosity about the world and traveled quite extensively. During my travels, I stopped in a small town to rest for a few days. I spotted a young lady, the most beautiful woman I had ever seen, helping some elderly people with some very menial tasks. I was intrigued. I made some inquiries and learned that her name was Theresa McMaster, she had no family, and she spent her time in the service of the church. In order to get to know her, I decided to extend my rest and get involved in helping people, as she was doing. I found many opportunities to speak with her and get to know her. It did not take long for me to become utterly infatuated with her. I asked her to marry me, but at first, she turned away my advances. She said that she wanted to stay in the service of the church."

"That was very commendable of her," Andrew said. "Obviously, you were not deterred by her rejection."

"The opposite actually," Talbot continued. "Her love for and desire to help other people was intoxicating. She would spend weeks on mission trips to various villages to help feed the hungry, take care of the ill, and build shelters for the widows and elderly. She was unlike any woman I had ever met in my life."

"Quite an impressive woman," Andrew said.

"That she was," Talbot agreed. "I loved her, and I admired her. After nearly a year of courting her, she finally agreed to marry me. We had been married for only fifteen years when she passed away. The sense of loss, the pain … it is nothing I would wish on my worst enemy."

"And you have never sought another wife?"

"I have entertained such ideas from time to time. In my position, it is a critical decision, for not only am I affected but the entire kingdom as well. If I choose poorly and should death capture my soul before hers, the kingdom could fall apart. These people are too dear to my heart for that to happen. It would be grand to have a son to succeed me to the throne, and in truth, that would be the foremost reason for me to remarry. However, should I never have a son, Marie will be more than fit to rule this kingdom. Indeed, she would put many rulers present and past to shame."

"It surely is a significant matter, and your prudence shall steer you true," Andrew said.

"What of you, Andrew?" the king inquired as he momentarily turned his eyes to the book on the table. "Have you ever taken a wife?"

"No, Your Majesty. Marriage is a dish of which I have never had the pleasure of partaking."

"Yet the idea sits well with you, yes?"

"At the appointed time, it will be welcomed," Andrew replied.

"I see." The king straightened up in his chair. "Enough talk of wives and marriage. Now let us address the reasons I brought you here this morning. I assure you it was not to discuss women.

"The qualities of yours to which I have been witness during your thus far brief tenure here have been pleasing to me. Your intelligence appears to well exceed that of the average man, and some of your ideas reveal much insight.

"I did not become king of this vast land by virtue of a simple mind. To the contrary, my intelligence and wisdom extend beyond that of the average man, as do yours. Part of wisdom is knowing its limitations and knowing that no man is omniscient. Considerable thought and planning have gone into the systems established in my kingdom. Year after year, they perform extremely well and have proven to be quite adequate, yet they are not beyond improvement. Understandably, I desire my kingdom to flourish even more, not for my own selfish gain but for the benefit of all who live in this land. Your ideas concerning agriculture are fresh and impressive. I desire to discuss them in more depth and possibly fashion a proposition for you."

"A proposition of what nature?" Andrew asked, his curiosity greatly aroused.

"If your ideas, once discussed in much detail, appear sound and plausible, I would like for you to work with Malcolm and possibly implement some of the ideas, then stay here to supervise them."

"Several years in the least would be necessary to bring such changes about and realize their full benefits," Andrew informed the king.

"Yes, that is true," Talbot agreed. "Would this be such a terrible place in which to live?"

"Not at all," Andrew replied. "What about Malcolm? Will he not be offended at a stranger taking over his duties?"

"I appointed Malcolm to his office, and I can remove him if I so desire. He has little say in the matter. Nevertheless, I understand your position. You will not be taking charge of his duties but will be working with him in a hands-on consulting role. I believe I can pacify Malcolm while utilizing your ideas and skills."

"Would the people be so ready to accept a stranger, someone who has been in their midst but a few days?"

"You need not worry about that. They like you well enough as it is. I had envisioned a gradual merging of you into the mainstream just so they can become more comfortable with you. You would start out by accompanying Malcolm throughout the land, visiting the families and talking with them. You could perform a few menial tasks for appearance's sake, to show that you are not opposed to literally dirtying your hands."

"This sounds well and good," Andrew said, "and I am honored that you hold me in such regards. However, I am first and foremost a warrior, not a farmer. I will not spend my days planting and weeding."

"Of course not," Talbot replied. "I expect you to do nothing of the sort. I have witnessed your expertise with the sword, and to let such skill go to waste would be unforgivable. You will also train with the other men under Angus."

"Forgive me for the appearance of arrogance," Andrew said, "but there is little if anything Angus could teach me."

"There is no arrogance in truth, Andrew. It was obvious that your skills exceeded those of Angus. Let me rephrase what I said. You could exercise with the men under Angus. Angus respects strong, disciplined men. Believe it or not, you gained respect from him the other day, though he will likely not show it. I would venture that, before long, he would have you second in authority to him and helping train the others."

"If I stayed here long enough," Andrew added.

"If you stayed here long enough," the king agreed.

"I cannot say for how long my visit will be," Andrew informed the king. "I am still uncertain as to my schedule and prior obligations."

"I would urge you to think strongly of this, Andrew," King Talbot said. "There is much here that can make a man happy till his years have run their course."

"I will consider your offer," Andrew answered, "but I can make no promises."

"Good enough," King Talbot said as he rose from his seat. "While you think the matter over, wander about the castle and village. Get to know the people and see how happy they are. See how happy you could be. When you are ready, come back to me, be it one day or several hence. I shall wait for your reply."

"You are most gracious," Andrew said. "Good day, my lord."

"And to you," King Talbot replied. Andrew turned and strolled toward the door, once again noticing the barrenness of the room. It was strange in the sense that every other room he had seen had been extravagantly decorated, and now there was this one, void of decor. As soon as he exited the room, his thoughts turned to the completely unforeseen conversation that had just ended.

It was indeed an interesting proposition, one that required much consideration. Just how important was his quest concerning the sword? Was it even remotely possible that he could fulfill it in light of the fact that despite the time thus far spent on his search, he had no hard clue directing him where to go next? For all he knew, the entire story could be just a fantastic legend with no truth behind it. Did he wish to end up as the former possessor of the sword had, old beyond his years with a life given in vain? Already he had spent five years of his life wandering through vast lands. The nomadic spirit was not his nature, and he had traveled enough to last two lifetimes. He wanted to find a place to call home once again, a place to fit in and have a family. The opportunity now stared him in the face. It would take some time to determine if he truly could become comfortable in this place and fit in as everyone else seemed to believe.

Andrew's trek through the halls had taken him to one of the castle's libraries. The double doors were wide open, an invitation to all who passed by. He remembered the room from the guided tour Marie had conducted and knew that, despite its size, this was not the largest of the three libraries. The room was approximately forty feet long by twenty feet wide. Wooden shelves, all filled with books, reached about three-quarters of the way up the twenty-foot-high walls. Above the shelves were numerous windows that provided adequate illumination when the day was sunny. To make up for the lack of sunlight on cloudy or stormy days and at night, several six-foot posts with candles on top were scattered about the room. Three large oak tables stretched down the middle of the room. Benches accompanied two of the tables on both sides, while the remaining table, at the far end of the room, had four cushioned, high-backed chairs surrounding it. Leaning against the wall to his right was a ladder that was just tall enough to allow a person of average height to reach the top shelf. There was no other person in the room.

Andrew turned to his right and began walking along the perimeter of the room, casually noting the books on the shelves. He ran a finger along some of the volumes and was surprised to find no dust. In fact, the entire room appeared to be quite clean. There were no books lying on the tables. The benches, as well as the chairs, were meticulously arranged around the tables. The floor was devoid of dust or trash. The unlit candles appeared to be new, and the floor around the posts displayed no wax drippings. The books on all the shelves were lined up almost perfectly, with not a single volume sticking out more than a quarter of an inch from another. As he finished his tour, Andrew could only conclude that the room was rarely used, if at all.

"Such a pity," he said aloud to himself. "All these books, all this knowledge craving to be caressed, yet it appears that not the least bit of attention is being afforded them. I wonder what types of literature decorate these walls." He began retracing his route around the room. At random, he pulled a book from a waist-high shelf and opened it. He browsed over the first few pages and carefully replaced it. "Philosophy. If that is the subject of all these books, it is of little wonder that I am the only soul here."

He continued down the wall and inspected several other volumes from different shelves. Their contents were all of a philosophical nature. "How boring," Andrew stated. "Is there anything interesting in here?" He was treated to a change of theme as the next book he examined proved to be one of science. "This is a bit better," he said after reading the first few pages. This particular book discussed theories behind different types of weather, from rain to snow, from heat waves to thunderstorms. He replaced the book and chose another. It, too, dealt with scientific matters, discussing the stars and cosmos. As Andrew continued his way around the room, he found books discussing medicine and agriculture, poetry and plays. They were all in distinct sections and apparently well organized. Finally, Andrew found himself back at the doorway, and he gave the room another scan.

"Not in this one," he murmured to himself and turned to leave. Deep in thought, he almost ran into Marie, who was standing in the doorway. Andrew stopped short, slightly surprised.

"Could you not find that for which you were searching?" Marie asked. Her eyes were not playful, and her tone bordered on accusatory.

"For what do you suppose I was searching?" Andrew asked in reply, not giving way.

"You tell me," she countered. "Obviously, it does not concern some of the better reading of recent times."

"Better or boring?" Andrew asked. "If indeed it is boring, then it is of no wonder that I am the only soul visiting this room today. If better, then I question the wisdom of those who live here, for to contain such wonderful literature, this room is most lonely and deserted."

"I assure you it is used quite often by numerous people, most often late in the day. It only appears unused because my father insists on every room being kept perfectly clean." Marie paused for a moment as a thought crossed her mind. Then she continued.

"You were disappointed at what you found, or rather what you did not find, on these shelves. I have become deeply familiar with the volumes of knowledge that lie herein and in the other libraries. The only subject of possible interest not represented in this room is that of history. That is for what you are searching, correct? History."

Andrew passed through the doorway and headed down the hall at a slow pace, with Marie walking by his side, then answered.

"I am intrigued by the past. As I have nothing else to do and considering the vast literary resources at my disposal, it would be a terrific opportunity missed if I did not indulge in a bit of casual reading."

"I see," Marie said thoughtfully. "Is there any particular time or place in which you are interested? Perhaps the last hundred years or so would be of interest to you?"

"I am interested in many places and many times," Andrew answered vaguely. "How did you happen to find me?" he asked, changing the subject.

"To find you, I would have had to have been searching in the first place," Marie replied coolly. "It just happens that I was passing down the hall and saw you."

"Of course," Andrew replied, though not believing her answer. "Your disposition seems foul today. Has the morning been unfair to you?"

"Not at all," Marie replied. "The morning has been fine."

"Then perhaps a tickling of anger from last night taints your mood."

"I do not understand," she replied with her most innocent of expressions. "Whatever could have happened last night that would render within me an unfair mood today?"

"Your father said you were quite disappointed that I was not around for dinner despite your invitation," Andrew responded.

"You are not obligated to dine with us every evening. I think it is good for you to spend time around the people and get to know them. I was not angered at your absence."

"Then I have misjudged your mood," Andrew gave in. "Forgive me."

"I believe this library will satisfy your taste for history," Marie said as she stopped and indicated a room to their right. It was a bit smaller than the library they had just left, and there was enough space for only one table. There was quite a bit of empty space on the shelves, and Andrew guessed that there were enough books to fill just half the walls. This room was as clean as the other but had no windows, and only two of the six candle stands were lit. They walked into the room, and as Andrew began inspecting the books, Marie lit all the candles. There were two smaller candles on the oak table, and assuming that Andrew would be some time here, she lit them.

"How are these ordered?" Andrew inquired as he pulled a volume off a shelf.

"I believe they are grouped by period. Those to your far left are the oldest we have and deal with the thirteenth century. As you make your way around the room, they become more recent, until you reach the last volumes, which speak of events over the last hundred years. As a matter of fact, I believe two new volumes were just added addressing the past fifty years."

"So roughly three hundred, perhaps three hundred and fifty, years of history are represented here," Andrew stated. He turned to Marie. "Does the main library contain any more books such as these?"

Marie shook her head. "As you saw before, the main library is mostly for decoration and art. That is also where some of the children are taught. It contains more general information. If you are to find what you seek, it will be in here."

Andrew turned back to the books and assumed that Marie would be leaving, but she remained in place. There were a few moments of silence.

"You are trying to discover who built the old castle, the one upon which we built ours," she stated. It was not a question.

"What prompts you to such a conclusion?"

"Yesterday, you mentioned your interest in those who lived here before. Your curiosity in these books is not purely coincidental."

"Would you not like to know whose ruins upon which you now live?" Andrew replied. "It could be fairly fascinating."

"It may be at that, but I assure you my father was most thorough when we arrived. If he could not determine who lived here, what moves you to presume that you can?"

"Are you so sure that he does not know?" Andrew asked, turning his head slightly toward her.

"He has never given any indication that he knows. Do you believe that he does indeed know?"

"I cannot say one way or the other. I will say, however, that I believe he knows something."

"What brings you to that conclusion?"

"Your very words that he locked away numerous articles found here and that it was odd he would not let anyone see them," Andrew reminded her.

"This is true," Marie said, her mind reaching into the past. "I have never stopped to think about it much. I assumed Father had his reasons and what they were held no importance to me."

"Some of these books appear quite old. Were any of them already here when you first arrived?"

"I could not say for sure," Marie replied. "I was quite young, and reading was not a skill I had fully mastered at the time. I could ask Joseph. He would know."

"Joseph?" Andrew repeated in question.

"Joseph has charge of the libraries and the education of the younger children. He is quite knowledgeable and has a most pleasant personality. I am sure he would give us whatever help we needed."

"We?" Andrew asked with a slight grin. "So you have given in to your curiosity?"

"I have nothing better to do," Marie replied straight-faced.

"That is not what your father said this morning," Andrew stated and turned back to the book in his hand.

"My father does not know everything I do," Marie said in her own defense. "What is important to me may not be so to him."

"Such as going away to study music?" Andrew asked.

"I happen to be very interested in music," Marie answered. "My father does not share my interest, but he has given his permission for me to go anyway. There are very few books here that deal with music. The best tutors are reluctant to leave their posts and students to come here and teach one young lady, even though she is a king's daughter, so I must go to them."

"That may be so, but from what I have seen and what you have said, there are quite a few books in these libraries that deal with other topics, such as religion, philosophy, and science."

"What do those things have to do with music?" Marie asked suspiciously.

"Very little. Other than they are all part of your great scheme."

"Scheme? I have no scheme," Marie innocently replied. "I have no interest in those other things."

"No interest?" Andrew continued. "You have told everybody, including your father, of your desire to study music when in fact your intentions are to study these other subjects."

"Andrew MacLean, I do not know how or why you have invented this ludicrous story, and I take great offense at being called a liar," Marie retorted defensively. "What is your motivation for saying such things? Upon what do you base these accusations?"

"Of course, it is no concern of mine what you do with your life," Andrew said, not giving in. "We all have passions and dreams. You shall do as your heart commands, regardless of what others think."

"I must say you are being a bit rude for a guest in this home. You know little if anything about me. You do not know my likes and my dislikes, you do not know what hobbies I have, and you certainly do not know what does or does not interest me. How can you stand there and accuse me of lying? Whether you saved my life or not, you are not at liberty to be so rude." Marie's voice was beginning to tremble with anger. Her eyes shot darts into Andrew.

"It is amazing what people will tell a total stranger," Andrew continued, although he knew he was treading on thin ice as it was. There was something about Marie, though, that motivated him to continue. "In a community this small, it is difficult to keep a secret, even among the closest of family and friends."

Marie did not reply at once. Andrew began to wonder if the story he had been told was true or not. During his conversation at the tavern the night before, he had sensed that Lawrence's disposition toward Marie was not completely favorable. Perhaps she had turned down his attempts at romance, and spreading rumors about her was his means of revenge. Andrew was about to apologize when Marie spoke in a quieter yet self-righteous voice.

"And even if such was my intention, although I am not saying that it is, why should I not do as I think best? Is it not my life to lead?"

"I am not necessarily saying that you should not. Is it right, though, to be deceptive?"

"If circumstances so dictate, sometimes it is necessary. For example, my father is quite against women taking part in higher education. He, as well as virtually all men, holds to outdated traditions that say women belong in the home, not in philosophical or theological circles. He has made clear that what I need to know to succeed him to the throne I can learn here, under the tutelage of himself and his counselors. If he knew of my intentions ..." She let the thought trail off, knowing she had just admitted to Andrew of her plan, then decided she did not enjoy being on the defense and attempted to change the direction of the conversation.

"What about you?" she asked. "Do you hold to the typical male view that women should remain ignorant of issues and ideology, never venturing forth beyond the threshold?"

Andrew considered his answer very carefully before giving voice to it.

"It would be an unforgivable act to intentionally hinder the learning opportunities for anyone. People have different abilities and gifts that must be utilized in different capacities. The question is, in what station in life can we best serve?"

"You did not answer my question," Marie said accusingly.

"I believe I did. You did not understand the answer because the question was too ambiguous."

Marie fumed. Now she was back on the defensive and getting sincerely agitated. She could never get a straight answer from him. She decided to rephrase her original question.

"Allow me to be a little less ambiguous. Are you of the mind that women serve best in the home, concerning themselves solely with domestic issues?" She had him this time.

"Do you recall much of your life before you came here?" Andrew asked in response.

"What does that have to do with my question to you?" Marie asked, confused and irritated.

"Answer my question," Andrew replied, "and I will answer yours. But the answer is neither short nor simple. Indulge me."

"No, I do not remember much of life before we came here. I have told you that I was but a young child at the time."

"So you know nothing but peace and tranquility, the kind of life you are living now, the kind of life you have lived for the past twenty years?"

"That is true," Marie answered, wondering what Andrew was up to.

"This is not the type of life the rest of the world knows, Marie. I have traveled to many places during my life, and I will tell you what is out there: war, barbarians, poverty, and death. People have turned away from what is good and right and now think only of themselves. They are getting stronger, overcoming the good yet weaker people. They will come here eventually. Maybe during our lifetime, maybe not, but be assured that they will come. When they do, this kingdom, and any other, must be prepared."

"Our men train daily," Marie said.

"This is true, but they lack in number. When the invaders come, they will come by the thousands. There must be thousands to defend against them, and not just physically strong men but men strong in moral character, men who can push back and destroy the tide of evil and be bright shining beacons of light that chase the darkness away."

"Tell me when you answer my question," Marie said impatiently.

"Where do you think such character is molded? On the battlefield? In the schoolroom? In soft, cozy fields while on picnics with friends?" Marie did not answer, so Andrew continued.

"It is molded in the home by the parents. The job is not any easy one and requires much work. It requires strong and wise parents. It requires a deep-rooted dedication to seeing good overcome evil. So to answer your question, I pose a question: Where do you and your friends serve best? In fields on beautiful summer days, in rooms full of books trying to gain knowledge of the world, or helping build a country by having strong, moral families?"

"There shall come a day in which I will be required to rule over my father's kingdom," Marie answered. "When that day comes, I would serve the kingdom best by being prepared intellectually and emotionally. As for my friends, they must settle their own minds. I do not speak on their behalf."

"I see," Andrew said. "Indeed, your situation and future are much different than those of your friends. I wish you well in your efforts."

Marie stood silently for a moment, surprised at Andrew's sudden ending of the conversation. Whether he finally gave in to her or merely tired of the subject she could not determine.

Growing weary of the direction their talk had taken, and not really caring for more conversation at the moment, Marie excused herself.

"I believe I will find Joseph and ask if he can help our search. Will you be spending much time in here?"

"I would think a few hours or until my stomach insists on lunch," Andrew replied. "I have no specific plans for after lunch."

"If Joseph is willing to aid us, I will bring him back here. If not, then perhaps I shall see you this afternoon." Without waiting for a reply, Marie turned and disappeared through the doorway. Andrew listened as her soft footsteps slowly faded to silence, then resumed his examination of the books.

Chapter 11

Andrew spent two full days in the library but found nothing that gave any hint to the identity of those who had built the original castle. During that time, he neither saw nor heard from Marie, which did not completely surprise him. Although he wished it were not so, he could not help feeling a bit disappointed. His eyes growing weary and his body aching from sitting hunched over books, Andrew decided to forego the research for a day. He stood at a window in his room, looking out over the rolling hills, and decided it would be a good day for a ride. The sun was already busy burning away the morning fog and promised to provide a comfortable day to rollick around. Andrew took several deep breaths and immediately regretted the last and deepest, as his chest stung with pain. While he examined the wound, a knock sounded on his door.

"Come," Andrew instructed the visitor, and Ian stepped into the room.

"Good morning," the physician greeted Andrew. "I came by to check your wound and change the bandage."

"Do not worry. It is still there," Andrew replied.

"How odd," Ian said. "Generally, a wound such as that heals within a few days. Perhaps you are just rotten inside, which is slowing the healing process."

"Me, rotten?" Andrew asked in mock astonishment. "Do not

allow such words to be heard by my mother. She would thrash the person who called her son rotten."

"As any decent mother should," Ian replied as he removed the bandage on Andrew's chest. "How does your mother fair these days?"

Andrew did not answer the question at once, which prompted Ian to continue.

"I am not attempting to pry where I should not," Ian said, as if reading Andrew's mind. "I wish only to make conversation. We shall discuss other things if you so desire, or not speak at all."

"Actually, I have no recollection of my real mother," Andrew admitted to Ian. He felt comfortable talking to the surgeon, and his instincts told him Ian could be trusted. He wanted to share at least part of his past with someone, and Ian seemed the most congenial of the people he had thus far encountered.

"No memory whatsoever?" Ian asked, surprised. "How did this come about?"

"You were correct concerning the seriousness of the claw marks on my chest," Andrew answered. "When I was young, perhaps nine or ten years old, my family was attacked by wolves. My parents and sister were killed, and I alone escaped, though obviously not unscathed. As one of the beasts leapt for my throat, a passerby shot it with an arrow. The dead animal crashed into my chest and sent me reeling into a tree. I was knocked unconscious. When I awoke, I could not recall anything from my past. Not even my own name. To this day, those memories have not returned. The man who shot the wolf took me as his own son and raised me from that day on."

"Such a tragic story," Ian said, shaking his head. "It must have been quite difficult, losing your past and suddenly being all alone."

"How hard could it be, losing something that you did not remember having in the first place? My senses were numb. I did not know what to feel. This man had a son who was my age, and we became brothers. If it were not for Donald, I hesitate to think what path my life would have taken." The memory of Donald's death came rushing up and flooded Andrew's mind. He closed his eyes and saw the sword pierce his brother. He saw the face of the man who had killed Donald as his own life slowly ebbed away. Then Andrew saw the beautiful sword that had changed the path of his life, an onerous path that bridled his aspirations for a more settled life.

"The wound appears to be well on its way to healing," Ian said as he finished wrapping the bandage around Andrew's chest. "I would suggest you stay inactive for another week at least. It needs time to heal completely." Andrew finished dressing as Ian gathered the old bandages together. "Will you be staying with us for a while, Andrew?"

"Are you asking if I have elected to accept the king's offer to remain here indefinitely?" Andrew asked in reply.

"It is a generous offer. There is no doubt as to that," Ian replied.

"That is the very fact that concerns me," Andrew said. "The king knows nothing of me, neither where I am from nor where I am going. We speak briefly on a few occasions only, yet he asks me to stay and take an active, though limited, part in his system. This would appear to be quite unwise and presumptuous on his part. What do you think?"

"My service to King Richard has spanned so many years I have lost count. Wisdom has always been a virtue of his, and he rarely has acted in a rash fashion. Were it that I knew him not so well, my reaction would be one of concern. Yes, it appears that the king has acted presumptuously. Nevertheless, know that he has given great thought to the situation. He has a most reliable intuition upon which past actions of his have been based, and with less evidence than what he has gathered on your character through your brief conversations. I cannot say that I would do the same in his position, but I trust him. I believe I trust you also. I am generally a good judge of character."

"Concerning my decision," Andrew replied, "let us say I am considering staying for a while."

"I hope you do," Ian answered. "Now, I must go and take care of some other patients. I will see you in a day or two so we can change the bandage again."

"You have done a good job. My thanks to you," Andrew said.

"Good?" Ian exclaimed as he walked toward the door. "Do not let my mother ever hear you say I did but a 'good' job. That woman's temper can be so terrible—" His voice faded to silence as he closed the door and walked down the corridor. Andrew smiled to himself and pulled his boots on.

"Humorous old man," he muttered. He decided the day would be too warm for a second, heavier shirt, and after making sure everything was straightened up, Andrew exited the room.

The warrior saw only a few other people roaming the castle as he ambled through the cool, lonely corridors. Finally, he reached an outside door and squinted his eyes as the brilliant sunlight overwhelmed his vision. He had exited into an alley between two of the buildings. As he stepped out from between the structures, Andrew was pleased to see a few dozen people walking around, talking and carrying on their daily chores. He had seen and spoken with fewer than a dozen different people during the last two days, spending most of the time in the library. Now, as he made his way to the stable, he found himself returning greetings to nearly every person with whom he made eye contact. Some of them he knew, but most of them were only vaguely familiar faces. As he reached the stable, Steven ran out to greet him.

"Will you be going out for a ride today?" the young boy inquired.

"It would be unforgivable to waste such a beautiful day doing anything else," Andrew answered. "I wish to do a little exploring this morning."

"Annon was wondering when you were going to pay him a visit," Steven said as he walked to where Andrew's horse was penned.

"Did he tell you this himself?" Andrew asked. "You know, it is of a bit of concern when you start talking to animals."

"Not so much as when they answer you," Steven countered quickly. "Did I not see you talking to him when you first arrived?"

"Ah, so you did. You have me there."

"He has been acting a bit fidgety lately, though he does calm when I give him a rubdown," Steven informed Andrew. "His appetite has been monstrous."

"Several years have gone by since he has been treated so well," Andrew said as he helped the boy prepare Annon for riding. "Spoil him, and he will refuse to leave."

"He is a very intelligent horse," Steven said. "He would be wise to stay here."

"By that, do you mean I should stay as well?" Andrew inquired.

"Why not? The people are friendly, the food is plentiful, peace rules the land, and there are women here who would make decent wives."

"Is that so?" Andrew asked, eyeing the lad. He decided to pursue the latter issue. "It seems that all conversations around here eventually lead to the topic of females."

"I can think of many other things to talk about," Steven replied in defense. "I was only pointing out some of the better reasons for staying here, and seeing how you are alone, I thought you might be interested in girls."

"Did you have a particular girl in mind?" Andrew prompted, playing along.

Steven shrugged. "Not really," he answered casually. "Heather is kind of nice though."

"What makes her nicer than the other girls around here?" Andrew asked as he hoisted himself into Annon's saddle.

"Perhaps it is just because I know her better than the others," Steven answered. "After all, she is my sister."

"The picture clears." Andrew nodded. Annon began moving about, giving an indication that he was getting impatient. "So you think I would be a good husband, she would be a good wife, and we could live happily together forever," Andrew surmised.

"Who cares about all of that?" Steven replied. "I am just anxious to see her leave home for good. She aggravates me to no end."

"How old are you, boy?" Andrew asked, slightly taken aback at the unexpected response.

"I am twelve years old," Steven answered proudly.

"If you wish to live to see thirteen, I suggest you cease trying to be so clever," Andrew advised. "If your sister heard such words …" He just shook his head without finishing the thought but managed a sly smile. Tired of being held back, Annon trotted forward without his master prompting him. Steven stared after the warrior for a moment, puzzled, then returned to his post in the stable.

Annon made it quite clear that he was ready for a good workout as Andrew tried to hold the stallion in check while they were still within the castle's walls. With his wound still aching, Andrew did not desire to embark on a jolting, all-out sprint. He leaned forward and patted Annon on the neck.

"I know you have a few days' worth of energy stored up and wish to let it all loose, my friend. However, we will not be galloping across the countryside like a raging storm this day. We are just out for a little fresh air and exploring." Annon snorted and shook his head several times but did not bolt as was his strong desire. Instead, he let his master choose the direction and speed. Andrew tugged the reins to the left, and Annon obediently followed the indicated direction at a leisurely trot.

The lake beside which the castle proudly stood was impressive in size. Even on this bright, clear day, Andrew could barely discern the opposite side. Not too far offshore was a small outcropping of rock that sported some trees and bushes. Nearly three hundred yards in front of him, a forest containing a beautiful mix of evergreens and hardwoods stretched to the very edge of the water. In fact, as far as he could see, the forest crowded the lake's shore, except for a few areas where small, sandy beaches refused to succumb to the trees. The sun glittered like a thousand tiny specks of light on the water's greenish face as a gentle breeze rippled the mirrorlike surface.

Andrew urged Annon closer to the water's edge. This particular area of the shore was a myriad of large boulders that were continually caressed by the rhythmic lapping of the tiny waves. A fairly large turtle was sunning itself on one of the flatter rocks and appeared to completely ignore the horse and rider. As they came to the edge of the forest, Andrew nudged Annon to the right, and instead of entering the woodland, they walked along its border. There were about four hundred yards of trees between the lake and the main road leading to the castle. As Andrew looked into the forest a sudden sense of déjà vu hit him. At first, he brushed it off as being a remembrance of when he had acquired the mystical sword. The feeling persisted though, and it became more ominous, more frightening. Try as he might, Andrew could not identify the source of the discomfort. A bead of sweat appeared on his forehead. Andrew quickly turned in his saddle, taking the feeling for a sixth sense warning him of danger. There was nothing of concern to be seen. He peered deeply into the trees, but again, nothing out of the ordinary was visible. As quickly as it came, the feeling departed. Annon gave no indication that he sensed anything peculiar, which convinced Andrew that whatever it was, the sensation originated within him. Puzzled, he faced forward again and decided to not become overly concerned with the momentary disruption in his otherwise calm state of mind. The horse and rider moved forward, and Andrew guided Annon toward the village. Although he had not originally intended to go into the village, Andrew suddenly felt the urge for a mug of ale and perhaps a little something to eat. Being the last building on the outskirts of the village, the tavern was quite close, and within five minutes, Andrew was wrapping Annon's lead around a post.

"Good day, Andrew," a soft, melodious voice called out. Andrew looked up and saw Heather approaching the tavern.

"Good day to you," Andrew greeted back.

"You have been scarce these past few days. People were starting to wonder if you had moved on so quickly. Has your wound kept you dormant?"

"It is but a small inconvenience," Andrew replied, shaking his head. "Hardly enough to keep a man confined."

"Oh," Heather said. "Then perhaps Marie's tours and tales have been the fetters to your freedom," she added a bit timidly.

"She gave me the grand tour for a few days after I arrived, but since then, I have seen little of her," Andrew answered.

Heather's bright eyes gleamed a fraction more. "Will you be staying until your wound heals?" she asked hopefully.

"I shall stay a few more days at least," he replied, committing himself to nothing definite. "Were you en route to the tavern?" he asked as he turned toward the door, changing the direction of the conversation.

"I am looking for my father," she answered and peered through the doorway. "Thomas Mulhaney's horse has lost a shoe, and he wishes my father to replace it at once. Unfortunately, my father's whereabouts this morning are a mystery. He disappears on occasion. He says he likes to get away and think when asked where he has been."

"I was about to have a bit to eat. Would you care to join me?" Andrew asked although he knew that she would have to decline from what she had just told him. Nevertheless, he felt it would be rude not to extend an invitation.

"I would that I was able to," Heather answered dejectedly, "but I must locate my father and deliver my message. I do not care to spend much time in the tavern anyway. The atmosphere is not quite to my liking."

"I understand. Perhaps another time, someplace where the atmosphere is more agreeable to you," Andrew suggested.

"Another time, yes, that would be nice," Heather agreed brightly. "I wish you a good day," she said with a smile and continued her search into town.

Andrew entered the alehouse, which at this time of day played host to a mere dozen patrons. As he settled himself at an empty table, a woman who appeared to be in her mid-fifties approached him from the bar. Her unkempt brown hair reached to a paunchy waist, and a snaggle-toothed smile greeted Andrew.

"What is your desire today, good sir?" she asked.

"A bit of ale and a bite to eat," Andrew answered.

"We have a gusty gallimaufry, which should be ready by now," she told him. "A bowl will be fetched out to you right away." She headed back for the bar before Andrew could inquire as to the exact contents of this dish. He resigned himself to accepting whatever it was and casually looked around the room.

He did not recognize any of the other people present, which was not much of a surprise. Of his time here, he had spent only a few hours out among the people. If he decided to stay for any length of time, that would have to change. The last thing he wanted was to be perceived as being in a state above the ordinary people or that he considered himself superior to the masses.

Andrew was not in so deep of thought that he failed to recognize Martin as the captain of the guard walked into the tavern. He moved over to the bar and began conversing with the rotund bartender, all the while offhandedly surveying the spacious room. He gave no indication that he recognized or even saw Andrew, but it was obvious that Martin had, as he broke off his conversation with the bartender and approached Andrew. For a moment, there was something familiar about Martin. Perhaps it was in his walk, or his posture, or how his eyes never seemed to rest. Andrew could not put a finger on the familiarity and decided it was his imagination. Without waiting for an invitation, he sat opposite Andrew, crossed his arms over his chest, and tipped his chair back slightly.

"Martin, please, take a seat and join me," Andrew said sarcastically.

"It is good to see you up and around, MacLean," Martin said, ignoring Andrew words. "I heard Angus gave you quite a cut."

"A small nuisance, nothing more," Andrew replied with a wave of his hand.

"Of course not. At least, not to a man of your measure. A lesser man would surely suffer miserably under similar circumstances."

Andrew did not respond to the bait but remained quiet and expressionless. He merely sat there and stared back at Martin, inviting him to continue.

"A most fitting day for a ride, is it not?" Martin said finally.

"That it is," Andrew agreed, trying his best to appear uninterested in any conversation. Martin was not about to leave, and what he said next caught Andrew's attention.

"In fact, I am reminded of a ride I took several days ago on an afternoon very much like this one. Only I was not out for a time of leisure, to be sure. I was on a mission to take captive several vagrants reported to be in the area. Vagrants who indulge in taking advantage of defenseless women." The waitress set Andrew's food and drink on the table, but he let his lunch sit while Martin continued.

"My men and I rode out to the scene of the supposed altercation where two men were reported to be tied up and a third dead. Imagine our surprise when we arrived only to find the area completely void of bodies."

"No bodies?" Andrew asked, surprised, stirring slightly in his chair.

"No bound men, no dead body, nothing," Martin told him. "It would move a man to question their actual existence."

"Their existence is as much in doubt as yours or mine, I assure you," Andrew responded. "You searched the area and found no signs of a camp, no tracks, no clues whatsoever? I find that difficult to accept."

"Our search was utterly thorough. Several hours were spent examining every stone, every twig for some distance."

"How peculiar," Andrew said thoughtfully. He reached for a utensil and began to slowly eat, although his mind was far from food.

"To say the least," Martin agreed. "Since we have three

trustworthy witnesses, there is no doubt that the incident took place or its exact location."

Andrew knew that Martin was well aware of just how many witnesses there had been. There was no doubt who, out of the four, Martin considered untrustworthy. The captain of the guard continued.

"It appears that the one who got away did not go far before returning and freeing his companions, then fleeing once again."

"And in the meantime, erasing every possible testament to their presence there. Why would three men, their lives only moments before nearly snatched away, take pause to remove anything that would indicate they had ever been there? That is difficult ale to swallow," Andrew said as he took a drink and waited for Martin's response. It was not what he expected.

"Did anything particular catch your eye about these men?" Martin inquired.

"Particular as in ..." Andrew answered, leaving the sentence for Martin to finish. It was encouraging to know that Martin could take taunting just as he dished it out.

"Their clothes, for one thing," Martin replied as he leaned forward in his chair. "Their weaponry, their accents, their ways of fighting, anything that might give some indication of their homeland. Knowing that you have traveled much, I had entertained thoughts that perhaps something about them reminded you of a certain place or people."

Andrew slowly chewed on another mouthful of food as he gave the appearance of being in deep thought. After fifteen or twenty seconds, he gave an answer.

"I would that I could be of some help," he said finally, turning his hands up in a gesture of emptiness and giving a slight shrug of his shoulders, "but I fear nothing specific about them impressed me." Andrew's tone of voice had an edge of innocence to it, underlain with an intimation of condescension. "If a remembrance should find way to my thoughts that might give you aid, I shall at once seek you out."

"I see," Martin said, leaning back in his chair once again. Andrew's tone had not been the least bit convincing, and Martin could not fathom whether he knew anything or not. Sensing that he was not going to make any progress here, Martin decided to conduct his business elsewhere. "Then I shall leave you to finish your meal in peace. As you continue your cozy, maidenly stroll, perhaps something will come to mind." Martin stood. "I bid you a good day."

"To you also," Andrew replied, and Martin marched out with a haughty stride, looking neither to his left nor right. It appeared that insults and sarcasm were going to be regular characteristics of conversations with Martin. It was a game Andrew preferred not to play, but if that was Martin's way, then Andrew would happily join the game. He immediately began turning the conversation over in his mind and tried to recall exactly what the vagrants had been wearing. The waitress interrupted his thoughts as she slipped up beside him.

"How is it?" she asked, referring to the plate of food on the table.

"Quite flavorful," Andrew replied. "I have only one question: what is it?"

"A bit of a mix," the woman explained. "Several types of meat, a few vegetables. A tasty hash. Would you care for more?"

"Not today," Andrew answered as he lifted his mug to drain away the last of the ale. "Another time." He dropped a few coins on the table, stood, and left the tavern.

"Good day to you too," the woman murmured sarcastically as she cleared the table.

Chapter 12

M artin was nowhere in sight as Andrew hefted himself onto Annon's back, but naïveté not being a component of Andrew's character, he was certain his every move was under close scrutiny. It was something to be expected and accepted. Having nothing to hide, Andrew did not concern himself with where those eyes were or to whom they belonged.

His original intention had been to explore the immediate landscape surrounding the castle, but upon Martin's report, Andrew changed his plans. He guided Annon up the street through the middle of the village and away from the castle. Even though Martin had been decidedly dogmatic in his assertion that he and his men had given the area a thorough sweep, Andrew wanted to inspect the site of the melee for himself. Perhaps by visiting the area, he would remember something important, something specific to help identify those loathsome, malicious men he had fought.

The best course of action, Andrew decided, would be to approach the scene in the same manner he had originally on that first day. By doing so, he could better remember the events as they had taken place. In little over an hour, the nearly flowerless trees that had been brightly colored on the day Andrew had first arrived in this land came into view, and Andrew dismounted when he reached them. He led Annon along the same path through the dogwoods and eventually approached the stream.

After he and his stallion refreshed themselves with a long drink of the cool, clear water, Andrew climbed back onto Annon and headed upstream at a casual pace. He continually shifted his gaze back and forth across the stream, from one bank to the other. Nothing peculiar stood out in the tranquil setting that would serve as an indicator of human passage. Being that a full week had passed since the fight, Andrew doubted that he would find any trace of the men. He focused his mind on the men themselves. Their appearance was the main issue. When he reached the immediate area wherein the action had taken place, he reined Annon to a stop and closed his eyes.

In his mind, he saw the three girls huddled together, clenching one another in vain hope of protecting themselves. The four men, with those lewd, lustful expressions on their faces, took positions around the girls. Andrew concentrated deeply, but nothing about the men's appearances grasped his attention. Their clothes were normal, average-looking garments. Their physiques had been a bit on the lean side, but that gave proof to nothing. Covering the face of each man was a scraggly, unkempt, dark blond beard. Andrew guessed the men to be near thirty years of age, yet he could not be absolutely sure. He concentrated a few minutes more, but that was all his memory would reveal to him.

Andrew opened his eyes and swung down from his horse. He slowly walked around, positioning in his mind where the men and girls had stood upon his arrival. He jumped to the point where the fighting had begun. The first two men rushed him and were quickly knocked out of the battle. The other two men joined the action. A whip snapped nastily at Andrew's back and cheek, the enemy rushed, a dagger appeared, a man fell, and the fighting was over. Andrew peered into the woods where the fleeing man had disappeared just a few days before.

"I doubt much would be benefited from giving search through the woods," Andrew said to Annon as he moved over to his stallion's side. "Several days have passed, and the area was given a thorough search already. There is nothing here for us." Andrew swung up onto the horse's back and guided him back to the road and the castle.

Fifteen minutes passed, and, his mind still working hard to recall the faces of the men who had attacked the girls, Andrew was surprised when Annon came to a dead halt and whinnied a warning. The rider instinctively reached for his sword even before he looked to determine the source of concern. Blocking the road, about thirty yards away, stood three horses and riders. Andrew nudged Annon, and the horse obediently strode forward at a cautious pace. The horsemen did not move. The horses were facing Andrew but were turned at a slight angle that allowed them to block the entire roadway. None of the men on the horses had drawn their weapons, which was a good sign, yet their posture indicated potential mal intentions. Andrew reined his horse to a stop five yards short of the strangers, his sense of danger growing.

"Did you find anything of interest?" the man in the middle asked Andrew casually, as if they were old friends. The speaker was rather burly, easily in his forties, with a long, full, dark blond beard but his head was shaven. Andrew had no recollection of ever seeing him before. The man to his right did not appear as old as the bald man. He was much leaner and sprouted a full head of dark, red wiry hair and a beard to match. This man, too, was a complete stranger. The third man was the youngest, appearing to be in his twenties, and although he tried to sit quietly, Andrew could see him fidgeting nervously. There was something about him that struck a chord of familiarity with Andrew. Several seconds passed as Andrew struggled to place the face, then it came to him. The boy was one of the men who had attacked the girls the week prior and whom Andrew had left bound. The other two men had not been part of that encounter.

"Nothing," Andrew replied, not even bothering to act as if he did not know to what the man was referring. Pretending innocence would have been a waste of time. "Your compatriots did quite an effective job of hiding any and all traces of their presence and identities."

"They were well-trained," the man replied.

"Hardly," Andrew countered. "Well-trained spies would not have allowed their primal urges to take control of them and sabotage their mission."

"You have a point, MacLean," the man answered.

"You know who I am?" Andrew asked in response.

"Aye, and if you think long enough, perhaps you will realize that you know who I am, too," the man replied.

Andrew looked at the man closely, seeking anything that would spark a hint of recognition. There was definitely something about the man that seemed familiar the more Andrew's eyes scoured him, but he could not place him. Seeing Andrew's hesitation, the man continued.

"I see five years of exile have taken their toll on your memory," he said, almost tauntingly. "Such a pity. Perhaps a name will loosen your memory. Gerard Peterson."

"Peterson," Andrew repeated. The name revived his memory and at the same time, set off an alarm bell inside him. "Ah, yes, Gerard Peterson. Edwin Gallard's master of espionage. What a coincidence that we meet again."

"No coincidence," Peterson responded. "You did not believe that King Gallard would simply let you run away and forgot about you, did you? We have had eyes and ears roaming the lands since the day you departed, waiting for you to step from the shadows. Several weeks ago I received word that you had been identified and were heading south. Young Nevil here and his three companions were sent to Durinburg in the event it was your destination. They were to report back to me if you were spotted. Unfortunately, as you said, they let their primal urges take control and it nearly destroyed their mission. But alas, here we are."

"Here we are," Andrew repeated. "Just to be clear, where is 'here'?" he then asked.

"Here is where you relinquish possession of the sword to us and we go our separate ways," Peterson answered. "We return to

King Gallard, our mission accomplished, and you return to whatever it is you are doing in Durinburg."

"We both know that Gallard will not allow me to live," Andrew countered. "Your mission is to obtain the sword and dispose of me once and for all."

"You were always an intelligent one," Peterson said, not bothering to deny the accusation. "Let us not make this more difficult than it needs to be. Though not authorized by King Gallard, I am willing to make you a deal for old time's sake. Give me the DuFay sword, and I will give you a full day's head-start to try and evade my sword. This is a one-time offer. Should you refuse it, I shall follow-through with my instructions to obtain the sword at any cost using any means I deem necessary. And, fully understanding that you would prefer to die than relinquish the sword to Gallard, I assure you that your new-found friends would be first to suffer for your obstinacy."

"You will not be afforded the opportunity to harm those who have befriended me in this land," Andrew replied firmly, not giving an inch. "Nor will Gallard be given the prize for which he seeks."

Peterson looked at Andrew, his mind considering what path to take. He looked at his companions. "Subdue him, but do not kill him," he instructed. "We need him alive."

The two men swung off their horses and drew their swords. Andrew could tell that Nevil was nervous and unsure of himself, undoubtedly remembering their previous encounter. The other man was obviously more experienced, and there was nothing but confidence in his stature. They slowly approached Andrew. Andrew swung down off Annon and unsheathed his long sword and a shorter sword. Hoping to take advantage of Nevil's lack of experience, Andrew wasted no time in launching an attack at the young man.

Nevil's eyes opened wide in surprise as Andrew quickly stepped forward and threw a powerful strike at him. Instinctively, Nevil stepped backward as he brought his own sword up to parry the blow. Andrew immediately swung the short sword at Nevil's mid-section, but the young man was able to dodge the blow. He tried to launch a counterattack, but Andrew would not allow it, stepping forward and throwing his right foot into Nevil's stomach. The boy stumbled backward, his breath momentarily knocked out of him. Andrew quickly turned and, thanks to his nearly inhuman reflexes, dodged the blow the second man had sent toward his head. The man let his momentum twirl him around, and he swung his right leg out, catching Andrew in his hip. Although it did not injure him, the blow knocked Andrew off-balance. The man quickly regained his own balance and stepped toward Andrew while sending a powerful sword stroke toward Andrew's hip. Andrew parried the strike with the short sword in his left hand and in nearly the same move, threw the butt-end of his long sword at the man's temple. The man tried to dodge the blow but was only partially successful. His head snapped to the side, and he fell backward, not unconscious but sorely stunned.

Nevil quickly recovered his breath and stepped back into the fray. As his compatriot stumbled backward and before Andrew could fully regain a defensive posture, Nevil lunged toward Andrew. Andrew instinctively raised his sword to ward off a potential blow, but instead of sending a sword strike at Andrew, Nevil dropped to the ground, rolled once, and swept Andrew's legs out from under him. Caught off-guard by the tactic, Andrew lost his balance and fell to the ground. Nevil quickly regained his footing and kicked at Andrew's kidneys. While the first kick successfully struck Andrew in the lower back, Andrew was able to dodge a second kick and grabbed Nevil's leg. While not being able to generate much leverage while on the ground, Andrew as able to disrupt Nevil's balance, sending the young man to the ground. As he stood, Andrew sensed movement to his side but was not quick enough to dodge a fist to the side of his face. Andrew spun-around, absorbing the impact and fighting to remain conscious and on-balance. He raised his sword to parry whatever blow might have been coming his way, but there was no strike from the man. Nevil stood and both men now faced Andrew once again.

"There is no escape," Peterson said to Andrew as the action paused. "The more you fight, the more intense will be the treatment your friends receive until you relinquish possession of the sword. Do not let your stubbornness and pride endanger them. Let us end this."

"End this we shall," Andrew replied, gritting his teeth. Knowing that the longer he fought the greater were the chances of him being beaten, he needed to end the fight quickly. He turned toward the man on his left and launched a furious attack with both swords raining down on the opponent. The man tried to counter-attack but was consumed with defending himself. Nevil ran forward to join the fray and present a daunting two-on-one attack on Andrew. Andrew saw the attack coming and was able to ward-off Nevil's strike. Momentarily pausing his attack on the second man, Andrew thrust his short sword towards Nevil's chest. The young man tried to dodge the blow, but Andrew's sword found its mark and struck Nevil just above the left pectoral muscle. The boy cried out in pain and stepped backward, momentarily leaving the action.

Andrew turned back to the other man and continued his attack. There was a furious exchange of sword strikes and parries. Andrew barely dodged several close calls. His opponent did as well, but nevertheless Andrew's sword found the man's upper left arm and right thigh. With his opponent pausing, Andrew twirled to check on Nevil. The boy had recovered from the shock of his injury and had vaulted himself toward Andrew. The attack was clumsy and badly timed. Andrew stepped into the attack, crouched, and lashed-out at Nevil's midsection. The boy's forward motion stopped. A look of astonishment crossed his face, then a look of realization of what had just happened. He dropped his sword and placed both hands on his stomach, but there was nothing he could do to stave-off the inevitable. He dropped to his knees, gave a final pained look at Andrew, then toppled over, lifeless.

Andrew turned to face the other man. Seeing his comrade fall did not give the second man hesitation, and he launched another attack at Andrew. Andrew parried two quick sword strikes sent his way, then sent his own back at the attacker. The fighting lasted another twenty seconds before the pain in the man's arm and leg caused him to slow-down just enough for Andrew to end the fight with a final thrust of the short sword at the man's torso. In defiance of his defeat, the man swung his sword weakly at Andrew, but Andrew easily parried the strike. After a few seconds, the man's lifeless body dropped to the ground.

Andrew did not relish in his victory but turned to face Peterson, knowing that the fight was not over. Before he could fully turn, a bone-jarring blow to the side of his head knocked him to the ground. He rolled onto his back and through eyes that were refusing to stay open, he saw Peterson standing over him with a smug grin on his face.

"It was always going to come to this," the man gloated. "Now, we will see just how tough you are and how much you value the lives of your friends." Peterson bent down and cocked his arm for the final knock-out blow to Andrew. The blow never came. Just before he blacked out, Andrew saw an arrow suddenly poke through Peterson's chest. With not even the fraction of a second for a reaction, Peterson fell over, lifeless. Before he could fully register what had just happened, Andrew's consciousness left him.

Chapter 13

A ndrew braced against the brisk breeze that greeted him as he left the blessed barrier of evergreen trees. He had no idea of how long he had remained unconscious, but a couple of hours must have passed, as evening was quickly approaching. The bodies of the men who had attacked him were gone. There was no trace of the melee nor of the person who had saved him. Only his headache and sore muscles could attest that anything had happened.

Time felt to drag as he approached the castle. He wanted to urge Annon to gallop and quicken their arrival to warmth and shelter, but that would only make him colder and his head ache more intensely. Instead, he hung his head and let the horse set his own pace. Finally, they crossed the drawbridge and automatically Annon headed for the stables. A stable boy was waiting as Andrew swung down from his horse. Not a word was exchanged while Andrew untied his prized sword. With an affectionate pat on Annon's nose, Andrew bid his horse goodnight and walked to the castle.

As if in answer to his prayers, a hearty fire crackled and hissed in its niche within Andrew's room. Its radiance of warmth reached out and welcomed the man home, inviting him to sit close and forget the unpleasant evening outside. For a minute Andrew did just that. He stood in front of the flickering flames and held his palms out to the heat. After becoming sufficiently comforted,

Andrew moved away from the fire and headed for his bedroom. He took his riding boots off and put on a pair of soft house shoes that had mysteriously appeared in his room one evening. On a daily basis Andrew found something new in his room, left by unknown persons. One day it was a pair of shoes, on another it was a shirt. Such small displays of thoughtfulness made Andrew feel more at home with the passing of each day.

In the bathroom, Andrew poured some water from a pitcher that was refilled every day, probably by the same person who left him the garments of clothing. He saturated his face and head several times, then dried himself. He stood over the washbowl, recalling the fight and Peterson's words. A knock on the door broke his concentration.

"Come," Andrew directed the visitor.

The door opened, and Marie walked in. "We are about to have dinner. I saw you ride in and thought that perhaps you would like to join us. Have you eaten this evening?"

"Not yet," Andrew admitted. The thought of food brought a rumble from his stomach. "I would be happy to join you." Marie led the way out of the room.

The first dozen steps were taken in awkward silence, as neither person knew exactly what to say. Their last conversation several days before had not been a merry one. Finally, Andrew spoke up.

"You have kept to yourself these last few days. I was getting accustomed to seeing you around."

"I had things to do," Marie answered vaguely.

"What nature of things?" Andrew prodded. "That is, if you do not mind me asking."

"Girl things, which you would undoubtedly find not the least bit interesting," she replied.

"You might be surprised at what interests me," Andrew countered, not referring entirely to her activities.

"I am sure I would. However, I doubt you would have much interest in sewing or child-sitting."

"The king's daughter, sewing and child-sitting? I would never have pictured you doing those things," Andrew said. "You have surprised me instead of me surprising you."

"And what manner of interests have been occupying your time?" Marie inquired casually, although she was dying to know where Andrew had been.

"I spent two entire days in the libraries doing nothing but reading. I believe I read more books in the last two days than I have during the rest of my life. Today I decided to get some fresh air, so I went for a ride."

"Did you discover anything that might shed light on the castle's previous dwellers?" Marie asked.

"Unfortunately, no," Andrew replied. "However, needless to say, I have not thumbed through every book available. That would take quite some time."

"Does that mean you have decided to stay with us?" Marie asked as innocently as she could.

"Do you think I should stay?" Andrew asked in reply.

"I do not know what is more important to you, settling in one place or finding this mysterious person for whom you seek. Since I know so little about your quest, I would not venture an opinion as to what you should do."

"Would you like for me to stay?" Andrew asked bluntly.

"It would be nice to have you around," Marie answered honestly, then added, "but in the long run, it does not really matter."

"And why is that?" Andrew asked.

"In a year, I will be going away to study. Even if you were still here at that time, we would not be in contact except for few and far between occasions."

"Oh yes, let us not forget your honorable ambitions," Andrew sarcastically responded.

"Have you no ambitions of your own?" Marie retorted defensively to Andrew's mention of a sore subject. "Do you desire to always fit in with the crowd, never excelling to greater heights or prominence, never making any kind of difference in this world? From what I have seen, your talents and intelligence are far above average. Do you not wish to use them, to strengthen them, to make yourself better?"

"For what purpose?" Andrew answered. "Am I such an undesirable person that I need to change? I think I am rather likable myself, not to be vain. Or perhaps you believe I should strive for greater heights so I can have people bow down to me, to treat me as an icon. Power and prestige have no lure to me. I do not desire to have people like me for what I have accomplished or what I have but for who I am. No, I do not wish to stand out, to rise a head above all others. If, during the normal course of life, things happen that set me apart from the average crowd, then so be it. However, my intentions are not to try to bring such events about. How do you know that what I am doing will make no difference in the world? It may just save the world as we know it."

"And what exactly are you doing? Trying to find the people who built this castle? What difference could that make in this world?" Marie argued. Her tone of voice changed and became sarcastic and mocking. "Perhaps I am mistaken. Your glorious contribution just may lie in this unknown person for whom you seek, this person with no face and no name."

"That may be so," Andrew answered shortly. They walked about ten yards in silence. Then Marie laid a hand on Andrew's arm, causing him to stop.

"You are not just researching to find who built his place. You are looking for something to help you identify this mystery person. That must be it," she deduced. Andrew did not immediately answer but resumed his march down the corridor. Marie hesitated a moment, then hurried to catch up. "Is this not true?"

Andrew knew that he needed to be honest with Marie. She was extremely perceptive, and if he lied, she would undoubtedly detect his dishonesty.

"That is part of it, yes," he admitted.

"You are looking into the past to help you find someone in the present," she continued as though working through a puzzle in her mind, discovering pieces of the puzzle and fitting them together. "What is it about the past that would give clues to a person who lives today?" When Andrew did not respond, she continued. "Why is this person of such significance that you would spend so many years seeking him?"

"I will not lie to you," Andrew replied, "but I will not tell you any more of my quest or of this person I seek, other than to say that many, many lives could hang in the balance someday if I do not find him."

"A man of that great importance, yet you refuse the genuine offer of assistance in locating him," Marie said almost rebukingly. "Does that not sound a bit contradicting?"

"You do have me there," Andrew admitted. "You will have to trust me, though, when I say that it is for the best that I traverse this journey alone. After five years, though, I am beginning to doubt its authenticity myself. I feel as if I am chasing a legend or fairy tale, one that could be as easily true as false. I am hoping to find something among these books that would lend the least bit of evidence to the reality of that in which I have become involved."

"If you would enlist the help of someone else, someone who is familiar with the past, then perhaps your questions could be answered," Marie suggested, making yet another bid to sway Andrew's resolve.

"That may be so," Andrew replied, "but it is best that I reveal as little as possible of my quest. Battles have been fought over and men have died for what I—" Andrew was about to say, "possess," but that would let Marie know there was something physical involved with his quest. He did not care to have someone snooping through his possessions and discovering the sword, even if nobody else knew of its history and importance. After a short pause, he finished, "—seek."

"Only Joseph knows these libraries better than I do. Share your secret with me. I know I can help," Marie pleaded. "It will take you so long to go through the libraries by yourself. Working together, we can cut that time by more than half."

Andrew thought about Marie's suggestion. It was certainly tempting to tell someone of his secret, to have a comrade in his search. He was convinced of her resourcefulness and ability to help. Also, the prospect of spending more time with her was not the least bit unpleasant. However, even if she swore to keep quiet concerning the matter, it would be only a matter of time before his purpose was made known to others. After all, he himself had already made known to her more than he had ever intended. It would be too great a risk.

"I would that I could tell you," Andrew answered, shaking his head, "but I must trust my instincts. I believe you are trustworthy and that you could be a great help. Someday I may tell you, or you may deduce it on your own. However, I know all too well how circumstances arise that force matters in directions in which we never intended to proceed. I have a feeling that if I confide in you, eventually, by no direct effort on your part, others will come to know my secret. That could prove to be disastrous if the wrong person became aware of my intentions. You must respect my needs and try to understand them."

"I will not cease trying to divulge your secret, Andrew MacLean," Marie said, giving in, "but I will respect your standpoint. Does this mean that you will be staying for a while longer, at least until you exhaust the resources here?"

"Up until now, my life seems to have been dictated to me," Andrew replied after taking a deep breath, his answer to Marie coming in a roundabout way. "I have never had many decisions to make regarding my path. It was always obvious to me which way I had to go, or I was forced in a certain direction," Andrew said. "Today it is different. Today I must choose where to go, and the decision is not an easy one. Do I continue this journey of mine, this seemingly impossible search for a complete stranger? Am I all but chasing a fairy tale and wasting my life for some fantastic ideal?" Andrew paused and shook his head. "I have been on the road too long. I desire nothing more than to find a home and settle down. However, if I give up on my quest, will I be at peace with myself for the rest of my life?"

"Trust your instincts," Marie advised him. "They are what you must believe in. If your desire is to put roots down, then do so. Who has called you to be the savior of the world?"

"Who indeed?" Andrew asked in reply. They walked in silence for a dozen steps or so. Marie did not know what else she could say at the moment, and Andrew was struggling with a decision that had to be made sooner or later. For the first time since he had stumbled across the sword and legend, he seriously considered giving it up. He felt queasy as the turmoil in his mind seemed to migrate to his gut. He wanted to shout, to lash out, to do something to vent his frustration. Only adding to his anxiety was the fact that, despite himself, he was becoming increasingly attracted to Marie, and just when he thought she was interested in him, she would push him away. Knowing that nothing would be accomplished by getting uptight, Andrew forced himself to relax, to let go of the building stress. He took a deep breath and slowly exhaled, though such an exercise rarely helped at all.

"I will stay for a while, but for how long I cannot say at this time," he said, finally answering Marie's original question.

"Will you tell my father this evening?" she asked.

"I would rather wait another day or two. There are a few things I would like to do before I get involved with whatever the king has for me to do. I have a feeling I will be quite busy after I inform him of my decision to stay."

"He will be pleased to hear that you have accepted his proposition," Marie responded.

"There is something for which I could use your help if you are still willing to help me," Andrew said.

"What do you need?"

"Do you recall seeing a mausoleum around here or any place

where people were buried prior to your arrival here? I have found no such place, though my search has been limited thus far."

"Why would you want to see a place like that?" Marie asked, then answered her own question. "Because it might provide information about the people who have lived here, of course." She thought for a moment. "Nobody of high standing has died since we settled here; therefore, we have had no need for a mausoleum. There is a cemetery down the road toward the village. The common people use it for their own dead."

"I am thinking more along the lines of royalty," Andrew informed her. "If I found the place where a king or queen was laid to rest, there would undoubtedly be evidence of their names or something to identify them. Common burial grounds would not provide the information I seek."

"I have discovered no such place within the castle's walls," Marie continued in deep thought, "but what you seek may lie outside the gates. There are several caves and caverns nearby in which I used to play as a child. Ten or so years have passed since I last visited them. They could very well have been used as a mausoleum, though I have no recollection of seeing anything to indicate such a use."

"It is doubtful that royalty would be buried outside of the protection of the castle's walls. That would allow for vandalism and desecration of the graves, which would not be tolerated. You are quite sure that there is nothing within these walls that could have been a burial chamber?"

"It is quite possible that such a place lies beyond my explorations. Although I have been in most every room of my home, there could very well exist catacombs beneath the castle's foundation upon which I have never stumbled."

"And the only entrance you are aware of that could lead to such a place has been barred by your father," Andrew stated as a question.

"That is correct," Marie affirmed. "He has forbidden anyone

from venturing into the lower depths of the castle for their own safety."

"I wonder," Andrew mused, believing that there could be other reasons for the king's barricading the heart of the castle. "There remains a chance that these caves of yours could hold something of minor importance. Will you show them to me in the morrow?"

"If you ask nicely enough," Marie answered alluringly.

There she went again, Andrew thought. One moment, she was warm; the next, ice; then warm again. He could not figure her out and was only vexing himself trying to do so.

"I thought I had done just so," he answered, not playing the game.

"You certainly did," Marie acknowledged less teasingly. "I will show you around tomorrow."

Their conversation ended as they entered the dining area. This place was new to Andrew. The room was about twenty-five feet long and fifteen feet wide, with a ceiling of exposed oak support beams fifteen feet above the floor. The floor was made of smooth slabs of oak so expertly laid together that in places it was nearly impossible to see the seams. Two circular iron chandeliers with three-foot diameters and holding fifty two-inch-thick candles each were suspended by chains over an exquisite dining table. The oak table was ten feet long and four feet wide with detailed carvings etched in a four-inch-wide border hanging from the edges of the table. Ten high-backed, padded chairs encircled the table, chairs that were similar to the ones in Andrew's room. Two candles, three inches thick, separated the table into three equal sections and were the only objects on the table. King Richard sat in the chair at the far-right head of the table, slowly sipping from an ornate silver chalice. He stood as the pair entered.

"I was beginning to wonder if you had become lost," Talbot said to Marie as she approached the table. "Andrew, sit here to my left. I hope you have brought your appetite. The cooks have prepared a fine meal."

"That I have," Andrew answered as he pulled the indicated seat away from the table. Talbot held his daughter's chair as Marie stepped up to the table, then pushed it in after she sat down.

"We have not spoken for a few days. How is your rest thus far?" the king inquired.

"Quite pleasing," Andrew answered as he sat down.

"I trust your wound is healing well."

"It is," Andrew replied, going along with the small talk. "Sometimes I forget it is even there."

"Wonderful," King Talbot said. "What have you been doing to keep yourself occupied?"

"Most of my time has been spent in the libraries," Andrew replied, although he was sure that the king knew good and well where he was almost every minute of the day. "You have a respectable collection of books."

"Thank you. We try to keep up to date on the new literature while also learning about the past. Some of the books and parchments were here when we arrived, remarkably well preserved in the libraries. Do you have a specific area of interest?"

"It is quite a coincidence that you mention the past. I tend to lean more toward historical texts," Andrew replied.

"History." Talbot nodded approvingly. "Only by learning of the past may we avoid making the same mistakes. By studying history, we know which philosophies have succeeded and which have failed. We know what makes a good administration and what makes a bad one."

"You appear to have a well-established domain here," Andrew noted. "Have you incorporated much of the past into your rule?"

"You could say that my kingdom's foundation is the past," King Talbot acknowledged. "After all, we sit upon ruins hundreds of years old."

"Evidently, the earlier inhabitants did not have too good of a system," Andrew said as a young lady placed a chalice of wine on the table in front of him, "considering the state in which you found this place."

"Do not be so sure of that," King Talbot countered. "As a matter of fact, they had an impressive system of society."

"Is that so?" Andrew asked innocently. His curiosity jumped at the king's words and the possibility of information that could help his search. "How could you know that? Did they leave books or other information setting forth their ways of life, their methods?"

"No, there is nothing in written form," the king answered rather quickly. "It was odd that of all the books and documents we found, none referred to any earlier inhabitants. What we know we have learned from the people. People around here are proud of their past. They pass information, legends, and ideologies from generation to generation. When you talk to them, if you are smart, you can piece together what the past has been like. If your eye is sharp, you can look around this region and see where old fortifications once stood and areas that could very well have been used for farming. Bits and pieces of information add up."

"That they do," Andrew agreed.

With those words, dinner was served, and the majority of conversation from then on was between the king and Marie. Andrew reflected not only on the things the king had said but also the way he had said them. He knew more than he elected to reveal; of this Andrew was convinced, and he was determined to find out just how much more. He would have to be discreet and cunning in how he went about divulging more information from the king. The last thing he wanted was to arouse suspicion.

Finally, the trio had finished dinner, and the plates and utensils were cleared from the table. Andrew leaned back in his chair and patted his stuffed stomach. He turned his head slightly to watch an attractive young female server leave the room through a door behind the king. A slight movement on the floor just beyond the king caught Andrew's attention. A huge dog lay on the floor, gnawing on a bone long since stripped of all meat. The animal held the bone between two huge paws and appeared to be doing its best to bite the bone in half. Andrew could not remember seeing the animal when he had first entered the room nor at any time during dinner. Talbot saw his guest's gaze and followed it to the dog.

"That is Sampson," the king informed Andrew, anticipating the question. He patted his right knee twice and whistled. Immediately the dog dropped his bone and walked to the king's side. Talbot put out a hand, let the dog lick it, then proceeded to pat the animal's head.

"He is the biggest dog I have ever seen," Andrew admitted. "I neither saw nor heard him enter the room."

"He does that quite often, sneaking up on me," the king said. "I guess that is the wolf in him. He is more wolf than dog. It has been over five years since we found him as a little pup, wandering around lost. He has stayed with us ever since. I will be in a room, reading or doing something that has my complete attention, turn around, and there he sits, just staring at me. On more than one occasion, I have nearly come out of my shoes he startles me so much. He gets a look about him at times. Maybe it is just the lighting or something in my imagination, but there are times when he has an evil look about him. He has never growled at Marie or me. He has never shown the least bit of aggression toward us, but he still scares us on occasion. Would you agree, honey?" the king asked his daughter.

"Wholeheartedly," Marie answered. "He makes me nervous for sure."

"Have you ever seen a wolf up close, or perhaps a dog that is part wolf?" Talbot asked Andrew.

"Not that I can recall," Andrew replied as he stared at the so-called dog. The top of the gray beast's head had to be over three feet from the ground while he was sitting by the king. His ears were pointed straight up, ever alert. His muzzle was a lighter shade of gray than the rest of his body, almost white. His upward slanted eyes were about halfway shut, but Andrew could still see the yellow eyes. As he looked at the profile of this majestic animal, a feeling of foreboding overcame him, and his heart began to beat faster. The dog turned its head and locked its eyes on Andrew. Andrew could only sit there, unblinking. A thin film of perspiration broke out on his forehead, and he could feel, and almost hear, his throbbing heart. The room was wide open, yet he felt trapped. Why did he want to flee? He was under no threat, yet the urge to escape predominated every thought, every feeling within him. A vision flashed before his eyes. Another wolf stood in front of him, one with a stained muzzle and lips pulled back in a vicious grimace, revealing dagger-like teeth. There was nothing else visible in this terror-fraught vision of raw bestiality. Andrew's hands began to tremble ever so slightly. In slow motion, the animal lunged for him with gaping jaws and minacious eyes.

"Andrew, are you all right?" Marie asked, breaking the flashback.

"What?" Andrew asked, snapping back into reality.

"I asked if you were all right. You appear quite flushed and are perspiring."

"I am fine," Andrew told her as he took a deep draw from his chalice.

"What came over you?" the king inquired. "I have never seen anyone display such a reaction to Sampson."

Andrew turned his head and looked over to the king. The dog was no longer by Talbot's side, nor for that matter visible anywhere else in the room.

"It was nothing," Andrew said. "Perhaps I ate something not too agreeable with me. I think I should retire for the evening, with your pardon."

"I was looking forward to talking with you more this evening, but if you are not feeling well, then we should wait until another time," the king said as he eyed Andrew closely. "You have my pardon. Shall I send the physician to you?"

"My thanks for the offer, but that will not be necessary," Andrew replied as he stood. "I believe a little rest should be all the medicine I need."

"I will accompany you back to your room," Marie volunteered, then looked at her father, "if I have your permission."

"You may go," the king consented. "We shall dine again tomorrow."

It was more an order than invitation. Andrew nodded respectfully to King Richard and walked out of the room with Marie by his side.

There was no conversation during the walk back to Andrew's room. Marie could see that Andrew had not fully recovered from whatever had struck him in the dining room, whether it was the food or something else. The silence was becoming uncomfortable by the time they stopped in front of Andrew's door.

"Why did you lie to my father and tell him that you have never seen a wolf before? You admitted the other day it was a wolf that inflicted those scars on your chest," Marie said as Andrew reached for the door.

"I did not lie," Andrew countered. "I said I did not recall ever having seen a wolf that close, which is nothing but the truth. I do not remember that event from my childhood." That was not entirely true, as his brief flashback had just proven otherwise.

"Are you sure that you will not be needing Ian? It would be no trouble at all for him to pay you a visit. He has some extremely effective remedies for upset stomachs. Perhaps it was the chicken. Chicken can make you sick if it is not prepared correctly," Marie said.

"It was neither the chicken nor anything else I ate."

"Then what?" Marie asked.

"Something else," was all that Andrew was prepared to admit. "Will you be free to show me the caves tomorrow?"

"I have no other plans," she replied eyeing him curiously, wondering why he refused to answer her question.

"Then I shall see you in the morning," Andrew said. "Good night." He entered his room and closed the door behind him.

Marie stared at the door for a few moments with a look of puzzled determination, then pivoted and headed back through the hallway.

Chapter 14

T he downpour began in the late evening hours and lasted throughout the following day. Andrew decided early on that he did not wish to spend the afternoon gallivanting about the countryside in the rain and therefore postponed his cave tours with Marie. However, he was not so intimidated by the wet weather that he was discouraged from taking a short ride to the tavern, which is precisely what he did. It was early in the afternoon as he strode through the pub's front door and glanced around the room. Obviously, he was not the only one who was willing to get a little wet for a mug of brew, as was evidenced by the crowded establishment. There was not an empty table in sight. Andrew was about to nudge his way to the bar when he spotted Lawrence and Louis at a table with an unoccupied chair. Andrew walked over to his acquaintances and grabbed the seat.

"Mind if I join you?" he asked as the two men looked up at the newcomer.

"Not at all, my friend," Lawrence answered. "Louis and I were just arguing as to who was going to buy the next round. Louis, is there not a rule that each time a new person joins a table, he must provide the next round of drinks?"

"I believe you are correct," Louis agreed, doing his best to appear serious. "That would mean the next round is on"—Louis looked around the table as if there were several other people present—"Andrew."

"Why do I get the feeling that this rule is of recent origin?" Andrew asked.

"Why, this rule has been in effect for at least"—Lawrence paused as if he were doing a mental calculation—"twenty seconds. Maybe longer, but time has such a habit of blending together it is sometimes difficult to tell."

"Is that the way it is around here, the days just blend together and drag on?" Andrew inquired as he signaled a barmaid.

"Sometimes, yes," Louis answered. "There are a few days throughout the year that are special, such as the two seasonal banquets and the Skills Contest."

"The Skills Contest?" Andrew asked.

"It is an annual skills competition between all the warriors," Lawrence answered. "It is actually a two-day contest that includes half a dozen events. You are awarded a certain number of points, which are reflective of your performance, for each event. What it all comes down to is who the best man is at the most things."

"Things such as ..." Andrew prodded.

"A javelin throw for accuracy, bow shooting, defense, galloping sword strikes, dagger throws, and endurance."

"Sounds fascinating," Andrew mused. "Tell me more."

"The javelin throw is self-explanatory," Lawrence answered. "A target is set up approximately thirty yards from the throwing line, and points are awarded depending on how close your javelin is to the center mark. The bow shooting is two events in one. First, you shoot at an immobile target. Then the target is set in motion, and you shoot at it again. Points are again awarded based on how close you come to the center mark. For the galloping sword strikes, melons are set on top of wooden poles of varying heights. Points are awarded for the quickest time through the course and the most melons struck in half. The dagger throw is nearly identical to what you and Louis did the other night. The defense event shows your skill at avoiding blows by your enemy. You are armed with two weapons of your choice. Two men surround you, each armed with a wooden pole dipped in dye. Their goal is to stain your tunic with dye. You must parry their blows. After a set duration, the number of stains on your tunic is tallied and counted against you." Lawrence paused and took a long swallow from his mug.

Louis continued where Lawrence had left off. "The endurance event is held last, due to its exhaustive nature. Sword fighting, a course of obstacles, running, and horseback riding are all included. It is grueling and tests the strength as well as willpower of every man who enters the contest."

"Tell me then. Who is the best man?" Andrew asked, lifting his own mug.

"The contest has been quite close for the past three years. The winning margin has not been more than five points during this time, so it is difficult to say who is clearly best," Louis replied.

"Allow me to venture a guess. Would I be correct in saying that you are not among those winners but maintained second or third best?" Andrew asked.

"You would be," Louis replied, eyeing Andrew suspiciously. "What has led you to such a deduction?"

"Your very own words," Andrew replied casually.

"How so?"

"From the first night we met, I gathered that you were not exactly the unpretentious type—that not meant to be a criticism of your character," Andrew quickly added, not wanting to offend Louis. "Therefore, if you had won, you would have been quick to say so in definite terms. The words that you chose to use, however, took some of the glory from the winner and placed it on those who fell short by such small margins. This seemed to be consistent with your nature. If you had not been one of the contestants to place next to the top, you probably would have simply named the winner. Therefore, I deduced that you must have been the second or at least third-place contestant."

"I am thankful that a battle of wits is not the contest lest Andrew win outright," Lawrence said, completely amazed. "I have never heard such a train of thought."

"My words could have been interpreted many ways," Louis said as he lifted his mug to his mouth. "Any one of which would make sense."

"Of course," Andrew replied as Louis's very words again reinforced Andrew's analysis of his character. "When does this contest take place?"

"Little more than a month hence," Lawrence answered. "Will you remain here long enough to compete?"

"I believe I will still be here," Andrew answered.

"Does this mean that you intend to settle here and accept the king's offer?" Louis asked.

"I have given it considerable thought," Andrew replied. "The offer is quite gracious."

"Indeed, it is," Louis agreed with a hint of bitterness.

"It does not sit well with you?" Andrew asked, noting Louis's toned reply.

"There are many hardworking, loyal, proven men who have served King Richard for most of their lives. To say the least, there would be some disgruntlement among the king's people should a complete stranger be installed in an authoritative position rather than one of those proven men."

"You stand opposed, then, to my staying and accepting the king's proposal?" Andrew inquired.

"Do not take this personally, my friend," Louis began, leaning over the table so as not to be overheard by a neighbor, "but for the first time in my memory of serving King Richard, I must question his wisdom in a matter."

"Which only proves that you are an intelligent man, for only a fool would allow himself to blindly be led," Andrew answered. "Are there many others who share your ill feelings?"

"A few," Louis answered as he leaned back in his chair. "Some more vehemently than myself, others less so. I would advise that you step carefully, however." There were a few seconds of tense silence.

"So, what is the prize of this contest?" Andrew asked, changing the subject and ignoring the warning. "What makes it worth the time and effort?"

"Land," Lawrence responded. "You are given the opportunity to choose twenty acres of the kingdom's land to be your own. You can do with it as you wish. Sell it, farm it, live on it, whatever."

"I have never owned land before," Andrew mused aloud. "It would be good to have a place of my own, to live and grow on."

"You sound as if you have already won the contest," Louis noted. "Are your skills so great that you need not even compete to win?"

"My skills shall speak for themselves when the time comes," Andrew replied. "I dare not speak for them, lest I have a day in which my eyes and hands do not quite meet and my words make a fool of me."

"Then here is to the contest," Lawrence interrupted, raising his mug, "a day on which our hands and eyes fail us not." Andrew and Louis joined in the toast. As they finished drinking, Rachel appeared beside their table.

"Would you gentlemen care for something to eat?" she asked.

"What is on the menu today?" Lawrence asked.

"Whatever you like," the waitress answered teasingly with a devilish grin.

"I see," Lawrence responded. "How about some bread and stew for now?"

"Same here," Louis put in.

"And how about you?" she asked Andrew with a glint in her eyes. "Perhaps you would care for a bit of the cheese today?"

Lawrence gave Andrew an amused look, waiting to see how he replied to the offer that was not about food.

"The day is not a good one for cheese," Andrew answered without hesitation, "but thank you for the recommendation. I believe I will have the stew."

"As you wish," Rachel said alluringly.

As she left, Louis spoke up. "How can you resist an invitation like that?" he asked incredulously.

"She has her eye on you," Lawrence added. "Rachel is very persistent."

"Her ladylike aggression is so appealing I wonder how long I can resist," Andrew answered, sarcasm riding his words.

"Ah, yes, that is her greatest quality, is it not, Louis?" Lawrence noted.

"That it is, my friend, that it is. I toast the aggressive woman: may her breed never depart this land." Louis and Lawrence noisily clanged their mugs together and followed with a long draw of lager. Andrew could not suppress a grin of amusement.

"I am curious, Andrew," Louis said after setting his mug down. "Just what kind of woman are you interested in?"

"He is interested in the type that goes on picnics, prances through the flowers, and has a certain royal quality to her," Lawrence answered before Andrew could respond.

"I see," Louis deduced. "In other words, the king's daughter. Ambitious, are we not?"

"Your imagination has gotten the best of you, Lawrence," Andrew subtly reproved him. "I have no desire for Marie in that respect."

"Yet you have spent a good bit of time with her, have you not?" Louis countered.

"She has shown me around the castle and grounds per direction of her father. I would have been content to explore on my own."

"And just what exactly are you interested in exploring?" Louis inquired, not particularly casually and just short of accusingly.

"Perhaps *explore* was the wrong term to use," Andrew responded after a moment of thought. "What would you call looking around, getting familiar with new surroundings, learning your way around?"

"Exploring," Lawrence answered, as if it were obvious.

"Then I was mistaken." Andrew looked Louis straight in the eye. "I believe *explore* was the correct word after all." Louis did not respond.

Rachel returned at that moment and served the men their food. As she set Andrew's stew in front of him, she spoke to the men, although it appeared that she was speaking more for Andrew's benefit. "If you gentlemen need *anything* else, I will be but a call away," she said with a flirtatious grin. With that, she disappeared into the crowd.

"Andrew, I believe we should get you drunk and send you home with her," Lawrence stated as he watched Rachel slide through the crowd. "I think it would do you good to spend some real quality time with a woman, especially that one. As your friend, I think it is my duty to watch out for your well-being."

"That would be such a kindhearted thing for you to do," Andrew replied. "The more likely scenario is that you would get drunk and end up going home with her."

"That is a better idea yet." Lawrence laughed and dug into his meal.

"As I have stated quite firmly previously," Andrew said, "my relationships with the opposite gender shall remain platonic until the day comes on which I am joined with a woman in marriage."

"Such a shame," Louis murmured.

"Are training exercises always discontinued on days of rain such as this?" Andrew asked, addressing neither man in particular, seeking to change the conversation.

"Not always," Louis replied. "If the foul weather continues for several days, we can be assured of getting our swords wet on at least one occasion. We have trained hard the past few days, and Angus has given us a brief respite. I would venture we shall return to exercises in no less than two days. That has been the historical pattern."

"Under what other types of adverse conditions do you train?"

"I know of no other adverse conditions," Louis answered with a quizzical expression, shaking his head.

"There are many conditions in which a man may be required to fight, and not all of them pleasant," Andrew stated.

"What is your point?" Louis asked.

"What is the key to one-on-one combat, the one thing that you must maintain in order to ward off blows and deliver strong, effective strikes of your own?"

"Balance," Lawrence quickly answered. "That is elementary."

"Exactly," Andrew continued. "What is the primary factor that lends to good balance?"

"Weight distribution," Lawrence again answered.

"And ideal weight distribution is a direct factor of footing. If your footing is off, then your weight is off, and you are rendered ineffective." Andrew paused for a moment. "What types of exercises do you engage in that challenge your footing, your balance?"

Louis and Lawrence maintained silence as they reflected on their past and all the training sessions that had been undertaken, but neither man could offer an answer. Their continued silence was the answer for which Andrew was looking.

"The situation is this: you have been taught that balance is of utmost importance; however, you have not been taught how to maintain your balance. Am I correct?" Andrew asked.

"Angus teaches us balance on a daily basis," Louis replied in defense.

"And you, as well as Angus, are naïve to believe that all battles will be fought on flat, unobstructed landscapes." Andrew took another mouthful of stew as he let his comments sink in. Louis and Lawrence eyed each other, knowing that what Andrew said was true.

"What types of conditions do you specifically have in mind?" Lawrence inquired.

"I have fought in fields littered with rocks, large and small. I have fought in forests where you can count on tripping over stumps and fallen trees. I have fought in fields of mud well over my ankles. I have fought in streams but a few inches deep and rivers that have swept past thigh-high. I have fought on sheets of ice in the very heart of a blinding snowstorm. These, gentlemen, are adverse conditions. You may never encounter the least challenging of them all, but to be the best warrior you can be, you must know how to handle them all." With that, Andrew leaned back in his chair and let his companions ponder his words.

"We have never been subjected to such conditions during training," Lawrence admitted. "The majority of our training takes place in the surrounding fields, which offer little if any opposition to solid footing."

"And that is a major deficiency in your training regime," Andrew pointed out matter-of-factly.

"Will you approach Angus with what you have just told us?" Louis inquired.

"It would not be my place," Andrew replied, waving his hand in negation. "However, I would not be uncomfortable with mentioning some of my concerns to the king if it comes up in common conversation. He in turn could address the subject with Angus, which would be far more appropriate."

"Do you speak with the king about such things often?" Louis asked slightly suspiciously.

"Not at all," Andrew returned. "My encounters with His Majesty have been few and situated around the dinner table. Conversation tends to be more casual."

"It appears that you have quite an opportunity at your disposal in that you are so close to the king's ear," Louis noted. "Properly taken advantage of, it could very well lead to more prominent positions at his side." Louis's words were laced with jealousy and envy. "Positions that generally take many years to ascend to."

"My intentions are not of power and prestige," Andrew firmly responded.

"Then just what are your intentions?" Louis fired back.

Andrew took a moment to think of a reply. What exactly were his intentions? Did he desire to remain in this kingdom, this land, and establish his own niche in the world? What about his quest? Was that to be pursued, even if he chose to stay here a year or two? Andrew could not come up with an answer.

"I would that I could answer you, Louis. At this precise

moment, however, I cannot. My path is not clear to me. I will tell you this: I do not intend on making enemies, but if men become jealous and hostile because King Richard solicits ideas from me and takes them to heart, then so be it. That is not my problem, I have no control over it, and I will not allow it to interfere with whatever future I pursue."

The edge that had been riding Louis's voice eased off, and he became nearly as friendly as when he and Andrew had first met.

"I believe those to be honest words," he said. "I will drink to them." The three men lifted their mugs and finished off the last of their ale. "Now we shall return to the dartboard and see whose eye is sharper today. Are you game?" he asked Andrew.

"Always game," Andrew replied and rose from his seat.

Chapter 15

S tanding at the bar, nearly finished with a mug of ale himself, Martin watched the three men weave their way around the dining tables as they headed for the dart-throwing area. He remained in place until the first few darts had been thrown and then turned and left the tavern. Undaunted by the rain, Martin untied his horse, jumped in the saddle, and headed for the castle at a quick trot. The unfavorable weather kept most people under shelter, and Martin passed no other villagers during his short ride. As he approached the stables within the castle's walls, a young boy ran out to meet him. After relinquishing the horse's reins, Martin walked over to the main entrance of the castle and disappeared inside.

Several corridors and one flight of stairs later, Martin came to a stop in front of a single wooden door. His sharp knock was immediately answered by a bid to enter. Martin complied and entered King Richard's study. The king sat in a plush chair in front of a warm, comforting fire, reading a book. Marie was also present, and she, too, sat in front of the fire, reading a book. The king looked up as Martin passed through the doorway.

"A most unpleasant day to be out riding, is it not?" the king asked. "You appear soaked to the bone."

"An inconvenience and nothing more, Your Majesty," Martin replied. "A man's business requires from time to time that he be inconvenienced."

"What business brings you out on such a dreadful afternoon? I trust it is nothing to be alarmed over."

"A routine report, Your Majesty, nothing more," Martin answered reassuringly. "No offense to the lady, but it may be best that I give my report to you in private. Surely you understand," he said to Marie.

"As the king's only child and heir to his throne, I believe my ears are fit for the kingdom's business," she replied tersely.

"Your Majesty?" Martin addressed the king almost pleadingly. "I respect your daughter most highly, but I would prefer to recite my report to your ears only."

Talbot thought for a moment, then spoke to his daughter.

"Marie, would you be kind enough to find someone who will bring us more wood for the fire? I fear it is dying, and the chill has slowly returned to the room."

"Yes, sir," she obediently replied. "I shall call one of the boys immediately." Marie left the room and shut the door behind her, but instead of carrying out her father's instructions, she quickly stepped several yards down the hall and into a room that bordered the study. She gently closed the door and carefully made her way across the dark room that had at one time been her mother's private study. The room was now for Marie's use, and she was about to use it well. She moved over to the wall common with her father's study and found the small opening in the stone barrier, the use of which Marie had never been sure. It could facilitate the passing of a book between the two rooms, or it could have been used for communication between the occupants of the rooms. For the moment, it was serving as an opportunity for eavesdropping. Martin's words and tone had ignited a flame of anger and damaged her pride; therefore, Marie was determined all the more to hear what he had to say.

"—just as you requested, Your Majesty," Martin was saying.

"And what have your patrols uncovered?" King Talbot asked.

"We still find no evidence of intruders anywhere within the king's lands. For over a week now, our patrols have been riding from one end of your kingdom to the other. Even I, myself, have led some of the patrols. We have encountered neither suspicious strangers nor signs of impending danger."

"Therefore, we have no more knowledge of the men who attacked my daughter than we did the day it happened," the king surmised.

"No, my lord," Martin replied. "All we have are the descriptions of the men from the young ladies and MacLean."

Talbot laid his book down. "You should speak with MacLean again. Perhaps there are details he failed to mention previously that could help identify those men. Something in the way they spoke or the way they fought, perhaps even the weapons they used, may lend clues to their homeland. MacLean's travels have been extensive."

"I spoke with MacLean recently," Martin replied. "He did not remember any details concerning the intruders' appearance that he did not reveal when I first questioned him. We know those men to have lighter-colored hair, beards, bluish eyes, and a rather mild complexion. One of them used an ax instead of a sword. Coupled with the men's most savage actions against our women—"

"Would lead one to believe they were Northerners," Talbot finished.

"My thoughts exactly," Martin agreed.

"If that be the case, it is most perplexing," Talbot mused. "The coast is at least a week's ride to the west. Those savages travel mainly by ship and rarely over land. What purpose could they have so far inland? I have never heard of the Northerners being so bold as to invade a country so distant from the sea."

"Nor I, but it appears that they have," Martin said. "It bothers me that the men were so careful to cover their tracks that not a single shred of evidence was found that would be a witness to their presence. Barbarians generally care not to hide their identity."

"Do you believe it to be a worthwhile endeavor to have MacLean return to the site of the melee in the event that his memory is spurred?" the king asked.

"He did just that yesterday, my lord. My men and I followed him most discreetly and remained hidden until he began his return. I then confronted him and inquired if anything of significance had been brought to his remembrance. He replied that he had no new information to offer."

"That is regrettable," King Talbot replied.

"There is something that does not sit well with me, sire," Martin continued.

"What might that be?" the king inquired.

"These men were either a scouting party for a potential barbarian raid, or they were indeed spies sent from another king. Either way, well, the description of the men is quite similar to MacLean if you reflect upon it for a moment."

"I had not thought about it, but you are correct," the king said thoughtfully. "The way he carries himself, and the way he thinks and speaks would, in my mind, eliminate the possibility of him being part of a barbarian horde. You believe Andrew to be a spy?"

"I do not accuse the man, but I have suspicions," Martin answered. "His sudden appearance in our land, his efforts to blend in, his hidden past, his extensive research within our own walls, it all points to sophisticated espionage. He could be determining our military abilities as well as agricultural production to see how well we could defend ourselves."

"This is most unsettling," Talbot said as he leaned back in his chair. "If he were a spy, why would he give us advice on bettering our system of food production and the training of our men?"

"That I cannot answer," Martin replied. "Perhaps he is only attempting to appear sincere in his desire to stay here."

"Perhaps," Talbot said. "I am not convinced that he is a spy though. Granted, his actions may be somewhat suspicious, but I am not ready to accuse the man. We shall keep him close and observe him. If he is a spy, he will give himself away somewhere, somehow. If he gives the appearance of leaving for an extended period, you are personally to follow him and determine if he is returning to his people. Should that be the case, you are to dispose of him before he can divulge any information. Do you understand?"

"Yes, sire, your order is clear."

"As long as he remains in our land, no aggression will be carried out against him, for to us, he is an invited guest."

"I understand," Martin replied.

"You have done well, captain of the guard. You have honored your position."

"The position honors me in allowing me to serve Your Majesty."

"You have my leave. Go, dry and warm yourself lest you become ill," Talbot directed.

"As you wish, my lord," Martin replied as he bowed humbly and left the king alone.

Marie quietly slipped away from the wall and gingerly walked across the room lest she stumble and give her presence away. She stood by the door as Martin's bold steps echoed into silence. The conversation she had just heard resounded in her mind and twisted her heart. She could not believe that Andrew was a spy of any type. His actions in saving the lives of her and her friends, their conversations, it all pointed to a mysterious yet sincere man. She would have to keep her ears and eyes open on Andrew's behalf. Convinced that the hallway was empty, she gently opened the door and, without making a sound, scampered down the hall to fulfill her father's request.

Chapter 16

A curtain of canescent clouds lingered across the late-afternoon sky, chasing away the remnants of comfort offered by the slowly setting sun and threatening to bring a cool, misty evening. A light breeze caressed the silent field and neighboring forest, gently lulling the land to a time of rest. The pacifying peace was interrupted by the faint whisper of an object cutting through the air, followed by a soft thud of impact. A nearby rabbit, startled by the sudden noise, took no chances and bounded away to safety. There were a few more moments of silence before the drumming of running feet rose into the air. They, too, ceased after only a few moments, and silence again followed but only momentarily.

"Bull's-eye!" a young boy's voice called out excitedly. The boy stood beside a four-foot-tall bale of straw, upon the front of which a brightly colored cloth was fastened. An arrow protruded from the center of the cloth, having pierced a small, painted, four-inch-diameter circle. The boy grabbed the arrow and tugged it from the target. He quickly ran back to the archer, who was standing nearly forty yards away.

"Another bull's-eye!" he exclaimed as he handed the arrow back to its owner. "That gives you six out of ten arrows shot. I have never seen such accuracy! How do you do it, Andrew?"

"Much practice, Steven," Andrew replied as he examined the projectile in his hand. "And a little luck," he added with a wink.

"I shoot all of the time, but I fear I shall never be as good as you," the young boy said. "I could not hit one bull's-eye out of twenty shots."

"Then I shall teach you how," Andrew said. There was a bow on the ground that was smaller than the one he had in his hand. He laid his weapon down and picked up the second one. He offered it to the boy, who reached out and took it.

"Take this arrow and shoot at the target," Andrew instructed. Steven complied and took a balanced stance. He placed the arrow against the string and gently pulled back as far as his strength would allow. He paused for five seconds then released his grip on the arrow. The arrow cut through the air and struck the bale of straw completely outside of the target area. A frown crossed his face.

"Not a bad effort," Andrew commented, "but certainly room for improvement. The first thing you must do is become comfortable with your equipment. You must be completely familiar with the bow and arrow. You must know every curve, every inch of your weapon. You must be able to picture in your mind every detail of it and how it feels. It must become like an extension of your own arm and feel completely natural. Otherwise, it will never be as formidable an ally as it could be." As Andrew spoke, Steven examined the bow and the arrow, turning them over one at a time and running his fingers along every inch of their length. He concentrated deeply, wanting to do well to impress his friend who was also gradually becoming his role model. When finished, he turned his attention back to Andrew.

"Now lift the bow and feel its weight; concentrate on how heavy it is. Do the same with the arrow. You must become intimately familiar with both before you will ever achieve the marksmanship you desire. Now lift the bow, place the arrow in its place, breathe slowly, and find your target. Shut out everything else. See only the target. Relax." Steven did as he was instructed. He took careful aim at the distant target, hesitated a few seconds, then let loose of the arrow. It sailed smoothly and unwaveringly across the field and struck the straw. It was not close to the center of the target, but it was at least within the target area. He looked up at Andrew, not entirely pleased.

"That is better. Do exactly what I have told you to do, every day, and soon you will find the bull's-eye," Andrew reassured him. "I think we have had enough for the day." Disappointed, Steven walked over to retrieve the arrow. The sound of trotting horses caught Andrew's attention, and he turned to see who was approaching. Marie and Heather reined their horses to a stop several yards from Andrew.

"Hello, stranger," Marie greeted Andrew.

"Good afternoon," Andrew replied.

"Heather, does this gentleman look familiar to you? I believe I have seen him somewhere before," Marie said to her companion as she looked closely at Andrew, her eyebrows slightly pulled together, giving her the appearance of deep thought.

"Now that you mention it, his appearance does tickle the back of my mind," Heather replied with an expression that mimicked her friend's. "It has been so long since I last saw him, I am afraid his name escapes me."

"Good sir, please tell us, do we know you?" Marie asked innocently.

"Where is the rest of your troupe?" Andrew asked in reply, throwing the girls into confusion.

"Our troupe?" Marie returned, perplexed. "What troupe do you mean?"

"The troupe of comedians that performed at the castle not three nights past. Surely you joined with them, did you not?" Andrew answered, not giving in to their teasing. "Your gift of humor would certainly be a great addition to their act."

"Where have you been keeping yourself these past few weeks?" Marie asked, discontinuing the jesting. "It seems you have all but disappeared."

"Since the moment I informed your father of my decision to postpone my journey for a time and remain here, I have been busy earning my keep," Andrew replied. "Malcolm has kept me plenty busy."

"And what exactly is it that the old farmer is having you do?" Marie asked.

"It would be simpler for me to list what he is not having me do. Suffice it to say that my hands have seen more than their share of dirt. Malcolm believes that everyone needs to start at ground level, no pun intended."

"That certainly sounds like Malcolm," Heather said. "I doubt he has ever had to scrape much dirt from his own fingernails."

"Have you been able to convince him to implement some of your ideas?" Marie asked.

"I believe he is beginning to see the logic of my suggestions. It should not be too much longer before we start a project or two of my devising."

"Hello, Steven," Marie called out as the young boy approached the threesome.

"Good afternoon," Steven replied, stopping beside Andrew.

"What are you doing out here, little brother?" Heather asked.

"I have been helping Andrew, *big* sister," he replied. He did not like being referred to as little.

"And what is Andrew doing that he needs the help of a stable boy?" Heather asked.

"Someone has to retrieve the arrows," Marie teased.

"He is teaching me how to shoot," Steven retorted in defense.

"Is he a good teacher?" Marie asked, looking at Andrew.

"The best I have ever had," Steven proudly replied.

"Would you be practicing for the contest?" Marie asked Andrew. "It is only two days away. You will be participating, I assume."

"I plan to take part in it," Andrew confirmed. "The prize is indeed worth the effort." He took the arrow from Steven and picked up his bow from the ground. "I have heard of the difficult nature of the contest, and I have seen the skills of many of the men who will likely be participating. It would be foolish not to practice as much as I can."

"Why, Andrew, that sounds absolutely modest," Marie said with feigned surprise. "What do you believe to be your chances of winning the prize?"

Andrew paused and reflected on the question momentarily.

"On any given day, a man can have great success, or he can have great failure," he finally responded. "When all is said and done, it is not up to him or his skills, but the plan of the Almighty. I can only strive to exercise what skills I have been given to the best of my ability, and then accept the outcome."

It was not the response that Marie had anticipated, but she did not push the conversation.

"Steven, it is time for dinner," Heather informed her brother, noting an uncomfortable silence in the air. "You can ride back with me. You know how angry Mother gets if we are late." Steven obeyed and climbed up onto the horse's back.

"I must get back also," Marie said. "If I stay away too long, my father will begin to worry. He only recently has permitted me to ride alone without an escort."

"In that case, I will see you later," Andrew said. The girls and Steven bid their farewells and began the ride back to the castle. Andrew notched an arrow in the bow, turned to the target, and quickly let loose. The others would have undoubtedly been impressed to see the arrow penetrate the center of the target.

Andrew walked over to the target and retrieved his arrow. He was turning to walk to his horse, which was grazing close by, when he caught sight of a figure disappearing over a not-too-distant swell in the field. Fearing more spies, Andrew quickly mounted his stallion and galloped across the range to where he saw the figure. Annon reared to a stop as Andrew tugged on the reins. The gently rolling landscape now dropped away quickly for several hundred yards until it again leveled out, but now it became a congregation of rocks and boulders, some small and some quite large. For a moment, Andrew saw no sign of life. A movement down the slope and to his right caught his eye, and he spotted the fleeing figure now on horseback. Andrew immediately continued his pursuit.

Strong and confident, Annon bolted down the hillside in what appeared to be an out-of-control, headlong dash to the doorstep of death. Andrew held on tightly as Annon agilely sidestepped the scattered rocks and an occasional bush, any one of which could produce a fatal fall. At the bottom of the slope, Andrew continued in the direction in which the mystery person had been riding. He could see that he was now in a shallow valley that was gradually becoming deeper and narrower. The horse and rider were nowhere to be seen. Andrew slowed his forward progress to a casual walk while focusing meticulous attention on the craggy cleuchs to either side of him. The quiescent hills offered no hint to the location of the prey that Andrew pursued. He continued his forward progress for several minutes before tugging on Annon's reins, prompting the horse to stop. Silence and stillness reached from the bottom of the valley to the top.

As Andrew surveyed the slope to his right, he became aware of an odd irregularity in the ground, barely noticeable. He looked away for a moment, then returned his eyes to where he thought the inconsistency was. At first, he could not discern it, and several seconds passed before he located it again. He did not shift his gaze from the spot and nudged Annon forward. As he approached the area of his attention, the irregularity became more obvious, and when he was fifty feet away, the mystery revealed itself: a cave. It was a well-camouflaged cave, both naturally and with some human help. When he had reached the opening, Andrew dismounted and tethered Annon's lead to a small bush. He drew his sword from its scabbard and cautiously advanced. The grass on this slope grew long and draped over the edges of the cave, making the opening difficult to discern from a distance. Someone had added to the camouflage by creating a curtain of grass and hanging it just inside the entrance. Andrew edged around the curtain and peered inside.

Blackness was all that he could see at first, but as his eyes adjusted to the lack of light, he could just make out a distant glow from a torch. Andrew crept forward, making as little noise as possible. The floor of the cave felt as smooth as one of the castle's hallways. The width of the cave provided for easy passage of at least two people side by side, and there were no low-hanging rocks that would pose a threat to one's head. The glow became brighter as Andrew moved forward, and soon he was at the opening to a large chamber. The origin of the light was in the far-left corner, a torch held by a bracket in the wall. A lone man was carefully inspecting the cold stone wall, and a horse patiently waited several feet away. Andrew surveyed the entire room before daring to reveal his presence. The room was approximately fifty feet long, but due to the lack of light, Andrew could not see its entire width. The ceiling was nearly twelve feet from the floor, and several wooden cross beams had been placed on top of man-made stone pillars to provide additional support for the ceiling. Although the torch was small and its illumination dim at best, Andrew could see that he was peering into a burial chamber. Numerous cavities had been cut into the rock walls throughout the room, and within those nearest the torch, Andrew was sure he could discern human figures. A large pedestal, six feet wide by eight feet long by three feet tall, occupied the center of the room. Upon the pedestal were two caskets. Assured that the two men were alone, Andrew broke the deathly silence.

"The day is not good for grave robbing," he remarked in a calm, nonaggressive voice.

The mystery man whipped around, and a menacing sword glinted briefly in the torch's glow.

"Who goes there?" he called out, looking in Andrew's direction.

"No one with whom you should be eager to tangle, nor one who wishes to fight you."

"What is your business in this place?" the man demanded.

"It is per chance that I stumbled upon this cavern, for its existence was not previously known to me. However, as I am here, the duty has been thrust upon me to protect the dignity and honor of those whose bodies have trustingly been laid here. Now I must likewise ask you your business in this dreadful, cold crypt, that I may know how to deal with you."

"Andrew? Andrew MacLean, is that you?" the man called out in recognition.

"It is," Andrew responded, intrigued. "I must admit that your voice is familiar, yet I cannot tie a face or name to it. Who might you be?"

"I am Carl Bergman," the man answered. "Heather's father."

"What are you doing in a place like this, Carl?" Andrew inquired as he slowly approached the man. Carl leaned his sword against the wall to show that he meant no malice.

"Is it not common for a man to pay respects to the deceased?" Carl replied.

"Not at all," Andrew answered. "Just as it is common for a horse to pay respects to the dead. It must have been a great man to earn such remembrance from a stallion," Andrew added as he stroked the horse's nose.

"I brought him here lest he remain outside and be stolen," Carl offered in defense.

"This valley is not exactly a major bed of activity," Andrew countered. "How often do you suppose someone wanders through here? Truthfully, it might appear that you simply did not wish your presence to be known. Now, I would have to wonder, why would a person not want someone passing by to know that he was here? Is this some sacred chamber, forbidden to be entered?"

Carl hesitated before responding. Andrew's instincts told him that there was something important here, something that Carl was trying to hide. Whatever it was, his determination to know of it was growing.

"Andrew, let not your mind become beleaguered with specious suspicions," Carl answered calmly, reassuringly. "There is no mystery encompassing my presence here, no foul intentions of disrespecting the dead. These are my people, my fathers. They were great people, and the memory of them is dear to me."

"I see," Andrew replied. He looked around the room. "This is not a resting place for the common man," he said as he gently rubbed his hand across the wall nearest him. A light layer of dust covered his hand. He looked to the low ceiling and took note of numerous cobwebs. "The appearance speaks of much usage in years past but little, if any, in recent times. Is this chamber no longer used?"

"It has seen all the dead that it will ever see," Carl acknowledged.

"What happens now when a person passes away?" Andrew asked.

"They are laid to rest, of course," Carl answered directly.

"Where?" Andrew prodded.

"In a field, in a graveyard, by a tree, wherever they desired before they died."

"In a cave?" Andrew continued.

"You certainly have a morbid curiosity," Carl countered. "Why are you so concerned about the disposition of the dead?"

"I have a great interest in history and its people. It is obvious that this land has a prominent past, and I wish to know more about it."

"I hear the castle has a respectable collection of books. Perhaps you should begin your research there, where it is warmer and far more inviting than this dreadful place," Carl suggested.

"I have combed the libraries most thoroughly, I assure you. There is no literature on those shelves that addresses the past of this land or its people."

"None whatsoever?" Carl asked, surprised.

"Not a word," Andrew confirmed.

"That is odd to say the least," Carl mused, turning back to the wall.

"Considering the quality and extent of the material in those libraries, it is a little more than odd," Andrew said. "It wears the look of intention."

"Intention?" Carl repeated. He looked at Andrew closely. "For what reason would such a thing be done?"

"These are your fathers, your people," Andrew reminded Carl. "If there is a reason to be known, surely you would have knowledge of it more so than I."

"Surely," Carl agreed and offered nothing more.

Andrew gave the appearance of being in deep thought as he examined the death-filled cavity in front of him. Carl remained motionless, waiting for Andrew to resume the conversation.

"Perhaps the reason is connected with King Richard's sealing off the older, deeper sections of the castle," Andrew suggested, fishing.

"That could very well be true," Carl responded.

"So, you do know of this," Andrew stated.

"I should. I am the one who forged the gate."

"Of course. You are the blacksmith," Andrew said as the correlation struck him. "Then you know what lies beyond those gates."

"That I do not know," Carl admitted quickly. "I was never permitted beyond them. A relationship may exist. To that much my reasoning will allow me to agree." He looked directly at Andrew, locking eyes. "Your casual curiosity is becoming disquieting, Andrew. Why are you here?"

Carl was not a simple man, and Andrew knew it. The question brushed aside Andrew's "just passing through" story and delved deeper into his motives for choosing to stay in the kingdom. He had thus far been careful with his words, but his actions needed at least as much attention, or else they were going to give his secrets away.

"I have searched quite some time for a home," Andrew answered, "and this region appears to be most inviting. I merely wish to learn as much as I can about the people with whom I may settle. That is why I tend to ask so many questions. Is that so strange?"

"I could not foresee someone being as thorough as you when

it comes to settling down," Carl replied. "However, if that is your way, I am not one to criticize it."

"That is indeed my way," Andrew confirmed. "I believe it is dinnertime, and therefore I will leave you to your business."

"It is that late?" Carl inquired. "I have been in here longer than it seems. If I miss another dinner, my wife will cease cooking for me. To miss one of her meals is a tragedy. You must come by for dinner one evening."

"That I will do," Andrew answered. Carl tugged on his horse's reins and led the way out of the cave.

Chapter 17

T he day could not have been better suited for outdoor festivities. The blissfully brilliant sun had chased away the morning mist by 9:00 a.m., and a whisper of a breeze stirred through the air. Faint wisps of smoke curled skyward from large cooking pits as the day's meals were undergoing preparation. The landscape was littered with people, old and young, as they milled about in eager anticipation of the day's main event: the Skills Contest.

Exactly one hundred men were silently encircled around a table at which five older men were seated. The seated men in turn recited the rules of one game each until all had spoken their piece. Once the game guidelines had been recited, the standing men were divided up into four groups in order that individual identification numbers could be distributed. The process of registering everyone and explaining the details of the competition took nearly an hour. The first men to sign up were restless and pacing about by the time the last man was given his number. Four of the five events were to be held that day, and the men's identification numbers dictated in which contest they would first engage. When the last man had registered, the other contestants began breaking up into their groups. Sensing that the contest was about to begin, the crowd slowly migrated to the bounded spectators' sections.

While most of the men congregated in packs of three or four to help relieve some of their nervousness, Andrew stood alone and inspected the weapon in his hand. It was an old crossbow given to him by his father. It had been well maintained over the years and appeared to be nearly new. Sunlight glinted off the polished, oiled metal as Andrew turned it over in his hands. A firm grip on his shoulder grabbed his attention.

"I take it that bow shooting is your first event," Lawrence noted as he came around Andrew's side. "It is interesting that you have chosen the crossbow rather than the standard bow."

"I grew up with this," Andrew said as he handed it to Lawrence. "I find it to be more accurate and effective."

"I know many other competitors here today who would disagree with you," Lawrence said, inspecting the weapon.

"Of them, there never has been a shortage," Andrew replied. "What is your first event?"

"The javelin throw, that cursed event. I have never been able to throw a spear with any decent accuracy. This is the event that kills me every year, no matter how much I practice."

"Perhaps you merely need someone to show you how to practice properly," Andrew teased.

"Aye, that may help indeed. If you run across someone, please do not hesitate to point him out to me," Lawrence countered.

"I hope you do well," Andrew said with genuine sincerity.

"Maybe, but you also hope that you do better," Lawrence responded.

"Of course."

"Then good luck to you also," Lawrence said as he walked to his position.

The spacious field was divided into sections that hosted the four events to be held that day. The contestants were divided up equally, so there were twenty-five men in each section. Three men competed at once in the javelin throw, bow shooting, and dagger throw and were given three turns in each event. There were two courses set up for the galloping sword strikes, allowing two men to compete at once. The endurance event would be held the following day.

A long, shrill blast from a horn signaled the beginning of the contest. A cheer of encouragement was born somewhere deep in the crowd and gradually evolved into a ground-shaking roar. Men, women, and children raised their fists into the air and made circular motions with their arms. The commotion lasted for an eternal minute before slowly dying away into a bearable murmur.

Andrew turned his attention to his first event. Three men lined up and took aim at the immobile targets approximately one hundred feet away. They fired their shots all at once and anxiously waited for the results. A judge for each target rushed over to his assigned target, marked the results, and pulled out the arrow. He then rushed out of the way and signaled for the contest to proceed. The same three men shot a second time, then a third time. There was a pause in the activity as three more men stepped to the firing line, took aim, and let their arrows fly. This process was repeated twice before it was Andrew's turn. He approached the line amid stares and snickers at his choice of weaponry. He stoically retrieved an arrow from the quiver on his back and carefully laid it in its resting place on the crossbow. No sooner had the judge given the okay to continue than Andrew quickly raised his weapon and discharged it. The arrow flew straight and true to the very heart of the target. His second shot landed just outside of the center circle, but his third shot found the center of the target. Silent stares of astonishment greeted him as he turned and took his place at the rear of the line.

After the last men in the group completed their turns, the targets were changed. Instead of a motionless bale of hay sitting on the ground, the archers were now faced with the task of hitting grass-stuffed canvas bags swinging from what looked like miniature gallows. The targets were moved in and placed nearly sixty feet from the firing line. Before the first men approached the line, Andrew could hear cursing as the bags were set in motion to test the devices. The only rule for this event was that the archer had to shoot his arrow before the target completed its third full arc. The first three contestants stepped to the firing line. Spotters pulled the targets to the side nearly shoulder height, then released them and darted out of the range. The three men took a second to time the motion of the bags and the anticipated flights of their arrows and released their arrows. This was repeated twice more, each time the bags being reset prior to the contestants firing.

By the time Andrew's turn came around, twelve men had fired, and only three were successful in hitting the target. By the end of the contest, Andrew had speared the target three times, and no other man had succeeded in hitting it twice.

"That was a very impressive display of shooting," one of the contestants commented to Andrew as they moved to the next section. "The first hit, I thought it nothing more than pure luck, but when your third arrow pierced the bag, I knew it was nothing less than skill."

"Thank you," Andrew responded. "My father was very insistent on me mastering this weapon as I grew up. Hardly a day passed when I could get away with not picking it up and practicing for at least an hour."

"I hope your father's persistence was not as great with the skills for the rest of today's tests," the man commented and moved on.

The next contest was the javelin throw and the one event for which Andrew did not care. While growing up, he had trained with many weapons and was extremely adept at most of them, but throwing a spear was not one of his better abilities. His performance spoke well of his inaptitude, as he never came close to the bull's-eye. Shrugging off the event, Andrew followed his fellow competitors to the next section.

Aside from bow shooting, dagger throwing was Andrew's next favorite event, and therefore he delightfully accepted the three daggers being handed to him. Evidently, word had spread of Andrew's proficiency with these weapons, for several dejected groans of defeat accompanied his approach to the throwing line.

He carefully analyzed the weight of the weapons, turning them over in his right hand and tossing them gently into the air. The target was a mere fifteen feet distant, closer than to what Andrew was accustomed. Within thirty seconds, each dagger had been thrown, tallied, and removed. Three daggers, three bull's-eyes.

"I see your accuracy has improved a bit, not that there was much need for betterment," Louis said as he stole up to Andrew's side.

"A man's aim is certainly truer when he does not have several mugs of ale floating behind his eyes," Andrew replied, "and a woman floating by his ear. I trust you have discovered that also today."

"Indeed, I have," Louis confirmed. "You matched my earlier perfection with the daggers. It is something only a few men will accomplish today. You will find men who are well prepared for one, maybe two of these events, but rare is the man who can master all five. You should not be too disheartened if you do poorly in two or three events. It is expected and by no means disgraceful."

"Of course. Even *second* place among such company as this is an achievement," Andrew said.

"It appears that my group is moving forward," Louis said, his voice marked with subtle malevolence. "I must join them. I wish you well with your remaining challenges."

"And I you," Andrew politely replied.

The next event challenged the competitors' abilities at striking stationary objects while at a full gallop. The course was comprised of ten wooden poles of varying heights, from four feet tall to six feet tall. The poles alternated sides of the riding lane, the first being to the right of the contestants and the second being to their left. Upon each pole, a large, round melon was set. It was the rider's task to gallop through the course as fast as possible and strike the melons. Points were awarded based on the number of successful hits and the quickness with which the course was completed. Successful navigation of the course gave evidence of the competitor's ability to ride, to control his horse, and to make accurate sword strikes.

Andrew watched closely as several of the men took their turns at the course. One man, halfway through the run, aimed a bit too low with a strike and embedded his sword in the wooden pole. Without missing a beat, he pulled a smaller, two-foot-long sword from its sheath on the horse and finished the course. It was an impressive recovery, but he lost points for the low strike. A second man completely missed two of the melons during his turn and just did nick two others, resulting in a low total score. A third man stretched a little too far and nearly fell of his horse. He passed three poles before he was able to right himself.

Annon snorted excitedly as Andrew approached him. The horse seemed to know that a competition was in progress and appeared eager to display his speed and agility. Andrew untied the reins and swung onto Annon's back. With a minimum of urging on Andrew's part, the stallion moved up to the starting line. Andrew leaned forward and spoke to his trusted steed.

"We must be strong but in control," he whispered. "Speed is essential, but accuracy is critical." He pulled his sword out of its sheath and pointed it within Annon's vision toward the targets. "We have done this before. You know what we must do." Andrew straightened up and waited for the starter's signal to begin. A young man placed a fresh melon on the last post and waved to the judge at the starting line. The judge turned his attention to Andrew.

"Ready yourself, contestant," he directed, and Andrew complied, leaning forward in anticipation of Annon's initial jump from the starting line. The starter held a two-foot-long pole straight up, on the top of which was a red flag. The anxious horse pawed at the ground. Andrew held tight the reins in his left hand and the cold steel in his right. He eyed the starter, waiting for the signal. The cheers and cries of the spectators became a dull murmur in the background. Andrew blocked out all thoughts other than the course immediately ahead of him and how he would navigate it. After a pause that seemed to last several minutes, the started abruptly slashed the air with the flag, and Andrew kicked Annon in his ribs.

The horse bolted from the starting line like a terrified cat. The first target was thirty yards away, and Annon galloped straight for it. Andrew held his sword so that it pointed to the rear, waist high and horizontal to the ground. As they came to the first target, Andrew smoothly brought the sword forward and in the blink of an eye successfully sliced the melon in half. Immediately he tugged the reins to the left, and Annon responded by swerving to the left and heading for the second target. Instead of circling around the outside of the next pole, which would have allowed Andrew to swing from his natural right-handed side and was exactly the method every other competitor had taken, Andrew switched the sword into his left hand and the reins into his right. As Annon galloped past the second pole, Andrew delivered another faithful strike to the target. Again, he tugged on the reins, switched hands, and shattered the third melon as he raced by it. Using this strategy, Andrew completed the course quicker than any other contestant and was successful in striking every melon.

The spectators, contestants, and judges stood in taciturn awe at this magnificent display of skill and dexterity. Annon sensed the admiration of the crowd and reared up in a pesade, his forelegs pawing in the air. Andrew casually wiped the sword on his trousers and stuffed it back into its sheath. He urged Annon forward, and the horse obediently returned to the starting area with what appeared to be a bit of a prideful prance. Not a word was said as Andrew rode past the open-mouthed, awestruck man who was next in line. He swung down from the horse's back and tied the reins to a post next to all the other horses. Conversation gradually returned to the incredulous crowd as the contests continued.

"Had not my own eyes witnessed such a feat, I would call any man who recounted it a liar," King Richard said to Angus as they watched Andrew take position to watch the other contestants.

"It was quite impressive," Angus admitted. "He is performing extraordinarily well today."

"Though the contest has two events to be seen, I would venture the winner has all but been decided."

"There are several others who remain within striking distance," Angus noted. "Should Andrew perform poorly in the remaining events and one of his trailers scores highly, it is possible for him to be overtaken."

"The only thing in danger of being overtaken is the contest's best-ever score," King Talbot said a bit tauntingly, "and if my memory is true to me, that was established by you more than a few years ago. Just before you were promoted to military adviser."

Angus threw the remaining ale in his mug down his throat and wiped a small trickle from the corner of his mouth as a look of determination crossed his face. He did not look at the king but scanned the field of competitors.

"He would have to suffer fewer than five strikes in the defense event and no less than fly through the endurance test to best me," Angus replied self-assuredly. "It is possible but highly unlikely. My performance shall stand."

"Being but spectators, we can only stand idle and see what shall unfold," Talbot said. "I must admit that I do not share your optimism."

"He will not succeed," Angus replied and stood up. "By your leave, sire."

"You do not wish to view today's final event?" Talbot asked.

"I would not miss it. I just feel it is time for a change in view," Angus answered.

"Then you have my leave," Talbot granted and watched Angus disappear into the crowd.

Andrew moved along with his group as they migrated to the final event of the day. The twenty-five men stood in a group and awaited the instructions of the judges. One of the judges, a man of gray hair who looked to be at least sixty years old, stepped forward.

"This is the defense competition," he announced loudly so all the competitors could hear him clearly. "The objective is to determine which competitors are best at defending themselves against multiple attackers. Each of you will face two challengers on a platform that is twenty-five feet by twenty-five feet. The challengers will each be armed with a four-foot-long wooden pole, the tip of which will be dipped in either red or yellow dye. As the defender, you will be allowed two weapons with which to protect yourself. It will be the challenger's task to strike the defender with their pole, anywhere below the neck. It will be your task as the defender to avoid their strikes. For every successful strike suffered, you will have a point deducted from the total that you have thus far accumulated in the contest. For every successful strike delivered, the challenger will be awarded a point. Each competitor, whether challenger or defender, must remain on the platform at all times. Should a competitor leave, or be knocked off the platform, he will suffer a ten-point deduction and will be eliminated from that round of competition. Each round will last two minutes. Are there any questions?" The judge looked around, expecting at least one question, but there was none. The competitors understood the rules and were eager to get on with the event. "You will each be given at least one opportunity to act in the role of challenger. Many of you will be given more than one opportunity, which will be determined by a random drawing."

At the bidding of the judges, the first three competitors stepped forward and scoured the table of weapons. Each man was offered a choice, although rather limited, of weapons to use for defending himself. The competitor could choose any of two weapons, but the choice was limited to a shield, long and short wooden swords, and a wooden pole. Once the choices were made and the defenders stepped onto one of the three platforms in the arena, two challengers armed with four-foot-long wooden poles stepped onto the platforms. On the ends of the poles were tied rags that had been saturated in either a bright yellow dye or a red dye. A small hourglass filled with sand served as the timing mechanism for the two-minute event.

As he scanned his surroundings, Andrew noted that there were more spectators at this event than there were at any of the other events. There was a grandstand built around the combat arena, and it was so cluttered that not a single empty space could be seen between the shoulder-to-shoulder spectators. Small pieces of paper were passed among the onlookers as wagers were cast on the combatants. The commotion off the field was a strong contrast to the serenity in the arena as the men began plotting their strategies and defensive moves.

With a resounding trumpet blast, the event commenced. Andrew watched the battles closely. Being new to the land and never having witnessed these competitions, he was extremely curious as to how they proceeded. He took note that, for the most part, there was no coordination, no communication between the challengers. Each challenger seemed to attack with no plan other than to bull-rush the defender in a very clumsy yet many times successful manner and strike out with his pole. Andrew's turn was not to come about until the last round; therefore, he had the opportunity to study the defenses that worked and those that did not. He also took his turn as a challenger in the third round and scored two hits against his opponent. After what seemed an eternity, he was called to one of the platforms.

"You know the rules of the game," the referee said as Andrew mulled over the weapons he was to choose from. "You must stay upon the platform. To leave the platform is an automatic ten-point penalty and the end of the event. Two challengers shall attempt to stain this white tunic that you are to wear. You are not permitted to grab their poles, just as you would not be able to grab the blade of a sword without losing fingers. When time has expired, the contest will be halted and the marks on your tunic totaled. Each strike will count as one point off the score you have thus far accumulated in the contest and will add one point to that of the challenger who delivered the strike. Have you any questions?"

"No," Andrew replied simply as he grabbed one sword, which

had a small, two-foot-long blade, and a second sword that had a blade three feet long. The normally razor-sharp edges had been dulled to prevent accidental injury to any of the men participating in the event. Andrew felt the weight and balance of the steel in his hands. Satisfied, he indicated to the referee that these were his weapons of choice.

"Very well. Take your place on the platform and prepare yourself," the referee directed and moved off.

Andrew complied and moved to the center of the specified platform. He waved the swords through the air and practiced a few defensive maneuvers as a warm-up. The other two competitors had also taken their positions and were likewise preparing for the event. Four challengers, each armed with a two-inch-thick, four-foot-long pole, approached the other platforms and split into pairs. Andrew's challengers appeared nearly two minutes later, striding boldly and confidently as if they were the center of attention in this event. As the men drew closer, a look of surprise and puzzlement crawled over Andrew's face.

Although he was not a participant in the Skills Contest, Angus approached Andrew's platform with a pole in one hand and determined eyes boring right through the defender. Andrew met the stare and did not move as a referee stepped in front of Angus. After a brief exchange of words, the referee turned and addressed Andrew.

"It appears that one of your challengers has suffered some type of injury that has required him to withdraw from this phase of the contest. The rules state that a substitute should be chosen in such circumstances. As the administrator of the Skills Contest, Angus has the authority to choose the substitute. As a past champion and honorary competitor, he also has the right to serve as a substitute. He has elected to fill the role of substitute himself. Do you raise any objections to his choice to participate in this capacity?"

"I have no objections," Andrew replied, knowing that if he did protest, it would make him appear cowardly or afraid.

"Then the contest shall begin," the referee stated and stood to the side. Angus and the other challenger took positions on the platform.

"Was your seat next to King Richard not close enough?" Andrew asked Angus as they waited for the starter's signal.

"I prefer to be closer to the action," Angus replied.

"Why?" Andrew asked directly. "What purpose of yours could be served by interfering in the contest?"

"You are doing quite well. Too well. These men are not adequate challengers for you. Your skills far surpass theirs, and therefore it was easy for you to score several strikes when you held this rod. I thought it would only be fair for someone with equal or better skills to oppose you. It is for the good of the game, of course."

"I see," Andrew responded, although he did not believe Angus's explanation. "When you find such a person, please send him along," he added with a smirk and turned his back on Angus. The men had no more time to converse as the starter called them to readiness. The crowd grew silent, and the men on the field braced themselves. Andrew looked at his challengers. He knew well Angus's capabilities in hand-to-hand combat and that it would take all his concentration and skills to defend himself against the much-determined challenger. He looked at the second challenger. He was one of the larger and stronger men in the competition, but as Andrew had noted earlier in the day, he was not the most gifted when it came to coordination. There was no doubt in Andrew's mind that this second challenger had been handpicked by Angus if for no other reason than to intimidate Andrew by the man's size. Andrew knew that in order to survive the competition without suffering a dozen strikes or more, he would have to eliminate one of the challengers. A strategy took shape in his mind, and he imagined the movements necessary to execute it. After a few seconds, a shrill trumpet blast commanded the round to begin.

Andrew stood in the middle of the platform with both arms outstretched toward his challengers. He did not look at either man directly but kept his vision forward, his eyes darting ever so slightly from side to side as he relied on his peripheral vision to guide him. Angus took a quick, though ineffective, jab at Andrew, hoping to catch him off-balance, but Andrew stepped backward, and the pole missed. The second man thrust his pole forward, but Andrew quickly deflected it with his short sword and reset himself. He needed to execute his plan now, before the action escalated and he found himself doing all he could to avoid being covered with red and yellow dye. In the blink of an eye, Andrew switched to an offensive stratagem.

He took several quick, and indeed unexpected, steps toward his second challenger, causing the man to backpedal in surprise while his reflexes brought the pole up in a defensive gesture. Andrew stopped the upward moving pole with the short sword in his left hand and powerfully struck up on the wood with the long, heavy sword in his right hand. The pole was knocked out of the man's seemingly strong grasp. It flew over Andrew's head and landed on the platform behind Andrew. Even before the pole hit the platform, Andrew had buried his shoulder in the challenger's midsection and knocked him off the platform ... and out of the event.

"You have found a unique approach to this event," Angus said as he picked up the pole lying on the platform. "I do not believe that I have ever seen a defender act as a challenger at the same time. I must say, it is most certainly a unique approach to the event, though perhaps not the wisest."

"Then perhaps it is time for you to entertain a reevaluation of tactics," Andrew replied as he readied himself to continue the battle.

Angus knew that Andrew was not innocently referring to the contest but was aiming his verbal blow at the training regime Angus had developed for his warriors. It did not sit well with him.

"It is quite the sense of déjà vu, is it not?" Angus asked, buying time as he readied himself for his attack on Andrew.

"The thought had crossed my mind," Andrew replied, undaunted.

"And I believe everyone here knows quite well the outcome of our last little confrontation," he continued.

"While I do believe in déjà vu, I do not believe in history repeating itself," Andrew said confidently. "Your best shall not be good enough today."

Angus wasted no more time. He immediately lunged forward, driving the pole in his right hand toward Andrew's chest while swinging the pole in his left at Andrew's feet. An average man would do well to skillfully wield even one of the challenger's weapons, but they were like willow branches in Angus's mighty hands. Andrew dodged, parried, and jumped as he narrowly evaded each thrust and strike. The two men battled with such ferocity and intensity as none had ever seen before in this "friendly" contest. On more than one occasion, Andrew was nearly successful in knocking Angus of the platform; however, Angus's strength and balance kept him in the fight. After what seemed an eternity to the competitors, the trumpet sounded to signal the end of the contest. Although he could not remember being struck a single time, there were two red and one yellow stains on Andrew's tunic. As Angus left the platform perspiring and breathing heavily, nursing bruised ribs and arms courtesy of Andrew's swords, he bestowed Andrew with a frustrated yet almost respectful glance.

"You son-of-a-dog!" Lawrence called out excitedly as he slapped Andrew on the back. "That was unbelievable. It was as though two gods were battling. The moves were so graceful, so flawless, fluid, and powerful. Did I not know better, I would say the whole skirmish was orchestrated."

"It was not the least bit staged; I can tell you that," Andrew said as he removed the white tunic. "If anything, it was completely dumbfounding. Why Angus chose to interfere is beyond my comprehension."

"There is no mystery there," Louis said as he stepped up beside Lawrence. "Many years ago, Angus competed in this same contest. In fact, he established a point mark that has never been equaled."

"And I am close to breaking that record?" Andrew asked.

"Close? It is a foregone conclusion that you will break his record. It is just a matter of by how many points you will outdo him. If you had suffered perhaps half a dozen strikes in the last event, it would have been close. That is why he stepped in. However, considering the results we just saw, all you need do is finish in the top fifteen during tomorrow's race, and the record is yours. For all intents and purposes, you won the contest today."

"After all these years, it remains that important to him?"

"It is not just the points," Lawrence answered. "You see, after he won the Skills Contest, Angus was named as Talbot's military adviser, replacing a man who was quite respected."

"I see," Andrew replied. "Then the man's concerns are well founded, although they do not justify his interference."

"Now it is time to feast," Louis declared as he moved toward the buffet table. "And for you, Andrew, undoubtedly many compliments on your performance as well as some subtle, and some not so subtle, tendering of affections from the young ladies. They always do that."

"You are nothing less than jealous that such affections will not be thrown your way this year," Lawrence teased.

"And you are not?" Louis countered. "Anyway, there are plenty of young ladies anxious to congratulate us on our day's efforts. Andrew, allow me to be the first to compliment your skills. They do indeed speak for themselves, and quite loudly at that. However, I will not be tendering any affections your way."

"I thank you most sincerely in both cases," Andrew replied as the trio headed for the banquet tables.

"After we have had our fill, we shall walk the course that has been marked off for tomorrow," Lawrence informed Andrew. "It is different every year."

"What does the course entail?" Andrew asked.

"Anything and everything," Lawrence answered. "Rough ground, even ground, hills, valleys, streams, forests. If it can be ridden across, and sometimes even if it cannot, you will encounter it during tomorrow's race. It is a grueling event that not every man and horse finishes. The strength and endurance of both man and steed are stretched to the limits."

"Who designs the course's path? Angus?" Andrew asked.

"Who else?" Louis replied. "He has designed courses that the devil himself would do well to finish. After the event has been completed and the exhausted stragglers start wandering in, Angus stands there watching them with arrogant amusement, so proud of himself for creating such an outrageously demanding challenge. I tell you, there are times I believe he has some of the devil in him."

"Of that there is no doubt," Lawrence agreed as they reached the food. "The man can be ruthless. Tonight, we shall drink a toast to him and his ego, and tomorrow conquer his course."

"I have noticed that the king's captain of the guard, Martin, is not participating in the event," Andrew said. "From what I know of him, he would likely be one of the leading favorites if he competed."

"That he would," Lawrence agreed. "He has competed in the past and performed well. However, it seems that this year his duties have kept him from participating."

"How so?" Andrew asked.

"It is apparent that since the day you arrived, the king has been somewhat fearful that his kingdom is being spied upon. By his instructions, Martin has established daily patrols to the kingdom's boundaries. Many of these patrols he leads himself."

"Does he not have enough competent men to lead these patrols without him having to go out?"

"There is no doubt that he does. There could be any number of reasons for him to go out himself though. He could simply take that high a level of pride in his job. Perhaps he is trying to impress King Talbot with his dedication." Lawrence looked around for a moment, then gave Andrew a sly smile. "Or perhaps he has a woman friend up north whom he visits now that he has an excuse to leave the castle on frequent occasions."

"Why up north?" Andrew asked. "Are there no pretty women to the east, west, or south?"

"I am sure there are," Lawrence replied. "I only said north because some of my friends with the guard complain that only Martin and two other men go on that patrol. The other men are required to go in the other directions, which are less scenic and more boring. I guess with authority come privileges."

"Evidently so," Andrew agreed.

"Gentleman," Louis interjected, "there is a buffet of food in front of us and a buffet of young ladies waiting for us to woo them with stories of the contest. If you do not mind, I am going to stuff my stomach while I think up some tantalizing tales with which to impress the girls. Feel free to stay here and talk though."

"By all means, lead us to the food and women!" Lawrence bellowed, and the men joined the throngs at the tables.

Chapter 18

T he cool, invigorating water chased away the remaining remnants of sleep as Andrew thoroughly soaked his face and head over the intricately painted porcelain bowl in the bathroom. Although he had been awake for less than ten minutes, Andrew was already reviewing the racecourse in his mind, recalling the terrain he would encounter and the areas in which he would have to exercise reasonable prudence in passing. His thoughts were rudely interrupted by heavy, anxious pounding on the door to his room. A young boy's panicky voice called out his name.

"Andrew! Andrew! Wake up!"

The alarm riding the voice gave Andrew a troubled feeling as he quickly crossed the room and opened the door. Steven, the stable boy, stood outside with his forehead layered with perspiration and his eyes screaming concern and fear. Even before Andrew could speak, the boy burst forth with his news.

"You have to come immediately! It is Annon! Something is wrong with him! I … I am not sure, but he is sick. I think he may be dying!"

"Dying?" Andrew repeated, numbed.

"I do not know for sure, but he is extremely ill. There is no time to waste! You must come now!"

Andrew jumped into his trousers, yanked his boots on, threw a shirt over his shoulder, and chased after Steven as the boy raced through the castle without speaking another word.

When Andrew and Steven reached the stables, a small, solemn crowd had gathered around Annon's stall. The people parted as they saw Andrew's anxious approach. When he reached Annon's stall, he felt his heart skip a beat and a pit form in his stomach as he caught sight of the horse.

Annon lay on a fresh bed of straw, his coat wet with perspiration as if he had just been through a rigorous workout. His heaving chest spoke of a constant struggle to draw every breath. His mouth hung slightly open, and his languid tongue drooped between his teeth. His open eyes remained motionless, and a faint haze dampened their normal vivacity. Ian had a hand on Annon's chest, trying to feel the horse's heart.

"What is wrong with him?" Andrew asked as he dropped to his knees at Ian's side.

"I am not quite sure," the physician replied. "The beating of his heart has slowed to an almost imperceptible rate, he is cold to the touch, and he is perspiring profusely. Such an illness I have never seen in an animal before."

"His health was perfect yesterday," Andrew countered, confused. "What sickness could befall a strong stallion so quickly and drag him to such a dismal condition?"

"I would that I knew," Ian replied, "for then I could administer medication and hope to snag him from death's grip. As it is, I am at a loss for a solution. I have no premise to proceed from." Ian looked around until he saw Steven. "Boy, come here!" he commanded. Steven approached apprehensively. "How long has this horse been ill?"

"Not long. He did not appear sick this morning as I filled his food trough. When I had finished with all the horses, I returned by this stall, and he was nervously moving about. Suddenly he crumpled to the ground and has not moved since. I came to you immediately."

"How much time elapsed from when you fed him until you returned and noticed his peculiar behavior?"

"Not long. Perhaps thirty minutes."

Ian stood and suspiciously walked over to the food trough. It was half-full of the morning's supply of oats. He ran his left hand through the contents and sifted the food through his fingers. He rubbed his thumb across his fingers and lifted his hand to his nose. Careful not to touch his hand to his lips, he inhaled. A slight grimace crossed his face. Ian turned to Steven.

"Have any of the other horses fallen ill?"

"None," Steven replied. "Only Annon."

"Did you feed them all from the same pile of oats?"

"That one in the corner," Steven replied, nodding and pointing.

Ian walked over to the indicated pile. He used his right hand and grabbed a handful of the oats and let them drain through his fingers back to the pile. Again, he rubbed his thumb across his fingers and sniffed them. After a moment of silent reflection, he spoke to Steven.

"Were you the only person in the stables this morning?"

"Yes, sir. It was my shift for the night watch and morning feeding. We take turns. The work only requires one person. Normally the person doing the feeding is the only soul present until well after feeding time."

Ian walked back over to Andrew's side and knelt. He looked at the suffering creature in front of him, his heart paining at the sight. There was no way of knowing if the horse was even aware of Andrew's tender strokes across his shoulders.

"This is no ordinary illness attempting to snatch your friend's life," Ian informed Andrew. "I believe he has been poisoned."

"Poisoned?" Andrew repeated incredulously. "That is absurd. Why would someone poison him?"

"That, I do not know. However, the reason for his condition is most obvious if you dwell on the facts for a moment. His appearance this morning gave no evidence of any malady before Steven fed him. None of the other animals have fallen ill as this one has, yet they ate of the same pile of food. When I examined the oats from Annon's trough, I noted a nearly imperceptible oily texture, which is not normal and was not in the pile from which he was fed. I have seen similar symptoms in men who have ingested poisonous substances. I tell you with no doubt in my mind that he has been poisoned."

Before Andrew could respond, the crowd parted, and King Richard appeared in its midst. He quickly strode into the stall and stood behind the two kneeling men.

"What has happened here?" he demanded.

Ian stood and answered. "Andrew's horse has been poisoned. It happened this morning after the boy fed him."

"Poisoned?" Talbot repeated, stunned. "That is a profoundly serious matter, Ian. Are you sure you are not mistaken?"

"My lord, I have been in your service for many years as a physician, a physician to man and beast. I have seen nearly every malady that could infect either. This condition has not resulted from natural causes. It is intentional."

"Will the stallion live?" Talbot asked, accepting Ian's judgment.

"For life to still be within him at this time is an encouraging sight. He is a strong animal, but it is impossible to know what kind of poison was fed to him or how much. I shall fetch a general antidote immediately, but how effective it will be I cannot say for certain. By your leave, sire," Ian said with a slight bow.

"Yes, of course," Talbot replied with a slight wave of his hand. As Ian hurried away, the king moved to Andrew's side.

"What vile, stone-hearted soul would do such a dreadful deed to this magnificent beast and for what reason?" he asked, though the question was directed to no one particular.

"I can think of one reason only," Andrew answered with bitterness rising within him. "The Skills Contest. It is somebody's desire that I not take part in the final event today. Why else would this atrocious act of villainy be so coldly consummated this morning? Perhaps one of my fellow competitors has taken exception to my proficient performance."

"If that is indeed the case, you have only five score of men for your suspicion to rest on," King Talbot said.

"Five score and one," Andrew countered as a menacing face flashed in his mind.

"If the identity of the culprit is discovered, I can assure you he will taste of the same death he has attempted to deal your steed," King Talbot stated firmly. "Such a barbaric act deserves no less punishment than its own evil ends. I shall not rest until this person is brought before my throne."

"Your concern is most comforting," Andrew said with genuine gratitude.

"I assume you will not withdraw as a result of this unfortunate incident?" the king inquired.

"And give the worm who did this the satisfaction of a job well done? No, I will compete. I will compete," Andrew vengefully replied.

"Excellent. There is only one horse here that is the equal of this one in terms of strength and heart. While I am certain you could ride any horse here and ride it well, I would not feel right if I did not offer this particular one for your use today."

"Any horse will suffice," Andrew replied determinedly. "Give me an old nag, a young stud; it matters not."

"Steven," King Talbot called out. The boy was immediately at the king's side. "Prepare my stallion."

The bystanders gasped in surprise at the king's most gracious offer, and a low murmur made its way about the stable. The king's horse, to be ridden by another man in a competition. It was unheard of. Steven looked up at the king, not believing what he had just heard.

"I said prepare my stallion," the king repeated authoritatively. "This man will need some time to become familiar with a strange horse." Subtly chastised, Steven bolted from the stable to carry out the instructions without further hesitation.

"This is an undeserved honor," Andrew said as he stood and faced the king. "You would let another man ride your royal steed?"

"I cannot tolerate cheating and evil deeds such as this," King Talbot replied. "If someone did this to your horse, there is no telling what sort of 'accident' they may arrange for you out on the course. Knowing that you sit upon the king's own horse may deter any further action against you."

"My gratitude is inexpressible," Andrew answered. "I am indebted to you, Your Majesty."

"Take care of him," King Talbot responded with a hand on Andrew's shoulder, then left the stable. The bystanders gradually dispersed, and Andrew was left alone with his suffering friend. Unable to aid the ailing animal, he walked around Annon and curiously inspected his saddle and other belongings hanging on the wall. Several articles were lying on the ground, which was unusual in that the stable boys were always careful to properly stow all gear. Andrew bent down and looked the items over without moving them. Straps on several large bundles were loose, and the flaps were partially open. He looked inside the bundles, then secured the straps and hung the items in their places. He stood and looked at the articles on the wall, his mind whirling at the recent events. A young lady's voice interrupted his thoughts.

"I have never seen the king offer his horse to another man for any reason. The honor he does you goes beyond hospitality. I must say I am perplexed at this turn of events."

Andrew turned around as Marie stepped out from behind one of the stall doors.

"No more so than I," Andrew replied.

"I watched you in the contest yesterday. That was, to say the least, an unprecedented display of skill you unleashed. I knew you would do quite well, but you easily surpassed even my expectations."

"I am glad that I did not disappoint you," Andrew responded.

"Judging from what just transpired, it appears that my father has taken a great liking to you. The door to opportunity opens wider."

"It would appear that way," Andrew agreed, eyeing Marie curiously. The young lady walked into the stall and stopped by Andrew's side. She reached out and touched one of the bundles on the wall, then turned and looked at Annon.

"Have you a person in mind who may have done this terrible thing?" she asked.

"I would that I knew," Andrew replied, not giving away his heartfelt suspicion. "He would not be in the best of health right now."

"One hundred men to choose from. If the culprit is among them, it will not be an easy task to determine his identity. Oh yes, I forgot," she quickly added innocently. "One hundred and *one* men. Has someone been searching through your things?" she asked, turning back to the wall. "You were a bit hesitant before replacing them."

"It is possible. The stable boys are quite conscientious about keeping things straight and in their places. Thievery is not unheard of, you know."

"Around here it is. If a person is discovered cheating or stealing, he is publicly beaten. It is a most humiliating experience and an effective deterrent."

"I will keep that in mind," Andrew said.

"Have you determined if anything is missing?"

"I only briefly looked through the pouches and bundles. All appears in order."

"Perhaps this person was looking for something specific and did not find it," she suggested.

Marie's probing questions were becoming disturbingly close to the truth. Had somebody learned of the legendary sword in his possession? Or was it indeed a common thief looking for anything of value? Considering the circumstances, the former situation was the more likely. Andrew decided it would be best to turn Marie's attention from what he might or might not have among his possessions.

"What do you suppose this person was looking for?" Marie continued.

"We do not know for certain that there was anybody here looking for anything," Andrew countered as he turned and knelt beside Annon. "Those bags could have easily fallen by accident.

Annon probably knocked them off while he was moving about. It would seem a more sensible scenario." He ran a hand along the horse's shoulder. "I believe Annon's health is improving a bit." The horse's chest had quit heaving so heavily, and his eyes were beginning to regain their sharpness. It was apparent that he was going to live.

"Do you suppose it was the same person who poisoned Annon?" Marie pressed, ignoring Andrew's plea of ignorance and attempt to turn the topic of conversation.

Andrew shot an irritated glare at Marie, but she did not back down. He knew that she would not give in until a satisfactory answer was given to her.

"Speculation will only breed suspicion, Marie," he warned. "We have no solid foundation upon which to base a theory of thievery or someone's curiosity of my belongings. I think it best that we assume nothing clandestine has occurred here and turn our thoughts to other things."

Instead of replying, Marie reached out and touched the items hanging on the wall. She pulled downward on two of the bundles, but they remained firmly in place. She pushed them to the side and let them fall back into place. As if satisfied with the results of her little test, she turned to Andrew.

"If that is how you wish to deal with the situation, then I will honor your decision and say no more. However, you cannot convince me that you genuinely believe it. You are too prudent to brush something like this off so easily. I have watched you closely during the past few weeks and know you better than you think."

She was completely correct. What he had just said was contrary to the actions and characteristics he had displayed since his arrival. If he did not back down, he would lose her trust, and for some reason, that bothered him greatly.

"The poison could have been a distraction, getting rid of the stable boy for a few minutes and rendering Annon harmless. That would permit a person enough time to quickly rummage through my belongings and disappear before the boy returned."

"What could be so important?" Marie asked. "What do you have that someone would be willing to go through that much trouble to find?"

"My possessions are quite meager," Andrew responded. "I have no more wealth than the average traveler and generally even less. I am a man of simple means. You have seen as much of my possessions as any other person. What do I have that another man would thoroughly covet? It is beyond me."

"Perhaps they were not looking for an object," Marie answered.

"Then what?"

"Information?" she suggested. "This person may have been looking for something that would reveal a little more of you and your past. You cannot deny that you have been somewhat of an enigma since your arrival."

"I do not deny it for a moment, as that has been my intention," Andrew responded. He looked curiously at Marie, as her words struck a chord within him. "Who wants to know more about my past, Marie? To whom is my history so important that they would stoop to such a level as this?"

"It was only a suggestion," Marie quickly defended. "I did not mean to imply it as fact. You are becoming paranoid, Andrew."

Her response did not convince Andrew. He stood and faced her, then firmly grabbed her arms as if to hold her in place. It was not enough to hurt her, but she knew that Andrew meant business.

"I have stayed alive these past few years by nursing a certain degree of paranoia and by some quite reliable instincts. At this moment, they are both telling me you are privy to more information than you have admitted. Tell me, Marie. What do you know?"

Marie was taken aback at Andrew's physical display and the determination in his eyes. His grip was neither painful nor threatening. Her first instincts were to retaliate and attempt to break free, but the look in his eyes held her in place. This marked a turn in their relationship that had thus far been strictly of a verbal nature. She did not know if the turn was for the better or worse. She looked around the stable and, satisfied that nobody had yet returned, answered.

"There is talk in the higher circles," she began. "People are questioning your secrecy, your delving into the past, your extensive exploring of the castle. There is also concern over the descriptions of the men who attacked Heather, Michelle, and me. Our descriptions and even your own. Andrew, your physical appearance is not much different than theirs. Your hair, your eyes, the shape of your face, they all seem to resemble those men. Everybody believed those men were spies."

The grim reality of her words struck Andrew hard. Suddenly it was obvious that he would have become suspicious, and he chastised himself for not foreseeing it. The very attention he had wished to avoid was hanging around him like a thick veil of cobwebs. If only he could as easily brush them aside.

"So, these 'higher circles' suspect me to be a spy?"

"No accusations have been brought forward, but great attention is being given to your habits and actions."

"What do you think?" Andrew asked, putting Marie on the spot.

"I believe you have reasons for your secretive nature, but I do not believe them to be espionage," she answered without hesitation. "That is an honest confession, Andrew. I do not believe you to be a threat to the kingdom … or me."

He had known that eventually this time would come, but its quickness upon him was unexpected. Andrew knew what he had to do.

"Accompany me to my room. There is something you must see." He released her and, with a final look at Annon, left the stable. Marie quickly followed without asking any questions and nearly ran into Ian as he was returning to Annon's stall. The physician shot the couple a curious glance as they hurried by without a word. He shook his head and proceeded with his business.

Several minutes later, Andrew and Marie stood in the middle of Andrew's room. The short trek through the castle had passed wordlessly, and only a few people saw them. Nobody was witness to the couple's disappearance into Andrew's quarters.

"Make yourself comfortable," Andrew directed, indicating one of the lavish chairs facing the fireplace. Marie complied and sat on the edge of the chair with her hands clasped in her lap, anxious to know what Andrew's intentions were. She remained silent as Andrew walked over to his bed and kneeled on the floor. He reached under the bed and pulled out the bundled sword. With sword in hand, he moved back into the main room and laid the bundle on the rug in front of Marie. He gently untied the straps and pulled the cloth to the sides, revealing the magnificent blade of steel.

"I do not understand," Marie said, looking at the sword, then at Andrew.

"Look at it closely," Andrew instructed. "Tell me if you have ever seen the like."

Marie dropped to her knees beside the weapon and inspected it. She picked it up and turned it over in her hands, admiring the intricate detail and designs, its perfection and beauty.

"It is indeed a unique sword with an exquisiteness all its own. I have never seen its equal. Is this why you brought me up here, to see a sword?"

"What you see before you is the secret I have been attempting to keep concealed, what you have desired to know since the day I arrived. This is no ordinary sword. This is that which expelled me from my homeland, drove me hundreds upon hundreds of miles across and through strange lands, and stole over five years from my life. This is my quest."

"I still do not understand," Marie said, pieces of the puzzle still missing from her mind.

"I stumbled across this sword more than five years ago during a battle. A dying man told me a story that even today I do not know if it is fact or fiction." Andrew paused for a moment, still not sure of how much of the story he should reveal. Although his instincts told him that Marie could be trusted, his better judgment told him to be careful. "He told me of a land long ago where there was peace and joy, where a king was so beloved that a sword, shield, and breastplate were forged for him. They were not ordinary pieces of armor; they were incredibly special. Within each piece was placed a spirit that would help the king and his descendants keep strong his land and people. The armor was passed from one generation to the next until they were lost during a war with barbaric invaders. Since that time, the land has been in chaos and strife, with no real peace. Legend has it that if all three pieces of the armor are returned to their rightful owner, back to an heir of the family that originally wielded them, then the spirits within the armor would be summoned, and the land would know peace again."

"To say such a tale sounds somewhat far-fetched would be an understatement," Marie said as she continued her inspection of the sword. "You chose to carry on the search, to sacrifice your life for this legend?"

"I chose nothing of the kind. I had no intention of giving my life to a fairy tale until the man I respected and loved, the man whose battles I fought many times, attempted to take the sword by force, even over my dead body. I realized that there may have been some truth to the story and fled, knowing that I could not return home. I cannot describe what has been pushing me these past years. I despise this sword and the life it has robbed from me, yet I cannot discard it. I have seen too much evil in this world. I must continue on until I find the one who should rightfully wield it."

"So that is your search. That is why you have become a student of history. You are trying to determine a family name or a clan," Marie surmised.

"I know a name, but it is hundreds of years old. I have not been able to reveal it or my quest for fear that once again someone would try to force me to relinquish possession of the sword. It is a lonely task but one I am compelled to complete."

"I will help you," Marie volunteered enthusiastically. "I can study and research without arousing suspicion."

Andrew knew that no matter how much he tried to dissuade her, it would be in vain. Marie was not the type of woman who would be told what to do or what not to do. She was headstrong and would try to figure out the mystery on her own anyway. The best thing for him to do was accept her help but keep a close eye on her.

"This matter must remain between us," Andrew warned her. "Not another soul is to know about what you have in front of you. Lives could be, and have been, lost over this sword. It is impossible to know who has knowledge of this legend and its potential effects on the land. Your father must not know of this, nor may your friends be told. An impenetrable veil of secrecy must surround this mystery we now share. Do you understand, Marie? This must be treated as something most intimate, something we share beyond words."

"I understand," she replied, nodding her head. "I would forfeit my honor before betraying our secret."

"Then let us speak no more of this today and proceed to the planned activities. We shall meet again and discuss our direction after the contest has ended."

"We will find the person whom you seek, Andrew," Marie said with complete confidence, "and we will put an end to your loathsome quest. I lack no confidence in this."

"I would that my doubts were as few," Andrew replied as he replaced the sword in its hiding place. "Five fruitless years have bred much pessimism in my heart. Perhaps our combined efforts will prove more successful than my own. Steven must have your father's horse ready by now," Andrew said, changing the subject as he walked toward the door. "We each should go about our business. The time of the race is not too far away, and I must prepare myself."

"Of course," Marie agreed as she stood. "My father has an extremely fine horse. You will do well today."

"We shall see. I am sure we will speak again before the day is ended."

"Yes, we will," Marie replied as she opened the door and stepped into the hallway. "In the meantime, I shall have one of the castle guards stand watch over your room to prevent anyone else from entering, one who has my highest level of trust. If they did not find what they wanted in the stall, they may try to search your room."

"That is a good idea," Andrew replied. "I will see you later." He closed the door behind her.

Andrew sat in a chair in front of the fireplace and pondered the morning's events and the conversation with Marie. Was it possible that there were more of Gallard's spies in Talbots kingdom? He had not spoken to anyone of his encounter with Gallard's men and his near-death experience. Who else would bother to poison Annon and search the bundles in the stall? He stood and began to pace around the room.

"That has to be it," he said aloud. "Peterson admitted that they knew I was here, or at least heading this way. He must have dispatched additional men to spy on me and try to discover the location of the sword. But who killed Peterson and saved me from what would have been a most severe interrogation? And furthermore, removed the bodies yet left me to recover on my own? Obviously, someone who did not want three strange bodies found decaying on the road, which otherwise would lead to Talbot increasing security. Surely it would not have been Gallard's men who killed their fellow countrymen, yet who else had knowledge of the sword? Why wait until this morning to search for the sword instead of waiting until I was out for a ride and the stall was empty?"

As soon as he asked the question, the answer was obvious: the Skills Contest. By waiting until this morning, they threw the suspicion on a hundred other men, and therefore nobody would think of outsiders. They must have been observing the contest and knew how well he was doing, which would all the more make the poisoning look like an act of desperation by a jealous competitor.

It was almost too easy to believe. If Gallard's men were in the area, why hadn't one of Martin's patrols discovered them? Were his spies that good at masking their presence? Given that the first group of spies had made their presence known to the girls in quite a savage manner, Andrew doubted that Gallard's spies were that good. He was about to get a headache when there was a knock on the door.

"Come," Andrew called out.

Ian stepped into the room. "I thought you would like to know that your horse appears to be slowly recovering. He is a strong one, which saved his life. A lesser animal would have succumbed to death almost immediately. He will probably be weak for several days, but I expect no permanent damage."

"I am indebted to you for your help, Physician," Andrew answered. "If I can ever be of assistance to you in any matter, all you need to do is ask."

"Steven has been looking for you for several minutes," Ian said. "He has King Richard's horse ready. That boy is prancing about more than the horse, I can tell you."

"I shall be down shortly, if you would relay the message," Andrew replied.

"Certainly. Before I leave, there is one more thing I wish to share with you." Ian paused and looked out of the door to ensure that there were no eavesdroppers. Satisfied, he stepped back inside and closed the door.

"I cannot be certain of the exact identity of the poison used on your horse, and you must understand this. I can only set forth my professional opinion based on experience, which encompasses many years and many lands. I may get a little confused at times when I recall places and events of the past."

"What is on your mind?" Andrew asked quickly, eager to get on with his busy day.

"I have seen the effects of numerous poisons on man and beast over the years, and I am sure there are even more that I have never seen. As I mentioned earlier, I have seen similar symptoms on men that Annon displayed this morning. I believe this type of poison may have a northern origin."

"A northern origin?" Andrew repeated. "You believe this poison comes from the north? I did not know that poisons differ in the north from the south, east from west."

"Usually that is true. However, this poison is a little different from most in that it is a bit more, how shall I say, barbaric? Not that I believe any poison to be less than barbaric. The main ingredient is the bulb of a flower, appropriately named the Devil's Kiss, that is found primarily far to the north. If it is the poison I am thinking of and have seen the effects of, its attack is quicker and more painful than most."

"I will take your opinion into consideration," Andrew replied.

"In that case, I believe I shall find where else I may be of use this day," Ian replied as he turned to leave Andrew's room. "The endurance event generally sends its share of patients to me. Good day."

"Good day," Andrew answered and was again left alone.

"Barbaric indeed," Andrew agreed. He marched out of the room to prepare for the physical challenge awaiting him.

Chapter 19

A wispy fog appeared to hang over the field of competition as the cool morning air transformed the anxious exhalations of one hundred men and their stallions into a mystical veil of vapor. The horses fidgeted in eager anticipation as their riders held them in close check at the starting line of the contest's final challenge. Each man casually reviewed the competitors closest to him and determinedly showed nothing but unabridged calmness and confidence. For many of them, the endurance event was a familiar nemesis. For a few who had participated only once or twice, it was but an acquaintance. For others, like Andrew, it was a completely new experience that was exhilarating yet foreboding. The path that lay before them promised to demand every bit of stamina, strength, courage, and willpower these men could muster from within. And sometimes that was not enough. By the end of the race, the victor will have reached into his inner depths and pulled out a determination that he never knew existed. It was a test of physical strength, indeed, but it also would test the resolve of every participant.

Andrew leaned forward and stroked the neck of the stallion upon which he sat. It was a magnificent animal not only in appearance but strength as well. Andrew could feel the shoulder and back muscles twitch as the horse pranced about gently, waiting for the great workout that lay before it. Being the king's horse, it was exercised often and trained far better than most other beasts of its kind. However, Andrew knew that there was no match for Annon, and he was disappointed that he would not be riding his own stallion in the race.

The endurance event was a series of challenges that would take even the winner nearly two hours to complete. The first leg consisted of a hard five-mile ride through the forest and the open plains, over rocky terrain and across a small river. Once the end of the first leg was reached, the riders would dismount and traverse on foot an obstacle course comprised of boulders, logs, water pits, and any other natural obstacle Angus could think of placing in the contestants' way. The third leg consisted of a two-mile run, at the end of which the contestants would arrive back at their horses. The men would then be required to take three dozen strong, swinging strokes with their swords at a hanging straw target, then remount and return to the starting, or finishing, line. It was not uncommon for injuries to rear their ugly heads during the event, and fighting among the contestants was forbidden.

Andrew knew that as a newcomer who had thus far seen great success in the contest, he was not held in high regard by his fellow competitors. It was entirely possible for several of the contestants who had nothing to lose to band together in an effort to impede his progress as much as possible so that one of their fellow countrymen could win the event. The thought was not a pleasant one. Although an honorable man would not stoop to such a level, Andrew was not certain of how honorable these fierce competitors would be. He decided that any man intentionally confronting him would not see the finish line this day.

The playing field grew deathly silent as King Talbot grandly strode to his seat of honor. Marie stood to his right, and Angus to his left. With a loud and commanding voice, the king addressed the crowd.

"Before us stand the bravest, strongest men in our humble kingdom. Each man has competed well, and while some have excelled above others physically, they are all equally courageous and have competed in all fairness and honesty. Every one of them deserves the highest respect and admiration." He turned his attention to the field of competitors.

"Gentlemen, you are about to embark on a physical challenge greater than many of you have ever encountered. Some of you may not finish. In that, there is no disgrace. Each of you has proven himself to be worthy of honor, and all shall be recognized at the end of the Skills Contest. I urge you to complete your competition in a manner worthy of the men you are. The road is clearly marked. Any deviation from it shall result in immediate disqualification and a public display of shame. This you should remember as you strive alongside your countrymen: you are competitors, not enemies. Any man unduly hindering the efforts of another shall be removed from the race and publicly shamed. There will be judges scattered all along the field of play, although I will not reveal their exact locations. The race will be closely monitored.

"Prepare yourselves, my friends. May each of you by far exceed his own expectations. May you give your kingdom a reason to be proud of its protectors. May the heart of the winner know humbleness and the hearts of the losers know pride."

King Talbot turned to a trumpeter to his right, and the man lifted the shiny brass instrument to his lips while keeping his eyes on the king. Talbot took one final look at the men lined up on the field. The world had become still. Even the horses ceased their nervous prancing, as if knowing that the moment of challenge was at hand. The king slowly turned his eyes back to the trumpeter and gave a short nod. The man inhaled deeply and then released a loud, resounding blast from his instrument.

The explosion from the starting line was easily exceeded by the roaring of the crowd as each person screamed for his or her favorite competitor. The riders leaned low as their horses jumped forward, and the field was ripped to shreds by the galloping beasts. The majority of riders strove to gain an initial advantage by pushing their horses to take a position at or near the very front of the pack. It was going to be a long race, and in order to conserve his horse's strength for not only the ride out but also the ride back, Andrew contented himself to remain in the middle of the group. There was much bumping and nudging at the start of the race, but gradually the competitors fanned out, and any interference from other riders was reduced to a small nuisance.

The first part of this event was not so much a test of the men's endurance as it was a test of how they handled their horses. The riders were faced with the task of pacing their horses to cover the most distance as quickly as possible without completely exhausting the animals. The five miles over which they had to travel was not a completely flat, smooth landscape. There were hills and valleys and many obstacles to ride through and over. The best horsemen would choose the paths that would keep them from having to dismount and lead their horses through any difficult terrain encountered.

The king's horse, although relatively inexperienced at riding over such challenging terrain, responded well to Andrew's directions as they leaped over small gullies and wove around boulders and fallen trees. As they neared the end of the first leg of the race, Andrew noticed some of the quick starters beginning to lose ground as their weary horses slowed down. With hardly a pause, Andrew and his horse plunged into the hundred-foot-wide, three-foot-deep river that was the final obstacle on the ride out. Several riders had fallen into the water and were frantically trying to remount their horses as Andrew passed them without a second glance. His horse burst out of the water, and after a short gallop of one hundred yards, they came to the area that was the transition point from the first to the second leg of the race. There were two dozen horses already tied up to posts as Andrew quickly dismounted and gave the reins to a young man who ran up to meet him. Without wasting any time, Andrew dashed for the beginning of the obstacle course.

The obstacle course was meant to stand as a challenge to a man's ability to maintain his balance over rough, uneven ground. A rolling field perhaps four hundred yards long lay covered with a carpet of rocks ranging from small pebbles to immense boulders, intermingled with logs and limbs up to nearly two feet in diameter. It did not take long to see that it was a challenge many of the contestants were not meeting with the greatest of success. Andrew had an advantage in this area, as he had trained under similar adverse conditions for many years. He passed several competitors who were picking themselves up off the ground for the second or third time. Most men were simply trying to run over the large rocks and logs as quickly as possible without exercising due care. The obstacles had a nasty way of rolling underfoot, throwing the racers to a painful collapse. Andrew moved quickly and carefully, gliding across the field with little difficulty, his experience guiding his steps. He had nearly traversed the course in perfection until he passed a little too closely to a competitor who was well on his way to a painful fall. As the man stumbled to the ground, he reached out by reflex and grasped Andrew's arm. Both men fell hard to the ground. Andrew reached out with his left arm to break his fall, but instead of contacting the ground, his hand struck a large rock. A searing pain shot through his arm as his wrist bent in an awkward position and he collapsed to the ground, his head narrowly missing a second, larger rock. Andrew did not bother trying to determine if the man had intentionally knocked him down. He quickly pushed himself up with his right arm and regained his footing. He took a brief look across the field and saw that less than a dozen men were still ahead of him. He quickly resumed the race without offering to help his competitor off the ground.

There was not much Andrew could do with his injured left arm. He examined his wrist as he continued across the field but could not determine if it was broken or only severely sprained. Normally he would have found a way to bind and protect the injury, but there was no time for that now. He held the arm close to his body, which negatively affected his balance and slowed him down. A slight feeling of nausea crept over him, and Andrew began to feel lightheaded. He fought through the discomfort and continued the race. He was not able to gain any additional ground on the field's forerunners as he completed the obstacle course and began the two-mile run.

Being warriors trained to stand and fight, the competitors were not acclimated to running long distances. The only extended running these men ever engaged in was while training for the Skills Contest. Andrew had watched these men during their numerous training sessions. There was no doubt that many of them were excellent swordsmen and marksmen worthy of respect, but that was all their training had encompassed. They had never been challenged with covering great distances on foot or having to pursue an enemy for any length of time. That was why Andrew considered their training to be substandard. He had been brought up to not only be able to fight an enemy toe to toe but also in skirmishes across great distances. Despite the hindrance his left arm had become, he could see that he was beginning to gain ground on the men in front of him. His pace would take him to the end of the foot race in about twenty minutes.

Andrew passed six individuals within the first half mile, as each had fallen back to little more than a fast walk. There was a trio of men barely a hundred yards ahead of him, and he concentrated on catching up to them. He need not have been concerned. Two of the men were obviously tiring quickly, as their pace substantially slowed, and within a minute, they were close to dropping behind him. However, as he closed to within three strides of the heels of the men, they picked up their pace. They ran with only a couple of feet separating them, which would force Andrew to go around them if he desired to overtake them. Andrew did not care to have the runners that close to him and therefore altered his direction in order to position himself to their right. No sooner had he done so than the men also altered their paths until they were directly in front of him. They dropped their pace a bit and forced Andrew to slow down. Irritated, Andrew again attempted to gain some clearance by moving off to the side. He also increased his pace. The two men wasted no time in blocking his path.

"So now the real game begins," Andrew muttered to himself as he contemplated how to handle the situation. "How did I know this was going to happen?" He decided to see just how intent the men were to keep him back. He moved up until he was almost shoulder to shoulder with the men. They inched closer so that Andrew could not pass between them.

"Nice day for a run," Andrew said in an offhanded manner.

"That it is," the man to the right responded. The man to the left replied with a snicker.

"The pace is a bit slow for me though," Andrew continued. "I prefer a little more strenuous workout."

"I find the pace quite satisfactory," the man on the right said. "How about you, Joshua?"

"I must admit, there is a mild pain developing in my side," Joshua replied. "I would prefer to slow the pace a little myself. Would you mind, Collin?"

"Not at all," the man on the right replied. "We want to make sure that we can at least finish the race even though we surely will not win it." The men immediately slowed yet again, and Andrew nearly tripped over their feet.

"In that case, do not let me interfere with your slow pace," Andrew said. "I would not want anyone to experience any pain that is not necessary. I will just go around you gentlemen and bid you a good day." Andrew's fourth attempt to go around the men was again thwarted. He decided that enough was enough. He looked around the plain but did not see any of the judges that King Talbot had said were monitoring the course.

Andrew dropped back behind the men about fifteen feet. Casually, he unhooked the sheathed sword from his side, which was not an easy chore considering his injured left hand. He held the weapon down by his side and sped up so that he was practically on the men's heels again. Joshua stole a quick glance to see where Andrew was but did not see the sword in his right hand. With a mean strike, Andrew swept the sword underneath Collin's feet, and the man immediately tripped and went tumbling across the ground. Before Joshua could react, Andrew turned and aimed a horizontal blow toward the man's shins. With a scream of pain, Joshua joined Collin on the ground. The third man, having stolen a glance back after hearing the screams of pain, exerted a burst of speed to increase his lead. Without so much as a cursory glance back, Andrew re-attached the sword to his belt and increased his pace to make up for lost time.

Andrew's legs were beginning to tire, and the ache in his left wrist was increasing due to the continual jarring from his running. Due to him having to increase his pace beyond what his initial strategy had planned for, his breathing was heavier than it should have been. Nevertheless, he eventually caught up with the next competitor in front of him. He was the man who had previously been in company with Joshua and Collin.

"It has been some time since I have had a workout such as this one," Andrew said to the man, panting. "How about you, Louis?"

"I would say it has been about a year," Louis replied casually between his own deep breaths.

"A nasty competition it can be too," Andrew stated. "I have seen several men take some quite painful-looking falls."

"Hazards of the course," Louis responded, breathing heavily. "It is not uncommon for injuries to occur. Some accidents are actually quite severe."

"This is true," Andrew answered. "In fact, I just witnessed two men hit the ground rather hard. I doubt that either of them will be finishing the race any time too soon." He followed with a grunt of laughter. "Actually, I doubt that one of them will be walking without a crutch for some time. Running can put quite a strain on the shins."

"And the arm," Louis said as he noted Andrew holding his left arm close to his body in an effort to keep it from moving as much as possible. "The obstacle course?"

"An unfortunate slip," Andrew admitted.

"That is too bad," Louis said, not even attempting to feign sympathy. He increased his pace. "Accidents happen."

"That they do," Andrew replied, keeping in step with his

competitor. "That is the interesting thing about accidents. You never know when or how one is going to occur." His voice took a bit of a threatening tone. "It would be quite easy for a man to step in an unseen burrow out in a field like this or trip on an unseen rock. One moment, you are running a race; the next, you are watching it go by you while lying sprawled on the ground. And no one close enough to determine what exactly happened." Andrew increased his own pace and moved several feet ahead of Louis.

"A wise man would watch his step carefully," Louis answered undaunted and matched Andrew's speed. The men raced side by side for the last two-tenths of a mile. Six other men had arrived only moments before and were beginning their sword strokes. Now Andrew was at a severe disadvantage. With his left arm injured, he would be required to take all thirty-six strokes with his right arm. The other men could use both arms, therefore avoiding fatigue and being able to quickly dispense with this part of the contest. Andrew unsheathed his sword even while still running and headed for the closest target. With an evil smirk, Louis attacked the next closest target, swinging strongly and quickly with his own weapon.

Sweat poured off Andrew's brow as he struggled to complete this leg of the event. He felt like he was holding two weapons instead of the one as he labored to swing the sword from side to side. He tried to grasp the handle with his left hand, but the pain was too intense. All too quickly, the muscles in his right forearm and hand burned with fatigue, and each stroke became a victory of the will alone. His arm was nearly numb by the time he completed the last stroke. A judge standing close by signaled that Andrew's strokes were acceptable and directed him to continue the last leg of the race. Andrew fumbled as he re-sheathed the sword and nearly dropped it twice. All seven other men had already mounted their horses and were well on their way as Andrew swung on top of his steed.

The immense spray caused by the horse plunging into the river was a welcome refreshment to Andrew. The throbbing in his left arm grew more intense as he wrapped the reins around his hand. There was no holding back as the horse burst from the water. Andrew kicked the animal hard in the ribs and leaned as far forward as he could. The horse responded by breaking into a full gallop.

Finishing the race first was no longer Andrew's primary goal. The delays forced upon him had all but thrown victory in this event beyond his reach. He now concentrated on one thing only: catching up to Louis. That Louis had orchestrated the delays for Andrew was not even questionable. The question was why. It was no mystery that short of not finishing the endurance event, the Skills Contest was Andrew's. And thus far, nothing had been done to remove him from the race completely. Perhaps the intent was to keep him from breaking Angus's long-standing record. With no other competitors close behind him, Andrew would finish well within the top twenty and still break the record. Knowing Louis's disposition toward him, Andrew decided that it must be a matter of pride. Maybe there was some significance or special honor in finishing the endurance event first of which Andrew had not been informed. He decided that at this point, the reasons were not important. The important thing was to finish the race.

Within the first two miles, Andrew passed three other riders. The king's horse was proving to be in excellent shape and showed no signs of weakening. Andrew knew that the horse would not be able to keep up the full gallop for the entire five-mile journey, but he would push the horse to its limits regardless of who owned it. As he crested a small knoll, Andrew spotted Louis about one hundred and fifty yards ahead of him. The horse on which Louis was riding did not have the speed King Talbot's horse had, and coupled with the fact that Louis was a good bit heavier than Andrew, the distance between them slowly shrunk.

By the time Andrew pulled to within a horse's length of Louis, they were only two miles from the finish line, and only one other rider remained ahead of them. The remainder of the ride was along a mostly flat path paralleling a forest of hardwood trees. The path was less than twelve feet wide in most places. A gully ran to the left of the path, and the forest was on the right. Louis had been riding in the middle of the path, but as Andrew closed, he maneuvered to the left side of the trail. This forced Andrew to pass on the right. Finally, the two riders were side by side.

No words were exchanged this time. If there was anything to be said, the men's riding would do all the talking. By now, the horses were nearing their limits and began slowing down. Louis knew that the king's horse was stronger than his own stallion and it was only a matter of time before Andrew left him behind. He gently pulled the reins to the right, and his horse obediently moved over until the distance between the two horses was less than two feet.

Seeing this move, Andrew could only assume that Louis was going to somehow try to knock him off his horse. However, Louis did not make any such threatening moves. He did not lift his arm as if to strike Andrew in any way but remained solid in his riding position. Louis did not even glance at Andrew but kept his eyes locked on the path in front of him. With his attention divided between the racecourse and Louis, Andrew did not notice how the path inched closer and closer to the forest's edge. If he had, perhaps he would have anticipated Louis's next move.

Suddenly, Louis urged a short burst of speed from his horse with a kick in its ribs and gained half a length on Andrew. He then pulled sharply to the right on the reins and cut Andrew off. The king's horse instinctively dodged to the right and off the race path. Andrew was immediately attacked by dozens of tree branches as they slapped him and nearly knocked him off the horse. While fighting to maintain his balance, he threw up his right arm to protect his face and yanked the reins to the left with his other arm. His wrist protested with a sharp, searing pain. The horse slowed and needed no encouragement to maneuver away from the stinging foliage.

This treacherous act gained Louis six horse lengths and

drained even more of the dwindling strength from the king's horse. Andrew could feel the welts on his bare forearm and on his right cheek. Their sting in no way matched that of knowing Louis was going to beat him in this race. Defeat was never more bitter than when tainted with the taste of chicanery. He resolved himself to finishing third in this event, a position in which there was certainly no disgrace. The Skills Contest was comprised of many different events, and his overall performance had earned him the ultimate victory. In this, there was much satisfaction.

The actions of Louis began to look even more childish as the finish line broke into view. Any resentment Andrew felt slowly dissipated until he was able to brush all enmity away like a frail cobweb. He looked behind him and saw the next competitor still nearly three hundred yards back. The end of the race was nearly the same distance away, and Andrew allowed the king's horse to slow its pace until it was proceeding along at a fast trot. He could see Louis gaining on the leader, but there was not enough strength left in his horse to overtake him.

A great roar erupted from the waiting spectators as the first contestant crossed the finish line. There was another thunderous wave of cheers as Louis crossed the line only a few seconds later. It took a couple of minutes more for Andrew to reach the end of the race, and he also received a respectful, yet not quite as enthusiastic, greeting from the bystanders. A throng of admirers crowded around him, patting him on the legs and congratulating him on a fine race. A young boy approached Andrew as he dismounted and took the king's horse to be cleaned and watered. Andrew had the same intentions for himself, although not in the same order. The group, now completely surrounding him, migrated toward a table set with food, wine, and water. Andrew lifted a huge bucket of water and, after taking a long, healthy swig, poured half of the contents over his head. He looked around the festive field and spotted Louis in the middle of a crowd at another table about fifty feet away. Andrew slowly made his way over to the man while kindly acknowledging the cheers from the people around him. Louis spotted Andrew working his way through the crowd and spoke to someone standing by his side. The man turned, and Andrew was greeted by Lawrence's mile-wide smile.

"Andrew!" Lawrence shouted. "Come, my friend! Drink with us in celebration of the end of that dreadful nightmare!"

"I believe I will," Andrew replied without hesitation. "A spectacular race it was, indeed, worthy of a toast in its honor. And a toast is in order for you, too, for taking the honor of first place."

"A small honor it is compared to being crowned Skills Contest grand champion," Lawrence replied. "It looks as if this last event nearly bested you," he continued after spotting the welts on Andrew's cheek and right arm as well as the way Andrew was holding his left arm.

"By no means," Andrew replied as he lifted a tankard of ale to his lips. "A few unfortunate mishaps at the most. Nothing that would keep a good man down."

"It was a rugged course," Louis said. "I doubt there is a man here who did not meet with the ground on at least one occasion."

"I will certainly vouch for that," Lawrence agreed. "That cursed trail where you could hardly see the ground for the rocks and trees took my balance a few times. I have bruises in places I would not show my closest comrade."

"I am sure he is grateful for that," Andrew responded. As the three men laughed and downed more ale, Angus approached the table.

"A race well run, gentlemen," he said as the crowd parted for him. "A most exciting finish for certain. Possibly the best in several years." He turned to Andrew. "MacLean, I must speak with you for a moment. Follow me."

Andrew gave his two companions a questioning glance, but they merely shrugged their shoulders in ignorance. Without setting his ale down, Andrew followed Angus. He was led to a small tent that was about eight feet tall and twelve feet square. Angus entered the tent, and Andrew followed. There was no one else present. In the middle was a small table with two chairs around it. Angus partially sat on a corner of the solid oak table and folded his arms across his chest.

"I have received a report from some of our judges," Angus began as he looked Andrew in the eye. "It is a most discouraging report of what appears to be less than honorable conduct on the part of one of the contestants. There is always at least one competitor who believes he is invisible and can run the race any way he chooses without regard to honor. Do you recall the king's words addressing conduct during the race?"

"I recall them quite clearly," Andrew confirmed, an uneasy feeling creeping into his gut.

"Then you know the punishment for unduly hindering another contestant's progress along the course?"

"I said I recall the king's words quite clearly," Andrew repeated as he returned Angus's cold stare without blinking.

"Three judges have come to me with concerns that such a thing has happened this day." Angus walked around the table and sat in one of the two chairs. He motioned for Andrew to take the other seat. At first, Andrew balked at the invitation, then reconsidered and sat in the chair while folding his arms across his chest.

"My concern is the integrity of the contest and the competitors. Therefore, I must ask you this question: do you feel that you were intentionally hindered by one or more contestants at any time during today's race?"

The question caught Andrew by surprise. He was so certain that he was going to be accused of foul play that he had not considered any other reason for being called aside by Angus. When Andrew failed to respond immediately, Angus prompted him.

"Specifically, as an example, during the final leg of the race when you were forced off the trail and into the trees?"

Louis's evil smirks and corresponding actions flashed into Andrew's mind. He had been intentionally interfered with; of that there was no doubt. Anybody who saw the race could see it. What sweet revenge this would be. What sweet revenge it could have been.

"That was an unfortunate mishap," Andrew replied casually as he stared back at Angus.

"Unfortunate? It was nearly deadly!" Angus retorted. "Your neck could have been broken had one of those limbs been any lower."

"True enough," Andrew agreed, "but it was still an accident. A dog leaped out of the gully as we thundered by, startling Louis's horse and causing it to veer into mine. My horse only reacted naturally to the dog and the other horse."

"If I asked Louis the same question, would he corroborate this story?"

"I do not know what Louis would report. He was so intent on the finish line I doubt that he even saw the dog."

"I doubt that anyone else saw the dog either," Angus replied. He could see that Andrew was not going to admit to Louis's unfriendly actions. Perhaps Andrew had other ways of dealing with the man in repayment. Angus could only shake his head.

"Very well then. Our business here is finished. You may rejoin your companions. I will relay your answer to the judges and the king. You will be announced grand champion at the banquet tonight." A mischievous glint formed in Angus's eyes, an almost friendly glint. "The grand champion is held in quite high esteem, especially by the young ladies. You will not spend the evening alone. I can tell you that from experience."

"It should be an interesting night indeed," Andrew replied as he exited the tent.

Chapter 20

The celebration was well underway by the time Andrew arrived in the great banquet hall. After the conclusion of the contest, Andrew had spent the afternoon getting his wrist examined by Ian (at the insistence of the physician, who was not to be put off), paying a visit to Annon, cleaning the remnants of the day from his body, and taking a well-earned rest. When he awoke to prepare for the awards ceremony, his body was stiff, his wrist was throbbing, and his stomach was growling fiercely. He mostly dreaded the attention that was forthcoming, but a small part of him, a very small part, would certainly enjoy it.

Andrew paused for a moment before entering the auditorium and being buried in the grand gala. The music that saturated the great room was livelier than any he had ever heard before and quite easily blanketed the hundreds of spirited voices fighting the music and one another. The middle of the room was a bedlam of dance as dozens of men and women twisted and twirled around one another in a joyful frenzy, more often than not colliding with one another and spontaneously changing partners. At one point, two burly men found themselves face-to-face and holding hands, at which point they quickly separated and located their female partners, who were close to tears from laughter. At the far end of the room, a troupe of acrobats was entertaining a small crowd of both adults and children. It was indeed a celebration the likes of which Andrew had never witnessed.

"The celebration is much more enjoyable if you actually enter the room," a feminine voice called out to Andrew above the boisterous revelry. Looking slightly to his right, Andrew spotted Heather approaching him from about fifteen feet away. It was immediately evident that she had spent a good bit of the afternoon preparing for the merry evening. Her golden hair, not a strand of which appeared out of place, gleamed softly in the glow of a thousand candles. Her cheeks had just a touch of rouge that was only noticeable when she stopped within three feet of him. Her eyelids were tinted just enough to make her exquisite blue eyes stand out like diamonds sparkling in the sun, and her eyelashes had been darkened just enough to give her a bit of an exotic look. Her lips spoke just a hint of red coloring. The fragrance of a thousand roses drifted over him like a mother's gentle caress. Her powder blue, lace-laden dress was but a shade lighter than her dreamy eyes and was accompanied by a beautiful royal blue, star-shaped pendant on a thin silver chain adorning her smooth, bronze neck. As Andrew's eyes drank in her splendor and his tongue fought to find the right words, any words, to respond, the reddish tint in Heather's cheeks noticeably deepened.

"It does appear as if everybody is having a most enjoyable time," he finally got out. He looked at her for a moment longer. "The competition this afternoon left me breathless, but I must say, you have taken my breath away. You are simply stunning tonight. That dress is most exquisite." Her cheeks now appeared as if they would burn to the touch.

"Thank you. I was not sure if I would have time to finish it before tonight. I begged out of my chores this afternoon so I could sew the last few pieces of lace on."

"You made that yourself?" Andrew asked in astonishment. "I remember your father saying that you were a seamstress, but I had no idea he meant of such a wondrous ability."

"You are too kind," Heather bashfully replied. After a few moments of awkward silence, she continued. "The musicians are playing quite well tonight. Would you agree?"

"Indeed. These melodies are unlike any I have ever heard. And they are played with such vigor and skill." It took about fifteen seconds for her unspoken hint to sink in, and Andrew mentally slapped himself for nearly missing it. "It appears that the people dancing are enjoying the music immensely. Dancing is not among my most proficient abilities, but would you care to join me in that mad throng anyway?"

"I would indeed," Heather replied without hesitation. The two threaded their way through the milling crowd and were quickly absorbed in the whirling mass.

The music seemed to go on and on without pause or interruption. People were constantly joining and leaving the swarm of dancers, and the floor remained rather crowded. In the madness, Andrew found himself dancing opposite three different females at different times but somehow always found Heather or was found by Heather; he could not be sure which was more accurate. The pace of the dance threatened to rival anything he had encountered earlier in the day. He was perspiring quite noticeably within a short period of time. After nearly fifteen minutes of constant skipping, prancing, and wheeling, Andrew was ready to make his excuses to Heather when the music thankfully came to an end. The crowd of bystanders quickly paused in their conversations as King Talbot stood from his seat of honor at the banquet table.

"Let us take brief pause in our merriment in order that we may acknowledge the occasion for which we have gathered. A toast is in order. Let us raise our cups in honor of the hundred men"—he briefly looked at Andrew—"the hundred and one men who have given us exhilaration and inspiration for the past two days. To the men who have exemplified bravery and chivalry, determination and resolve; to the men who have tested their endurance and abilities and excelled beyond their own expectations. Let us drink to the men who did not shirk from the challenge but rose to it. Men of the Skills Contest, we drink to you!" An enormous thunder of approval erupted within the great hall as Talbot raised the chalice to his lips. Letting the revelry continue for a few moments, the monarch looked over his people with a smile of satisfaction stretching across his face. He finally lifted his right hand, and the noise abated.

"And, of course, when there is a contest, there must be a victor. This year, the victor is someone new to our land, someone who has made contributions to us in a myriad of ways. He has shown that might of mind and might of arm make a formidable combination. Indeed, he has well earned his victory and in a manner that impressively surpassed every winner of the contest since it was established fourteen years ago. Let us congratulate this year's victor, Andrew MacLean!" Another explosion of praise filled the immense chamber, and Andrew felt his back pounded time and time again by enthusiastic admirers. The crowd in front of him slowly parted, leaving an unobstructed path to the king. Reluctantly, Andrew left Heather's side and approached the king's table amid the shouts of adoration. As usual, Malcolm, Angus, and Marie were seated close to the king. Malcolm's expression was scrupulous as usual, although it had softened somewhat in the last week or so. Angus maintained a rather neutral facial expression, which Andrew considered a great accomplishment at this juncture. Marie sported a friendly smile of congratulations and gave him a short nod of approval.

"To you, Andrew, I bestow this medallion in commemoration of your victory." King Talbot leaned across the table, and Andrew did likewise so that he was within the king's reach. Around Andrew's neck, Talbot slid a bright gold medallion attached to a deep burgundy loop of velvet. The medallion was embedded with several small representations of the events in the Skills Contest. His name was also impressed in the medallion. "Your name shall be inscribed on the Wall of Honor in the foyer at the main entrance to the castle for all to see, just as the name of every other winner in years past.

"As you know," King Talbot continued, "the grand prize for the victor is the choice of twenty acres of land in the kingdom to be his own. Of course, land owned by others is excluded, as is the castle and land within two miles of its walls. But otherwise, it is your choice. Tell me, have you chosen which land shall be yours from this day forward?"

"I must say I have not, Your Majesty. I was far from convinced that I would finish among the top contestants, and to win was beyond a dream. If I may, I would request a few days to lay claim to the prize so I can recover from the excitement of this honor and carefully consider my options."

"Of course, you may take as long as you like. It is indeed an important decision to make and should be diligently deliberated. Let us now enjoy the rest of the evening in celebration. Musicians!" Immediately another energetic melody arose from the players, and the people quickly resumed their dancing. Andrew was unsure of just what to do next. As he looked over the crowd, Marie made her way around the table and to his side.

"For someone who does not wish to stand out above the crowd, you certainly have become quite popular," she noted.

"So I have," Andrew acknowledged reluctantly. "So I have."

"It was a good thing you arrived when you did. Heather was well on her way to offending every man in the room."

"What do you mean?" Andrew asked.

"She was one of the first few dozen people to arrive this evening. Not long after entering the room, she casually slipped to a position within clear sight of the doorway. There she stood idle for nearly twenty minutes, her eyes never wavering far or long from the entrance. At least a dozen young men invited her to the dance floor, and she turned each one down, which is quite a feat considering how much she loves to dance. It was sad, the long expressions on their faces as they walked away from her. She barely moved until you stepped into the doorway. Once you appeared, she moved so quickly it was as if a snake had suddenly crawled across her foot."

"You believe she was waiting for me? Certainly you have read more into the matter than the simple truth. I would venture the truth to be that the music was not to her liking, or perhaps she wished to absorb some of the atmosphere before joining in."

"No, the music was much to her liking, I am sure. The matter was that the proposing partners were not to her liking."

"Well, it could be that she merely wanted the first dance with the winner of the contest," Andrew replied innocently. "Look, she is dancing with the other young men even as we speak. It appears that she will not be disappointing any more of them this evening." He nodded in the direction of the middle of the dancing pack. Sure enough, Heather was partnered up with one of the other young men who had competed that day, and they appeared to be having a grand time.

"Andrew, you may know a lot about fighting and farming and other things, but you are much underread and quite naïve when it comes to young ladies. She may be dancing, but I promise you her partner is not of her preference. I warrant that throughout this entire evening, she will not stray far from your vision."

"I do not recall seeing you venture onto the dance floor thus far this evening," Andrew stated, changing the subject of their conversation.

"Dance invitations for the king's *independent* daughter are generally few and far between," Marie answered.

"Then I shall remedy that. Would you care for a little exercise?"

"It would be a pleasure," Marie replied, and the two headed for the dancing area.

The celebration lasted well into the night. Food was constantly brought to the tables, and the wine jugs routinely refilled. At one point, a second group of musicians replaced the first and played with equal skill and energy. Andrew split his time between dancing with the young ladies, including a few more trysts with Heather, and joining many of the men in recollections of the Skills Contest. As usual, Lawrence and Louis put away their share of wine and then some. Andrew was listening to Lawrence brag as to how he had mastered the obstacle course when Heather's father, Carl, approached him.

"I know that you have heard this many times today and are likely weary of hearing it, yet I must offer my congratulations on your performance in the Skills Contest. I have either participated in or witnessed every event that has been held, and no man has ever come close to your performance. Well done."

"Thank you," Andrew answered, indeed weary of the compliments.

"You have a great choice ahead of you," Carl continued. "Twenty acres of land. There are few here who own such a vast amount of land outside of past contest winners. Have you any preference on the type of land you wish to have? Perhaps good cropland or forest? Possibly pasture?"

"As I mentioned to the king, I have not thought much on the issue," Andrew replied as politely as possible, considering he had been asked the same question at least a dozen times already. "Perhaps something with a nice stream running through it."

"Yes, that would be nice," Carl agreed. "There are quite a few highly desirable parcels of land around the kingdom. Some are not so desirable. In many places, the soil is very rocky and hard. It would be difficult to build a home or farm on such land. In other places, the ground is infected with caverns and sinkholes, dangerous to man and beast. You certainly would not want a piece of land where you could fall through the earth in the beat of a heart and be lost forever."

This caught Andrew's attention. "Caverns, you say?"

"It is not uncommon in this part of the country," Carl said, nodding his head. "I would venture that in your time here you have seen at least one of them yourself. The stone beneath the earth tends to be soft and erodes quite easily. Sometimes the openings to these caverns are obvious and hold few mysteries. I would say that most children here have ventured into more than one of these caves and pretended great adventures." Carl lifted his mug and took a long draw of wine.

"So I have heard," Andrew said, his curiosity aroused.

"Other times, the openings are not so obvious. Most people

could walk within twenty feet of a cave and not know it was there. Such types as these can go many years without being stumbled upon."

"Most people," Andrew repeated. "I am sure there are those who know of the existence and locations of such places. People who have lived in this area for many, many years."

"That would be a logical conclusion." Carl suddenly appeared to change the direction of the conversation. "My daughter spent an inordinate amount of time on that dress of hers," he said, catching a glimpse of her among several other young ladies. "I am glad it is finished. Perhaps now she will be able to complete her chores."

"It is a beautiful dress indeed. She wears it well."

"That she does," Carl agreed. He turned to face Andrew again. "My family would like to extend a dinner invitation to you, Andrew. I realize you are quite popular right now and must have many people seeking your company; however, it would be our pleasure to entertain you one evening this week."

"It would be my pleasure to visit your home," Andrew replied.

"How does the evening two days hence sit with you?"

"I look forward to it," Andrew confirmed.

"Then we shall see you the evening after the morrow," Carl said and offered his hand. Andrew shook the outstretched hand, and Carl disappeared into the crowd.

Having had enough of the revelry and attention, and his body aching from the beating it had taken during the day, Andrew elected to retire for the evening. After bidding farewell to his friends and one last bow to the king, Andrew made his way out of the room. Marie saw Andrew heading for the exit and hurried after him.

"I take it you have had your fill of celebration this evening," she said as they simultaneously reached the large doorway.

"That and more," he acknowledged. "I could not stand to have another person tell me how greatly I performed and how impressed they were. I almost wish I had foregone the contest and stayed in the shadows."

"*Almost*," Marie repeated teasingly. "I could not help but

notice that Heather's father held your attention for more than a few moments."

"An immense room filled with hundreds of people, and you could not help but notice two particular people conversing for but a few minutes?" Andrew asked cynically. "I would venture that you were watching me to keep count of how many times I danced with Heather."

"Six that I saw," Marie replied undaunted, "including that one lovely, slow ballad where a person would have been hard-pressed to see a glimmer of light between the two of you. But you were not dancing with her father."

"Being that his wife was but a few steps away, I did not feel it would be appropriate," Andrew countered. Becoming weary and wanting to be left alone, Andrew gave in to Marie's unspoken question. "He simply offered his congratulations on my performance and recounted several past contests. I was also offered a dinner invitation that I felt would be rude to reject. That is the simple matter of our discourse."

"I see," Marie said. She remained silent for all of a half dozen steps down the hall. "When shall we continue our discussion of this morning?" All day, she had been eagerly waiting for a chance to broach the subject and would not have been able to sleep that night had she not caught him.

"The day after tomorrow. We can talk then. I believe I should spend tomorrow considering the choice my victory has presented to me."

"I understand. I shall corral my curiosity for another couple of days. Sleep well, Andrew," she said as she turned to head back to the celebration.

"And you," he politely replied.

"One more thing," she said over her shoulder without stopping. "Congratulations on an excellent performance in the Skills Contest. I was most impressed."

Andrew shook his head and could not suppress a faint smile of amusement.

Chapter 21

Marie and Andrew sat in her private study, their voices a bit lower in volume than if they had been engaged in casual conversation elsewhere in the castle. It was late afternoon, and they had been speaking for the better part of three hours.

"So throughout five years of travel, you have never stumbled across any references to the DuFay family? I find that difficult to believe if he was as great a king as this legend purports," Marie said.

"You must understand that in my travels I have not been privy to such literary resources as contained within this castle. Most of my investigation has been conducted through casual conversation with commoners who themselves have not much education. Had I been able to access detailed libraries along the way, it is possible that I could have discovered that for which I search—some mention, either directly or indirectly, of the DuFay name. However, it has not been so. Even the people with whom I spoke had little knowledge of the name, and most of them believe it all to be a child's fairy tale."

"Perhaps the name died long ago. That could very well explain why it is not known today. Or you simply have not traveled far enough. How have your travels been guided thus far? Have you simply roamed about at random, hoping to stumble upon some bit of information to lead you in another direction?"

"For nearly half a year after the sword fell into my possession, I did just that, riding whatever road lay before me as long as it took me farther from my home, which had become an unwelcome place for me. I struggled greatly with the destruction of the only life I had ever known and the fairy-tale final words of a dying man. I was utterly lost.

"One evening, about six months after fleeing my homeland, I was riding through a small village, a village like a hundred others through which I had passed. As I approached the edge of the village, I was startled as several terror-filled screams shattered the peaceful evening. Looking up, I saw three vile, filthy men running from an alley between two small buildings. I leaped from Annon's back and ran to the alley. At first, I did not see them, but as I peered into the darkness of the alley, I saw two forms lying still on the ground in the waning shadows of the evening. As I got closer, I could see that they were young females, much younger than you. Pretty girls—or at least they had been. Out of politeness and respect, I will not describe to you what I saw, but my heart sank into the deepest part of my chest. One of the girls still had breath in her, and I knelt on the ground beside her. I will never forget the terror in her eyes—the terror of what had happened and the terror of knowing that her life was slowly draining away. I took her in my arms to try to provide some comfort for the last few moments of her life." A deep sadness began to overtake Andrew as the memories resurfaced. He had tried to forget that terrible day, to wipe it from his memory and convince himself that it had been simply a nightmare and never happened. The awful feelings he felt that day came back upon him in a rush, and he could not avoid them.

"She told me what had happened," he continued with a mist hovering just behind his eyes, "how the men had lured her and her sister into the alley to show them some beautiful dresses they wanted to sell. There were no dresses in that alley, only death. The men beat and violated the girls, stole what little money they had, then stabbed the girls over, and over, and over. She died in my arms, crying for her mother." Andrew took a deep breath to compose himself. Marie only stared at him in sad silence.

"It was as if a veil had suddenly been lifted from my eyes. I knew in a moment what I had to do. I knew that if there was even a hint of truth to this legend, that if there was the remotest possibility of finding one who could help drive the evil from the land, I had to seek out this person. I knew that if I did not at least try, my soul would be tortured for the rest of my life. Then and there, my journey began. In every town and village I passed through, I would ask whomever I could if the name DuFay was familiar. I read whatever books or parchments or documents I could get my hands on, praying to God that He would give me a hint or clue as to where to go. My journey has been led more by determining where not to go as opposed to where to go. I was able to eliminate different peoples and countries based on the limited histories I gleaned from the few books I came across. I did find a few minor and very vague references to great kingdoms of the past; however, they were so vague as to not even mention any names. I could only gather a general direction from the information and therefore would alter my path accordingly."

"And that is why you came this way, because you believed a great kingdom had once encompassed this land?" Marie asked as Andrew paused for a breath.

"I would not say this land particularly. I was headed more in a direction than to a destination. I just happened to stumble upon this place."

"And just in time to save the lives of me and my friends," Marie mused as she tried not to picture Andrew's tragic story. There was a moment of silence before either of them spoke again. It was Marie who continued the conversation.

"The symbols on the hilt of the sword surely have some significance," she pondered aloud. "It is quite possible that they could hold an important clue."

"Only if they directed us to the doorstep of a DuFay descendant," Andrew replied. "The sword is hundreds of years old. Whatever importance the symbols had would likely be obsolete by now."

"Perhaps. Perhaps not," Marie replied, holding on to her theory. "I would like to study the sword in greater detail, with your permission."

"By all means. I would like to know what the symbols represent, if not for curiosity's sake alone." Andrew looked out one of the windows lining the west wall of the room. "It is near time for me to depart for dinner. If you will accompany me back to my chamber, you may inspect the sword. Better yet, bring along a piece of paper and something with which to write. You can copy the symbols and study them at your leisure. Be sure that no one else sees the paper though. I would hate for questions to arise."

"I take it that you are off to Heather's home for dinner," Marie stated rather than asked as they left her study. "I would venture that she eagerly awaits your arrival."

"I doubt that," Andrew replied modestly. "I believe most people enjoy my company to some extent, but I cannot imagine it having that kind of effect on someone."

"I do not believe you are as modest as you would have us believe," Marie answered. "You have seen how the young ladies look at you and the young men look up to you. Steven and many of his young friends hold you in quite high esteem, though you have been here but what, two months and a few days? The soldiers on the field watch you train and strive heartily to emulate you. There are many fathers who would readily give their daughters to you rather than to most of the other men who have lived here all their lives. Though you may not want to admit it, your presence here has caused a stir the likes of which has not been witnessed in the last four years."

"Are you referring to the strangers who came by several years ago and ended up falling under your father's wrath?"

"No, that happened about eight years ago. I am speaking of the time when Martin first ventured upon our land."

"Martin?" Andrew repeated. "Somehow I was under the assumption that he had either lived here all his life or came with your father."

"Neither is the case. Your situation is eerily reflective of his. He came this way a little over four years ago, simply passing through by his own admission. He elected to remain and rest from his travels for a few days. A few days became a few weeks. During that time, he became immensely popular with the common people, helping wherever he could. He assisted in building homes, harvesting crops, and in anything else where there was a need. He, too, was quite adept at combat. Four months after his arrival, he took part in the Skills Contest, and although his performance did not match your own, he fared quite well. My father was impressed with him and offered him a modest position under Angus in the castle guard. Nearly six months later, Angus named Martin as captain of the guard, where he has served quite well. He, too, had quite an impact on the people during his first year here."

"Well, that is understandable considering his immensely cordial personality," Andrew cracked sarcastically.

"In social circles, he still maintains an enjoyable demeanor, although I will admit it has changed over the years. He has become a bit more impassive. I always attributed it to his responsibilities as captain of the guard."

"He was here less than a year and part of the guard for but six months, and Angus made him captain of the guard?" Andrew asked suspiciously. "You would think that there were other men easily as qualified as Martin available for the promotion, men who had lived here all their lives."

"That could very well be true. Back then, I was less involved in such matters than I am now. Did bitterness exist among the other men? Likely, but I would guess no more than what you have encountered in your own situation."

"There has been some resentment; this is true. Only from a few, but like a wildfire, it could spread quickly and become dangerous. I do not wish that to happen. I believe it would be wise for me to move out of the castle as soon as possible. Did Martin stay in the castle also when he first arrived?"

"No, he was not presented with the opportunity. Yours was a special case. Martin had no heroic exploit to warrant the offer of a room in the castle. He stayed at the inn for several weeks before moving into the bachelors' quarters. That is where he has remained to this day, although being named captain of the guard has granted him the privilege of a more private room."

"From where did he come, and to where was he traveling?" Andrew asked.

"I believe he indicated that his homeland lay many weeks to the south, although I do not recall him specifying any more particular of a region. As for his destination, to that I cannot testify. If it was ever mentioned, it has long escaped my memory."

"It is strange indeed, the similarity of our beginnings here. Then again, people are always seeking a better life in a better land, and travelers are commonplace. Perhaps my and Martin's situations are not as uncommon as one would imagine." As Andrew finished speaking, they arrived at his room. Upon entering, he proceeded directly to the huge fireplace, which was quiet, and after bending over, stepped into the pit. He straightened up, and all Marie could see of Andrew was his waist to his feet. He stepped onto one of the large iron cradles that held the firewood, and even more of his body disappeared. Just as Marie was going to ask him what he was doing, Andrew dropped back to the floor and exited the fireplace. In his hands he held the magnificent, mysterious sword that was slightly blackened from the soot and smoke of prior fires. Andrew cleaned the sword off and handed it to Marie.

"A little paranoid, are we?" she asked as she accepted the weapon.

"I prefer to call it being careful," Andrew replied. "After Annon was poisoned and my belongings in the stable searched, I decided it would be wise to hide the sword. It would be far easier to rummage through my room than it was Annon's stable. After you copy the markings, I will return the sword to its hiding place."

Marie proceeded to copy the sword's symbols onto the piece of paper she had brought along with her.

"You know, the closer I look at these markings, the more I cannot help but suspect that they are actually words or letters. I do not know from which language, but it appears they are just that."

"I guess it is a good thing that you have an interest in studying languages," Andrew remarked. "This should keep you busy for some time."

Marie finished her copying and handed the sword back to Andrew, who promptly replaced it in the chimney. She folded the piece of paper and stuffed it into a hidden pocket in her dress.

"I am eager to begin my research," she said, "and I would presume you are eager for your dinner appointment. Therefore, I shall head for the library and leave you to your evening. I am certain you will find the company of the Bergman family most enjoyable."

"It should be an interesting evening for sure," Andrew replied as Marie exited the room.

The courtyard was rather calm and quiet as Andrew left the castle. The stable boy had Annon ready to go and was walking the horse out of the stable as Andrew approached. With no more than a courteous greeting to the young lad, Andrew took Annon's reins and hefted himself onto the horse's back. With a mild nudge from the rider, Annon proceeded across the courtyard.

Chapter 22

A gentle and somewhat cool breeze caressed Andrew's cheeks as he rode into the early-evening sunset. It should have been a short, relaxing ride, but Andrew's mind was racing: the contest and the banquet; his quest; Marie; Heather; Marie's description of Martin's appearance in the kingdom and Martin's obvious contempt for Andrew; and last but not least, the king's scrupulous eyes. And then there was the rather mysterious conversation in which he had engaged Heather's father at the banquet. There were so many things that he could not get out of his mind. Without any clues to lead him on, Andrew had a deep-down suspicion that he was somehow making progress toward his goal.

The ride was soon over, and Andrew dismounted Annon in front of the Bergmans' home. There was a short post at the side of the house to which Andrew tied Annon's reins. He had not even knocked when the door was opened from inside. Carl Bergman stood in the doorway.

"I thought I heard someone approach. How are you this fine evening, Andrew?"

"Quite well, thank you," Andrew replied politely.

"Good, good. I trust you have brought your appetite. My wife is in rare form this evening in her preparations of the meal. I should invite guests over more often," Carl said with a smile. "Come inside and meet her."

Andrew followed Carl into the house. It was an average-size

dwelling, not much different from many others Andrew had seen in the area. There were three separate rooms, although there were no doors filling the entrances to the two rooms off the main room. Instead of doors, there were long pieces of fabric hanging from the tops of the doorways. The main room served as kitchen and dining room, with a modest but sturdy wooden table set slightly off-center of the room to the right. There was room around the table for about eight people to sit comfortably. A large fireplace in the far wall, about twenty feet from the front door, served dual purposes. First and foremost, it heated the home during the cool evenings. Secondly, it was used for cooking. At the present time, it was doing both. A large cauldron hung over the licking flames, and an appetite-arousing aroma filled the room. Carl's wife was fussing over a smaller table set about three feet to the right of the fire, with her back to the main door. She turned around as the front door closed.

"Good evening, Andrew, and welcome to our home," she said with great sincerity.

"Good evening, Mrs. Bergman. It is my pleasure to be here," he replied.

"Do not 'Mrs. Bergman' me, young man. Annette will do."

"Thank you. I will try to remember that," Andrew answered.

"Good evening, Andrew," a soft, sweet voice called out, and Andrew turned to catch Heather floating through one of the veiled doorways.

"Good evening," Andrew replied. "You look very nice tonight," he added politely.

"Thank you," she replied, blushing a bit. Andrew had no idea that she had spent two hours preparing for his arrival.

"Heather, please run over to the stable and inform Steven that dinner is ready," her mother directed. With a barely perceptible pout, Heather obeyed without delay and headed out the front door.

"Would you care for a glass of wine, Andrew?" Carl asked as he pulled a large decanter off a shelf.

"Yes, thank you," Andrew replied and accepted a mug of a strong red wine that had a somewhat fruity taste to it.

"I would ask how you are doing, but with your success in the Skills Contest and the choice of twenty acres of land, the answer is quite plain," Annette said as she began placing food on the table. The delicious aroma, which had previously seemed to simply taint the air, now saturated it with the promise of a most filling meal. Andrew's appetite immediately escalated, and his stomach growled in anticipation. "Plus, you seem to maintain a full day with your other responsibilities."

"That is quite true. Malcolm and Angus keep me busier than I have ever been in my life," Andrew replied. "It is hard work, but I have to say that I enjoy it. The worst part of it all was getting Malcolm to look at me other than as if I were covered by leprosy."

"Ah, yes, Malcolm has such wonderful skills with people," Carl noted. "I would venture that he offered no more congeniality to his own mother than that which he offers you. To this day, he hardly nods if we pass along the road, and I have known him for what must be nearly twenty years now."

"It does not take an educated man to tell that he is none too pleased to have me around," Andrew stated.

"Do not take it personally," Carl advised. "Those men of Talbot's are quite the prideful bunch and are easily threatened by someone of intelligence and ability. As you appear to have both, it is no wonder that you are not held high in their sight."

As Carl finished speaking, the front door opened, and Heather reentered the house, followed by Steven.

"Hi, Andrew!" Steven called out, excited to see his friend and instructor.

"Hello, Steven," Andrew replied. "I have not seen you in a few days. Has your father been keeping you busy with chores?"

"Every day," Steven answered a little sullenly. Then he brightened up. "But I have been practicing with my bow! I can hit the target almost every time now!"

"Excellent!" Andrew replied. "You just might be ready for the Skills Contest next year. Keep practicing."

"Andrew," Carl said, eager to start eating, "you may sit here, to my left side. Steven, you may sit next to Andrew. Heather, across from Steven." As they took their seats, Annette finished filling the table with food and sat down beside her husband.

"Father, may I give thanks?" Steven asked. At the boy's words, a sudden rush of déjà vu overwhelmed Andrew, and for a moment, he felt like he was in a dream. Carl replied in a voice that sounded to Andrew as if he were far, far away.

"Very well, Robert. You may give thanks."

"Robert? Why did you call him Robert? His name is Steven. Is it not?" Andrew asked with a confused look as he turned to the boy.

"Yes, his name is Steven," Carl replied with a curious look at Andrew. "Who called him Robert?"

"Did you not just call him Robert?" Andrew asked. "You said, 'Very well, Robert. You may give thanks.'"

"No, I called him Steven," Carl countered. He looked at Andrew with a bit of concern. "Are you feeling well, Andrew?"

Andrew looked around the table for a moment and was hit with looks of concern and confusion from Heather and her mother. He returned his gaze to the young boy. He shook his head a little, as if waking from a dream. "Yes, I am feeling okay. I just thought—" He paused for another moment before fully recovering, thinking back on what he thought he had heard. "No, I am fine. I must have simply misheard you. I have eaten little today, and this wine must have gone to my head rather quickly. That, coupled with your beautiful daughter across the table, must have made my head swim a little. Forgive me for interrupting."

Steven giggled, Heather blushed, and Annette let out a little laugh to help ease what must have been an uncomfortable moment for Andrew. Carl managed a polite smile but was not totally convinced of Andrew's explanation. After a moment, Steven proceeded with saying grace, and the group jumped into a meal that was better than anything Andrew had eaten since his arrival in this land. The dinner conversation was pleasant, and more than once, Andrew stole a glance at Heather. It seemed that every time he looked at her, she lifted her eyes to him at the same moment. Dinner was over too quickly in his opinion, even after two helpings of nearly everything on the table.

"That was possibly the best meal I have had the pleasure of eating in the past five years, if not my life," Andrew complimented Annette as he patted his stuffed stomach.

"That is very sweet of you to say," she replied with a bit of an embarrassed smile.

"Now that you have filled your stomach, would you care for a little after-dinner drink, a little something I make myself that puts just the right finishing touch on such a gourmet meal?" Carl asked Andrew.

"I believe I might be able to find a little room left for a drink," Andrew replied, "but very little room at that."

Carl walked over to a shelf on a wall and retrieved a metal flask about ten inches tall and three inches wide. He took two small cups and filled them with a deep red, sweet-smelling liquid. After handing one to Andrew, Carl motioned for Andrew to join him outside the front of the house.

"A grand evening this is," Carl said as he sat down on a bench under a huge oak tree. "This is the nicest time of year in these parts. Your arrival was well timed. Had you arrived two months hence, I fear the chill in the air would not be too inviting for us to sit outside like this."

"It is most favorable," Andrew agreed politely. He was eager to get beyond casual conversation since he felt that Carl had something particular he wished to discuss, but being the guest, Andrew decided to let Carl lead the conversation.

"My wife is a fabulous cook. I am glad you found her meal most satisfying." He patted his stomach that, although not large, did form a bit of a mound over his waistline. "I definitely do."

"It was the best that I have eaten since my arrival. I am surprised that Talbot does not have her cooking for him."

"She would be most flattered to hear that," Carl said, although Andrew could tell that his mind was wandering far from food.

"Tell me, Andrew, how long has it been now since you first ventured into our hamlet?"

"Well over two months," Andrew answered.

"You have met many people and have seen the daily routines of the village, correct?"

"Yes, that is correct," Andrew agreed, his curiosity continuing its rapid rise.

"Through the years of your travels, I would venture that you have met many people and seen many lands and countries."

"I have traveled through many places and met many people," Andrew agreed again.

"How would you compare this kingdom and its people to the many other places through which you have traveled?"

"Compare in what sense?" Andrew asked.

"Life in general. The attitudes of the people, their moods, their strengths and weaknesses, the produce of the land, the weather, those kinds of things."

"I would venture to say that most are quite comparable. The primary differences would lie in the faiths of the people. Of course, a person's faith has quite an impact on how he or she lives his or her life, their moods, their strengths and weaknesses. But overall, I would say that this place is hardly that much different than other places I have seen."

"And in the past five years, what is the longest amount of time you spent in any one other place?" Carl continued.

"I would say perhaps several weeks at most," Andrew answered, still unsure of the purpose of Carl's line of questioning.

"And yet you have been here over two months," Carl noted with a bit of a knowing look, a look that said he was about to make a point.

"Yes, that is correct."

"Why?" Carl asked point blankly.

"What do you mean?" Andrew asked, although he knew very well what Carl was asking.

"You admitted that this land is not much different than most others you have visited. You stated that the longest period you have spent in any one place during your travels is several weeks at most. Why have you tarried your travels in this place for significantly longer than any other place, even accepting a position in the administration of the kingdom, if there are no visible, significant differences?"

"I believe I have felt more welcome by the people here than most other places," Andrew responded, which was true. "Also, I must say that my indoctrination into this land was a little different than any other place I have visited."

"Yes, I should hope so," Carl said. He sat silently for a few moments as he contemplated what to say next.

"But in all truth," he continued matter-of-factly, "the people and their reception of you really play only a limited role in your decision to remain here for as long as you have."

"Pray tell, then, what has been the prime factor?" Andrew asked challengingly.

"That you would have to tell me," Carl answered. "I have seen you walking around and riding around quite frequently since your arrival. You have roamed nearly every inch of this village and some distance beyond, more often than not without company. And the expression on your face during those times never changes. It is the look of a man searching. Your eyes never rest. They are always moving, searching, looking for something. Tell me, Andrew, what is it that you seek?"

"I think you are mistaken," Andrew replied, his defenses starting to rise. "I am but a man in new surroundings, trying to understand where he is and what his place is. If I am looking for anything, it would simply be my well-being."

"Hmmm," Carl replied. "From any other man, I could accept

that. But not you, Andrew. You are no mere wanderer who was looking for a home, a man out seeking his fortune, or a hero looking for a damsel to rescue. You have purpose about you, and I can see it. It is in your eyes, it is in your voice, and it is in your mannerisms. So the question is, what is your purpose?"

Andrew stared at Carl for a few moments, not sure of how to proceed. Carl was a very perceptive and determined man. Of course, Andrew could continue to deny having any specific purpose for being there and attribute it to his being tired of wandering from land to land and desire to settle in one place. It was a perfectly reasonable rationalization of his decision to stay in this land. He then remembered seeing Carl in the cave a few weeks earlier and what appeared to be Carl's own search for something. And despite being a blacksmith and a commoner, there was an air of authority about Carl that Andrew picked up on quite easily. He decided to answer the man's question without giving away his true mission.

"I am looking for a man," Andrew said finally. "I have been for some time."

"I see," Carl replied. "Does this man have a name?"

"I do not know the name of the individual for whom I search," Andrew continued. "All I know is an old family name that may not even exist today."

"And this name is …" Carl prodded.

"DuFay," Andrew answered as if the name itself was magical.

Carl tried to show no reaction; however, he stirred ever so slightly. "DuFay?" Carl repeated. "You are correct. That certainly is an old name."

"Then you know of it?" Andrew asked a bit excitedly as he tried to hide his enthusiasm.

"I know of it," Carl admitted indifferently. "Why do you seek this man of the DuFay line?"

"I was commissioned nearly five years ago by a man who wished to return a certain personal possession to the DuFay family. Sort of a family heirloom, if you will."

"It must be quite valuable. And your compensation for this task must be quite large for you to spend five years of your life wandering from land to land."

"Its value would vary depending on the person possessing the item, I would think," Andrew replied guardedly.

"Tell me, Andrew. Which piece of the armor is it?" Carl asked casually as he took another drink from his nearly empty cup.

A stunned Andrew could only stare at Carl in complete silence. A thousand questions raced through his mind, and he could not ask even the simplest of them. He knew that to continue his charade would be in vain.

"You know," he finally said. "You know. How?"

"You are not the first person who has ventured this way seeking the DuFay legend, and I doubt the last. I would say that in my lifetime here, I have seen at least a dozen men venture through this land who were on the same mission as you. It is not difficult to spot them. They all had that same nomad-like quality. That same look in their eyes, the way they explored the land in detail. I can spot a man on the DuFay trail a mile away."

"You know about the legend and the importance of the DuFay Triad," Andrew stated.

"The DuFay Triad?" Carl asked questioningly.

"The DuFay Triad," Andrew answered, "although I do not know if that is the official name of the armor. The sword, the shield, and the breastplate. The DuFay Triad."

"My boy, I do not know where you obtained your information, but there is more to the legend than a sword, shield, and breastplate," Carl replied. "There is a helmet, a belt, and boots. The six pieces have been known as the DuFay Armor for many years. And yes, I know of the legend and the DuFay Armor. I have known about it since I was a child. Most people around here know of it, although most think it is just that: a legend and bedtime story."

"What do you think?" Andrew asked.

"I think there is some truth to the legend. After all, it is a story several hundred years old and is bound to change over time as it is repeated from generation to generation. I do not believe in spirits and magic. I can tell you that right now," Carl answered.

"What do you believe?" Andrew pressed.

"I believe—" Carl started, then paused as he stared at Andrew and reflected on what to say. "I believe that a long, long time ago, a wise and righteous king ruled this land from where the sun rises to where it sets and beyond. I believe that his sons and his sons' sons were righteous. Somewhere along the line, they became proud and arrogant. They ruled to satisfy their own egos and attributed the goodness of the land to their wisdom. The Almighty judged them for their pride and brought in another nation to subdue them. I also believe that someday another king will arise who is righteous and wise, and he will restore the goodness and abundance of the land."

"What role, then, does the DuFay Armor play?" Andrew inquired.

"That I do not know," Carl admitted. "I do not believe them to be magical, yet I do believe that they are significant in some manner. I also believe that they are the reason for Talbot's presence here."

"You think that Talbot knows of the legend then," Andrew said.

"I am quite certain of it," Carl affirmed.

"How so?" Andrew asked.

"I told you, I can spot a man on the DuFay trail from a mile away," Carl replied. "There are a number of things that convince me of his intent." He scrutinized Andrew for a moment, then continued. "What do you know about Talbot and how he came to our village?"

"I was told that you were being raided by a band of barbarians who stole the produce of your crops and your livestock. One day, Talbot came on the scene and promised to chase the barbarians away and protect the land if the inhabitants would take him as their king. He did as he said he would do, and in addition to that, he improved the produce of the land through new farming techniques. To this day, the land has known peace and plenty."

"That sounds about like what I would expect a stranger to know," Carl replied. "Now let me tell you the truth. Before Talbot came to this place, I had lived here my entire life, which up until that time was thirty-five years. In all those years, this land never failed to produce plentiful crops, and no person went hungry. I cannot recall one bit of trouble from nomads or barbarians during that time either. It would appear quite convenient for the land to suddenly decide to go bad and then at the same time for these raids to start and what we were able to harvest being ripped from our stomachs. Then our savior miraculously appears, a man whom no one had ever seen or heard of before. There was one mock battle with these barbarians, and they are never seen or heard from again. I say mock battle, for the engagement between these barbarians and Talbot's men was nothing more than the training exercises you have witnessed during your stay here." Carl paused to catch his breath and finish the contents of his cup. Andrew silently waited for Carl to continue.

"Talbot then set up his administration and proceeded to commence excavation and rebuilding of the castle. Through his *ingenious* agricultural ideas, the land once again produced bountiful crops. The people hailed him as their savior and a miracle worker and placed him on a pedestal upon which he still sits today."

"You are none too bitter about it. I can see that much," Andrew noted with a bit of sarcasm.

"It is all a charade," Carl replied bitterly. "Talbot cares not for this land or the people here. He cares only for his ambitions and obtaining the DuFay Armor. He came here and took control of everything without bothering to consult with the leaders of the village. He apportioned crops and herds and land as if none of us had ever lived here, and many of us have lived and worked here for several generations, even more. Crops and livestock are wealth to him, and I would venture that not far from here, he has an entire army supplied from our land ready to go to battle over the DuFay Armor."

"I heard how Talbot failed to take any of the local elders into his administration when he arrived," Andrew said, ignoring for the moment Carl's speculation of any army in hiding. "While that may not have been entirely wise of him, it certainly was not an unusual thing to do. From what I was told, it was of little matter anyway, as three of the four elders met with unfortunate accidents that took their lives."

"Accidents? Ha! If those were accidents, then I am the pope!" Carl exclaimed.

"What do you mean?" Andrew asked. "Lawrence Morecraft told me how the men died. His father was consumed by a fire in his home that was started when a candle accidentally tipped over. One elder drowned in the lake, and another was trampled by his own horse. In truth, I have known a number of men who have died by these very same means."

"Yes, that is how the men died, but those were no accidents. I warrant it. Justin Morecraft was extremely cautious. He had many, many books and parchments in his home, and he was aware of how easily they could catch fire. He generally kept them in a room well away from any candles or lanterns. When he read, he would set the candles on stands and not on the table where the books and parchments lay. I spent many evenings in his house, and I knew his habits. Also, after the fire, I personally went through the ruins. Although I have never told this to anyone before, I am telling you now. Someone had removed nearly all the books and parchments before the fire was set. The remains of a few books were scattered around, but they were hardly a fraction of what you would normally find in that house on any given day."

"Why would someone do that?" Andrew asked, bewildered.

"Justin had collected much of his reading material from the castle's ruins. Somebody knew that and wanted those documents. Someone wanted them badly enough to murder a harmless man. I would venture Justin was killed while he slept, the books and parchments removed, then a fire was set in the house to give the appearance of an accident."

The Legend

"And you believe it was Talbot?"

"Perhaps," Carl replied carefully. "Justin's reading habits were no mystery to the people of this land. There was no reason for one of the local people to do such a thing. It had to be someone strange or new to our village, someone who had some knowledge of those reading materials and valued them more than a man's life."

"What about the other two elders?" Andrew inquired.

"Patrick Jergen was supposedly trampled by a horse. Patrick had lived his entire life around horses, training them and breeding them. He knew their habits, their moods, their instincts. He could break the wildest of horses. Now, I know that horses can get spooked quite easily, and a man caught off-guard can be seriously injured. Normally that would be enough to support the theory of an accident. However, what not many people know is that the horse Patrick was supposedly trampled by was an old, nearly blind nag that was as docile as a mouse.

"Finally, you have Connor O'Banion, who drowned in a lake. Again, normally such a thing would arouse little suspicion, as it is not uncommon for people to drown in such a large and deep body of water. However, Connor was terrified of water deeper than his ankles. As a child, he nearly drowned in the lake, and for forty years, he would venture no closer to the lake than a stone's throw. For him to get close enough to drown, well, it would have had to have been extreme circumstances."

"You make good arguments," Andrew commented. "Considering how new I am to this place and the fact that I was not present at the times of these events, I could not dispute your opinions. Yet I must ask, who would have a motive for committing these murders? Why would someone go to the trouble of stealing Morecraft's books and hiding their actions in a fire when they could have simply asked to read them? And what would have been the motivations to kill Jergen and O'Banion?"

"The shield," Carl replied simply.

"The shield?" Andrew asked incredulously. "How were Morecraft, Jergen, and O'Banion connected to the shield?"

"As I mentioned before, most people around here know of the legend. Morecraft, Jergen, and O'Banion did not simply know about the legend; they prided themselves as experts on it. All three had explored the ruins of the castle at great lengths long before Talbot arrived. As it happens, on one of Morecraft's forays into the depths of the ruins, he came upon a cache of armor, weapons, books, and many other items of great age and of great historical value. One of those items was a beautiful shield of such exquisite artistry that no man had ever seen its equal. He knew at once what he had found and immediately informed the other elders. They desired to explore the ruins in even greater detail and had targeted a corridor only recently uncovered. However, it was at that time Talbot arrived on the scene, and the elders could no longer search the ruins in secrecy. They formulated a plan wherein Morecraft would convince Talbot to allow him to supervise at a minimum the partial excavation of the ruins in preparation for the building of the castle. It was not a difficult chore, based on Morecraft's knowledge of the ruins. Once in place, Morecraft would not only steer the excavation away from this new corridor, but he would also see to it that Jergen and O'Banion were granted secret access to the corridor in order to continue their explorations. The fourth elder was intentionally omitted from the plan as a safety precaution in the event the other three were discovered in their activities and deemed to be a threat to Talbot. If those three were jailed or executed, then at least one would remain to continue the search however he could."

"I take it then," Andrew surmised as Carl paused, "that the three were discovered."

"At this point, conjecture takes over," Carl replied. "They were never approached, never questioned by Talbot or any of his men as far as anyone knows. Morecraft, Jergen, and O'Banion did feel as if they were being watched, though, and elected to suspend their explorations. Unfortunately, they never were afforded the opportunity to explore that one corridor they intended to excavate. I was commissioned by the king to build a gate barring entry into the very same corridor that the elders were exploring. There were always two guards present while I was working, presumably to ensure that I did not set off on my own little journey into the corridor. Not long after that, Justin died in the fire. Patrick was trampled. Connor drowned. All very quick, convenient, and to the unsuspecting mind, accidental."

"What of the shield?" Andrew asked.

"Justin had it in his home, hidden away among his books. Whoever set the fire and took the books stole the shield as well. I warrant it."

"And you believe that Talbot now has the shield," Andrew concluded.

"That is exactly what I believe," Carl confirmed. "I cannot prove it beyond a doubt; I realize that. But in my mind, there is no doubt."

"Do you still believe that the depths of the castle hold secrets worth knowing?" Andrew inquired.

"I do not know," Carl admitted. "Talbot has the shield, and you have ... actually, you never answered that question. Which piece do you have?"

"The sword," Andrew answered.

"The sword," Carl repeated. "That is not surprising. There had been rumors that it had been found. It is unlikely that the other pieces of the armor are here since all six were supposedly scattered during the barbaric invasion."

"I believe that my former king, Edwin Gallard, has the breastplate," Andrew said. "The day I found the sword during battle, Gallard tried to force me to relinquish the sword to him. The man I obtained it from told me of the legend, and that moment changed my life. Something inside of me, I cannot explain what it was, knew that I could not give the sword to my king. Under penalty of death, I had to flee my homeland. That morning, though, before the battle, I entered the king's tent, and he had three of his advisers with him. They were having a conversation, which abruptly stopped the moment I entered. I saw something on the table in front of the king, something that was large enough to be the breastplate, but it was partially covered. The king moved quickly to cover the object, but I could tell that whatever it was, it appeared to be golden in color. Now it makes since that it was the breastplate."

"I suppose you are correct," Carl said. "In truth, I was quite surprised that the shield was here, back where it all started. The only secrets that may remain in those dark depths would be clues as to the exact importance of the armor and perhaps something to help identify the DuFay family and rightful heir. It is not out of the question that Talbot has discovered all there is to discover in there."

"Are you so certain that this truly is the land, the very kingdom, where the legend started?" Andrew asked. "Is it not possible that DuFay's kingdom was far from here, and the shield somehow made its way to this place over the years?"

"Oh, there is no doubt in my mind that this once was DuFay's domain," Carl replied. "I was privy to all that Morecraft, Jergen, and O'Banion discovered and learned in the depths of that stronghold. There was plenty of evidence to prove DuFay once ruled here. I will concede it is entirely possible that the shield left this land only to return many years later. Perhaps many years ago, someone else was on a quest similar to yours, a quest that ended here for whatever reason."

"Why was the castle not plundered over the years? How is it that the shield and all those books and other items remained hidden, undisturbed for so many years?"

"All of the corridors leading to the lower levels of the castle had been blockaded and covered," Carl answered. "A person simply wandering around would not and could not know what lay in the depths of the ruins. It took a serious, concentrated effort to locate and uncover the hidden passages."

"Tell me, Carl," Andrew started with a bit of a knowing smile in his eyes, "who exactly was that fourth elder who has avoided any life-robbing accidents over all these years?"

"A simple man, really," Carl replied, returning the knowing grin. "A man who knows when to keep his mouth shut and goes about his business as discreetly as possible."

"A man who secretly explores burial caverns with his horse," Andrew added.

"It could be such a man," Carl admitted.

"You have found nothing in those searches to help solve the DuFay mystery, have you?" Andrew asked.

"Unfortunately, I have not. I really do not believe that what needs to be found is to be found among the dead. I believe that if there is any information in this land to help discover the secret of the DuFay Armor, it is held in the depths of the castle."

"That is what I feared you would say," Andrew said with a sigh. "I saw that gate when I first arrived here while Marie was giving me the grand tour of the castle. You did a fine job, blacksmith. That gate is solid, and no man could get by without the key."

"Yes, it is one of my finer pieces of work, I must say," Carl said with pride in his voice. "But getting by it is no problem."

"Do not tell me you have a key," Andrew said, shaking his head.

"Of course I have a key," Carl confirmed innocently. "No respectable blacksmith would forge a lock for which he did not keep a spare key."

"Of course not," Andrew added. "Now all you need is someone who has access to the castle to continue the search abandoned by your friends so many years ago."

"My voice has grown tired of telling tales," Carl said as he stretched. "Tell me about yourself, Andrew, and we will see if you are that man."

"Very well," Andrew answered and commenced with the story of his life.

Chapter 23

M arie laid the piece of paper on the desk in front of her and stared at the markings. For two days, she had studied the markings and diligently searched through the castle's libraries. From memory, she could write out the symbols perfectly, yet they remained as mysterious as the first time she had scribbled them on the yellow parchment in Andrew's room. She had returned to her private study, where she could think without being interrupted. She knew that simply staring at the paper would not magically reveal the meaning of the markings and having exhausted all of the resources at her disposal, she knew that she would have to go beyond books if her research was going to continue.

She looked around the room that had once been her mother's study. It was beautifully decorated, attesting to the eye and taste of her mother, who had furnished the room herself. The furniture was all meticulously crafted, every piece unique and one of a kind. Exquisite portraits decorated the walls along with colorful tapestries. Attesting to her mother's curiosity and quest for knowledge, nearly two hundred books were packed together in shelves spread around the room. Memories of countless evenings spent in this room with her mother skirted through Marie's mind. She could almost envision her mother sitting in her favorite cushioned chair, with her feet folded up under her, reading a book, or sitting at her desk while writing. She had spent a lot of time writing, which was never something that had struck Marie as particularly odd in her youth. In retrospect, Marie realized that she had never seen or read what her mother had written. She had asked her mother once what it was that she was writing, and her mother had said that she was simply writing down her thoughts. Marie had never asked to read the journal. Evidently, it was not for anyone to see because Marie remembered her mother placing the journal among several inconspicuous books in one of the bookshelves, as if to hide it. Her eyes floated over to the area where her mother used to stand when she would retrieve or replace the journal. She could almost see her mother standing there, reaching up and putting the book in its place. After her mother died, Marie's father had closed off the study for several years. It was only when Marie had reached her teens that her father realized she might need some privacy from time to time and had allowed Marie to use the room. By that time, Marie had forgotten about the writings of her mother, and it never occurred to her to try to find and read the journal. Her eyes scanned the bookshelf, and suddenly her innate curiosity got the best of her. She stood up and walked across the room.

Her hands gently passed over the books on the shelves in a reverent manner, as if the books were religious icons to be respected and treated with gentleness. She began pulling books out one by one and opening them. None of them appeared to be anything other than ordinary books of a scholarly nature, the same kinds of books that could be found in any of the castle's formal libraries. After perusing two dozen such books, her eyes fell on one that, upon close scrutiny, appeared to be a bit more worn than the others, as if it had been handled more frequently. She pulled the book out and looked at the cover. There were neither markings nor words on the front cover that indicated what the contents of the book might be. She walked over to her mother's desk and sat down. She gently opened the book and looked through the first few pages. At first glance, it appeared to be just like any of the other books. However, after flipping through a few pages, Marie came across a loose page that blended in quite well with the fixed pages. She pulled the page out and looked at it. The writing was quite elegant and quite different from what was contained in the other pages of the book. She did not recognize the language and therefore could not read what was written. She continued to flip through the book and came across a few other loose pages very similar to the first one. She pulled out each piece of loose paper she came across, and by the time she reached the end of the book, there were easily three dozen pages on the desk. She looked at the pages one by one, intrigued. She could only assume that the writing was that of her mother. Marie had never known that her mother knew a second language. As she picked up the fifth page, her intrigue turned to excitement.

In the middle of the page, noticeably separate from the writing before and after them, were the symbols she had copied from Andrew's sword. Marie quickly picked up the piece of paper upon which she had copied the symbols and compared it to her new discovery. The markings were identical. Her hands shook from the excitement that engulfed her. She briskly looked through the other loose-leaf pages and discovered another set of symbols like the first. Marie abruptly stood and hurried back to the bookshelf. She began fumbling through the remaining three dozen books on the shelves and quickly came across another book that contained loose pages. Again, she sat at the desk and looked frantically, although carefully, through the book. When she reached the end of the book, another three dozen sheets of paper lay on the desk, and one of them contained more of the mysterious symbols. Marie anxiously looked around the room and nearly ran to another bookshelf on the far end of the room. With heart-pounding excitement, she fumbled through the several dozen books on the shelf. Her hands were shaking when she came across a third book that contained thirty or so more loose pages and yet another set of the strange markings. Having searched through every book in the room, she closed her eyes and tried to picture her mother in the room. Was there anywhere else she may have hidden her writings? Was there anything else she did that, in retrospect, seemed out of the ordinary? Try as she might, Marie could not recall anything else that was suspicious about her mother's actions in this room. Then again, many years had passed since she and her mother last lounged in this room together, and those memories were less than fresh in her mind. She opened her eyes, walked back over to the desk, and leafed through the papers again.

The curiosity over her mother's written thoughts was overwhelming. Somehow, she had to figure out in what language her mother had written, yet ironically, for privacy's sake, she did not want to share her mother's writings with anyone else. An idea leaped into her mind. She pulled out two blank pieces of paper and a pen and then chose one of her mother's pages at random. From the middle of one of the pages, she chose a line of writing and copied it down as best she could on the blank piece of paper. On the second sheet of paper, she copied the three new sets of symbols along with the original set from Andrew's sword. When finished, she returned the loose pages to the book and then placed the book back in its place on the bookshelf. Continuing with her plan, Marie left the study and sought out Joseph, the castle's librarian and scholar.

Joseph was repairing a damaged book when Marie walked into his study, which doubled as a workshop. Books in various stages of deterioration or repair covered just about every horizontal surface in the room. It looked like chaos to Marie, but she knew that, to Joseph, everything was organized perfectly.

"Ah, young Marie, how pleasant a surprise this visit of yours is," he said, looking up as she walked into the room.

"Good afternoon, Joseph," she replied cordially. "You appear to be quite the busy one today."

"Today, yesterday, tomorrow, it matters not. There is always more to do than can be done."

"I would say that you need an assistant, but I know you would never let anyone else touch your children."

"Yes, yes, that is true. These books are like my children. They need nurturing and caring, and nobody else can do it as well as I can." He reached out to pick up the book he had been working on, and as he lifted it off the table, it literally fell apart. Pages scattered across the floor. He looked at Marie with a sheepish grin. "Of course, some children can be a little difficult from time to time. So how may I be of service to you today?"

"I could use a little education this afternoon," Marie replied, trying to think of the best approach with Joseph that would not give her true intentions away. "I have come across some writing, and I do not recognize the language. My curiosity is getting the better of me, and therefore I am hoping you will be able to tell me what language this is."

"I will do my best," Joseph offered. "Show me what you have."

Marie handed Joseph the piece of paper upon which she had copied the sentence from her mother's writings. Joseph looked at the writing for maybe twenty seconds and then looked at Marie.

"The first line is an old form of Greek. It reads: 'requires even more diligence and perseverance.' Needless to say, it does not make much sense, being but a fragment of a sentence."

"How true," Marie agreed. "I was more interested in the language as opposed to the interpretation, truth be told." With a little doubt and battling second thoughts, she handed Joseph the second piece of paper.

"What about these other writings? Do you recognize them?" she asked innocently.

Joseph looked at the piece of paper in his hand for a few seconds, then turned a curious eye to Marie.

"Where did you say you saw these writings?" he asked.

"Oh, I ... I saw them in an old book," she replied truthfully.

"In one of the libraries?" the librarian inquired.

"No, it was not in one of the libraries. It was somewhere else."

"Hmm," Joseph murmured as he continued to gaze at her for a few seconds, then turned his attention back to the paper. "I do not know the meaning of these symbols. However, this is not the first time I have seen them."

"You have seen them before?" Marie asked a little too enthusiastically. "Where?"

Joseph replied slowly, as if considering each word carefully. "Here, in this very castle." He turned from Marie and disappeared into a small side room. "It was soon after we first arrived," he continued as he appeared to be searching for something. "Your father found a number of old books, parchments, tapestries, et cetera that contained what appeared to be writing just like this. I was not able to read the writing, but strangely enough, your father could. He said quite emphatically that the writings were evil and of Satan and that all books and parchments and any object inscribed with this writing must be destroyed, lest our village be infested with evil. Ah, here we are," he said triumphantly and pulled an extremely old and worn book from a shelf. "By your father's decree, we gathered all such things, and we burned them. I did so reluctantly, as you could imagine, being the scholar that I am and having such a love for books. It was quite the painful chore. However, I carried out your father's orders. We were most thorough in our search, and you will not find a single book or object in this castle that bears that language." He looked at the book in his hands with perhaps a little guilt. "Well, there is one small exception." He opened the book and showed it to Marie. The pages were full of symbols remarkably like those she had copied. She took the book in her hands and with great care turned several pages.

"It truly is a language, just as I suspected," she said.

"Yes, it is a language," Joseph acknowledged. "From what I can gather, it is an ancient language. I have not been able to determine what language or even begin any translation. I have many other responsibilities and projects that have taken the bulk of my time, and to be honest, I had nearly forgotten about this book." He turned an inquisitive eye to Marie. "I am understandably most curious as to where you found the book that contains this writing. You say it was not in any of the libraries?"

"It was in a private collection of books," Marie replied without a pause. She bowed her head a bit and diverted her eyes toward the floor in a mock movement of shame. "I ... I did not exactly have permission to go through this private collection," she said, which was about a half-truth. "I would rather nobody know about this, lest it become an embarrassment to me." She looked back at Joseph with her most innocent, trusting, little-girl look. "May we keep this between ourselves, my friend, my teacher?"

Joseph looked into Marie's eyes and paused for a moment before addressing her. He knew there were only three people in the castle who maintained any semblance of a private collection of books, and he was quite sure he knew the content of those collections. One was that of the king, a second was of the late queen, and the third was his own vast collection. He knew the king's private study was locked and off-limits to everyone, including his daughter. Having provided the late queen with all her books, he was intimately familiar with the collection and knew that there were no books in the queen's library that contained this writing. His gaze nearly became accusatory, but it very quickly turned soft. "Of course we will," he answered gently. "We shall have our little secret. Perhaps one day you will be able to tell me more of where you saw this book without the danger of your integrity being compromised. Until then, I shall quell my curiosity."

"Thank you," she said with an expression of relief.

"In return," Joseph added as he took the book back from Marie, "I will ask you to keep what I hold in my hands unto yourself and not reveal it to anybody, especially your father. If he were to learn that I possessed this book, it would not go well for me. I am showing it to you because of what you have brought to me, and I am showing it to you because you have a love of learning and knowledge that reminds me of your mother. I had great respect for her."

At the mention of her mother, Marie's heart skipped a beat. Was it merely coincidence that Joseph mentioned her here and now, or did he know of her mother's personal writings?

"It shall remain our secret," she agreed. "Why did you keep this book, knowing that my father would be angry should he learn of it?"

"Curiosity," Joseph replied. "I was not convinced that the writings were of such an evil nature as your father believed. If they truly were evil, why were there no physical representations of evil anywhere in the castle? What I mean is, we saw no statues, no paintings, no depictions of demons or Satan or anything of an evil nature. Based on the sheer number of books and tapestries and other objects we found bearing the same writing, if they were truly evil, one would expect to find carvings or statues or other manifestations of evil beings. There was not one to be found. I could not help but question your father's conclusions. My curiosity took hold of me, and I kept this one book so that I may someday learn the truth."

"Well then, perhaps we can help each other," Marie replied. "I have time to do the research, but I have exhausted my resources. I do not know where to go from here. Do you have any suggestions, any at all?"

Joseph thought for a few seconds.

"I have an old friend in Habersham whose knowledge of languages far surpasses mine," he answered. "It is—what, maybe two days from here? I would wager he would be able to interpret the writing for you. I would be happy to pen a small letter of introduction and request for you, if you would like to go see him."

"That would be wonderful!" Marie exclaimed. "Thank you so much!" She stepped forward and hugged the elderly librarian. "You are such a wonderful teacher and friend."

"And you are a wonderful student and friend," he replied in kind as she released him. "I will have the letter ready for you by the end of the day."

"Then tomorrow I shall continue the search for the both of us," Marie said. "I will return for your letter after dinner." She turned and left the room.

"It is my pleasure," Joseph replied and watched her leave. He stared at the empty doorway for a few minutes after she had disappeared, then bent over to pick up the pages that littered the floor.

Chapter 24

L awrence slowly approached his opponent. A lone bead of perspiration dripped from the end of his nose, and his challenging eyes bore into the man standing ten feet away. His massive right hand grasped the hilt of his tremendous sword with a grip no man could break. The muscles in his right forearm looked to be hard as a rock. His left hand slowly flexed open and closed, as if not sure what to do. He stopped his approach and stood at a slight angle to his opponent, with his left shoulder and hips slightly ahead of those on his right. The sword pointed to the ground slightly behind him. His eyes and tone demanded a response. A menacing smile stretched across his face.

"How are you feeling this morning?"

"Strong," Andrew replied, not the least bit intimidated by the aggressive approach of Lawrence. Although his body appeared relaxed, it was anything but. His muscles were poised and ready for action. All it took to set them in motion was the slightest impulse from his ever-alert mind. "And you?"

"Invincible," Lawrence replied as his smirk slowly faded and his muscles started to tense. He raised his sword, and his left hand joined his right with a vicelike grip.

Andrew's eyes scrutinized Lawrence. He studied Lawrence's eyes, his posture, his balance, even the rising and falling of his chest. Every part of Lawrence's body provided Andrew with information that was invaluable in assessing an opponent's strengths and weaknesses. Unfortunately, Lawrence had grown in skill to the point that few weaknesses could be found in his fighting techniques. Andrew could acknowledge without fear or damaged pride that Lawrence was nearly his equal on the battlefield—the key word being *nearly*.

The two men slowly circled each other, one man trying to get a stronger position, the other trying to thwart those efforts. Their feet constantly felt the ground, feeding their brains with the information that was necessary for them to maintain ideal balance on the rolling, somewhat rocky terrain. Their brains compared the weight of their swords to the strength of their muscles, calculating their best and quickest moves and reflexes. Their hearts beat a little quicker, feeding blood to the massive muscles in preparation of the melee. Their adrenal glands began pumping out the chemicals that would make them faster, stronger, and more enduring. Their muscles tensed, waiting to leap into action.

"Then let it begin," Andrew commanded and lunged toward Lawrence. Lawrence easily stepped out of Andrew's reach while deflecting away Andrew's weak sword stroke. Andrew backed up a step, and Lawrence quickly went on the offensive with several lunges and sword strokes. Skillfully, Andrew dodged and blocked each stroke. After about twenty seconds, the men paused in their match.

"Surely that is not the limit of your skill," Andrew taunted. "If so, then I have done a poor job of training you."

"On the contrary, I have learned much," Lawrence replied with a menacing grin. He again attacked, this time with more ferocity. The battle raged as both men defended, then attacked. Several times, Andrew managed to break through Lawrence's defenses and either poke or slap him with his sword. They continued for about ten minutes before pausing once again.

"I see that you indeed have learned much," Andrew stated as he caught his breath, though not relaxing completely.

"Evidently not enough," Lawrence replied as he lifted his right hand to a slightly painful point on his left shoulder, then looked at his hand. He wiped his stained hand on his trousers.

"My apologies," Andrew said, noting the injury. "It was not my intention."

"It is nothing but a scratch," Lawrence replied casually. "When I return the favor, know that it is not intentional on my part," he added a bit maliciously.

"Of course not," Andrew replied with a knowing grin. "Your skills have improved greatly; of that there is no doubt. I am confident that you could best any man in the kingdom. There is one last bit of instruction I can give to you, though, and in truth it is something that cannot be learned."

"You must mean confusing your enemy with senseless statements," Lawrence replied, anxious to resume the melee.

"It is this," Andrew said with all seriousness. "You must rely on your reflexes, on your instincts, when in battle. I realize it may sound as though I am stating the obvious, but to truly be the best warrior you can be, your body must work before your mind can think."

"How philosophical," Lawrence responded, not at all impressed.

"Allow me to demonstrate," Andrew said. "Let us pause our contest for a moment. Stand there as we did in the beginning." Lawrence took the same position he had before they started fighting. Andrew moved in front of Lawrence. "Now, block my strike." With great quickness, Andrew swung his sword toward Lawrence. Lawrence easily parried the blow, and their swords met about a foot from Lawrence's midsection. "Good. Now, I want you to close your eyes and keep them closed until I say open them." With a questioning glare, Lawrence obeyed and closed his eyes. Andrew walked around him.

"You should feel the presence of your opponent at all times. Your mind should be anticipating his next move. However, your body must be able to work independently of your mind at the same time. When that happens, your reflexes are taking over. You must be able to give in to those reflexes and not think about them but let them happen." Andrew moved back in front of Lawrence and took a position from which he could attack. "Now open your eyes."

No sooner had the last word escaped Andrew's mouth than he swung his sword at Lawrence in the same manner as but a few moments before. Before he had an opportunity to think, Lawrence's arm lifted his sword and again blocked Andrew's sword, but this time, much farther from his body.

"That is what I am talking about," Andrew said approvingly. "We all have reflexes; this much is true. But the best warriors have reflexes that are much sharper than the average fighter. When are your reactions the quickest? It is when you see something coming at you out of the corner of your eye. It is when you unknowingly touch something that is burning hot and jerk your hand away. Those reflexes are the ones that save your life, and those are the ones you must hone and trust for battle."

"Are we to talk all afternoon, or are we going to finish what we have started?" Lawrence asked menacingly, readying himself to resume the fight.

"If you are in such a hurry for a sound beating, by all means, let us continue," Andrew replied, backing up a couple of steps. "At your leisure."

Lawrence wasted no time in launching another attack. The action was fast and furious. Both warriors floated back and forth between being on the offensive and then being on the defensive. It was like a dance as the men moved in closely, then backed away, twirling and leaping, swords slicing the air in all directions. Both had successful strikes against the other, though none of the strikes were of a dangerous nature. The battle lasted what seemed an eternity to the fighters. Andrew began to realize that Lawrence was no longer a lesser-skilled student but now a true peer of equal, if not greater, skill. Soon, Andrew's left wrist began aching from the workout, it still not having healed 100 percent from the injury received during the Skills Contest. Lawrence noted the weakness and attacked Andrew's left side. Despite his constant attempts to maneuver back to a position of strength, Andrew could not move to a position of offense. Lawrence slowly wore him down until Andrew could no longer protect himself. With a mighty swing, Lawrence jarred Andrew's sword loose, and it fell to the ground several feet away. Immediately Lawrence's sword was at Andrew's neck. Both men stood panting heavily, staring into each other's eyes for several seconds. Slowly, Lawrence lowered his sword and retrieved Andrew's.

"What was that talk about a sound beating?" he asked Andrew slyly as he handed his opponent his sword.

"I was motivating you," Andrew replied with a sheepish grin. "Apparently, it worked."

"Aye, it did," Lawrence agreed, patting Andrew on the shoulder. "It did." Andrew grimaced at the touch of Lawrence's hand. He reached up and rubbed his shoulder and was surprised to see blood on his hand. "Oh, sorry about that," Lawrence said, smiling. "It was not my intention."

"I believe that about as much as I believe you have given up ale," Andrew replied.

"It is about as true," Lawrence answered, still smiling. "Now let the victor buy his opponent a mug of ale for a battle well fought."

"Lead the way," Andrew accepted, and the duo headed for the tavern.

As they neared the outskirts of the village, Andrew caught a glimpse of three men riding out of the village, heading north. He could tell that it was Martin and two of his guards.

"Time for the daily patrol," Andrew murmured to himself, although it was just loud enough for Lawrence to hear.

"Yes, there goes Martin and his boys. Right on schedule. Protecting the kingdom from spies and invasions," Lawrence replied with a semisarcastic tone.

"Has anyone determined why only he patrols the land to the north?" Andrew asked.

"I do not believe anyone has thought of it as enough of a concern to make an inquiry," Lawrence replied. "In fact, there are probably few who even notice or care."

"It is definitely odd," Andrew mused as he watched the men ride from sight.

"Perhaps," Lawrence agreed. "However, I am one of those who does not care. I have other things to harness my attention. Let the captain of the guard do as he wishes. I am going to pay a visit to the blacksmith. He is forging a new sword for me, and I am anxious to see his progress. I shall buy you a mug of ale another time. Would you care to accompany me? Perhaps Heather will be out taking care of some chores," Lawrence said teasingly.

Andrew gave Lawrence a bit of an annoyed smirk but did not reply.

"Come now, Andrew. I have seen you in her company on several occasions, especially since the night you had dinner with her family. A blind man could see that you two enjoy each other's company. Just what may be smoldering there?"

"It would take a lot more heat for anything to smolder right now," Andrew replied casually. "However, should I decide to start a fire, I will certainly let you know."

"You are a tough one to figure out," Lawrence said, shaking his head. "It is obvious that Heather has you in her sights, and any man here would give all he has to be in your position. Yet you remain rather aloof in the matter. How can you not take advantage of her interest?"

"Timing, Lawrence. It is all about timing. Sometimes the most preferred route is not the ideal route. For now, marriage is not the ideal route for me, though it may be the preferred route. There are things that have my attention focused elsewhere right now, things that I must attend to first."

"Such as why Martin patrols the north region?"

"That is part of it."

"What is the rest of it?"

"The time will come when I will tell you the rest of it. I am certain of that. Now is not a good time."

"Clandestine as ever," Lawrence noted aloud, shaking his head again. "I shall hold you to it, MacLean. You will tell me your story, or I will not hold back the next time we joust." Lawrence turned his horse in the direction of the blacksmith's shop. "And I just might romance Heather away from you out of spite."

"You would be wasting your time. She is only interested in gentlemen," Andrew called after Lawrence, who replied only with a wave of his hand over his shoulder.

Andrew nudged Annon and tugged on the reins to turn the horse in the direction in which Martin and his cohorts had disappeared. After traveling several hundred yards, Andrew caught sight of the trio ahead of him. He slowed Annon enough so that he would not gain any distance on those whom he followed. Fortunately, this road was somewhat winding, and the forest encroached upon it rather closely, thereby aiding Andrew's attempts to remain undetected. It was not a road upon which Andrew had traveled for any extensive length, and despite his urge to survey his surroundings, he kept his attention focused on the road and riders ahead.

Two hours later, the terrain began to transform from rolling hills and forest to a wide-open plain. This was not good, as Andrew would become exposed, and the chances of him being seen would rise dramatically. As he approached the last vestige of cover, comprised of a grove of small trees at the edge of a forest, Andrew reigned Annon to a stop. He could still see Martin and his two men, who were nearly five hundred yards away. They had stopped, and for a moment, Andrew was certain he had somehow been spotted. However, the men did not turn in his direction. Instead, Martin's companions dismounted. Andrew could not be completely sure of what they were doing; however, it appeared that they were driving a stake into the ground. After several minutes, the two men pulled themselves up upon their horses and continued along their original path. Andrew waited in place for about ten minutes. Then, curiosity getting the best of him, he prodded Annon in the ribs and set out to see what the men had been up to.

As he approached the area where the men had stopped, Andrew could see that it was a sign that the men had constructed.

It was rather simple in nature, with one board driven into the ground and several other boards nailed to it horizontally. Although the design of the sign was simple and unimpressive, the message was quite bold: "Danger. Area infected with deadly plague. Do not enter." A skull had been painted on the sign to enforce the warning. Andrew looked down the road, but Martin and his men were nowhere in sight. If the area was plague infested, why would they continue? He was tempted to continue along the road, but he decided that he had pressed his fortune enough for the day and headed back home.

It took nearly three hours for Andrew to reach the village. He had purposely stretched his trip back in order to allow him time to reflect without distraction on the events of the past few days and weeks. His after-dinner conversation with Carl Bergman the other evening had given him much to consider. Had Talbot truly ordered the execution of the three elders so many years ago? Did he really have the shield? There was no question that Talbot had gone to great lengths over the years to hide something—and what else could it be? Andrew knew that he had to sneak into the lower levels of the castle and look around for himself. There still had to exist clues that would shine light on the darkness that continued to cloak his quest.

Chapter 25

T he note read: "Meet me in the third-floor library after the sun
sets this evening." The signature at the bottom was that of
Marie. Andrew had discovered the piece of paper on his bed upon
returning to his room in the castle. Instead of returning to his
room directly after his ride, Andrew had occupied himself for the
remainder of the afternoon taking care of a few of his rather
mundane but necessary work responsibilities. He looked out the
window in the bathroom and saw that the sun was nearing the
end of its daily trek. As part of his daily routine, Andrew walked
over to the fireplace and checked to see if the sword was still in
place. Satisfied that his prize was undisturbed, he returned to the
bathroom and washed off the little grime that had accumulated
on his face and arms from his earlier activities and changed into
some clean clothes. By now, the sun had nearly disappeared from
sight, and Andrew made his way to the secretive meeting.

Marie was already in the library when Andrew passed through
the doorway.

"Your message was certainly short and vague," Andrew said
as he walked over to the table where Marie was sitting, reading a
book. "I was not sure how to dress."

Marie looked up as he approached, and Andrew could see the
excitement in her eyes. "If you would, please close the door," she
instructed without responding to his statement. With a
questioning glance at Marie, Andrew complied with her

direction. His curiosity was piqued, to say the least. He returned to the table and sat beside her. Sitting on the table beside the book was the piece of paper she had used several days before to copy the markings on the sword. Below the markings was additional writing.

"I see you have been busy," Andrew noted, nodding toward the piece of paper.

"I have figured out what the markings are!" she exclaimed, her eyes gleaming with excitement.

"You have?" Andrew replied in excited astonishment. "Why am I not surprised? How did you figure it out?"

"In truth, I had help," she admitted. Seeing a look of concern cross Andrew's face, she quickly added, "Oh, but I did not reveal where I got the symbols. Your secret is still safe. I have not told anyone."

"Good," Andrew said, still not 100 percent reassured. "Please continue."

"Like you, I was completely baffled by the markings when I first saw them. I had never seen anything like them, and believe me, I have read and studied many books and subjects over the years. The more I looked at the markings, the more I was inclined to believe that they were more than likely words. Therefore, I searched the libraries for books on different languages. I found several books in other languages, but none seemed to resemble these markings much at all. I felt that I had exhausted all my resources, and the only thing I could do was inquire of someone who was more educated than myself. Therefore, I paid a visit to Joseph."

"What did you tell him?" Andrew asked suspiciously.

"I showed him the piece of paper on which I had copied the markings from the sword. I told him that I had seen these symbols in an old book and was wondering if he knew what they were. After a few moments of deep thought, he disappeared into one of his private study rooms, and when he came out, he had a book with him. It was an old book, well-worn and ready to fall apart.

He opened the book, and it was full of symbols resembling those on the sword. My theory was correct; the markings were words from another language. It is an old language and has never been spoken in or near this region. Unfortunately, neither Joseph nor I were able to decipher the words. There was no key available for translation. Joseph then suggested that I send the piece of paper to an acquaintance of his in Hambersham who is a scholar and expert in linguistics. Hambersham is a large borough about two days' ride west of here. In secrecy, I dispatched my most trusted and loyal aide to find this man and see if he could provide a translation of the words. Just this afternoon, my aide returned, successful in his charge." Marie paused to catch her breath. She took the piece of paper and set it on the table in front of Andrew, where he could plainly see it. Andrew reached out and picked up the piece of paper and read what was written. There was a phrase written directly under the strange symbols and below, the phrase appeared to be an alphanumeric code of some type.

"'Sword of the spirit,'" Andrew said, reading the first line. "Sword of the spirit," he repeated softly, entranced in thought.

"What do you think that could mean?" Marie asked with her eyebrows furrowed.

"I am not certain," Andrew replied. "The legend surrounding the armor speaks of a spirit of wisdom that was imbued upon the sword by its craftsman. However, I do not subscribe to such fairy tales. Inanimate objects cannot possess or be possessed by spirits or souls or the like. Perhaps King DuFay was known as a *spirit* or *spirited* in tribute to his courage or boldness, and the writing was meant to identify the sword as his."

"Perhaps, but it would strike me odd that the blacksmith who forged this sword would place a nickname on it instead of the name of his king. Evidently, the smith had a great love and respect for his king."

"I cannot disagree with that thinking," Andrew answered, still in thought. "What about the rest of this?" he asked, moving to the second line of writing. What does *eph617* mean?"

"I am completely mystified by that," Marie admitted. "Perhaps it refers to a date?"

"Possibly," Andrew replied. "Did the translator offer any other information?"

"None," Marie replied. "My aide said that a helper took the paper back to the translator and returned it not long thereafter. He never saw the translator in person."

"You would think that this translator would have provided some indication as to what language this is," Andrew said as he pointed to the original symbols. "That information might be of some importance."

"I could send my aide back and have him inquire," Marie offered.

"That may be a good idea. Perhaps in another day or two, we will do that." Andrew drifted off into deep reflection, staring at the piece of paper he still held in his hand. After nearly a minute of silence, he looked to make sure the door was closed and turned to Marie.

"There is something I must do," he said in a somewhat hushed tone, as if fearing he would be overheard by someone passing the room. "I must search the lower levels, the ones your father had blockaded. I cannot help but think there is something worth learning in the bowels of this castle."

"What moves you to believe there is something here that would shed light on the sword or the mystery behind it?" Marie inquired.

Andrew hesitated for a moment. He struggled with how much to tell Marie. He did not want to tell her about his conversation with Carl, lest his revelation somehow put the man in danger. Yet he knew that Marie was extremely perceptive, and he could not fool her by fabricating facts. Considering how much she already knew and how she was now somewhat of a partner with him, he knew he would feel guilty by not telling her the truth.

"I spoke with someone recently who knows of the DuFay legend," Andrew began. "You will understand if I do not reveal his name." Marie nodded, and Andrew continued. "This man has significant knowledge of this land and its history. He knows much about the castle and the secrets it holds. He also knows that some years ago, the DuFay shield was found here. He saw it himself. Through questionable circumstances," Andrew said, trying to be as careful as possible, "the shield disappeared. This man is convinced that DuFay himself once ruled this land, from this very spot. And I am convinced that this man was telling the truth."

"I see," Marie replied, deep in thought. "If this was indeed the DuFay castle, I fail to see how my father did not discover that during his excavation of the ruins and construction of the new castle." Andrew did not reply as Marie looked at him as though she were expecting him to respond. Andrew said nothing, but his eyes were not silent.

"You believe my father knows," Marie deduced from Andrew's silence.

"I believe he knows," Andrew admitted.

"Yet I have seen nothing in this castle that even alludes to the DuFay line in the least way," Marie said. "I have looked most carefully since you first revealed that name to me, hoping to find something to help you solve your mystery. One would think that with a king so great, there would be some evidence of him and his reign."

"Yes, one would think so," Andrew agreed. "Of course, if someone were to gather together and hide all such evidence—" he continued, leaving the thought unfinished.

"But why would my father do that?" Marie asked.

"Perhaps he knew of the legend and was on his own quest," Andrew offered. "It could be that he wanted to keep it a secret and therefore removed all references to DuFay from the castle. You admitted that when you were young, your father had a gate installed to prevent you from going into the lower levels and exploring. Is it not possible that his motivation for barring the lower levels extended to keeping others out, and not just yourself?"

"I would have to admit that possibility," Marie replied.

"You also told me once that during your explorations, you discovered numerous items, such as books, art, weaponry, and armor. Do you believe your father would leave items of such historical value locked away for no one to see and study?"

"To do so would certainly appear odd," Marie admitted, her mind whirling. She tried to envision her long-ago escapades into the depths of the castle. Try as she might, she could not recall specific details of what she saw. Andrew continued.

"What motivation could there be for hiding these things, leaving them to be untouched and unseen for years upon end? They would certainly have historical value and undoubtedly monetary value. If these items are still down there, the monetary value is obviously not an issue. So why would a person want to hide items of the past?"

"To prevent others from learning of the past," Marie concluded.

"Precisely," Andrew said. "Therefore, I believe that whatever is down there does have historical value and could very well provide information as to the history and purpose of the armor and who the rightful heir is. It could mean an end to my seemingly endless quest. Now you understand why I must go there."

"My father has made it very clear that no one is to venture beyond the gate," Marie informed Andrew. "If you were discovered, it would not go well for you."

"It is a risk I must brave. I have run out of alternatives."

"How do you plan to get by the gate?" Marie asked. "It is quite solid and would take a team of horses to pull down."

"One does not need a team of horses when one has a key." Andrew smiled as he pulled the key out of his tunic.

"I would wonder where you got that key; however, I recall you spending an evening not too long ago at the home of the blacksmith who forged the gate himself," Marie said with a knowing smirk.

"I do not believe it would be appropriate for me to reveal just how this key fell into my possession," Andrew replied. "If it was given to me by someone, then that person would know much trouble if my intrusion into the forbidden area and the key were discovered."

"I understand," Marie said. "Speaking of intruding into forbidden areas, when do we go?"

"We?" Andrew repeated. "I believe I should take this risk on my own. It would be best if you did not accompany me."

"On the contrary, I believe it would be best if I did accompany you," Marie countered. "I have been down those corridors and could help guide you. And if we happened to be discovered, it would be less likely that you were accused of spying should I be in your company. I believe it would not be too difficult for me to talk our way out of trouble should we be found out. Therefore, I am going, and I do not believe the subject requires further discussion."

"I see," Andrew responded. "How easy would it be for the king's daughter, his one and only child, to slip away from ever-watchful eyes in order to scurry around in dark, damp passageways for several hours? Would your absence not cause some alarm?"

"Andrew, do you really believe it would be the least bit difficult for me to disappear for a few hours without causing any suspicion or alarm? Trust me, it would be no great task. In any event, I doubt that you had planned to set off in exploration during the middle of the day. A midnight investigation, when everyone is sleeping, would likely be best. Was that not your plan?" Marie looked at Andrew with a somewhat smug expression, as if she had just solved some great mystery. It was a look Marie had displayed on several occasions, and it was a look that irritated Andrew every time.

"It is an option," Andrew replied a bit caustically. "I believe in considering and maintaining different options. For example, I could also go during the middle of the day, and my absence would not raise a single eyebrow. It would be quite simple to slip down the corridor unseen. No one would know that I was down there. I could go tonight, I could go tomorrow, or I could go three days hence. My flexibility in the matter is great."

"That it is," Marie replied. "However, it would likely shorten your time down there and reduce your chances of being caught if you were to choose a time when I could accompany you. I could take you to the rooms where I discovered all those relics, and you would not waste your time looking through empty chambers. I am certain you would prefer to learn as much as you can as quickly as you can and solve this mystery of yours as soon as possible."

"Very well," Andrew conceded, tired of their banter. "Meet me at the head of the passage leading to the lower levels tomorrow night after the second changing of the guards. Dress warmly. Bring along some paper and a pen in case we run across more strange symbols that must be interpreted. Be absolutely certain that no one sees you. Do not carry even the smallest of candles with you. If you are seen by anyone, you must return to your room and give no indication of where you were going. Do you understand?"

"Yes, I understand," Marie answered excitedly. "I will ensure that I remain unseen."

"I will wait for you only a short time; therefore, do not tarry. If I do not see you soon after the shift change, I will proceed without you."

"Fair enough," Marie acknowledged.

"Then I will see you tomorrow night," Andrew said as he stood up. He indicated the piece of paper on the table. "You did well in your research and figuring out the strange writing. I am impressed."

"Thank you," Marie replied politely. "There is still the mystery of the second line to resolve. I will continue to work on it."

"I would be surprised if you did not find the answer, and soon," Andrew added as he turned to leave the room. Before he got to the door, he hesitated as a thought crossed his mind. He turned back to Marie.

"Tell me, what do you know about the plague to the north?"

"Plague? What plague?" Marie asked with mixed curiosity and concern.

"The plague that infects the land to the north, about two or so hours from here. Do you not know of it?"

"I have heard of no plague," Marie replied, her concern deepening. "What type of plague is it?"

"I do not know," Andrew answered. "I was hoping you could tell me."

"This is rather disconcerting, to say the least," Marie said. "If there was a plague anywhere near here, I am sure it would be common knowledge. I have heard no talk of a plague. Where did you hear of it?"

"I did not hear of it," Andrew replied. "I saw a sign along a road that warned of a plague. I did not see anyone around of whom I could make any inquiries."

"A sign?" Marie asked. "What kind of sign? What did it say? Where did you see it?"

"It was a rather rudimentary sign. It simply warned of a deadly plague and for travelers to not venture any farther. A skull was painted on it to better make the point. It is just about two hours from here to the north along the main road, not far from where the forest ends and the plains begin."

"How odd," Marie mused. "There are no significant dwellings or towns for at least two, maybe three days' ride to the north, nor is wildlife exactly abundant in that area. There is nothing there to be infected."

"Apparently someone believes there is," Andrew stated. "The sign appeared to have been erected not too long ago." He did not want to tell Marie that it was Martin who had put up the sign. His instincts told him to keep that information to himself for the time being.

"I shall ask my father about it first thing in the morning," Marie informed Andrew. "He will certainly send someone to learn the truth as to whether there is indeed a plague or not."

"Let us hope it is some prank and nothing more," Andrew said. He once again turned to leave the room. "Good night."

"Good night," Marie replied and watched him leave.

Chapter 26

The pale radiance of the full moon joined with the fluttering flames of four lonely candles to cast a gloomy mood inside the vestibule of the resting castle. Silence engulfed nearly every corridor and every chamber of the stronghold as its inhabitants slumbered with fanciful visions fluttering behind their sleeping eyes. The faint protest of an opening door called out into the dark silence, followed by the echoing of soft footsteps. Four men entered the castle and stopped in the middle of the large vestibule, allowing silence to momentarily return to the darkened domicile. Within a few minutes, four other men entered the vestibule from inside the castle, each from a different corridor, and joined them. There were a few moments of brief, hushed conversation. The newcomers separated and disappeared down the four corridors from which the other men had emerged, while the second group left the castle. Soon all footsteps faded into the night. Cautiously, a lone figure slid out of a side room and silently glided across the stone floor where the guards had met. The figure paused in the shadows, peering deep into the darkness and silence with its eyes and ears. Satisfied that it was alone, the figure stole down a little-used, often-ignored corridor and stopped after about twenty feet.

"Andrew, are you here?" Marie called out in a barely audible whisper.

"I had a feeling you would be quite punctual," a hushed voice called back in answer. A yellowish glow appeared about twenty more feet down the corridor. It offered just enough light for Marie to see Andrew's darkly dressed form.

"I have been waiting for no less than an eternity for the guards to change," Marie replied. "I was greatly tempted to get here some time ago and just wait for you." She looked at the light in Andrew's hand. "That is a strange lantern you have there. Where did you find it?"

"I made it," Andrew replied. "I took a normal lantern and simply inserted extra thin panels of steel in three of the four sides. The panels limit the shining of the light to one direction. The interior sides of the panels are polished rather well and help reflect the light. Hopefully, this will reduce the chance of someone seeing our lantern from behind. It also helps brighten our intended path. I kept it covered with a small, dark cloak until you arrived."

"Impressive," Marie said. "At least you can see where you are going."

"Do not worry. I brought one for you," Andrew informed her as he handed a second lantern to her. He took the candle out of his and lit the one in her lantern. "Until we get a good distance from this entrance, keep the lantern pointed down the corridor. We would not want to accidentally reveal our presence should one of the guards happen to walk close by in the next few minutes. Are you ready?"

"Lead the way," Marie replied, suppressing the excitement and tinge of fear that filled her. She was suddenly cast into the past, and instead of a full-grown woman, she was a young, brave girl venturing into the dark unknown. Andrew turned and continued down the corridor.

"What did your father say about the plague?" Andrew asked quietly. He had barely been able to curtail his curiosity all day.

"To my surprise, he knew about it," Marie answered. "I cannot imagine him knowing and not telling me. He said that it slipped his mind, but nothing slips my father's mind. He said that a couple of days ago, Martin came to him after one of his scouting patrols and reported there were rumors of a plague to the north. My father instructed him to erect a sign warning of the plague and to send patrols farther north to verify the rumors. There has been no additional word since then."

"Hmm," Andrew mused to himself. "Interesting." They continued for another twenty yards before encountering the iron gate that barricaded further progress. Andrew held the lantern in his left hand and with his right retrieved from his tunic the key given to him by Carl Bergman. He inserted the key in the lock and with little effort unlocked the gate.

"That is strange," Andrew mused as the gate swung open with only the hint of a squeak of protest.

"Strange?" Marie echoed. "Why is it strange that a key meant to unlock a gate actually unlocks the gate? Were you expecting something different?"

"I am surprised at the ease with which the gate opened," Andrew answered. "You would think that after all of these years down in this damp corridor, the lock would have corroded a small bit and would have been more difficult to open. Yet this lock opened with only a small effort, as if it has been in constant use and has not had the opportunity to become even the least bit decayed."

"That is definitely interesting," Marie replied, peering at the lock and gate. "As far as I know, only you and my father have a key. Then again, it is certainly possible that more keys were made and someone else has been coming down here," she offered in conjecture.

Andrew took his lantern and inspected the lock more closely. "The person who gave me this key did not mention any other stray keys wandering around. Perhaps your father continues to make routine visits to the depths of the castle."

"That would have to be the most likely scenario," Marie agreed. "But for what purpose?"

"I would venture the very same purpose that has brought us down here," Andrew replied. "The search for answers."

He directed the light to the floor of the corridor immediately in front of the gate. He examined the floor and the walls, then the gate once again. "I do not see immediate evidence that anyone has passed this way in the recent past," he said. "Not that someone's passage would necessarily be readily evident though. We shall proceed but with much caution." After Marie stepped through the gate, Andrew closed and locked it. "Would you prefer leaving it open so we may be followed?" Andrew asked in response to Marie's questioning glance.

"Of course not," she replied. "It will be spooky enough down here without having to worry about someone sneaking up on us."

The duo slowly proceeded down the damp, daunting corridor as their lanterns chased away the darkness in front of them. The floor of the corridor was rather smooth, giving evidence of much usage in its past. Empty yet ornate sconces dotted both sides of the corridor, having last yielded illuminating flames many, many decades ago. The walls of the corridor were otherwise unmarked and quite plain. It was not long before they came upon the first room. A black doorway interrupted the monotonous wall on the right. Andrew stood in the doorway and directed his lantern into the room. It was empty. The room was quite small, perhaps fifteen feet square.

"As I recall," Marie said, still in a hushed voice, "the majority of the rooms down here are rather small and mostly empty. I believe other than a few scattered and broken pieces of furniture, there was nothing of note in them. There are a couple of larger rooms somewhere down here, and those are the rooms where I saw everything."

With a final cursory glance at the room, Andrew withdrew the lantern and continued down the hallway. True to Marie's memory, they quickly came across several other rooms that were quite similar to the first. None held anything of interest. They came to an intersection where they were forced to make a decision as to whether to go to their right or go to their left.

"What do you think?" Andrew asked as he shone the light

from his lantern down each corridor. The light pierced the darkness for less than three dozen feet before being completely engulfed by blackness. "Does your memory prompt you one way or the other?" Andrew asked.

Marie looked to the right, peering deeply into the darkness, then looked down the corridor to the left. She concentrated deeply, striving to recall her ventures as a child through the lonely halls. She closed her eyes for a moment, trying to picture in her mind her childhood explorations.

"I can remember different rooms, but I cannot remember exactly where they are. I am afraid I do not know in which direction to go," Marie replied, disappointed in her failed memory.

"In that case, it was a good thing I elected to bring this," Andrew said and pulled a piece of paper from under his cloak. As he opened it, Marie could see that it was a rather rudimentary map of the lower levels.

"A map? And just where might that have come from?" Marie demanded, taken completely by surprise.

"I would that I could tell you, but again, I must keep my source in confidence," Andrew answered, bemused that he had been able to surprise Marie.

"You and this secret source of yours," she retorted. "As though it would take a genius to figure out who it is. You have spent a good bit of time over at the Bergman residence in recent days, have you not? You would not have me think all that time was spent in the company of Heather and Heather alone?"

"Of course not," Andrew answered. "Not if it would upset you," he added with a smirk.

"I can think of no reason why that would upset me," Marie copped innocently. "The Bergmans are a nice, pleasant family. I can understand perfectly well why a bachelor would spend so much time over there."

"You may think what you will," Andrew replied obscurely. "I know and have spent time around many people in this area.

Remember, the people of this land were here long before you, your father, and his entourage appeared. This castle and its secrets are more widely known than you or your father may otherwise believe."

"I never thought of it that way, but you are likely correct," Marie answered. "I must have thought that since the castle was practically in ruins when we arrived, it had been abandoned and forgotten for generations. I never considered that these people, or at least some of them, could have histories here for even more generations than that." She paused for a second, then changed the subject back to the map. "Why did you not simply consult the map to begin with rather than asking me which way to go?"

"You have firsthand knowledge of these passages. I wanted to see how much you could remember," Andrew answered. "According to the map, there are a few larger rooms down the corridor to the left. Perhaps those are the rooms that we seek. Let us explore those first."

Without argument, Marie followed Andrew as he turned and walked down the indicated corridor. They walked slowly and carefully, examining the surrounding walls and the floor before them as they proceeded deeper into the bowels of the castle. An occasional drip of water striking the stone floor somewhere within the darkness provided the only sound other than the soft scuffle of their feather-light footsteps. They encountered few cobwebs stretching across the passages, as this dark, damp atmosphere did not exactly provide a smorgasbord of prey for spiders. The deeper they probed into the darkness, the mustier the air became. There was the unmistakable essence of age that became stronger with every step they took. They passed several rooms without doors that held nothing of interest but soon came upon four doors that were closed about halfway. The doors were hinged so that they swung out into the corridor to open. The five-foot-tall doors were made of wood, and each had in its midsection an iron bar, four inches wide and nearly a half-inch thick, that extended beyond the left edge of the door about six inches.

Attached to the stone wall to the left of the doors were iron cleats. The bars on the doors were attached with hinges, and it was obvious that they served as locks for the doors.

"I assume that these were quarters for people who had been somewhat naughty," Andrew surmised as he fully opened the closest door. Inside the ten-foot-by-ten-foot room was what appeared to be the remnants of a rudimentary cot, although as broken as it was, it could have easily been nothing more than a pile of kindling for a fire. Though neither numerous in number nor impressive in design, there were various markings etched into the walls, born of the boredom thrust upon those sentenced here for their unlawful deeds. "Not very ornate, to say the least."

Marie looked upon the room with disgust. "No person deserves to be locked away in the damp darkness like this, no matter what he has done. This is nothing more than brutish barbarianism."

"I saw no other prison facilities in or around the castle," Andrew said as he withdrew his head from the cruel chamber. "What is done with those who break the law in your father's kingdom?"

"Naturally, it depends on the nature of the crime. If a person murders another, then the murderer has his life taken from him. If a person steals, he is required to pay back twice what he stole, or he must serve his victim until he works out his debt. There is also public humiliation for lesser crimes, which can also be a great deterrent. Keeping a person locked away is not something needed around here very often."

"I shall most certainly watch my step so as not to resurrect this miserable place," Andrew said jokingly. "It appears that it could be quite lonely."

"Do not worry," Marie replied in kind. "If you manage to commit such a dastardly crime, I shall still come to visit you from time to time. And if you are kind enough to me, I may even be persuaded to show you a secret way out."

"A secret way out?" Andrew repeated. "You could not

remember where the room full of artifacts is located, but you can remember a secret way out? What a selective memory you must have."

"Comments such as that seem to fog my memory, so you best hope you are not cast away down here," Marie replied slyly as she turned and took the lead down the corridor.

"My memory is neither selective nor fogged, and as I recall, you told me previously that you knew of no other way into these lower levels," Andrew said as he followed Marie. "Am I to suppose that the memory of this secret way out just suddenly came to you?"

"Of course not," Marie replied. "You will recall that when we had that conversation, you were all but a stranger to me, and I knew nothing of your plans and intentions. It would have been nothing less than complete foolishness to tell you of the secret passage."

"That would make sense," Andrew admitted. "Sometimes it seems that it was only a couple of days ago that I arrived here."

The explorers had walked perhaps another thirty yards when they encountered a set of closed double doors. These doors were about six and a half feet tall, four feet wide, and appeared to be quite sturdy. Unlike the doors of the prison cells, these doors were designed to open into the room behind them. Iron plates decorated the exterior of the doors and held together the individual wooden slats that comprised the doors. Two large iron sconces hung to the stone walls outside of the doors, and long-extinct wooden torches sat in their grasps. A third, smaller sconce protruded from above the doorway.

"I remember these doors!" Marie exclaimed as she ran her hands over the ages-old wood. "Yes, I distinctly remember these doors. This is the room where I saw everything." Her heart began to race as memories flooded her mind. She was once again a little girl, exploring the dark unknown, facing a door that had to be opened.

"Then let us waste no more time and go in," Andrew said as

he pushed on the doors. However, the sturdy barriers failed to yield to his hand. He pushed a little harder but achieved no more positive results. He handed his lantern to Marie and shoved on the door with both hands, putting the fullness of his body weight behind him, but the stubborn doors did not budge.

"I believe we have encountered a small setback," Andrew said as he examined the boundaries of the doors. There were no visible handles or knobs with which to open them.

"Set the lanterns on the ground and help me push on the door," Andrew said to Marie.

"I think not," Marie replied. "Those doors look rather filthy. Perhaps if you stood back a few steps and lunged at the door, you could force it open," Marie suggested.

Andrew looked at her for a moment, then took two steps back, which was all the narrow corridor would allow. He rushed forward and planted his shoulder against the door, yet it did not move an inch. The sturdiness of the door told him it would be a waste of energy to continue such an effort.

"Apparently what is behind those doors shall remain a secret for now," Andrew said as he reached for his lantern.

"I have an idea," Marie said. She pointed up to the sconce above the doors. "Reach up and pull down on the sconce. Perhaps it will unlock the doors."

Andrew looked up at the sconce and then back at Marie. Having nothing to lose by trying, he reached up and pulled the metal sconce down. To his amazement, he heard the scraping of metal against metal on the other side of the door. With a shove, the doors swung inward without further resistance. He looked at Marie, and the light from the lanterns revealed a mischievous grin on her face.

"Why do I feel your suggestion was more than a desperate guess?" Andrew asked as she handed him his lantern.

"It was odd how I suddenly remembered that," she replied, "just after your brute force failed. How is your shoulder, by the way?"

"My shoulder is fine," he answered. "Payback for the map thing?" he asked.

"Payback for the map thing," she confirmed with a smile.

Andrew shook his head and entered the room. The combined light from the two lanterns illuminated a room cluttered with many items of furniture, mostly chairs and tables. The walls in this room, like the walls of the corridors, held many iron brackets for torches. A chandelier of melted candles hung from the ceiling, candles that had burned out their useful lives many decades, if not centuries, ago. Two large wooden shelving units, five feet wide and seven feet tall, decorated the rear wall. The shelves were barren. There was nothing in this room that appeared to have any great value and nothing in the room indicated that it had ever been a place of importance.

"I do not understand," Marie said as she looked around the room dumbfounded. "I am certain this is the room. But it is all different. Everything is different."

"You are certain this is the room you are thinking about?"

"I am very certain," Marie replied, looking from wall to wall.

"What do you remember of this room?" Andrew asked as he walked to the far end, which was about fifty feet from the main entryway.

"I do not remember specifics," Marie answered as she looked around the room. "It is but a pale vision in my mind."

"Do you remember what used to be in here?"

"Unfortunately, no," Marie replied dejectedly. "Perhaps some furniture, perhaps some wooden crates. I just do not know."

"It must have housed something of importance; otherwise, why the sturdy doors and clandestine opening mechanism?" Andrew pondered. "What importance could this room have had so many years ago, way down here beneath the castle? So far, all rooms have been sparse and simple. What was this room meant to hide?"

The duo continued looking around the room. After a few minutes, Andrew stopped and set his lantern on a table that appeared to still have some strength to it. He pulled the map from his tunic and laid it on the table so both he and Marie could see it.

"We are in this room," he informed Marie, pointing to a large square on the map. "This is the largest room indicated on the map. There are just a few more rooms down this corridor, and then the map ends. Let us explore as far as the map goes and then come back here and decide how to proceed."

Marie agreed with Andrew's suggestion, and they left the room, being sure not to close the doors behind them. They followed the corridor for another thirty yards before encountering the next room. It was like many others they had already investigated: small and sparse. They encountered two more closed doors before the corridor branched to the left. Andrew pushed on the door to his right, and it yielded with but a little resistance. Again, the room did not have much to offer. He then turned his attention to the room on the left side of the corridor. The door to this room was partially open. He pushed it fully open and peered into the darkness. Although his lantern revealed nothing of interest, Andrew walked into the room and around its perimeter. Satisfied that the room was nothing more than a vacant space, he moved back into the corridor.

"Anything?" Marie asked hopefully.

"Nothing," Andrew answered as he peered toward the turn in the corridor. "Let us explore farther down the corridor."

The twosome continued for another few minutes, but there were no more rooms, and knowing that their time was limited, Andrew led Marie back down the hall. When they were about sixty feet from the large room that had been resistant to their entry, Andrew suddenly stopped. Marie nearly ran into him.

"What is it?" she asked quietly, afraid that he had heard or seen something ominous. He backed up a couple of steps and turned his lantern to the wall on his left.

"Shine your lantern on this wall," he directed, and she complied. He looked the wall up and down, then took several backward steps down the corridor. "No, stay there and keep your lantern on the wall," he directed as Marie moved as if to follow him. She looked at him curiously and then followed his intense gaze. She could see nothing of interest.

"What are you looking at?" she asked. "It is but a wall."

"I think it is more than that," Andrew answered. "Here, trade places with me." He moved forward, and she moved back to where he had been standing. "Now look right here," he instructed, pointing to an area on the wall. "Now look a few feet to the right and left." She complied but could not see whatever it was that he was seeing. "Do you see?"

"I see very well," Marie replied, "but evidently, I do not see what you seem to see. What has captured your interest?"

"There is something not right with the wall in this area," he replied, running his hand over its surface. "It is difficult to see, but if you look closely enough, you can tell that the wall bends in ever so slightly right here and then returns to its correct position a couple of feet over here."

"I do not see—" Marie began, but just then Andrew shifted his lantern, and she saw the wall in a different light. "Wait, wait, you are right. I see what you are saying." She moved over to the wall. "There is definitely an indentation in this section of the wall."

Andrew bent down and examined the floor. "Look," he said, pointing to the floor. "You can see how the floor in the middle of the corridor has been worn slightly smoother than at the edges of the corridor. That is from people walking up and down the corridor, of course. But look right here where the indentation is in the wall. The worn area of the floor extends right to the wall, as if it went through the wall itself."

"How can that be?" Marie asked, then answered her own question. "Because there used to be a door here. It must have been enclosed a long time ago."

"And what a fantastic job it was," Andrew noted as he stood again. "You cannot tell of the work unless you see the wall from the right angle with the right lighting. Somebody did a great work of concealment here."

"I wonder what is beyond that wall," Marie contemplated.

"The map shows no room at this particular point," Andrew said as he looked at the parchment he had pulled from his tunic. "Let us go back to the room just down the hall and examine it a little more closely." He led the way down the hall, with Marie right on his heels.

"Now, this is the room we are now in," Andrew informed Marie as he pointed to the drawn square on the map. "These three squares are the rooms we just visited," he added as he pointed to the appropriate boxes. "There are no other rooms shown to be in this corridor. We have visited four rooms, and there are four indicated on the map."

"Perhaps the person who drew this map had no knowledge of the hidden room," Marie suggested.

"Yes, that could very well be. We could very easily have missed it ourselves. I do know that the person who drew this map had firsthand knowledge of this place and had spent much time down here. It could be that he did know of the room but elected to not include it on the map."

"Why would he do that?" Marie inquired.

"To hide it from others should his map be stolen or lost."

"Then that would indicate something of significant importance lies behind that wall," Marie stated. "Of course, to be certain, you could always ask the person who gave you the map to begin with."

"Yes, that is true," Andrew agreed. "But he is not here, and my curiosity is not a patient partner. My instincts tell me there must be another way into that room. We just have to use our brains and figure out where it is."

"That suspected doorway is not far from this room," Marie said, her mind turning over the facts they had in hand. "Maybe sixty feet. The wall of this room extends about thirty-five feet from the door in that direction. It is likely that these two rooms share a common wall."

"For all we know, there could be ten or twenty feet of rock and earth between the two walls," Andrew stated.

Marie ignored his pessimism. "This room was meant to be somewhat secure, considering the concealment of the opening device for the doors. That would indicate this room was of some importance at one time," Marie continued. "Perhaps the two rooms are connected somehow."

"I see no doors along that wall," Andrew said as he turned his attention away from the map.

"Then again, you nearly did not see what we suspect to have been a doorway at one time in the corridor," Marie reminded him.

"Then let us look more closely at the wall," Andrew said as he picked up his lantern and headed over to the end of the room. He began at the edge of the wall closest to the corridor and held the lantern within a foot of the wall as he ran his hands over the stone blocks. He could see no evidence of an existing or former doorway. Marie stood back from the wall, holding her lantern up and looking at the wall from different angles. She moved closer to the wall, then backed away from the wall. She walked toward the end of the wall farthest from the corridor. She looked down along the wall toward Andrew, trying to see if there were any irregular lines. Meanwhile, Andrew looked along the floor to see if what he had spotted in the corridor's floor existed along this wall. He scrutinized every square inch of the wall and saw nothing to indicate any kind of connection with another room.

"I see no signs of passage to another room," Andrew said, disappointed. "Our hidden room theory may just be a figment of our imaginations."

"No, I believe we are correct in that there is a room there," Marie countered. "We just have not found the way into it." She directed her lantern away from the wall and back into the room. "Look at the arrangement of the furniture in this room," she said, shining her lantern around. "Do you see?"

"I see quite well," Andrew replied, mimicking Marie's response from out in the hall several minutes earlier. "The furniture is scattered all over the place, most of it broken beyond recognition. What is your point?"

"What pieces of furniture in here are not damaged and appear to be exactly where they are intended to be?" she asked. Andrew looked around the room, trying to see what she evidently saw, but he saw nothing out of the ordinary. He was about to give in and tell her to make her point when he saw it.

"The shelves," he answered. "Everything else appears to be scattered around and damaged to some degree, but the shelves are not. They are tight against the wall and in rather good condition."

"And does that not appear odd?" Marie asked. "You would think that this room had been ransacked at some time, considering how everything is upended and broken. Look, over there along the far wall, you can see where two other shelving units were knocked over and broken. Yet these two were not. Why?"

"That is a good question," Andrew replied as he moved closer to the shelves. He ran his hands along the side of the shelving unit where it met with the stone wall. He looked down to the ground at the base of the unit. The stone floor was a patchwork of mildew. He wiped the crud away with his hands and moved the lantern closer to the ground. "Look," he said, pointing to the floor. Marie moved closer. After adding the light of her lantern to Andrew's, she could see what he had discovered. There were faint markings etched into the stone floor, as if something heavy had been pulled across the stone numerous times. Andrew stood and grabbed the side of the shelving unit and pulled. At first, nothing happened. He stood to the side of the unit, braced his backside against the wall, and shoved on the edge of the wooden structure. With a creak of protest, it moved. Excited, Andrew pushed even harder, and the unit moved a few more inches. He turned around, grabbed the backside of the unit, placed his left foot against the wall, and pulled. The unit moved another foot, and it was now over twenty-four inches from the wall. Marie moved around to where she could see behind the structure.

"A passage!" she exclaimed. Her light revealed a dark hole in the wall, four feet square. She moved closer. "It turns to the left! Andrew, I believe we have found our secret entrance!"

"There is only one way to find out for sure," he replied, dropping to his hands and knees and crawling into the dark passage. Marie quickly followed, eager to see what secrets lay at the end of the mysterious tunnel.

Chapter 27

T he cool, damp darkness of the secret subterranean passageway made for a most uncomfortable and foreboding atmosphere. The walls were about three feet apart, and the ceiling was four feet above the floor. The claustrophobic nature of the close quarters urged Andrew to move forward quickly; however, his sense of safety and caution kept him at a rather slow and deliberate pace. Several times, Marie's impatience nearly caused her to bump into Andrew.

"Andrew, if you went any slower, you would be moving backward," Marie touted. "We do not have all night, you know."

"Forgive me for exercising a little prudent caution," he replied. "You would rather I rush headlong into the unknown, throwing safety to the side and risking the danger of setting off a trap that would bury us under tons of rock and dirt?"

"Trap?" Marie asked a little nervously. "What do you mean a trap?"

"Obviously, somebody has gone to great lengths to hide something. For all we know, this could be the only access to that something. If so, it would only stand to reason that this passage be protected against unwanted visitors."

"You are just being paranoid," Marie replied, brushing off his explanation. "We have seen nothing down here that has the appearance of a trap."

"That is the beauty of traps," Andrew countered. "They are

designed to be concealed and undetected. If a trap can be detected and avoided, well, it rather defeats the purpose of the trap in the first place. However, if you would prefer to take the lead, throw caution to the wind, and scamper your pretty little princess self into the darkness, I would be more than happy to step aside and let you pass. And when you get trapped behind an impenetrable wall of rock and dirt, I will be sure to let your father know where you are. Now, if that does not sound too inviting, we can do this my way and exercise a little life-preserving care."

"Ha! I knew it!" Marie exclaimed triumphantly.

"You knew what?" Andrew asked, confused and a little perturbed.

"You think I am pretty."

"It was just an expression," Andrew countered casually.

"Oh, so you do not think I am pretty? Then you must find me repulsive."

"I believe *irritating* would be a more appropriate term," Andrew responded. Before Marie could retort, Andrew's lantern illuminated the end of the passageway about ten feet ahead. There were no turns but just what appeared to be a dead end. He continued forward until he came to the far wall and stopped. Marie moved as close to him as possible.

"A dead end?" she asked.

"I do not believe so," Andrew replied, looking at the wall to his left. There was an opening in the wall similar in size to the one that had granted them access to the secret passage. However, it was blocked by a wooden structure on the other side. Andrew surmised that the passageway was not meant to be readily detectable from the secret room either. Marie moved forward until she could see the opening.

"That must lead to the sealed-off room," she asserted. "Do you think we can move whatever is blocking the opening?"

"There is but one way to find out," Andrew answered. He sat upright in the corridor with his back to the wall opposite the opening. He then braced his feet against the wooden barricade and pushed. The barricade did not budge. Andrew repositioned himself to provide as much leverage as possible. He again pushed with his legs. After a few seconds, the obstruction moved several inches. Again, Andrew adjusted his position and pushed as hard as he could. The barrier moved another foot, and the opening was now wide enough for Andrew's torso to fit through. He squeezed through until his back was flush against the wooden object. He braced his hands against the stone wall and pushed. The barricade again moved several more inches. There was now plenty of room for him to maneuver past the obstruction, and he crawled out of the passageway with Marie on his heels. The explorers stood, brushed themselves off, and stared with silent wonder at the awesome sight before them.

The room was nothing less than a museum of antiquities with hundreds, even thousands, of objects filling the space from wall to wall. There were weapons of all sorts. Hundreds of crossbows, swords, lances, maces, axes, shields, and other arms lay about the room, enough to outfit a regiment of soldiers. A host of body armor pieces were stacked against the walls as if lying in wait for their long-lost warriors to return. There were heavy leather vests and armbands, light chain mail vests and breastplates, helmets, arm and leg plates, more than could be counted. Many pieces appeared to be made of, or at least covered with, gold. Along the walls stood dozens of bookshelves filled with hundreds and hundreds of books. Lances with tattered and faded pennants rested against the walls where they had been left many, many years ago. Several decaying tapestries hung from the walls, refusing to succumb to their age and fall to the ground. Dozens of pieces of furniture were scattered around the room, including many heavy, locked chests. Andrew and Marie had found a treasure of untold value.

"Oh Andrew, look at it all!" Marie whispered breathlessly as she marveled at the room. "Just look at it. This is history. Nobody has been in here for hundreds of years. I am afraid to move lest I touch something and break it."

"It is amazing indeed," Andrew agreed, just as awestruck as Marie was. "Simply amazing. Is this what you saw as a child?"

"No, no, I never saw anything like this. I mean, nothing as grandiose as this. This is magnificent. For some reason, it makes me feel small and insignificant."

"Shall we have a look around?" Andrew suggested and moved farther into the room. He stopped by a table upon which several books were stacked and set upright two fallen candleholders. "A little more light would certainly be helpful." He produced two extra candles and placed them firmly in the candleholders. Using the flame from his lantern, Andrew brought to life the candles on the table. The dancing flames brought forth an eerie illumination to the room and cast the far reaches of the space into spectral stirrings.

"Where do we begin?" Marie asked incredulously. "There is so much to see, so much to learn. We could spend a month down here and still not see everything."

"That is the problem. We do not have a month. In fact, I would say we have only a couple of hours before we must return to the main level of the castle, lest dawn breaks and you are missed."

"There is always tomorrow night, and the next night, and the next," Marie said. "It is not as though this place is going anywhere."

"True, but you must understand that despite whatever measures we employ to maintain the secrecy of our explorations, the more often we venture down here, the more likely we will be discovered. It is not a question of whether we would be discovered but one of when we would be discovered. Therefore, we cannot be leisurely in our search. We must move quickly and not be distracted by the wonder of this place."

"Not be distracted?" Marie replied incredulously. "The room is full of nothing but distractions."

"We must stay focused," Andrew replied. "We are looking for ..." Andrew paused. For what exactly were they searching? They already knew DuFay's name. Finding that name tucked away amid the thousands of artifacts would not be surprising and in fact would be expected. The name alone would be of little use. What could possibly be contained in this room that would aid him in his search for the rightful heir to the DuFay lineage? "We are looking for any kind of emblem or family crest that marked the DuFay family," he finished. "I fear it is the only tool that would offer us any aid in finding the DuFay descendant for whom I search. I will work my way around the right side of the room. You work yourself around the left side. We shall meet on the far end, and hopefully one of us will find information of value."

Andrew turned his attention away from Marie and started moving off to his right. Marie stared after him for several seconds, then moved off to her left. Her lantern provided a warm glow to her surroundings, and the flickering flame gave rise to dancing shadows on the objects around her. The sense of awe that had gripped her so tightly immediately upon entry to the room would not leave her. Lightly and with respect, Marie ran her fingers over objects hundreds of years old. It was all so amazing. She fantasized of the time these objects were new and tried to picture the people who had created them, possessed them, and used them every day. A bookcase appeared as the glow of her lantern illuminated the wall to her left. In fact, there were several bookcases containing hundreds of books and parchments. With great gentleness and care, she pulled a book from one of the shelves. The ancient pages protested her intrusion, crinkling as she turned them one by one. She did not know the language in which the book was written, which was disappointing but not unexpected. With just as much care as she had exercised in removing the book, Marie gingerly replaced it. Oh, that she had the time to peruse every book and parchment! Reluctantly, she turned to her right, and at least a dozen life-sized statues leaped out of the darkness. The sculptures represented what appeared to be various people of prominence. Some of the statues were carved from what appeared to be marble, and others from solid wood. All of them were magnificently detailed and ordained with jewelry appearing to be made with gold and precious stones. She lightly ran her hand over the closest figurine, a six-foot tall man exuding much pride and authority. The face was very lifelike and gave testimony to the inordinate skill of the artist. Marie inspected closely the several rings carved on the fingers of this statue. This had apparently been a man of much prestige. She had seen royal rings before, and these were most certainly the rings of royalty. The desire to examine every statue consumed her, but she only gave the others a cursory glance before continuing her search.

Andrew could not suppress a feeling of hopeful anxiety as he walked around the room. There had to be something hidden within this room that would aid him in his quest. It would be unthinkable to make this wondrous discovery, only to leave the room empty-handed. He knew he would come down here time and time again until he had searched every square inch of the room if that was what it took to find the least bit of relevant information, the smallest clue, that could possibly help him discover the identity of the DuFay descendant. Andrew believed firmly that somewhere among all these wondrous things, there had to be something that showed the DuFay family crest. Such a symbol would most likely be depicted on a piece of armament or a painting or tapestry. He tried to focus his search on those types of objects, and there had to be literally hundreds of those types of objects scattered around the room.

After nearly an hour of fruitless searching, Marie ventured upon what appeared to be a box covered with a canvas. She slowly and softly pulled away the canvas and moved her light close to the box. The lantern's twinkling glow chased away the darkness and revealed a box of portraits. There was quite easily a dozen of them in this box alone, and she could tell that there were several other boxes behind this first one. She reached out and touched the frame of the first portrait. It was hand carved and fit for a royal palace. With great caution and gentleness, Marie lifted the first portrait from the box and set it on a table behind her. The portrait was that of a woman, apparently one of much importance, judging by her elegant raiment. Marie retrieved the next portrait, and this one was of a young man, perhaps in his teens. Again, based upon the fine clothing, she judged him to be another person of prominence. Perhaps she was the woman's son, Marie mused. The third portrait was that of an older gentleman with a grand gray beard and piercing blue eyes. There was no doubt that he was an authoritative man, a man of prestige. The artist had captured well the inner power of this man. Marie's hands began to quiver as she wondered if she was staring at the face of Reginald DuFay. She picked up the fourth painting and set it on the table. This one was larger than the first three. While the portraits of the individual people measured probably eighteen by twenty-four inches, this painting was easily thirty inches by thirty-six inches. Upon illuminating the artwork, her eyes widened, and the pace of her heart nearly doubled. She bent closer to the surface of the painting, and with the gentleness of rubbing a butterfly's wings, she moved the tips of her fingers over the canvas.

"Andrew!" she called out. "Andrew! Come see this!"

"What have you found?" Andrew replied, pausing in his own search and looking in her direction.

"It is a painting! You must see this! Come quickly!"

Sensing a magnificent discovery, Andrew quickly wove his way through the stacks of archaic relics and hurried to Marie's side. He set his lantern on the table and gazed at the painting. It felt as though his heart skipped two beats.

In the top-center quadrant of the painting was the portrait of a kingly man. A beautiful golden crown embedded with dozens of sparkling jewels adorned a full head of grayish hair. The beard that reached to the man's chest was nearly fully gray, much more so than the hair on his head. His deep-set eyes appeared to gaze right through the person viewing the painting. The painting stopped below the man's shoulders, but what little could be seen of his clothing indicated a royal nature to them. In the bottom-left quadrant of the painting was a sword. Even in the dimness of the lanterns' light, Andrew could immediately tell that the sword in the painting was the very sword he possessed. The painting was so detailed that he could see the representation of the inscription on the sword, although it was so small as to be indecipherable. To the right of the sword, in the bottom-center quadrant, was a shield. It appeared to be golden in color, with exquisite carvings around its entire perimeter. As with the crown, the shield appeared to be embedded with dozens of jewels of all different sizes and colors. There appeared to be writing in the center of the shield, but it was just the representation of writing, as it was too small for the artist to have made it readable. The third object on the painting, in the lower-right quadrant, was a breastplate. As with the sword and the shield, the breastplate was adorned with unbelievably elaborate decorations. Andrew could also make out what appeared to be golden boots and a greatly ornate golden belt within the artistry.

"He was right," Andrew said under his breath, but Marie heard him.

"Who was right, and about what?" she asked.

"There is more to the DuFay legend than a sword, shield, and breastplate," Andrew answered. "There is also a helmet, which in this painting must be the crown, along with a belt and boots. They are all here in this painting."

Toward the bottom of the breastplate, Andrew could see yet again what appeared to be a kind of writing. But it was not the writing that captured his undivided attention. Above the writing, in the center of the breastplate, appeared something with which Andrew was extremely familiar. It was more than just a decoration. It was that which he had hoped to find from the very first moment he had stepped into this room. Though deliciously sweet the fruits of their search, bitterness soon crept into Andrew's stomach as the fullness of their discovery washed over him. He stared at the painting, not wanting to believe what he saw.

"This is DuFay," Marie pronounced, barely above a whisper.

"This must be DuFay!" she repeated. "The sword, the shield, the breastplate—all six pieces are here! Together! Andrew, this is it!"

"It is indeed," he replied somewhat solemnly.

"And there on the breastplate. That must be the family crest! We have found it!" Marie could barely contain her excitement.

"That we have," he said with constrained concurrence. "That we have."

"Are you not excited?" Marie asked, looking at Andrew with eyes full of exhilaration. "You wanted to find a family crest or an emblem to identify the DuFay family, and you have it! Now you know what to look for, and you can continue your search!"

"There is no need for me to continue my search," Andrew replied, his excitement having turned to disappointment. "I have seen that crest before."

"You have seen it?" Marie asked in reply. "Is that not good?"

"Only in that it tells me my quest is over."

"I am confused," Marie stated, her eyebrows furrowing a bit. "Where exactly have you seen this symbol? Why do you say your quest is over?"

Andrew looked into Marie's eyes for a few moments. He stretched his right arm out over the table as if to pick up his lantern but stopped short of grasping it. With his left hand, he pulled the sleeve up to his elbow. Marie broke eye contact and peered down at Andrew's arm. Her eyes widened in astonishment, and she felt as though her breath had been taken away.

"I ... I do not believe it!"

Chapter 28

M arie could not contain her excitement.

"Andrew, this is incredible!" she exclaimed as they retraced their steps in return to the main castle area. "It is beyond incredible! You are a descendant of King DuFay! You could very well be the very heir for whom you search!"

Andrew continued down the corridor without responding. After all these years, he finally knew for whom he searched. His mind was numb.

"Andrew! Do you know what this means?" Marie asked.

"I know very well what it means," Andrew finally responded. "It means that my five years of wondering, my five years of traveling from one land to another have been in vain. Five years of my life have been completely wasted."

"What do you mean?" Marie asked. "How can you say that? You have accomplished your mission!"

"Yes, I have accomplished my mission. I have learned the identity of the heir to King DuFay," Andrew replied somberly.

"Then why is your mood suddenly solemn? Is this not that for which you have so earnestly searched? Are you not excited that you are the very person for whom you have searched so long and hard? While the sweetness of success is certainly tainted with the bitterness of irony, I would expect your excitement to be overwhelming."

Andrew took several steps without replying. On the one hand, he was indeed greatly excited that the mystery had been solved. He had discovered who the heir to DuFay was. He had achieved success. But considering the circumstances, it was indeed all in vain. The knowledge was of no use but to stir old, painful memories. He paused and looked at Marie, then stated matter-of-factly, "The heir of DuFay is dead."

"What do you mean?" Marie asked, confused. "You are the heir. The scar on your forearm proves it."

"It proves nothing insofar as my interest is concerned," he replied. "I am no more the heir of King DuFay than your father's dog. The rightful heir died over five years ago on the battlefield. I should know. I saw him die."

"Andrew, I do not understand."

"You know that the scars on my chest were the result of me being attacked by a wolf when I was around ten years old. A family was passing through the area and saw the wolf preparing to leap upon me. The patriarch of the family shot the wolf as it soared through the air, killing it. However, the beast still slammed into me, and my head slammed into a tree, knocking me unconscious. When I awoke, I had no memory of who I was or where I was. I had no memory of my family. I was a stranger to myself, as were those around me. The people who saved me adopted me into their family. As was the custom of this family, the oldest son was branded with the family crest down through their generations. The man who rescued me was the oldest of his brothers; therefore, it was his responsibility to brand his son. When I was adopted into their family, I was given the brand to establish my identity with the family."

"You have no memory of your true family?" Marie asked. "No memory at all?"

"None. I was shown the body of my sister who had lived for a short time after the attack, but I did not recognize her. To this day, I have no memory of that awful day, of my parents, or of my past to that point."

"So, who is the rightful heir? You say he is dead."

"The rightful heir was the son of the man who adopted me. He was slain in battle the day my quest began. I saw him fall on the field. I tried to save him, but I was too late. I chased after the man who had dealt the fatal blow, and it was then that I found the sword. That dying man told me of the legend and charged me to continue the quest he had dedicated his life to in vain. That is where my journey began. Here is where it ends."

"What of the man who adopted you? Is he still alive?" Marie asked.

"He was killed ten years ago in battle."

"Did your brother, or rather half brother, have any children? Perhaps a son?" Marie asked.

"Yes," Andrew said, internally chastising himself for momentarily forgetting his brother's son. "His name is Alexander."

"Then would he not now be the heir, the honor having passed from his father upon his death?"

"Technically, yes, that would be the case," Andrew answered. "But Alexander would be no more than twelve years old and certainly in no position to claim a throne hundreds of years vacant."

"Nevertheless," Marie continued, "he is now the heir."

"It would appear so," Andrew admitted. "Yet he is not close to manhood, and he is many years away from being mature enough to understand or deal with the responsibilities that would be thrust upon him once he is revealed as DuFay's descendent. I do not know if my brother even knew about the significance of the family's heritage and what might be required of him one day, or his sons after him. Nothing of the sort was ever mentioned in my presence. Alexander was only seven years old when his father was killed."

Marie thought for a moment, not willing to end the debate.

"Very well. You do not wish to involve your nephew, despite his rightful place. You cannot allow your journey to end this way, and if you feel as strongly about the nature of the world today as you have claimed, with its evil and wickedness, you must act. You have the emblem on your arm. Nobody would know that you were adopted. Nobody would know the difference. You could reveal yourself as the heir."

"I would not participate in such a lie," Andrew responded. "I would not take something that is not rightfully mine."

"But imagine what good you could do," Marie argued. "You told me yourself that what I have seen of the world is far from what the world actually is. You said that there is much evil in the world. What better opportunity could a man have to do something meaningful, to start addressing the evil and chasing it away? To help prevent young girls from being lured into dark alleyways by men who are hardly more than demons in disguise. To help prevent mothers from losing their sons and wives losing their husbands in senseless wars founded upon greed and jealousy."

"Do you believe that your father would simply hand over the keys to the castle to me and remove himself from the throne?" Andrew asked. "You know as well as I do that he would do no such thing. You have praised Durinburg as a place where there is peace and plenty, where the people are happy, and it is all due to your father. Do you believe that they would tolerate another man, someone barely more than a stranger to them, taking his place? No, they would not. I have no desire to sit on a throne. There is no royal blood in my veins, and that sits quite well with me. I thank the Almighty that my quest is over. Perhaps now I can live a life of peace and contentment. I have land of my own in a land of plenty. I have friendship. Perhaps I will find a woman, and she will give me five or six children. I desire nothing more. Let other men of greater wisdom be the changers of the world."

"Oh, yes, I nearly forgot. You have no desire for fame or fortune or to be a leader of the people. You desire only mediocrity, to blend in, to have a life of ease. You could be a great leader of the people, Andrew. You have much wisdom and strength, though you will not admit it to yourself. But others see it in you. They look up to you. They see in you a man in whom they can place their trust."

"Just because a person is wise and trustworthy does not automatically make him a leader of people," Andrew replied. "It takes much more than that. It takes desire, dedication, and sacrifice. The ability to lead a country, a people, is a gift. I do not possess that gift, nor do I desire that gift."

"Oh, Andrew, you have the gift. I have seen you training with the other men. They watch your every move with an intensity I have never seen. You could tell them to stand on their heads and cluck like chickens, and they would not hesitate to do so. They respect you and admire you. You have a natural charisma that attracts people."

"So *that* explains why you were so insistent on coming down here with me this evening. You are attracted to me and my natural charisma," Andrew replied teasingly, hoping to lighten the conversation.

"As the king's daughter, I have been trained to resist the enticements and entrapments of the common people," she replied. Then she added with a smirk, "Sometimes it can be difficult, but then there are times such as this."

"Keep on telling yourself that, princess. One day you may actually believe it."

"Just as you have told yourself so many times that you are not a leader of men that you have come to believe it?" Marie asked, not allowing Andrew to steer the conversation away from her desired path. "Tell me you were not at some point in the past a leader of men. I can see it in your words and actions. I have seen you sparring with Lawrence and others. I have seen you take some men aside and provide them instruction beyond that which Angus provides. They drink your tutoring as though it were the sweetest of ale."

"Ah, now you are trying to wrangle from me more information of my past," Andrew replied. He paused for a moment to contemplate his response, then answered Marie's question. "Yes, there was a time when I held a position of leadership within an army. You are correct in this. You must understand, though, that leading men in battle is a far cry from leading a country. There are no politics among fighting men, no backstabbing, no lying or cheating. They are trained to follow instruction, to follow those men who have been appointed as their leaders."

"Ah, so we are back to the point that all politicians are backstabbers, liars, and cheaters," Marie stated, as though not surprised.

"You put words in my mouth," Andrew replied tartly. "I did not say all politicians are like that. But the majority I have met are willing to say and do almost anything to keep their positions, even to the point of destroying the character of a good man through their lies and deceitful tongues."

"Then why do you not get involved and change that which you see to be such a large problem? Perhaps the ideal man to govern is the man who does not wish to govern," Marie said.

"And that makes sense in what way exactly?" Andrew replied, furrowing his brow and giving Marie a questioning glance.

"The man who does not aspire to greatness in governing is not concerned about keeping his position at the expense of others," Marie answered. "He will do what is good and righteous and fair and just. He will expose corruption where it exists and will not be afraid of the volley of falsehoods launched toward him. He will stand firm and deflect such attacks as one flicks a fly from his arm. He may not desire to achieve immortality as some legendary politician, but he will desire to see justice spread over all people as a blanket is spread over a bed. And it is this very desire that motivates him to do what is right."

"I have said it before, Marie. Power corrupts. The best and most innocent of intentions can, over time, be strangled by the seductions of prestige."

"You do not feel that you would be immune to such seductions?"

"If I was not, instead of this conversation, we would be discussing how to break the news to your father that I am the descendant of King DuFay and rightful ruler of this land."

"Well, then, I guess your point is proven," Marie stated, despite not being convinced of Andrew's arguments. "I guess—"

"Listen!" Andrew said in a hushed tone as he stopped and held his hand up to hold Marie in place. Marie stopped immediately without making another sound. They were probably a hundred feet from the gate leading back into the castle. Her heart pounded in her chest at the thought of them being discovered in an area that had been declared off-limits to everyone. Excuses and explanations began flooding through her mind as she tried to figure out what she would say to her father. She was less concerned about what would happen to her than with what would happen to Andrew. He could no longer use the excuse of being an uninformed visitor. Her father would pry Andrew's secret from him one way or another. She was seriously considering taking Andrew back down the corridors and deep into the bowels of the castle when he lowered his hand and moved closer to her, gently and noiselessly.

"Do you hear anything?" he asked in a barely audible tone less than an inch from her ear. While at any other time such proximity would be enticing, right now she was full of anxiety and could feel nothing else. All she could manage to do was shake her head from side to side ever so gently, afraid of making any noise at all. Andrew waited several more eternal seconds before speaking again, still in a hushed voice.

"I thought I heard something ahead, a metallic sound as though the gate had just closed. You did not hear it?"

"No," Marie was barely able to get out, still afraid to even breathe.

"Let us move on but slowly and without additional conversation. We shall douse our candles and move by feeling. It may have just been paranoia prompting my imagination, but I would rather catch someone by surprise than be caught by surprise. Hold the back of my tunic, and I will lead the way. If I stop, you stop. If I move to the side, then you do so also, but quietly. Now blow out your candle." Marie followed Andrew's instructions, and both candles went out almost simultaneously. The darkness was complete. It had been a long time since Marie had been enveloped by such blackness, and with the thought of them not being alone in the corridor, the blackness was very frightening. Marie heard Andrew draw a short sword from its sheath, and then he crept forward ever so slowly. Marie followed closer than a shadow on a sunny day. Suddenly, she was afraid of someone, or something, sneaking up on them from behind. It was an unreasonable fear, she knew, but nevertheless it pounced upon her as a lion pouncing on its prey. She was powerless to chase the feeling away. Despite not being able to see her hand in front of her face, she turned her head to look back down the corridor and immediately felt silly for doing so. Her eyes were useless in the pitch-black corridor. She then cocked her head ever so slightly to the left so that her left ear was pointing more behind her than to the side. At least she felt like she was doing something proactive, and that alleviated a small bit of the helplessness she had been feeling.

It took what felt like an hour to travel the final one hundred feet to the gate. The tip of Andrew's sword scraped against one of the iron bars, and he nearly cursed himself for being so careless. He should have been reaching into the darkness with his hand to find the gate instead of using his sword for some level of protection. He froze in place at the sound of metal on metal, and Marie nearly bumped into him. Andrew sheathed his sword and felt along the gate until he located the locking mechanism. He gently tugged on the gate and was somewhat relieved to find it fully closed and locked. Part of him had expected to find it unlocked. At least that way he would have known for sure that someone else had been there and most likely was aware of their journey into the lower levels. However, with the gate locked, there was no way he could be sure one way or another. That uncertainty would nag at him for days; of that he was certain. He reached into his tunic and retrieved the key. Gently he inserted the key into the lock and turned it ever so slowly. The release of the lock made a barely audible noise, but to Andrew, it sounded like the whole gate had fallen. He paused to make sure there was no reaction from beyond the gate, then pushed it open. He stepped through the gate, with Marie still grasping his tunic, then turned, closed, and locked the gate. They continued a bit less carefully through the corridor, both being anxious to get out of there. The end of the hallway came into view as the glow from candles in the common area reached into every corner of the room. Andrew and Marie paused and carefully peered around the corner and into the room.

The room was deserted. They could see through several nearby windows the faint glow of the approaching dawn and knew they needed to get back to their individual rooms as quickly as possible. It would only be minutes before the daily activities commenced in and around the castle.

"We must move quickly and quietly," Andrew informed Marie. "We shall get together and talk more about our discoveries in a couple of days. I wish to be certain that nobody has discovered our explorations."

"Very well. Good night," Marie said and lingered for just a moment, though for what reason she was not certain. It was as if she had something else to say, yet no words came to mind. With a final glance at Andrew and another into the common area, she stole into the shadows and made her way back to her room. Andrew watched carefully as she left. Feeling confident she was unseen, he melted into the shadows and made way toward his own room. As he entered a side hallway and left the common area, he paused out of instinct and turned to look back into the room he had just left. There was nothing but silence and stillness. The flickering of the few candles caused the shadows to dance slightly, and for a moment, Andrew thought he saw something move. He remained motionless for a few more minutes but saw nothing. Convinced that his paranoia and lack of sleep were causing him imaginations, Andrew turned and proceeded down the hallway toward his quarters.

Chapter 29

I t was the second day after his discovery, and although on the surface Andrew believed his quest was over, deep down he wondered if his adventure had truly come to an end. It seemed to lack a degree of finality, and it was most certainly anticlimactic. He continued his internal debate on whether to return to his homeland, as dangerous as that would be, and explain to his nephew just who he was and what history expected from him. The day before, he had performed his daily duties in a bit of a numbed state of mind, having taken some time during the middle of the day to make a report of his findings to Carl Bergman. The blacksmith had been enthralled at the telling of the tale and desperately desired to make his own foray into the depths of the castle, but he knew that such a thing would be extremely risky and could very well cost him his life. Therefore, he resigned himself to continuing his pursuit of the DuFay Armor legend via other means. There was still much to be known about the armor and its meaning.

Andrew, however, was less enthusiastic. His quest had provided him with purpose and direction, and no matter what task was at hand, there was always the DuFay Armor in the back of his mind. Not that they were completely removed now, but they certainly seemed to carry less importance. There was always the potential for someone to obtain all six pieces of armor and claim the DuFay throne, but while he possessed the sword, that chance was extremely remote. And since he knew Talbot had the shield, he could not allow the sword to fall into his possession. For all Andrew knew, Talbot could also have other pieces in his possession. And then there was the mystery of the inscription on the sword. Although he had an interpretation of the writing, there was still the lack of meaning. But did the meaning of the inscription still bear importance since the true heir was dead? These questions swirled in Andrew's mind as he got dressed for his daily routine. As he pulled his boots on, a knock sounded on his door. Before Andrew could answer the knock, the door opened. Martin and two of his men walked in.

"Come in," Andrew stated sarcastically as the two men took station by the door and Martin approached Andrew. "To what do I owe the pleasure of this visit?"

"The king would like a meeting with you this morning," Martin replied with a slight smirk on his face. "He requested that I bring you to him."

"It must be a very important meeting for him to send the captain of the guard and two of his men."

"That you will have to discuss with the king," Martin answered. "If you please?"

Andrew stood and followed Martin out of the room. There was an irritating smugness to Martin's attitude this morning, and that did not make Andrew feel comfortable. It was very odd for the king to send Martin and two of his men to call Andrew to a meeting. Usually, it was either Marie or a house worker who was sent to summon him. This did not bode well. Andrew could only surmise that somehow the king had learned of Andrew's trip into the bowels of the castle, and he would now have to answer for it. He wondered if Marie would be at the meeting as well.

After several minutes, the men arrived outside of the king's private strategy room. One of the two guards who were always posted at the door when the king was inside opened the door. Andrew and Martin, along with the two escorts, entered the room. King Talbot was sitting in his personal chair at the end of the lone table in the room, and his mood looked less than fair. Marie was nowhere in sight. Martin motioned for Andrew to approach the king. Andrew did so and stopped just short of the table. Talbot, who had not looked up but had maintained his attention on some documents on his table to this point, finally looked up and fixed his eyes on Andrew.

"There are many things in life that make a man who he is," the king started out. "Some things are beyond his control. Where and when he is born, who his parents are, whether he is tall or short or has brown eyes or blue eyes—those are just to name a few. But the foundation of a man, that is up to him. A man decides to be honest or dishonest, to be loyal or to be disloyal, to be trustworthy or untrustworthy, to love or to hate, to be wise or to be foolish, to be strong or to be weak. A man decides what his character is going to be and if he is going to live a life of honor or dishonor. Our decisions in life are based on our character. A man of strong character makes strong decisions, the right decisions though at times they may be tough decisions. A man of questionable character makes questionable decisions, which more often than not are the wrong decisions. There are times, though, when a man of good character makes the wrong decision. No man is infallible. Sometimes that man is made to suffer the consequences of his poor judgment, and sometimes that man is given the opportunity to repent of his error before he is forced to face the consequences." The king paused in his speech, and Andrew remained stoic, showing no signs of emotion or uneasiness. After a few moments of deafening silence, the king continued.

"It did not take me long after meeting you, Andrew, to surmise that you were a man of good character. Your intelligence was obvious, your manners were excellent, and you carried yourself with a self-confidence that bordered, but did not pass into, arrogance. You have demonstrated your abilities and skills time and time again. Therefore, I still believe you to be a man of good character. Therefore, I am going to ask you once again and give you another opportunity to tell me why you are here in my kingdom. What brought you to us, and why have you remained here with us?"

"My lord," Andrew answered without a pause, "my reason for being here has not changed since the day I arrived. I have been a wandering soul for many years with no homeland, no people, no family. My path was guided not by my own intent but by the Almighty. Perhaps it was simply to save your daughter and for no other purpose. Perhaps it was to settle in this land and become a part of your people. Perhaps I will be led away again. I do not know. I have remained here because I have found rest, warmth, and friendship. Your Majesty himself invited me to stay and take a place among the people. There is every reason for me to stay and no reason for me to leave, at least none that I have been aware of up until this morning."

"That is all you have to say?" the king asked, obviously not receiving the answers for which he had been seeking.

"I believe I have answered Your Majesty's questions quite clearly and fully; however, if you have additional questions, I shall of course answer them."

The king walked out from around his table and approached Andrew, stopping several feet away. One of Martin's men stood between the king and Andrew and just off to the side. He was obviously positioned to protect the king should Andrew prove to be a threat.

"Allow me to be quite clear myself. Allegations have been brought forth against you, Andrew. You have been accused of being a spy. If indeed you are a spy and you confess your guilt, and if you pledge your loyalty to me, then I shall be merciful to you. Perhaps more for my daughter's sake than anything else, for she has taken something of a liking to you. To choose to be a spy for a king you serve is an honorable thing and shows great love and loyalty. I myself have spies in many lands, and they are highly valued men. I chose them because they are strong and loyal. All kings have spies they dispatch regularly. They are necessary to the survival of any kingdom and of any people. If you confess, then you shall be treated fairly. If you do not confess and it is proven that you are indeed a spy, then you shall be treated with much contempt, and it shall not go well for you no matter what my daughter or any other person thinks of you. Now tell me, Andrew, have you been sent to spy on me?"

Suddenly Andrew recalled his conversation with Marie several days before when she warned him that certain people were murmuring about him possibly being a spy. He had hoped that such suspicions would die away and not grow to the point of accusation. Obviously, that was not how things were playing out.

"My lord, I am no spy. As I said before, prior to my arrival here, I had no king, no land, no people. If it would place your heart at ease, I will confess that I was driven from my homeland by the king I had devoted my life in service to because I refused to act in a dishonorable way upon his command. However, if I were a spy, I would hardly confess to it, and I certainly would not betray my own king. A man who would betray his beloved king is not much of a man at all. It is the man who betrays his king who should be treated with contempt and disdain, not the man who maintains his loyalty."

The king slowly walked around Andrew, but Andrew remained motionless and did not turn to face the king.

"Why were you roaming the forbidden chambers and corridors beneath the castle the other evening?" the king asked.

"I did not know that it was not permissible to explore those areas. Your Majesty invited me to explore the castle and make myself familiar with it and all that is in your land."

"Your midnight excursion would seem to indicate that you did not wish to be detected. If that were not sufficient, did the locked gate not speak loud enough that the area beyond was not to be entered upon?"

"I must confess it did give me pause, but my curiosity soon overcame my hesitancy," Andrew answered. "After all, I could not be certain if the gate was ten years old or ten times ten years old. As to the timing of my exploration, there have been thoughts on my mind regarding my daily responsibilities that have made sleep somewhat difficult from time to time. It is not the first time that I have wandered around the castle and grounds at night with a troubled mind."

"I see," the king said. "And from whom did you get a key to open the gate?"

Andrew did not fall into the king's trap. "I had no key, Your Majesty, other than my own experience and skill. As a lad, I developed quite the talent for picking locks. I never stole anything, of course; it was just the challenge of opening locks that I enjoyed."

"You have spent much time with the locksmith, Bergman. Is it possible that you obtained a key from him?" the king inquired, ignoring Andrew's response. "Perhaps your visit to him yesterday was to return the key to him. Although I instructed him to make one and only one key for that lock, which I would maintain in my possession, I know locksmiths and would expect that he made a duplicate for himself."

"Your Majesty, I do not know what keys Mr. Bergman has or does not have. It is none of my concern. You are correct that I have spent much time with him and his family of late. The reason for that, if you truly must know, is his daughter, Heather. She is an exceptionally fine and beautiful young lady, and she has captured my heart. Naturally, I wish to spend as much time around her as I can. With twenty acres of prime land at my disposal, I am now looking to start a family. My visit to Mr. Bergman yesterday afternoon was for no other reason than to inquire if I may formally court his daughter."

"I see," the king replied, not at all convinced by Andrew's argument. He decided to switch the questioning back to Andrew's descent into the lower levels of the castle. "For what were you searching the other night?" the king continued.

"I was searching for mystery, for the thrill of the unknown. I find it exciting if not exhilarating to explore areas of great age and darkness. You never know what you may find."

"And did you find anything interesting during your exploration?" the king asked.

"Beyond dark hallways and dark rooms, nothing, my lord," Andrew replied. "It was quite the boring and unfulfilling venture in retrospect. Quite a pity, I must say." Andrew found it interesting that Talbot had yet to make mention of Marie having accompanied Andrew. Even if he were going to interview them separately and compare their stories, why would he leave her out of his conversation with Andrew? Did he not know that she had accompanied him? Surely he did. If the king knew that Andrew had explored the lower levels, he had to know that Marie had accompanied Andrew. It was something Andrew would have to ask Marie at a later time.

"When you first arrived here and gave an account of the men who had attacked my daughter and her friends, you, and the young ladies as well, provided quite a detailed physical description of the men. Have you ever considered the fact that the description you gave of those men could fit yourself as well?"

"The similarities had not dawned upon me," Andrew answered innocently but not exactly truthfully, "but now that you mention it, I can see that there could be a distinct likeness or two."

"And this does not seem an odd coincidence to you?" the king asked.

"Not at all," Andrew replied. "It would be quite arrogant of me to think that I was the only handsome man in the land, and as you pointed out earlier, I am not an arrogant man."

"Do you believe this to be a game, MacLean?" the king asked heatedly. It was the first time Andrew could recall the king addressing him by his family name and not his surname. Whether a conscious move or not, it was the king's way of pulling back his familiarity and friendship. "I assure you it is not. These allegations are quite serious and carry quite serious consequences."

"No, Your Majesty, I do not think this to be a game," Andrew replied boldly. "I think it is a waste of your precious time. These false allegations are based on nothing more than a paranoid mind creating suspicions based on innocent, everyday occurrences. If I am guilty of anything, it is of bad judgment and intruding into a forbidden area of the castle. For that, I shall beg the king's forgiveness and mercy. However, in no other way have I crossed Your Majesty. I would like very much to know who my accuser is, that I may deal with him myself."

Talbot had made his way back to the table opposite Andrew. It was plainly obvious from the expression on his face that he did not believe Andrew. He peered into Andrew's eyes for a few moments before reaching down behind the table and retrieving a leather vest, which he tossed onto the table.

"Yesterday, we apprehended two spies about a half-day ride to our north. They had been seen riding around our land on quite a few occasions, and they had been in various small villages asking questions about our kingdom. The questions would be innocent enough to the average person, but they just happened to ask the wrong questions to the wrong person. I have many men posted about my kingdom in different towns and villages, specifically trained to identify foreign spies. These two men casually conversed with one of my men, and he became suspicious of them. He befriended them and led them to believe that he was a grand source of information on our country. After several days, while the two spies were otherwise occupied, my man entered their quarters and discovered written documentation these men had been keeping pursuant to their detailed conversations about the kingdom, the number of inhabitants, the estimated strength of our army, et cetera. A detail was dispatched yesterday, and the men were taken into custody. In their quarters were vests nearly identical to this one. It appears to be an ordinary vest, but when one looks on the inside of it" — the king turned the vest inside out — "an inscription is revealed along with what appears to be a kind of family crest. It depicts a stallion on its two hind legs, pawing at the air with two standards crossed in front of it. We cannot read the inscription yet, but it is identical on the two vests. Can you tell me what the inscription reads?"

"No, my lord, I cannot tell you what the inscription reads," Andrew answered truthfully.

"That is a bit surprising, to say the least," the king replied.

"Why so?" Andrew asked.

"Because this is your vest, Andrew. It was discovered in your room," the king said accusingly. "It can be no coincidence that we discover two spies with nearly identical vests bearing the same inscription and crest as a vest that was found among your possessions. Do you wish to provide an explanation for this too?"

Andrew looked at the vest. He had never seen it before this very moment. Someone had obviously planted it in his room, someone who was determined to see that he was arrested as a spy. He was being set up, and unfortunately for him, the pieces seemingly all fit together. If he denied having ever seen the vest, Talbot would not believe him. In fact, Talbot would be expecting Andrew to deny having ever seen the vest. For all Talbot knew, the vest was indeed Andrew's, and he would expect Andrew to say whatever he could to disassociate himself from the captured spies. If Andrew denied owning the vest, Talbot would not believe him. If Andrew admitted to owning the vest, he would basically be incriminating himself. Andrew decided to take the riskier route for an answer.

"My lord, I have traveled through many lands and kingdoms during the past few years of my life. I have purchased many articles of clothing during that time. I cannot remember exactly where and when I purchased that vest. I knew of the inscription when I purchased it but assumed that it was simply the signature of the one who made it. I saw no use for further inquiry into its meaning. Is it not possible that these two men also visited some of the same boroughs that I visited, and is it not possible that they purchased vests from the same craftsman from whom I purchased my vest? As you can see, it is very well made and a desirable piece of clothing."

Talbot smirked. "You seem to have an explanation for everything, MacLean. Your answers make perfect, reasonable sense. You are very sharp on your feet. If this ended here and now, there would be no way one could prove that you were a spy. At least, not beyond a reasonable doubt. Fortunately, though, we are not through." The king nodded to the guard standing at the door, and the guard opened the door. A man in shackles shuffled his way into the room, prodded on by two trailing guards. He was rather unkempt in appearance, with dirty clothes and dirty hair. It could be seen, though, that his hair was similar in color to Andrew's, and they had similar facial bone structure. The complexions of their skin, save for the dirt covering the prisoner, were also quite similar. The prisoner stopped beside Andrew, facing the king. Talbot spoke to Andrew, although he looked at the prisoner, who was staring at ground.

"This is one of the spies we took into custody yesterday. He has been very cooperative during interrogation. Indeed, he has provided us with some remarkably interesting information. I believe you will be quite interested in hearing what he has to say." The king spoke to the prisoner. "Prisoner, tell us who you are and what your mission is."

Without lifting his eyes, the prisoner replied quietly, as if ashamed to speak. "My name is Gregor McBride. I was dispatched by my country several weeks ago to carry out two objectives. The first was to gather as much information as possible on Your Majesty's country. I was to determine most of all the strength of the army protecting this kingdom. The second objective was to make contact with one of our spies who had been dispatched many weeks earlier and to receive his report on the land, which I was then to carry back to my own country."

"And did you succeed in your second objective?" the king inquired.

"No, my lord. I was preparing to make contact when I was captured."

"And who was this man with whom you were to make

contact?" the king continued. The prisoner did not answer immediately. "You will answer me, McBride. Who was this man with whom you were to make contact?" Again, the prisoner was reluctant to answer. The king looked at one of the guards and gave a quick nod. The guard stepped forward and punched the prisoner in the kidneys with a strong blow. The prisoner grunted loudly and sank to his knees. Two guards reached out and, grabbing him by the arms, lifted the prisoner back to his feet.

"I will ask you once more, prisoner, and then the next blow you feel will be from the tip of a sword. Who was this man you were to meet?"

The prisoner slowly lifted his eyes toward Andrew with what appeared to be genuine remorse. "I am sorry, my brother," he whispered. "I cannot stand the beatings and the pain any longer." He looked at the king. "I was to meet this man, Andrew MacLean."

Andrew stared at the disheveled man in total shock and disbelief. He had never seen this man before. How could this man know his name and, even more, claim to have been on a mission to meet him? It was insanity. It was total insanity. Whoever was setting him up had gone to extreme lengths to ensure his appearance of guilt. But what was their motivation? Why would anyone want him to be imprisoned or even potentially executed for being a spy? The only answer Andrew could come up with was the sword. Someone wanted him out of the way so they could find it among his possessions. Only two people in the whole land of Durinburg knew that he had the sword: Marie and Carl Bergman. Andrew immediately ruled both of them out as suspects. If the king knew Andrew possessed the sword, he would come right out and say so and demand that Andrew give it to him. He then remembered his encounter with Gallard's spies. Was this man another such spy, and his capture intentional in order to have Andrew convicted of espionage, and possibly ransomed back to Gallard? And who was it that saved him from Peterson, and why? Andrew turned his eyes to Martin. Martin stood there and returned Andrew's gaze. Although Martin maintained a facial expression that was neutral and revealed nothing of what he was thinking, he could not completely control his eyes. There was something in his eyes that spoke of triumph. Andrew was convinced that Martin was behind this conspiracy, but whatever his motivations were would remain a mystery for now.

"Do you wish to explain this away?" Talbot asked Andrew, breaking Andrew's silence.

"What would you have me say, Your Majesty? It appears your mind was made up on the issue long before I stepped into the room," Andrew replied.

"I would have the truth!" the king yelled as he slammed his fist into the table.

"You have the truth!" Andrew replied firmly. "You have asked me if I am a spy. I have truthfully replied that I am not a spy, yet you do not believe what I say. What else can I say? If I tell you that I do not know this man and have never seen him, will you believe me? I think not. Yet it is the truth. I do not know from where he has come, I do not know how he knows my name, I do not know of any mission he is on, and I do not know if he is even a spy himself. A lousy spy he would be, giving up his name and mission and revealing the identity of a fellow spy. But I am not a spy. Believe me, or do not believe me. Use those *instincts* of yours and believe what you will."

The king continued glaring at Andrew for a few moments, trying to decide what his course of action would be. The evidence against Andrew was quite convincing, yet then again, so was Andrew's argument. He decided that he would need time to think about the matter.

"Martin, take Andrew down to the old prison, down beneath the castle. As Andrew is curious about what is down there, we shall allow him to spend some time there by himself. Make sure the door to his cell is sturdy and securely locked. Post two men outside his cell, and post two more at the main gate. Only I will have the authorization to pass the main gate. Nobody else may pass. Not my daughter, not someone claiming to have my permission, no one else is allowed down there. Do you understand?"

"I understand perfectly," Martin replied. "I will have my best men standing post." He turned and spoke to Andrew. "I believe you know the way, spy." Andrew looked at Martin, then stole a final glance at Talbot before turning and leaving the room.

The walk to the dungeon was made in silence, but the smug look on Martin's face spoke volumes. In less than ten minutes, Andrew, Martin, and Martin's four guards were standing outside one of the cells in the dungeon, one that Andrew had actually visited during his and Marie's expedition.

"Your new home," Martin said as he motioned for Andrew to enter the diminutive room. "Not quite as luxurious as your previous accommodations, would you not agree?"

"It does lack a bathroom," Andrew replied. "But I am sure I will be able to make do."

Martin chuckled. "I dare say, it will not be long before a filthy body is the least of your concerns," Martin said. "Succulent feasts are a thing of the past. Your food will be what the dogs did not want. Your water, well, it will not exactly be freshly drawn from the well. You will not know if it is day or if it is night. There will be no books for you to read, and there will be nobody to share your thoughts and dreams with. Your daily rides upon that fine stallion of yours are a thing of the past. I have to wonder, what shall happen to that beast of yours?"

"If any harm comes to him ..." Andrew started.

"What?" Martin replied with a malevolent look. "What would you do, locked away in this cold, dark, damp hole? Nothing, I would think."

"I shall not be here very long. I can assure you of that," Andrew responded firmly. "And when I leave this place, should any harm have befallen Annon, the person responsible will wish that he were locked in this very room instead of facing the wrath that I would bring down upon his head."

An evil grin spread across Martin's face. "Let it not be said that I am not a compassionate man," he said as he withdrew two unlit candles from a pouch at his side and threw them into the cell. "After all, it would be cruel to leave you down here in the dark." He took a lit candle from one of the guards and passed it to Andrew. "Goodbye, MacLean," Martin said as he closed and locked the cell door. Andrew heard Martin give orders to the guards. Then his departing footsteps slowly faded.

Andrew looked around his cell. At least this cell had what appeared to be some fresh straw on the ground where he could receive some insulation from the stone-cold floor. He sat down with his back against one of the walls. He could not fathom who had set him up or why. He thought back to the day that the DuFay sword had come into his possession and the quest that was passed on to him. He thought about the five years that he had spent as a nomad, traveling from one land to another, seeking a man who, as it turns out, was his dead brother. Five years wasted, adding who knows how many years to him physically and emotionally. And for what? What had he accomplished other than discovering a hoard of antiques and treasures that most likely would end up in Talbot's personal collection? Then he thought about Marie, and Heather, and Elizabeth and how he had first come upon them. If he had not been there, they would have suffered such unspeakable atrocities. For a moment, the memory of two dead young girls in a dark alley what seemed a lifetime ago flashed through his mind. He laid his head back against the wall and closed his eyes.

"Father, if saving these young women was the sole purpose of my journey, then it has been worth it. It is not for me to decide who is worthy of the sword or who rises to rule lands and kingdoms. I am not wise enough or worthy to make those decisions. I leave that in your hands. I can only ask for your mercy and that you not turn your eyes from your humble servant. If this is where my journey ends, then so be it. Grant me peace in my circumstances."

Exhausted both physically and mentally, Andrew stretched out on the straw, no longer worried about a sword, or a descendant, or what tomorrow held for him. For the moment, he was at peace, and sleep came quickly.

Epilogue

With barely a whisper, the man moved along the tree line, keeping pace with his prey. He was thankful for the tweets and chirps of the forest's inhabitants as they began their daily activities, for they would help mask any sound that he might make. He watched her as she walked without a care in the world, singing a capricious tune, practically oblivious to her surroundings. He had a feeling of where she was likely heading, and that gave him at least ten minutes to carry out his plan. Not another soul was in sight. It was so foolish for her to be out by herself. What a short memory she must have, and what a false sense of security she must have felt. One part of his plan had been successful. Now he had to carry out the second part of his plan.

After ensuring that no other people were near, he slipped soundlessly out of the forest and carefully walked up behind her. He pulled from a pouch at his side a rag and then a small bottle filled with a liquid. Cautiously, he saturated the rag with the liquid, ensuring that he held it downwind, and then returned the bottle to the pouch. He increased his pace. In less than a minute, he was but a few feet behind her. He glanced one more time to his sides and to his rear, making sure nobody else was around. Satisfied that they were alone, he took two quick steps and was upon his prey. He wrapped one arm around her torso, pinning her arms to her body. With his other hand, he covered her face with the rag. She tried to scream, but the rag muffled her cries. She struggled violently, at one point nearly breaking free, but her attacker was too strong. He gripped her tighter, and slowly, her struggles became weaker. The bright morning sun seemed to grow dimmer and dimmer to her, and her arms and legs started feeling as if they had heavy weights tied to them. No matter how hard she tried, she could not keep her eyelids open. Within thirty seconds of being attacked, the woman's body went limp. With a final look at their surroundings, the man picked up the sleeping woman and disappeared into the woods.